NORTHFIELD

NORTHFIELD

CALVIN FISHER

Cover design by Geoffrey Bunting
Interior formatting by Bodie D. Dykstra

To Bailey,
My greatest supporter.

PROLOGUE

Despite all these years, the smell could still make Mark Northfield nauseous. He inhaled, and discomfort pricked his stomach like a sewing needle. The scent made him think of someone pouring sweat into an aged water bottle and holding the bottle to his nose.

While exhaling, he wondered why he continued expending energy on being annoyed at the gas mask. Had even one day passed when he didn't have a mask plastered to his face for however many hours a day? After pondering the thought, Northfield supposed that the mask only really bothered him on long escorts like this one. Being cooped up in a truck, plus being stuck sucking air out of a filter without a single break, drove him up the wall and then some. At least his gas mask only covered his nose, mouth, and cheeks; most people wore the full-face masks, and if he had to subject himself to such a stuffy and sweaty hell each day, he would've offered himself long ago as fertilizer for the vegetation outside that taunted the last stubborn remnants of humanity.

He turned his head on the torn leather headrest to look out the passenger side window. Short, stubby shrubs jutted out of the ground alongside the road, their deep-green leaves stabbing into the gas.

The gas. The omnipresent gas that acted like it paid rent, gently glowing in its ominous yellow-orange glory.

1

He looked out of the sideview mirror and caught a glimpse of the massive gray transport vehicle he rode in. Five wheels kicked up dust on the road. The barrels, neatly arranged in rows and columns on the flatbed, were covered by a black tarp, keeping him from catching a glimpse of any labels that might indicate what the barrels contained.

He stretched his legs as well as he could in the cramped confines of the seat. Why the designers of the truck couldn't have made a single inch of legroom in such a large vehicle was beyond him.

Sighing, he rolled his head to look at the driver. He was a burly man with prominent arm hair that weaved like waves, a man who carried himself with a brazen confidence that constantly threatened to break out of his puffed-out chest. Northfield imagined him waking up each morning and challenging the world to a one-versus-one bare-knuckles brawl, even though a bowl of soggy cereal could probably throw him down to the ground and pin him.

"What are you hauling?"

The driver turned slowly and glared at him through the glass lenses of his gas mask, his eyes burning with unwarranted contempt. Northfield had met more of this type of man than he could count. Enough to know the exact trajectory of the conversation he had started.

"I reckon that I'm payin' you to guard the cargo, not pester me about the contents," the driver said. Pleased with such an adequate answer to what he perceived as a stupid and out-of-the-line question, he turned his eyes back to the road.

Northfield massaged his forehead and let his eyes fall shut, allowing himself one breath before reopening them. "Look, man, I don't personally care what you're hauling. Just a friendly piece of advice for next time: when you're taking these dangerous roads, and you're taking a flatbed truck with the cargo as exposed as it is, you really should hire two guards. Better yet, invest in a semi-trailer with a reinforced flatbed. Yellowbacks can hit from either side of the road, and I can't keep track of the blind spots well enough on a vehicle like this to make sure no bullets hit the cargo."

"What the fuck am I payin' you for, then? I thought you mercs were supposed to be the best."

"I can take on as many Yellowbacks as you can throw at me—if I can see them, that is. I can't take on a Yellowback humping some bushes while firing a couple potshots that hit an oil drum, blowing us all to hell. So I just want to know what we're hauling so I can figure out how to best protect you and your cargo and get us to the Network outpost in one piece."

"'Best protect you,'" the driver repeated. "Let's get one thing straight, pal. I'll worry about me. I'm not payin' you to worry about me. You worry about the cargo. But find a way to do it quietly."

"Suit yourself," he muttered. Shaking his head, he thought, *As perfect of a day to die as any.*

Two more hours passed in silence, both inside and outside the vehicle. Despite Northfield's weary bones and lead eyelids, he kept a vigilant eye on the road and surrounding fields. Stubborn pride in performing his job well and the desire to keep himself and the driver alive, regardless of the driver's bullish disposition, prevented him from drifting off or succumbing to sleep. It had been a long drive, alright.

A brown blur rustled through the knee-high yellow brush past the bushes and skipped across the road in front of the vehicle. Northfield propelled his hand out and commanded, "Stop!"

The driver, reacting as if he'd been thrashed by a whip, slammed on the brakes. His eyes moved to the brown object, which now stood frozen dumbly in the middle of the road. After a moment, both men realized that they were looking at a deer.

"A deer? You're stoppin' me for a fucking deer? This vehicle could run over ten in a row without even wincin'."

Northfield continued to stare, marveling for what seemed like the thousandth time at how nature soldiered on, unimpeded by the toxic gas. Meanwhile, humanity had to suit up in gas masks, surely designed by a sadist, just to go outside and walk across the street.

Northfield said, "Why run over a deer?"

"Oh, now you're lax. Thought you were paranoid about my cargo. Ain't you worried about an ambush?"

"Last I checked, the Yellowbacks didn't train deer to run across roads as distractions. I'll keep my head on a swivel, but we're fine, man."

As they impatiently waited for the deer to pass, Northfield noticed blotches of red on the side of the road. *The hell?* he thought, his eyes moving down the road as they followed a trail of blood consisting of intermittent pools with small rivers connecting them. His fingers tightened around the grip and foregrip of the Vector submachine gun on his lap. At the end of the trail, a man with a black gas mask lay face-down; the blood oozing from his midsection painted his white T-shirt like a crackhead's rendition of modern art. The somberness Northfield felt at seeing the man was immediately replaced by distressed hope as he spotted the man's ring finger twitch.

His head snapped around to the driver as he dug around his backpack for a first aid kit.

"Hang on. You see that wounded guy ahead?" Northfield asked.

"Yeah," the driver said with complete apathy, like Northfield had asked him if he'd spotted a fly. "What about him?"

"When that deer moves, don't drive off," he said. "I'm gonna try to help him."

"Are you crazy?" the driver cried. "Hell no! Stopping for a deer's one thing. That guy is a whole 'nother world. That wound could be ketchup or beet juice as far as I know. He could be a Yellowback." He punched Northfield's shoulder. "And don't you think of goin', either. You damn well know that if you leave the truck and I drive off, that'll be a breach of Network contract, and your ass is dead."

"He's not a Yellowback." Northfield's hands found the first aid kit. "He's not wearing the uniform."

"You're decidin' if he's a Yellowback or not based on his fuckin' fashion choice?"

"Yeah, I'd bet the farm on it. Uniform's part of their whole cult mentality," he said, pulling the first aid kit out of his backpack.

"Then he's probably runnin' from them, and I'm not about to sit here till they come."

"Christ," he muttered. The guy outside might be taking his last breaths, yet here he was, arguing with the driver. "I've seen enough Yellowbacks to know how they work. They're not after him anymore. Look at him. He doesn't have anything on him. They'd only kill him for his belongings. Without anything on him, there's no point. They probably swiped his stuff already."

"That's your opinion," the driver said, pressing on the gas pedal. The truck lurched forward. "I pay you for your gun, not your brain. Yellowbacks could be any damn where. Fuck him."

"Wait," he cried. "I'll pay you, alright? You keep the money you'd pay me for this job. You hear me? Just let me try to save him and it's yours."

The driver braked. "All of it?"

"All of it."

With a sigh, the driver shook his head. "Fine. Guess if I die, you'll probably be dead, too. Small consolation."

Northfield flew out of the door and sprinted to the man, submachine gun in one hand and first aid kit in the other. Upon Northfield's approach, the man let out a defeated cry, akin to a wounded animal watching encircling predators close in.

"It's okay, it's okay," Northfield soothed. "I'm here to help you, alright?"

As gently as he could, he rolled the man onto his back, eliciting a groan. "I'm sorry, buddy. I know that hurt," he said, his fingers fishing around the first aid kit. He didn't have much inside the kit, only some gauze, antiseptic wipes, and painkillers, the last of which he couldn't give the man without removing his gas mask and killing him. The best he could possibly do would be to slow the bleeding and help the guy hold out until someone who was better equipped could help. He'd somehow have to convince the driver to let the man tag along to the Network outpost, but he'd figure out that problem after he fixed the man up the best he could.

"This's gonna hurt, too," he warned the man, applying the wipes to his stomach wound. The resulting cries were sharper than the first, although paradoxically, they were more distant, like a drop of lighter fluid being poured onto a fading ember. Northfield wrapped the gauze around the man's midsection as tightly as he could. When he pulled away to examine the man and assess what to do, his teeth gritted in defeat as dark blood spread across the gauze like a rabid infection.

"Damn it, I'm sorry," he told the man, holding his hand for comfort despite fully knowing how inadequate the gesture was. He whispered a soft prayer as the man drifted off, holding his hand even after his soul had gone elsewhere. Northfield remained on his knees for a moment longer, staring off at nothing in particular before grabbing his first aid pack and submachine gun and hurrying back to the truck.

When he got into his seat and closed the door, the driver scoffed and said, "Bet it feels pretty shitty to lose those credit cards now, huh?"

"Nah, I'll just strip on the side," he muttered, his voice too soft and quiet to put much emphasis on his sarcasm. If exhaustion was a mouse nibbling on him before, now it was a bloodhound. Cognizant of his weariness, he doubled down on keeping his eyes focused on the road and his surroundings. If Yellowbacks were close, they weren't going to catch him by surprise—they weren't. He saw the driver shake his head in the reflection of the glass before turning his own eyes to the road. Neither of them spoke for the remainder of the drive.

CHAPTER 1

A high-pitched noise that sounded like the shrill cry of a robotic bird freed Mark Northfield from the frenzied grip of his nightmare. The dream faded from memory almost instantaneously, and he struggled to remember if he was falling, descending, drowning, or choking. It hardly mattered; while the scenes, scenarios, and characters changed, the overall formula of the dreams stayed the same, as if they were directed by a lazy filmmaker who made one good flick in his life and fundamentally re-created the same movie ad nauseam.

He remained still for a few moments, staring with no small magnitude of grogginess and disdain at the source of the high-pitched alarm: a gray rectangular device with an array of switches and blinking lights plastered to the wall. The device had two different alarms: one to warn if something was wrong with the power and one to warn if the air was unsafe to breathe. The latter alarm was significantly louder than the former. Seeing as he still had his ears, and seeing as he wasn't dead and didn't feel like he was gonna get there any time in the next minute, he gave himself a moment to take a breath and will himself to begin the day.

Turning on his side, he cast his gaze on a four-by-four-inch picture within a rusted frame propped up next to his stained and decrepit mattress.

"Morning, Love," he said to the picture, in which a brunette woman sat in the soft shade of a barren tree. She was surrounded by bright red and yellow leaves not yet disturbed by the inevitable hand of decay. The leaves ate at her white dress, which curved in the shape of a crescent.

He rolled off his mattress, which had no bed frame to speak of. He picked himself up off the floor.

After quickly stretching his back, he made his way across his log house to the blaring device on the wall.

Silence blissfully greeted him after he turned off the alarm. He examined the electronic display above the array of buttons and switches.

He read off the display: *NO INCOMING ENERGY: 20 HOURS OF SAFE AIR LEFT.*

He turned toward the picture on his floor and said, "Something from the storm last night is probably blocking the blades. I've gotta go outside and check. Wouldn't want you to get stuffy in your frame, Jess. Or, you know, for me to die."

Northfield's log house was small, comprising one main room along with a small bathroom. He walked into the bathroom and looked at his reflection in the cracked, dirty mirror as he washed his face. He ran his hand through his long and ragged dirty-blonde hair and beard, staring into his crisp, lightning-seared blue eyes to examine how much life remained in them.

"No graying. The rugged good looks haven't left me yet, Jess," he said.

He returned to the main room. Along with his mattress and the window, it contained a table with two chairs, a couch, a bookshelf, and a black chest. Ghost-white spiderwebs drooped off the wooden ceiling, both speckled by dust. The floorboards were illuminated by faint morning light that shined between a handful of raindrops too stubborn to dry on the house's lone window. It was bulletproof, which was always a weight off his mind; he didn't need to worry about some broken glass being the death of him.

He opened the black chest. He grabbed a baseball jacket, beanie, Oakley gloves, cargo pants, and boots. The jacket was light blue with light-red lines running across the arms, and the jacket had the word *Spoonbills* written across the center in red cursive letters. The beanie, similarly, was red and blue and had the Spoonbills logo across the front. After dressing himself, he reached back into the chest and grabbed a Gl-17 pistol and a holster. He holstered the weapon to his ankle and reached into the chest one final time to grab two more items: his gas mask and an extendable rake.

He put on the gas mask, then proceeded to open the heavy steel door by twisting the handle, pulling out, then pulling down hard. Three high-pitched warning sounds shrieked from the rectangular device on the wall. He proceeded to push the door open slightly, just enough for him to fit his body through. The air filter hummed with exasperation as it worked furiously to purify the air contaminated by incoming gas from the opening. After he exited the house, he shut the door behind him, which clicked sharply as it automatically locked.

The gas, as always, inhibited his vision so that he could only see a couple of football fields ahead. The thick grass reached his knees, licking his calves and leaving crisscross marks of dew on his pants. Fifty feet in front of his dwelling, an oak tree rose out of the grass, its leaves weaving in and out of the gas. The blades of grass at the edge of the field brushed against the first row of trees in a forest, but he could barely see the thick line of trees due to the gas. He appreciated the forest; its greenness provided a visual break from the glowing yellow and orange. Plus, being so near the forest provided him a welcome degree of privacy. However, his current area of interest was on the opposite side of his house as the forest.

Behind his house, he passed his motorbike, which was chained to the side wall. His boots splashed in a handful of small puddles surrounding his house. Along with a smattering of branches and leaves atop the grass, these puddles served as the only traces of the prior night's storm. By midday, the puddles would be entirely gone, but due to how wet this time of year was, the grass wouldn't stay dry for long.

Twenty feet away from the back wall, a river ran parallel to his house. Tubes snaked from a generator to the river, in which there was a turbine with three blades. The river's current spun the blades around the turbine's rotor, collecting energy that the generator converted to electricity to power the air filter in his house. The added water from the storm made the river flow faster than normal, but Northfield didn't need to step any closer to the river to see why his turbine wasn't generating any power.

A giant log, which looked like the better part of a tree, had gotten itself wedged in the river. One end of the log was jammed between rotors while the other end was firmly stuck in the widest part of the meander on the opposite side of the river.

Mesh netting held by metal rods was supposed to keep anything from getting near the blades. Evidently, the netting forgot how to do its job.

Rake in hand, he approached the edge of the river and stopped directly above the turbine. The semi-clear water was only a few feet deep, although the river still had a strong current.

Immediately, he could see that the netting needed to be replaced, even if the log hadn't busted through it. Intact strands of netting were stretched and thinning in many areas, and aside from the gaping hole left by the log, there were a number of smaller holes. Considering the condition of the net, it was a small wonder how the log managed to break through.

He looked upstream and shook his head. The storm ended hours ago, which meant that the log probably also entered the river hours ago, when the heavy wind was more apt to transporting logs.

After hours of traveling miles upon miles down the river, probably getting stuck and unstuck any number of times, the log had still somehow found the weak points in Northfield's net.

God's trying to kill me again. Northfield smirked. *Sorry, Pops, you're gonna have to try harder than that. Next time, try a bolt of lightning.*

He fetched a pair of brown waders sitting near the generator and returned to the river. He jammed the butt end of his rake under the log.

Using the rake as a lever, he pushed downward with a groan. The log stubbornly remained in place for a couple of seconds before the nearest end popped up. Now free to move, the log realigned itself parallel to the river and continued floating downstream.

The rotors didn't look damaged, and they started spinning with a low-pitched hum. He turned his attention to removing the net from the rods around the turbine.

Satisfied with his work, Northfield climbed out of the river and shed his waders. He went back to the heavy steel door. On the keypad, he typed a four-digit passcode, and after three high-pitched warning sounds, he opened the door and entered his house, then quickly shut it behind him. Upon entering, he examined the air filter, which now read, *POWER RESTORED. TWO HOURS UNTIL FULL BACKUP POWER IS CHARGED.*

He took off his gas mask but didn't put it back in the chest. Instead, he set it on the floor; he would need to put the mask on again shortly.

While he dug around the chest, he spoke to the picture near his mattress, "All done, Jess. Not dying today. At least not yet."

He pulled three credit cards wrapped in a rubber band out of the chest. A frown spread across his face. "Only three credits left. Gotta head to the outpost and get a new net. More importantly, I gotta see if they have any work."

He set the cards down and rummaged through the black chest again. His fingers scraped across the bottom until he found a pair of electronic earplugs. Relieved that they hadn't found a nice spot to hide, he inserted them. They were capable of lowering sounds of high intensities to eighty decibels while retaining the sharpness of his hearing; he could still detect faint whispers or rustles that were audible to him without the earplugs. Acute hearing was paramount to detecting Yellowback ambushes, and he took what precautions he could to protect his ears. Otherwise, he'd eventually be either dead or out of a job.

Next, he took a pair of quad-lens goggles out of his chest. The goggles had hybrid functionality, and they were capable of utilizing night and thermal vision. Night vision was useless during the day, but thermal vision could help him spot Yellowbacks if they tried attacking. He never liked traveling anywhere without them. The lenses rested well enough on his beanie.

He reached into the chest and took out an empty black rucksack before grabbing his Vector submachine gun. The weapon was converted to fire TAP rounds, total armor penetration, instead of the standard .45 ACP rounds. The TAP rounds, developed and used by the United States military before the bombs dropped, could penetrate every type of body armor he'd ever seen. Additionally, the Vector had a holographic sight, a laser sight, a black strap, and a silencer. The silencer primarily served to protect his ears in case he ever had to fire without earplugs rather than serving as a stealth tool, as the gun still fired loudly with it.

He set the weapon down next to the rucksack, which he filled with extra magazines in addition to food and water, flashbangs, smoke grenades, a spare gas mask, and other various supplies. He took off his Spoonbills jacket and put on a light armored vest before putting the jacket back on. The vest primarily defended against knife attacks instead of ballistics. The Yellowbacks had access to TAP rounds, too, which made vests that protected against bullets a moot point. Lastly, he put his three remaining credit cards in his pocket. Paper money fell out of style after the bombs; people preferred a less easily destroyed form of currency to compensate for the world around them. Credit cards, useless after the concept of credit disappeared, fit the bill for the new form of legal tender.

After closing the chest, he stood up and slung the submachine gun and rucksack over his shoulder. He looked at the picture and said, "I'll be back in a few hours, Love."

Northfield left the house and began his trek to the outpost, which was four miles away. Although he could use the motorbike chained to the side of his house, he chose not to; to say that fuel was expensive would be a gross understatement. Furthermore, the Yellowbacks often watched the roads on the other side of the forest. He'd heard multiple stories of travelers being robbed or killed if they put up any resistance. No other roads within any reasonable distance led to the outpost, so he had to contend with potential ambushes. The motorbike was loud; he preferred to make as little commotion as possible.

The outpost belonged to the Network, an organization established years ago, maybe two or three after the bombs dropped. Back then, various factions and groups constantly warred with each other in the anarchy that followed America's fall. The Network surfaced—from whom or where, he didn't know—and it served as a mediator between groups and their interests. As the years passed, factions formed and dissolved, but the Network remained constant, only growing over time. Today, the Network mediated transactions between customers, shops, apartments, and hotels in the few rebuilt cities in the Midwest region's five districts, and it acted as the arbiter between parties for contract jobs in and outside of the cities. Furthermore, the organization produced and sold gas masks, filters, and filtration systems, items so widely needed that only the Network, with its vast resources, could adequately meet the demand. According to the Network, at least. Of course, the organization could have simply eliminated the competition; people managed to survive in the wasteland before the Network came along.

Despite the Network's growing power, the organization still pushed the "agendaless mediator and supplier" narrative. Northfield had his doubts; he knew that once you started climbing the ladder of power, it was hard to stop climbing. However, as a Network mercenary, someone who took contracts mediated by the Network but didn't directly work for the organization, and as someone living in the middle of nowhere, he had little concrete information about its goings-on aside from the contracts it mediated between private parties and mercs. These contracts were dealt to mercs through various Network outposts placed around the Midwest region. Jobs included protecting clients and their cargo and often escorting them across the region, usually as a safeguard against the Yellowbacks. A fair number of assassination jobs were offered by anonymous clients through the Network, too, but Northfield stayed clear of hits. Life in the former land of red, white, and blue might have descended into a nightmare of unmeasurable proportions, but he would let his body die before throwing his soul that far into the dirt.

As his shoes crunched on twigs, he thought, *Wonder why God would try to kill me this morning. What could I have done to incur the Big Mighty One's wrath? Maybe he's jealous that Jess is taking up more imaginary conversation time in my head than he is.*

A crossroads lay past the forest, one of the Yellowbacks' favorite hunting spots between his house and the outpost. Before exiting the forest, he hid behind a tree and put his goggles over his eyes. He scouted out the crossroads using thermal vision. Determining that the coast was clear, he walked to the crossroads and took the most familiar road.

Hey, but I managed to avoid taking Network wetwork jobs up to this point, and I haven't hurt anyone who hasn't tried to hurt me first. That's gotta count for something. God's gotta throw me a bone at some point, right? Maybe by casting me off this hellhole early to be with Jess.

The outpost was initially a faint silhouette obscured by the gas before he drew nearer. The main structure was a small, log-cabin-looking building enclosed by a barbed electric fence and guarded by a watchtower. Atop the watchtower, a guard manned a mounted machine gun at all hours. A dirt path led up to a gate in the fence.

He smirked behind his gas mask. *Or maybe I'm just bored as hell on this walk and I'm overthinking random crap to keep my mind occupied. Yeah, that's probably it.*

A wooden post with an intercom stood in front of the gate. He pressed a red button on the intercom and said, "This is Mark Northfield. Operator code 1285."

There was a pause before he heard static. A deep, gravelly voice growled through the intercom, "Gate's openin', Northfield. Hope it hits ya on the way in."

Classic Francis, he thought. *Don't suppose you'd consider smiting him, huh, God?*

A high-pitched creak pierced through the sky as the gate opened. Northfield could feel the guard studying him from the watchtower. He reached the building, where he heard three warning beeps before the door opened; the building had a similar, albeit more advanced, air filtration system to his house, rendering gas masks unnecessary inside the building. He entered, and once the door closed, he took his off.

There wasn't much to the building's interior. In the main room, there were tile floors, white walls, and a few dim lights hanging from the ceiling. Two wooden tables with benches sat in the middle of the room. At one sat a middle-aged blonde woman who ate some sort of gray sludge that vaguely resembled something edible. On the wall opposite the door, a bulletproof window stretched from waist to head height. Francis resided past the glass, in a smaller room with various weapons mounted on the back wall. Through a closable opening at the bottom of the window, he exchanged credit cards for food, weapons, and supplies. In addition, he distributed jobs and assignments.

Francis was a portly man with patchy brown facial hair that had touches of gray. There was a black mole near his left nostril, and his beady little eyes always seemed full of resentment, an effect exacerbated by the perpetual downward fold of his bushy eyebrows. Currently, he was flirting with the woman eating her porridge. Northfield couldn't hear the last half of what Francis was saying, but he'd bet the farm that whatever drivel came out of Francis's mouth was sleaziness of the highest degree.

Don't get involved again, you idiot, he told himself. *Shit like this always blows up in your face. Just let it go. None of your business.*

He took a few steps forward and heard the woman say, "You're damn lucky I'm busy eatin' this slop and you're behind that glass. Say that shit again."

He studied her; aside from a rusted revolver in a waist holster, he didn't notice any other weapons on her person. The pistol indicated that she could probably take care of herself, but her lack of heavier weaponry led him to assume that she was one of the farmers struggling to feed the starving survivors both inside and outside of the boonies they lived in.

Despite the presence of the gas and its semi-opaqueness, which one might think would interfere with the photosynthesis of vegetation, crops could still grow. Rather, the chronic shortage of food in the wasteland could be attributed to the deaths of most farmers, like so many others, when the bombs dropped, leaving many inexperienced people having to fill the void. Not to mention, the machinery and irrigation systems necessary for running large-scale farms were either destroyed or rendered inoperable due to lack of maintenance in the following years.

Although the Network could probably alleviate these issues, the organization took no action, claiming a myriad of excuses that he didn't bother to remember. He'd bet a stack of credit cards thicker than a bus that the real reason had to do with power. People who were worried about getting their next meal didn't have the time or energy to concern themselves with the Network's machinations.

Even if she can take care of herself, that doesn't guarantee the next person to enter this outpost will be able to. Can't let this behavior slide and let a situation like this get worse. Not like last time.

He spoke up. "You better be talking about Network affairs, Francis, or we're gonna have some problems."

Francis directed his gaze from the woman to him, and with a scowl, he said, "None a' your goddamn business, Northfield. Who died and made ya watchman of the wasteland?"

He shook his head and said, "Not watchman of the wasteland— watchman of you. I'm not letting you pull your bullshit on another person. Don't need to see someone else go through that. Not again."

The woman, after finishing her porridge, put on her gas mask and stood up. As she walked toward the exit and past Northfield, she whispered, "Thanks."

He nodded almost imperceptibly, and the door opened and shut swiftly. *The fact that she ate her porridge here and stomached this overcooked Muppet's lechery probably means that she lives far away from this outpost and she needs food between the trip here and back. A long-ass journey, across some dangerous roads, just to order new tools and supplies.*

Francis said behind his bulletproof glass, "Don't make me have to report you to the Network, Northfield."

"Sure. If I kick your ass, you could report me. Get me in a lot of trouble, even. But if I kick your ass, you'd have to eat through a straw for a couple months. So there's that. Plus, I'm sure you'd love explaining your side of the story after I give mine."

They stared at each other tensely for a few moments. Northfield approached the bulletproof glass and softened his tone. "That's what I thought. Let's get this over with and we can both get out of each other's hair."

"Fine," Francis said, exhaling exaggeratedly. "What do you want?"

Northfield pulled out his three credit cards and said, "I want a week's worth of food rations and a net."

He slid the credit cards through the glass opening, and Francis slid the requested items through.

"Pleasure doin' business with ya," Francis said, sarcasm pricking each syllable like a porcupine's needles.

"Hang on. I'm not done," he replied. "I need a contract. What Network jobs are available? Any of my regulars?"

"I only got one," Francis said, grabbing a clipboard. "Assassination contract."

"You know I don't take those jobs," he said. "You don't have anything else? At all?"

"Stop bein' such a righteous pussy, Northfield," Francis said. "If you like eatin', take the job and stop bein' the only living blockhead in this hellhole whinin' about what jobs he will and won't take."

"I'll have to pass on your ever-enlightening advice, Francis. I'll check back tomorrow and see if you have anything else."

"Oh, what a joy for me," Francis growled.

Northfield left the outpost without spending another wasted word on him.

Along the way home, he thought, *Did I earn any redemption points for that one, God? Win myself any favors I can call in? If so, any chance you could stop logs from jamming my turbine? Or, the hell with it, maybe you should send logs into my turbine, take me out of my misery. I guess it depends on the day you ask me.*

After crossing the forest to reach his house, he connected the new net to the rods in the river.

Inside his house, he set his gas mask on the ground next to the black chest and pressed a small button located beneath the mask's chin. A loud hissing sound came from the left and right sides. The gas mask was a gadget, like his earplugs, that he'd spent a small fortune on. Most filters for gas masks protected the user for twenty-four hours of exposure before needing to be replaced; most people in the wasteland had to fork over large portions of their daily earnings just to buy bundles of filters from the Network. The expense, along with exorbitant prices for the scarce food and crowded living spaces, was a primary cause of poverty. His mask, in contrast, came equipped with reusable filters that could be cleaned by the mask itself. By pressing the button underneath the chin, the mask used energy acquired from small, nearly indistinguishable solar panels to suck in air and blast it at high pressures to clean the filters on either side and keep contaminants from clogging them. Eventually, the filters wore out from the high-pressured air, but they could last for months before having to be replaced.

Northfield had been accumulating the filters over time in case he couldn't get any more from the Network for whatever reason, be it a war that halted the Network's sale of them or if he ever found himself on the organization's hit list. With his current stash, he could last for years without having to visit another Network outpost. After stashing the rest of his gear in the black chest, he lay on his mattress and turned to face the picture.

"Francis was an asshole today, as usual. Caught him creeping on another woman. Can you believe it? I warned him, but I just pray that what happened last time won't happen again . . ."

He paused, then said softly, "Anyway, I missed you today, Jess. More than usual. Maybe it was just how big of a jerk Francis was. I don't know, but I just want you here with me. Or me with you. Either of the two works for me."

His eyes moved to the bookshelf next to the black chest, searching for escape in the cracked and bent bindings of the yellowing books. He'd read every one dozens of times at least. Books were a rarity in the toxic world, especially religious texts and fantasy novels. Whether the widespread disappearance of literature could be attributed to Network tampering, hatred for stories borne out of bitterness and resentment for how the world turned out, or the world's tendency to destroy ever since the bombs dropped, he wasn't really sure, but he nonetheless lamented the lack of stories to melt into, and he made a point of ac-quiring new books at every opportunity.

He snatched a copy of the complete *The Lord of the Rings* trilogy off the shelf and returned to his mattress, starting the story from the beginning. He let himself fade from his mattress and materialize in the Shire, hours passing as the pages turned.

Feeling a headache spawn in the center of his forehead, along with a good dose of tiredness, he returned the book to the shelf. Glancing at the picture of Jess one final time, he said before closing his eyes, "I'm gonna sleep, Love. As always, I hope you'll be in my dreams."

* * *

Four miles away, just before the end of Francis's shift, a truck arrived at the outpost. The gates opened, and the truck pulled up to the main outpost building. A man stubbier than a cigarette butt exited the truck with a sheet of paper in hand and entered the building. He took his gas mask off and approached the bulletproof glass windows.

"Two new contracts," the man said, sliding two slips of paper through the opening to Francis. "Escort mission and assassination mission. The first is protecting cargo from a possible Yellowback assault as it travels to Michelle's outpost. The second is a hit in Cumulus."

"Thanks, George," Francis said as the man turned around and left the building. He attached the slips of paper to his clipboard.

He looked down at the two new contracts. Assassination mission. Confirmation number 4456. Escort mission. Closed. Confirmation number 3328.

He smirked and muttered bitterly, "See ya tomorrow, Northfield."

CHAPTER 2

Northfield awoke from his slumber early and headed to the outpost as soon as he could. If Francis had received an escort or protection mission, he didn't want another Network merc nabbing the job before him. After hearing the loud creaks of the opening gate and the three warning sounds at the door, he found himself standing in front of the bulletproof window, staring at Francis's ugly mug.

"Have anything for me, Francis?" he asked.

"Lucky fer you," Francis said, pulling out his clipboard. "One came in last night. Escort mission. Open. Reward: fifteen credit cards."

Escort and protection missions could be open or closed. Open missions were available to all certified mercs. The person hiring the merc for an open mission could, if he chose, pay an additional fee for the next mission and specifically request the same merc, which closed the mission. If the merc refused or otherwise didn't take the mission within an allotted time, the mission would return to an open state.

Northfield made most of his income through closed missions, and they were how he managed to avoid taking assassination contracts. He'd gotten a lot of people out of scraps they had no business surviving; those same people tended to rehire him. Still, his location in the boonies gave his work an ebb and flow; if the escort and protection missions were far away from the merc's location, the Network tacked on a distance fee to accommodate the merc's transportation needs. Many clients, not desiring to pay an additional fee on top of the fee to request a merc, chose to simply hire mercs closer to the job. Right now, he was in a dry spell.

"Good," he said. "I'll take it."

"Confirmation number 4456. Ya know the drill, but always, as per Network policy, I gotta read ya the rules a'gin."

He nodded.

"If ya take the mission, an escort truck will arrive at yer house. You still live in that house by the river?"

"Yeah."

"Okay. An escort truck will arrive at yer house with a package. Ya tell him that confirmation number: 4456. He'll give ya the package containing specific details about the mission. Once ya take the package, yer officially accepting the mission. Ya gotta do it or ya will be killed. The package is deliver'd to yer place to protect the privacy of the client, so if ya disclose the contents to anyone, ya will be killed, too. Clear?"

"As a crystal."

"Good. I'll message the Network now to deliver yer package," Francis said, "Remember the confirmation number—4456."

"Got it," he said.

"Whoopdee-fuckin'-do for ya. Now get outta my outpost."

Not bothering to come up with a witty retort, Northfield left. As he made his way home, the deep orange sun rose from the horizon like a fireball launched from the surrounding trees, enhancing the soft night glow of the gas. He looked around and drank in his surroundings, a sense of sublime rising within him in tandem with the sun. The ever-present gas surrounded him but only spanned from ground level to a couple hundred feet in the air; it was evidently designed to remain stagnant and settle on the ground.

Due to the relatively low density of the gas, the sky and its clouds were still visible, albeit with a yellow-orange tint. The sun retained the same fiery-orange intensity that he recalled from watching sunsets on the beach years and years ago; if you squinted, you could almost mistake the light from the sun and the swirling gas for the glow of a forest fire past the canopy of trees on the horizon. As he observed, he became acutely aware of the gas mask over his mouth, remembering that if he took it off for even a few moments and inhaled, he'd be dead. Whoever designed the gas was a sick puppy, alright.

He entered his house and, after stowing away his gear, took a brief respite on his mattress. He grabbed the picture and brought it nearer to his face.

"God's looking out for me, I think," he said. "When I run out of credit cards and can only buy one more week's worth of rations, an escort mission falls in Francis's lap for me to take. What luck, right? Guess my good behavior might finally be paying off instead of royally bending me over."

He rolled onto his back, taking the picture with him and holding it over his face to look at.

"Or maybe I'll end up being shot by a Yellowback on this escort mission, end up bleeding out on the side of the road while drowning in that toxic gas. Then I'd be with you, at least. Or maybe I should stop being so negative. That's what you used to always tell me to do. This is positive, right? This is good."

He stared at the picture for a few more minutes. He set it down and said, "Alright, Love. Thanks for listening."

He stood up from the bed and ate a portion of the food rations he'd purchased with his credit cards. Now all he had to do was wait for the Network truck to arrive and receive his package. He occupied himself by picking up where he had left off in *The Lord of the Rings*.

Sure enough, in the afternoon, he heard rustling in the grass near his house; it was just loud enough to be audible over the sound of the humming air filter. The sound likely came from the Network employee. Trucks couldn't make it through the dense woods, so the employee probably parked the truck somewhere secluded, where Yellowbacks wouldn't easily find it, and walked here. The occurrence was common with drop-offs to his house. But just in case, he grabbed his pistol and gas mask from the black chest.

A knock at the door. He put on his gas mask, and with his pistol in hand, he opened the door. A stout woman with a gas mask that concealed her entire face stood with a sealed yellow envelope in her left hand. A pump-action shotgun was slung over her shoulder.

"Name, confirmation number," she said with a slightly impatient tone that implied she had a lot more packages to deliver that day.

"Mark Northfield, 4456," he replied.

She handed him the package and, without another word, turned and walked away, presumably heading back to her vehicle on the other side of the forest.

Good talk, he thought, shutting the door. He checked the air filtration system. After determining that the air was breathable, he took off his gas mask and stowed it in his chest, along with his pistol. He sat on his mattress and examined the thin envelope, which had no labels aside from the confirmation number written in black ink. He opened the envelope, and his eyes widened in tentative fury.

What the hell? he thought while yanking three documents out of the envelope.

In big, bold letters at the top of the first document was *X4456*. The X indicated that the job was an assassination mission. E would indicate an escort mission, while P would indicate a protection mission.

The target: some guy named Nathaniel Salb. Five-ten, brown eyes, black hair, olive-colored skin. Place of residence: Heaven's Rebirth, Cumulus. Reason for job: blank.

Of course it was left blank. To safeguard their anonymity, clients who hired the Network for assassination jobs didn't need to write down why they sent out the hit. Even the location of the outpost that received the hit contract was randomly chosen to protect the client's identity. Unlike escort and protection missions, assassination missions were always open to all certified mercs.

Oh no, he thought as he seethed, barely resisting the urge to crumple the documents. *This will not do. This will not do at all.*

He needed to clear this up. Right away. If he didn't, he'd have to complete the job within seventy-two hours. If he failed or refused, he'd be killed. A harsh and incredibly twisted policy, but one that had heartless logic: mercenary work was one of the few ways people could earn enough credit cards to do more than simply scrape by, and the list of people wanting to get merc certification was long as a result. If he was killed, another five people would be begging for his piece of the pie.

The envelopes crackled as he shoved them into his backpack. His fingers felt numb and clumsy while he packed his supplies and threw on his gear. Lastly, with a dark and uncomfortable feeling swirling in his chest, he decided to bring his picture of Jess. The straps of his backpack pulled sharply on his shoulders.

He left his house and slammed the door, then jogged toward the forest at the fastest pace he could maintain.

Clouds infested the late-afternoon sky, steadily growing in number as more moved into view. A few beams of sunlight pierced through the clouds to the west as the sun behind them grew nearer and nearer to the horizon.

Each of his breaths was extraordinarily heavy by the time he reached the outpost gate; he might have set his personal record for the fastest four miles traveled.

"This is Northfield," he said between breaths into the intercom. "Operator number: 1285."

"Ah, look. The esteemed one's returned," Francis's voice crackled through the intercom.

"Funny," he replied. "Open the damned gate."

After the gates opened, he wasted no time walking to the main outpost building. He waited impatiently for the three warning beeps of the door, then yanked it at the soonest possible second and stormed up to the bulletproof window, tearing off his gas mask. Francis just stared at him, smirking.

"I got an assassination mission," Northfield said. "Fix it."

Francis's smirk only grew wider.

"The hell's that jackal grin for?" he asked, his eyes narrowing.

"I just don't see the problem here," he replied with a shrug. "Ya gave the Network yer confirmation number. Took the job."

Northfield's eyes narrowed even further. "You son of a bitch."

The Network's complete-the-job-or-die policy did have a workaround, and that workaround was through outpost managers like Francis. The Network, like any other organization, occasionally made mistakes. Confirmation numbers could be fudged, packages could be delivered to the wrong people, and so forth. As such, if a Network mercenary was ever given a job they didn't sign up for, they could report the problem to their outpost manager, like Francis, and get it sorted out. Northfield had a sickening suspicion that the job he was given wasn't exactly a mistake. Worse still, he suspected that Francis would take no measures to rectify the situation.

"You did this on purpose, didn't you?" he said, terrified by the implication. If Northfield tried to report Francis with no third-party witness, the Network would side with Francis.

Francis leaned forward, his whole face darkening as his eyes narrowed and his smirk fell to a scowl. He said, "Yer such a righteous boy scout, Northfield. Turnin' yer nose up on jobs that fathers would give their children up fer. All fer some sort of higher purpose or God that any sane person would have given up on lon' ago. Thinkin' it's yer job to patrol me and these women yer so devoted to protectin'. Figured it was time fer someone to change yer view. Maybe after this job, when yer morally stained like the rest a' us, ya will get off yer porcelain high horse."

He took a moment to absorb what Francis had said. Then his teeth flashed in anger. "I have half a mind to find a way to break this bullet-proof glass and then break more than just the glass."

Francis leaned even farther in, to the point where his nose almost touched the glass. He said, "An' I wouldn't even report ya. Because that won't change anythin', and ya know that. Beat me an' run like an angry little boy, an' the Death Corps will be sent after ya all the same if ya don't do the hit."

The Death Corps were the Network's private army, and they enforced the rules of the Network in the region. The intimidating name, despite being at first glance contrary to the Network's "neutral adjudicator" public relations stance, was justified by the Network's claim that the Death Corps worked for the people by "protecting" trade and society from whoever posed a threat to them. If Northfield either refused to complete the hit or botched it, breaking the contract and consequently the Network's rules, the Death Corps would be sent after him.

His hands clenched into fists so tightly that they shook.

Francis continued. "Maybe yer best option is to just take the damned job. Fuckin' earn yer livin' like the rest of us."

Northfield didn't have any words; anger inundated his body to the point that it choked his throat.

Francis, delighted by his silence, said, "Ya need me to get ya transport?"

Cumulus was a long haul from their outpost; the random choosing of outposts for each hit contract often resulted in contracts being assigned to outposts far away from targets. If Network mercs decided to take distant contracts and didn't have transportation, they resorted to hiring drivers.

Due to the randomization of hit contracts, the contracts included an automatic distance fee, which covered the cost of a driver. Because mercs were paid after completion of the contract, payment to the driver was typically deducted after the contract was completed. Open escort and protection contracts, in contrast, were usually sent to outposts closer to the mission to avoid the distance fee. This meant that, most of the time, mercs could make the trek on foot, rendering transportation a nonissue.

In effect, by asking if Northfield needed to pay for transportation just to reach the damned target, Francis was rubbing salt in the wound he had so treacherously dealt.

Desiring to be the bigger man and retain at least a shred of dignity, Northfield mustered his strength and remained silent. He put his gas mask back on, turned around, and left the building. The clouds dumped on him; each raindrop that hit his body felt like a slap. As he walked to the gate, he realized that he could have taken his motorbike and saved himself the run over. The situation was certainly urgent enough to overcome his reluctance to ride it. However, he figured his forgetfulness didn't matter. With his luck, the damned bike would break down the next time he sat on it.

You really did me over here, God, he thought, kicking a pebble in frustration as he waited for the gate to open so he could leave. He walked through the gate, continuing his rumination. *Try to do the right thing, try to stop Francis from targeting another woman, and you do me over. What's new? What was I expecting? I mean, it's Tuesday, right? Maybe I should find some random tree stump and kick it for a few hours, see if that makes me want to kick Francis's head in less. Probably not. Yeah, if the Death Corps are sent after me for this garbage and I run into that fat bastard, I'm gonna give him a beating hard enough to make his grandchildren regret what he did—if any woman would willingly set foot in a room with him, that is, let alone get into a bed with him. That damned mole is the size of Antarctica.*

He stopped walking and looked up. Through the orange-yellow tint of the gas, he watched rain plummet from the darkening blue-black sea of clouds.

Put aside the anger for a second, he told himself. *I've got a question to answer: what am I gonna do? I made two promises to you, Jess. The first being that I would find any way to live without you, that no matter what, no matter how bad it got, I would do everything in my power to live and keep going. The second is that I wouldn't lose myself, who I am, because when I come up there with you, you want me to be with you, not some monster the world's turned me into. Not someone who loses what makes him feel human in the first place, what makes him feel right.*

His eyes fell from the clouds, and he continued walking. He held his Vector submachine gun, ready to use it at a moment's notice. Yellowbacks liked to prowl for victims at night; he had to be prepared.

He followed the road from the outpost to the crossroads, but he walked in a ditch with waist-high grass to keep hidden.

That puts me in a pretty fat pickle, doesn't it? If I don't assassinate Salb, the Death Corps will be sent after me, and that's a death sentence. If I don't kill him, I'm essentially forfeiting my own life. That would be breaking promise number one. And if I assassinate a guy without even knowing the reason why he's being assassinated, that would be breaking promise number two. What the hell do I do, God?

I could try to run, grab my bike, head anywhere but Cumulus, and never return. I'd be on the run from the Death Corps for the rest of my life. Best outcome, I'd only delay my death. I've got my supply of filters, but what about food and water? Even if I had a supply of them, too, I couldn't bring all that shit with me on my bike. Even if my stock of filters means I can avoid visiting Network outposts, I'd still have to interact with people in some capacity to get my other essentials. Even if I can get a fake ID, that doesn't change my face, which will be plastered on enough dumpsters to build a mountain. The Network offers a hefty reward for Death Corps targets, and the Death Corps is ruthless and unrelenting in their hunt.

Sooner or later, they'd get me; there's no doubt about that. And I'm sure that God would piss on me at every turn, making my life come to its inevitable end all the sooner. I'd be killing myself if I ran. But maybe running would count as trying to live and not breaking promise number one. I'm not sure . . .

He was getting close to the crossroads; soon, it would be visible.

Man, I wish you were here, Jess. You always would talk me through decisions, parse and organize my thoughts, and help me figure out what to do. But I guess if you were here, I wouldn't have this problem in the first place, would I? I wouldn't have promised you anything.

BRRRAP! BRRRAP!! BRRRRAP!!

He dropped to his stomach, his body instinctively reacting to the gunfire before he even recognized the sound. Determining that the gunfire came from in front of him, he aimed his Vector submachine gun in that direction despite being incapable of seeing past the thick grass. He heard another flurry of gunfire, but he didn't hear bullets impact anywhere near him. Because of this, he determined that the gunfire wasn't aimed at him. That meant one situation was incredibly likely; some cargo truck or travelers had been moving without an escort, and the Yellowbacks had jumped them at the crossroads. Credit cards weren't plentiful, and despite the always-present danger of attack on the roads, many travelers opted out of escorts to save their cards. Sometimes, that decision had a cost.

Don't you dare, Northfield. Keep your head down and get home. You always butt into stuff like this to help, and you always get reamed. Look how you got into your present situation. Just let it go. Let someone else come along. Or no one. How many people would help you in this world?

He looked down at the grass and mud.

But there's promise number two rearing its big buck-toothed head. I've screwed myself over following number two, and after I've already done that, I'd be damned if I quit abiding to promise number two now. Hey, maybe for testing me so much, God will at least take me out to dinner before screwing me again.

With that logic, I guess I'd have to not go through with the hit, wouldn't I? Then again, I couldn't see Jess wanting me to lie down and let Francis's bad action bring about the end of me. It wasn't my choice to take the hit. It was his. Should I really die for something bad that he did?

One thing at a time, Northfield. Help whoever is getting shot at. Then you can figure out what to do next.

He flipped down his quad-lens goggles and switched them to thermal vision, brushing the water off the lenses. From his prone position, he pulled himself into a crouch and crept through the long grass on his way toward the crossroads.

With my luck, there's probably ticks in this grass that'll give me Lyme disease or some other nasty crap.

The grass appeared navy blue through the goggles; the night sky was a dark blue that approached black. The ground had an upward incline that proceeded to dip sharply before the crossroads. From his position, he couldn't see the crossroads; he needed to reach the top of the hill to survey the situation.

More gunshots. He hurried his pace; if travelers had been jumped by Yellowbacks, he didn't know how long they could hold out. He reached the top of the incline, and he could see the crossroads below. A large steel post was bent sideways in the back-right corner of where the roads met. The bumper of a pickup truck with an attached trailer wrapped around the post. The right side of the truck faced Northfield. Mud covered the tires.

Four men appeared. Through his goggles, they were bright red and yellow blobs. They approached the vehicle at a slow, measured pace. Their backs faced Northfield, and they held assault rifles, which they fired at the truck in short bursts. He could see two big tanks strapped to each of their backs. Yellowbacks.

If he lifted his goggles, he'd be able to make out the all-too-familiar yellow and black uniforms that covered their bodies from head to toe. The source of their name, however, came from their yellow air tanks, which had tubes connecting to the masks on the front of their uniforms. The Yellowbacks didn't believe in inhaling gas-contaminated air during combat, even when filtered through gas masks. Instead, they breathed "pure" air from their tanks.

Yellowbacks had the notion that the "pureness" of this air invigo-rated their bodies and strengthened them to levels beyond what their "gas-breathing" counterparts could attain, bullshit Northfield didn't buy for one second. He'd run into a lot of Yellowbacks, and none had managed to kill him yet. The production and breathing of pressurized air had one key benefit that made the whole process worth the hassle: to be outside, the Yellowbacks didn't have to buy Network-made fil-ters for gas masks, allowing them a degree of autonomy not afforded to many others.

At what ragtag lab their "pure" air was whipped up in, Northfield didn't know for certain, although he had come up with some theories in the copious amount of time he had to think.

He suspected that the Yellowbacks were nomadic, frequently moving their bases of operation and labs from one place to another, with lookouts keeping an eye on nearby roads. This way, they could pack up and leave a location before a Death Corps force large enough to threaten them could show up. They could produce their air, prob-ably using materials stolen from the Network, and fill enough sup-plies of air tanks to sustain them when outside. Northfield suspected that the majority of Yellowbacks lived separately from the main base, traveling to it when necessary to acquire supplies, drop off stolen goods, and resupply air tanks. In whatever shelters the Yellowbacks lived, they likely used stolen Network filtration systems repaired and maintained indefinitely by capable technicians, affording them yet further autonomy from the Network. In addition, the breathing of "impure" air in their homes wouldn't violate their doctrine, as their bodies didn't need to be "strengthened and invigorated" when out of combat.

When entering combat, the Yellowbacks also turned on glowing lights that circled their gas masks and tanks, another instance of their cult-like mentality; they thought that "glowing" with their comrades would instill fear into their enemies.

Northfield couldn't see who, but someone on the other side of the truck returned fire; a pair of hands popped over the bed and blind-fired an AK-47. His suspicions were all but confirmed.

The Yellowbacks had jumped the truck, firing to take out its tires, and caused the truck to crash into the post. Mud was dripping from the door and bumper of the truck, and the front tire sunk into the ground; the driver must've gotten stuck in the mud, and he or she exited out of the passenger side door. Now, the driver desperately fended off the incoming Yellowbacks.

Wonder if that poor bastard will give me any credit cards as thanks for this, he thought, rising out of the grass and looking through the holographic sight of his Vector. He centered the red dot on the left Yellowback's chest, then pulled the trigger five times. Immediately after firing, he lowered himself into the cover of the grass. A cry rang out, and gunfire erupted in his direction. He moved backward, using the hill as a shield to break the Yellowbacks' line of fire.

He crept through the grass rightward, hearing more gunfire from the direction of the truck. Once he put about thirty yards between himself and the location he had fired from, he slinked back over the hill. He wiped the rain off his goggles before he popped up, watching as the Yellowbacks tactically rushed to his previous position.

There were three hostile gunmen; the fourth lay at the crossroads, face-down as blood poured out of a wound in his back. Northfield fired four shots at the nearest Yellowback. After seeing him fall, he swiveled to the second-nearest Yellowback and pulled the trigger three times. Northfield couldn't tell where the third shot connected, but it certainly hit the Yellowback. He watched the Yellowback recoil and tip backward, disappearing as the grass enveloped him.

The final Yellowback screamed in response, launching a burst of gunfire in Northfield's direction. But Northfield was already on the move, sprinting in a crouch as bullets whistled past him. He popped out of the grass and, while running, fired four more shots at the Yellowback. His enemy glowed bright red and yellow through the goggles, contrasting with the surrounding shades of blue. The Yellowback ducked to avoid the return fire, and he lost sight of Northfield for just a moment. But it was enough; Northfield disappeared into the vegetation again, leaving the Yellowback frantically searching for his assailant.

Fifteen yards away, Northfield popped up and pumped off a few more rounds in the Yellowback's direction. The bullets tore through the grass and mud surrounding the Yellowback.

The Yellowback remained unharmed, but after seeing the fate of his buddies, he didn't have the inclination to stick around. He spun around on his heels and sprinted away from the crossroads, cursing and swearing through his mask between each inhalation from the air tanks on his back.

Two down, one on the run, and one at the very least injured. He had to make sure the injured Yellowback wasn't going to fight, one way or another. He hoped he could patch up the Yellowback and send him packing, but even as the thought occurred to him, he knew that it was a stupid dream.

He sneaked through the grass, weapon at the ready, closing in on the location where the Yellowback had fallen. When he drew close enough, he heard a sound that kicked his heart down a cliff.

Thick, wet coughing. Agonizing, raucous coughing. Coughing so violent and crimson and rapid that Northfield knew the Yellowback couldn't even get out a scream of agony.

A lonely gunshot roared, jolting every one of Northfield's muscles into tenseness. This tenseness faded after a moment, replaced by a loose and exhausted somberness.

He reached the body of the Yellowback. As he expected, one hole from his Vector. Because of the angle, the bullet grazed the Yellowback's face but didn't cause serious damage. It would have been better if the bullet did; instead, it broke the Yellowback's mask, allowing toxic air to seep in. A final bullet from the gun in the Yellowback's now-limp hand had finished the job.

Blood surrounded the Yellowback's head. Northfield had no doubt the Yellowback had thrashed around in every direction while the gas invaded his body, ripping apart his lungs and sending the scarred and bloody remains through his throat.

He didn't suffer long. For him, however, the agony probably felt like an eternity. Funny how time worked like that. Another one of God's little treats for the earth.

You didn't deserve that. Not one second of that did you deserve.

Northfield had an urge to just stay there and not do anything for a little while, but he forced himself to keep going.

In a crouch, he checked his surroundings before tentatively standing up and doing the same from above the thick grass. Aside from the dead Yellowback on the road, he didn't see any warm bodies through his thermal vision; the other bodies were concealed by the grass. The heat signature of the Yellowback on the road was fading from a bright red to a cool purple and would soon be indistinguishable from the blue pavement beneath him.

He stared at the body, feeling again the somberness that never really left. *I don't take any satisfaction or joy in this. I hope you know that. I hate it as much as the first time I pulled the trigger, but I couldn't let you take an innocent person's life and possessions. For what it's worth, I hope you're all in a better place.*

He turned his attention to the driver camped out behind the truck, whose return fire at the Yellowbacks had ceased shortly after Northfield's offensive began. Northfield could only guess as to the reason for the absence of fire: the driver could have decided to hunker down behind the truck and wait out the commotion, or the driver could have attempted an escape, running from their side of the truck and into the cover of the grass. He doubted the latter, because if the driver worked for the Network, they would be killed for an unsuccessful delivery of cargo. Or the worst case could have happened: the driver could have taken a bullet and was either rolling around in pain or dead in a puddle of blood and water by now.

Just leave it. You already did your boy scout duty for the day. Jess would be proud. God might even be proud that I saved someone, although he'd probably lecture me on how the Samaritan didn't lug around a submachine gun. The Yellowback that ran away is probably on his way to get enough reinforcements to make Normandy look like a birthday party. You really wanna be here when they show up? And if I go near the truck, whoever's behind it may think I'm trying to steal their stuff, like the Yellowbacks, and put a .45-caliber bullet between my eyes. Wouldn't that be a pitiful way to go out?

He switched off his thermal vision, flipped his goggles off his eyes, and rested them on his Spoonbills beanie. Then he studied the truck, which was thirty or so yards away from him. He realized that the truck had airless tires, a detail he didn't previously observe due to the obfuscation of the tires by mud, his distance away, and his negligence to pick up the detail due to the sheer rarity of the sight.

The airless tires were expensive. To save enough money to afford them, drivers had to cut out the expense of a Network merc. Due to how dangerous the roads were, most drivers didn't make it long if they opted out of taking a merc. He realized that the driver taking cover behind the bed of the truck was likely a deliberate maneuver. The driver wanted to draw fire away from the front of the truck, where the engine resided. Because the truck was already stuck in mud, the Yellowbacks prioritized hitting the driver rather than further disabling the vehicle. He hoped the Yellowbacks failed to achieve their goal. Well, he had only one way to find out.

Ah, the hell with it. I've already waded into this pond. If the truck driver was hit, and they bleed out, then what the hell was the point of this? Gotta make sure the driver's okay.

He made his way out of the grass and walked to the middle of the crossroads. A thin black snake of smoke rose from the hood of the truck and swirled around the steel pole, poised to choke it.

"You're safe now," Northfield called out. "The Yellowbacks are gone, at least for now."

He figured that he'd wait ten or so seconds for a response before repeating what he said. If he didn't hear a response soon after, he'd assume the driver was incapacitated or killed, and he'd go to the other side of the truck and investigate. Otherwise, he was tentative about moving toward the truck; he didn't want to startle the driver and catch a few bullets in his sternum.

Five seconds passed. A man popped up over the bullet-kissed bed of the truck, pointing the barrel of his rusted AK-47 at him. He was tall and sturdily built with light-brown skin, and he wore a red flannel shirt with the sleeves rolled up past his elbows. His gas mask had an opaque visor. Rain splashed off his bald head.

Northfield resisted the self-preserving urge to point his submachine gun as the man demanded, "What the hell do you want?"

"Nothing," he replied. "Just wanted to make sure you were alright before I head on my merry way. You weren't shot or anything, were you?"

"I don't like this," the man said, shaking his head. "I don't like this at all. You're telling me this was some do-gooder shit? I don't buy that."

"Honestly, I don't care if you believe me or not. Just wanna make sure you don't pump lead into my backside the second I turn around. Now answer my question: are you alright? You're not hurt, are you?"

The man hesitated before he said, "No, I'm not hurt."

"Good. You gonna be able to get this truck out by yourself? My place isn't far from here, and I might have some supplies if you need them."

"I've got floor mats with extra traction for shit like this," the man said, tilting his head toward the front of the truck. He added, "Why are you doing this?"

"I saved your ass. If Yellowbacks come back and you're still here, then I would have wasted my time and effort saving your ass in the first place. Gotta cross the finish line, you know?"

"Not good enough. What's your angle? What are you looking to gain here?"

"Nothing. Well, nothing you've got on that truck, that's for sure. Either way, doesn't really matter. If your truck will get you where you need to go, my work's done. I just need your assurance that you won't pull the trigger the second I turn around and expose my back."

The man lowered his weapon slightly. "Whatever your reason, you saved me. I gotta respect that. You have my word."

"Good talk," Northfield muttered, turning around and taking a few steps away from the truck. He felt the man's eyes needle him. Fear curled up his spine like barbed wire. The image of a bullet piercing his back appeared awfully vivid in his mind. He thought about facing the man and walking backward until he was out of range of the AK-47, but he resisted; he had enough faith in humanity to believe that this guy wouldn't just shoot him in the back for no reason. He wasn't going to lose his trust in people and become cold and aloof;

43

he'd seen enough people fall and lose everything about themselves by that first step.

"Hey," he heard the man call out after he traveled a few paces, encouraging him to turn around and face the truck once again. Once the stranger saw that he'd caught Northfield's attention, he asked, "You want a job?"

"What kind of job?" Northfield asked after a pause.

"My truck ain't exactly in pristine shape, and there's always the danger of Yellowbacks on these roads. If you come with me as added protection, I'll give you half of the credit cards I earn for this job. It's not as much as other protection jobs, but it's something."

Of course, I get a job offer I want only after I'm shafted with this assassination bullshit. Tell me, God, is it really that fun messing with me, or are you just that bored?

Out of curiosity, he asked, "Where's your destination?"

"Cumulus," the man said.

Northfield's eyes widened. *Here I am, deliberating about whether to do the job or run, and a ride to Cumulus just appears here in front of me. You've got a funny way of working, God. A really funny way.*

"What's your name?" he asked.

"I'm Jake Jameson," the man said, walking around the truck to Northfield's side. "What should I call you?"

"Mark Northfield," he said, extending his hand to shake Jameson's.

As they shook hands, Jameson asked, "Is that a yes, then?"

This better be some sort of sign, God, because I'm taking it as one. If you're gonna give me a damned ride to this job, I'm gonna assume you're pushing the universe to make me do this for whatever bizarro omniscient reason you have. I'm sorry, Jess. I promise I won't let it change me. A stain on a shirt's a stain, alright, but it doesn't destroy the rest of the shirt.

44

He nodded in response to Jameson's question. "We should get out of here before trouble finds us."

"Agreed," Jameson replied. He handed his newly hired merc floor mats before he climbed into his truck. Northfield placed the mats behind the trailer's wheels. Fortunately, the wheels were still mostly on the road and not embedded in mud. "Let's hope those thugs didn't hit anything vital," Jameson muttered, turning the ignition.

Northfield took a step backward as the truck revved, and he kept an eye out for Yellowbacks as Jameson reversed the vehicle. The tires spent a second spinning in the mud before they gripped the mats. Jameson let out an excited shout, and he realigned the truck on the road. He beckoned for Northfield to enter the truck.

After Northfield slammed the passenger door shut, Jameson muttered, "Hope you like R&B. Only disk I've got left." A crackle emitted from the truck's aged speakers before guitars strummed. Without looking back, Jameson took the road that led to Cumulus.

As the last echoes of the engine faded from the crossroads, the dead bodies were left with only the company of swaying grass and broken glass.

CHAPTER 3

The two men sat without speaking for a couple of minutes. Eventually, Jameson asked, "You ever been to Cumulus?"

Northfield was staring out the window; he initially tried to keep on the lookout for Yellowbacks, but the staring quickly became absentminded. The day had been long. "Yeah. Couple times. Not a place I frequent, though. Got out of the urban areas not too long after everything fell apart."

"Must be nice, huh?" Jameson muttered, his eyes gazing far ahead like he was staring off into a dream, "Livin' up in those skyscrapers, bein' able to step out on a balcony and breathe actual fresh air."

"It ain't all it's cracked up to be. Most of them are packed in apartments like sardines in a can."

Jameson scoffed. "We're all packed in rooms or houses like sardines in a can. Or are you not?"

"Nope. Got my own filtration system."

Jameson's eyes widened, and he took his eyes off the road to look at Northfield. "Hot shit. You must be a Network merc, right? Gun skills like that against the Yellowbacks. Able to afford your own filtration system. I ain't no Nancy Drew, but the pieces come together."

"Yep. With this truck, I take it you're a Network driver?"

"You got it."

"I see those airless tires you've got," he said. "Do you usually skip taking an escort?"

"Yeah. Before the gas, I used to drag race."

"Really? Were you any good?"

Jameson chuckled and said, "I was okay. Point is, I'm used to taking the odds. I calculate which routes to take an escort and which routes to not take one. Lately, I've been realizing that I'm getting too old for playing so fast and loose with luck. I was planning on taking a merc on every job after I finally saved up for a bigger place and my own filtration system. Almost reached my goal, too. Before today."

"And then shit happened."

"And then shit happened," Jameson echoed before adding, "But bein' a merc. Damn. That must be exciting, with all those gunfights and battles."

Northfield let out a soft laugh. "It's not all that it's cracked up to be. Most days it's just sitting around and waiting. Or walking and waiting. Or driving and waiting. Lots of waiting."

Jameson laughed. "Still, though. Hard to beat the pay. You like the job?"

Northfield's demeanor darkened slightly. "Not particularly. I got tricked into doing a job that I don't want to do."

"What? How does that even happen?"

"Long story. Suffice it to say, I'm in kind of a bind right now."

"I'm sorry to hear. If you're in a bind over this job, don't you have to be somewhere? I mean, why did you take my job when you've already got one?"

"Yeah, I do need to be somewhere. Cumulus."

"No kidding. What are the odds of that?"

"Pretty damned low, I'd say. Makes me wonder if ol' magic eight ball in the sky is looking out for me. That or just messing with me."

"Nah, man, God left this earth a while ago."

With nothing left for either of them to say, silence ensued. Jameson kept his eyes on the road while Northfield stared out the window, watching dark-green trees and shrubs and grass pass by. The glowing gas slithered through the greenery like a serpent. Jameson, apparently not someone that relished silence, spoke up again.

"I hate the name Cumulus. Liked the old one better. Cumulus sounds pretentious to me."

"Yeah, well, when you're one of the few cities left in the Midwest, I guess you deserve a little pretentiousness."

"Not when the rent's so high for those high-rises above the gas. You know how much those cost?"

"No, how much?"

Jameson laughed. "I actually don't know diddly squat about how much they cost. That was a serious question."

"Oh." Northfield laughed. "I don't know how much they cost, either. Probably expensive as hell. I mean, think of it: they're some of the only places you can live and breathe fresh air. All I know is that the Network handles apartment rentals and stuff like that. But then again, Yellowbacks live in the city."

"You know, I've always wondered how the hell Yellowbacks get away with being in the city with such a heavy Network presence."

"From what I've heard, they usually dress as normal people instead of their bargain-bin Power Ranger getups and sneak into the city. From there, they kick out, threaten, or kill the occupants of an apartment and set up shop there. As long as the Yellowbacks continue to pay rent, the Network doesn't usually notice that the apartment's changed hands. Or, hell, the Network probably just doesn't care. I wouldn't be surprised if there was some sort of deal between the Yellowbacks and the Network. Maybe they just pay for rent instead of kicking people out. Rumors are rumors, so who knows how true they are."

"Sheesh," Jameson said, shaking his head. "You'd think with how much the Yellowbacks screw with the Network, the Network would try better to make sure not even one of those deranged loons steps foot in the city."

"Thing is," Northfield said, "the Yellowbacks don't mess with Network operations in the city. They're not that dumb. They know they'd have Network reinforcements sniffing their asses if they tried to tamper with a Network operation in-city. It's easier to employ their hit-and-run tactics in the boonies. Maybe the Network figures that if the Yellowbacks are in the city, they're less of a problem."

"Maybe less of a problem, but still a problem. Those fucking Yellowbacks are a problem wherever you go."

"Some of them. Maybe most of them. Good and bad in every lot that big, I guess."

"Maybe," Jameson said. "But if I see a Yellowback, I'm gonna keep my barrel pointed in his direction. All of them I've met are dog shit. Murdering, stealing thieves, all of them."

"Hopefully whoever I'm after fits both of those criteria."

Jameson averted his eyes from the road to look at Northfield. "'Who I'm after'? Ah, geez, is the job a hit? You know, I've never understood how you mercs can do those jobs. I mean, I've done a lot of bad shit to survive, but I couldn't imagine doing that day in, day out. But a man's gotta eat, I guess. Does it get easier?"

"Wouldn't know." Northfield looked out the side window wistfully. "I've made it a point to never take assassination missions. Sometimes there's too much dirt for the gold underneath to be worth it, you know? Someone screwed me over to make a point."

"Damn," Jameson muttered, shaking his head. "That's some cold shit. I'm sorry."

"It's alright," he said, turning to look out the windshield. "I'll get in, do the job, get out, and get paid, then wash my hands of it and move on."

"Yeah, man. Ain't no shame in earning credit cards in whatever way you can out here. Harsh world and all, you know?"

"Sure, but I'm afraid of what you said: jobs like these becoming easier. This is only one mission, but the slope is damned slippery. If I do more hits, well, that changes someone."

"I don't know, man. Most people I know ain't got the smallest scrap of humanity in them. From what you did for me, I can tell that you're a good person, but out here, that's dangerous. Maybe change wouldn't be the worst thing."

Northfield lounged back in his seat and said softly, "I'm not ready to believe that. Not yet."

He scanned his surroundings for any Yellowbacks or traps that would wish them harm, but his mind was elsewhere, reliving memories with Jess. The sparks of joy he felt from each replayed scene quickly faded into painful reminders of reality.

CHAPTER 4

"**O**ur chariot has arrived at the kingdom," Jameson said sardonically. "The south Cumulus entrance."

Northfield stretched his aching muscles, pulled himself from a slouch into an upright sitting position, and stared out the windshield. Masses of buildings broke through the ocean of glowing gas and basked in the clear night sky above the surface, a sky he hadn't seen untainted by yellow and orange in several years.

The city was encircled by a twenty-foot-tall electric fence with barbed wire. Guard towers were posted at steady intervals. Faint candlelight ebbed from a sparse number of the buildings' windows. The road led to a gate with one guard tower on each side, along with a small kiosk that acted as a wedge between the road's incoming and outgoing lanes. Two guards stood on both sides of the right lane, which was designated for traffic going into the city. Each guard held an assault rifle.

Jameson pulled up to the kiosk. Shielded by concrete and bulletproof glass, a member of the Death Corps stood inside the kiosk. As part of the Death Corps' duty to enforce the rules of the Network, it controlled entry into and exit out of Cumulus. Looking up, he could see a Death Corps soldier posted in each guard tower, both manning shielded miniguns, which were currently pointed at Jameson's truck.

"Papers," the guard in the kiosk said. His electronically scrambled voice was unnaturally deep. Death Corps soldiers had voice modulation software in their helmets that made them sound like, well, agents of death. *There must be some sort of compensation game going on between the Corps and Yellowbacks. Man, they've got some whacked-out uniforms,* Northfield thought, smirking behind his gas mask.

The guard, like all Death Corps soldiers, wore a solid-black faceplate with vertical red and blue lines running over where the eyes would be. Death Corps soldiers could see through the faceplates, but to an outside observer, the plates were opaque, betraying none of the wearer's features. Although the faceplates were devoid of eye or mouth holes, the plates had three slits on both the right and left sides for six in total: part of the Network's advanced air filtration system that replaced conventional gas masks.

Soldiers additionally wore black body armor that had the same red and blue line patterns as the faceplates. The armor protected the soldiers from most calibers of bullets, save for TAP rounds. However, due to how expensive TAP rounds were, few people had access to them.

There were only two groups that the Network, and subsequently the Death Corps, had to worry about possessing TAP rounds: mercs, particularly ones they hunted for failing contracts, and Yellowbacks, who acquired the rounds through theft, such as by hijacking supply vehicles. Northfield suspected bribery could be another source.

They don't even look human, he thought. *Makes it easier to shoot them if things go south.*

As Jameson handed the guard his Network identification card, Northfield searched his backpack for his own, thinking, *What the hell are you going on about, Northfield? Even if you fail or refuse to complete the mission, you're not shooting any Death Corps soldiers.*

You're running. You're running and not looking the other way. Man, I must really be losing it.

After finding his card, he handed it to Jameson, who passed it to the guard. While the guard inspected the card, the two previously on the right side of the incoming traffic lane opened Jameson's trailer and searched it.

Alright, Northfield, buck up. You're not going insane. You're not. Jess wouldn't like it any better if you get unhinged and meet her up in those white clouds as a psycho instead of just a morally bankrupt guy doing hits for money. At least if you're the latter, she can chew you out for losing yourself, and you won't be too far off the deep end to understand what she's talking about.

Or is that your big cosmic plan, God? To screw with me so much that I go insane. I'd be mad, but hell, that sounds like a wildly interesting thing to watch. If I was an angel or some random guy in heaven, I'm sure I'd get a kick out of that. Maybe you get watch parties together for this week's episode of How I'm Going to Mess with Mark's Life Next . . .

"You both check out," the guard said after receiving a nod from the two searching the trailer. He handed Jameson the identification cards. "If you're going to the South Network Facility to drop off your cargo and collect your payment, go straight for two blocks, then take a right. The building will be on the next street."

"Thanks," Jameson said and handed Northfield his card. After a few moments' delay, the gate opened slowly, emitting a loud rusted creak that rattled Northfield's teeth.

The truck passed through the gate and entered the city. As Jameson continued forward two blocks, Northfield observed the city through his window. The asphalt road and the sidewalks on both shoulders had deep spiderweb cracks from years of neglect.

Dim cones of fragmented light flickered from the cracked street-lights; the glass that covered the bulbs on the streetlights was broken, leaving them half-exposed. The luminescent orange-yellow gas glowed even brighter as it slithered around the streetlights. The Network provided electricity for the city, although most apartments were left unpowered or unused to save money. Instead, lamps were used to illuminate living spaces.

They were in one of the most populated areas of the city; citizens walked on both sides of the street despite the late hour. Though the pedestrians were tall and short, male and female, and all shades of skin colors, they all had one thing in common; they wore gas masks. Some were military-grade while others were homemade or shoddily crafted by the store owners and merchants in the city. Those who could afford weapons armed themselves, usually with a handgun strapped to the chest or in a hip holster. Although crime and violence in the city were relatively low due to the Network's presence, guns were used as intimidation and gave the holder a degree of power when negotiating for prices on food, water, and other materials.

"God, what a depressing sight," Jameson muttered as he drove.

"I know. Nobody's wearing Spoonbills gear," Northfield replied, looking down at his red and blue jacket and gloves.

Jameson laughed and said, "I've always been partial to the White Sox myself, so I can't agree with you there."

"We made it this far, Jameson. Don't make me shoot you," he said dryly.

"Give it your best shot," Jameson said while chuckling. "I've survived in this hellhole for a decade. I'm not gonna get killed by a fucking Spoonbills fan."

The truck turned right, and the two main structures comprising the South Network Facility came into view. The first was a concrete building with two-story windows encircling the top floor and a steel beam that rose from the roof. The silhouette of the building resembled the Empire State Building, albeit smaller, leading to the nickname "Little Empire." Many high-level Network employees worked in Little Empire; Northfield could only guess what was going on in there.

The second main structure of the South Network Facility, a fifteen-story parking garage, connected to Little Empire. The Network repurposed the parking garage for various tasks like coordinating incoming and outgoing deliveries of supplies, organizing contracts, and managing living spaces in the city.

A barbed-wire fence surrounded the South Network Facility in the shape of a rectangle. There was a guard tower in each corner. On the side of the fence nearest to the parking ramp, a kiosk stood in front of a gate, which was almost identical to the gate and kiosk that allowed admittance into Cumulus.

Jameson drove to the kiosk and presented his identification along with Northfield's, in addition to his delivery papers. The Death Corps guard read the ID number at the top of the delivery paper, and he checked his clipboard. Trucks had designated drop-off floors based on their cargo.

Without looking up, the guard said, "Floor five." After he radioed to one of the guard towers to open the gate, Jameson drove through. Between the fence and the two buildings, a well-kept grass lawn added to the aesthetic appeal of the facility. To Northfield, the grass existed as a sort of oasis in the middle of a jungle of machine guns, armored vehicles, and barbed wire fences. In the sporadic light that illuminated the field, he could see the grass lightly undulate in the breeze.

"You could make a mighty fine baseball field in here, couldn't you?" Jameson asked.

"Yeah. Yeah, you could. Maybe I should challenge some Network guys to a home run derby to get out of this contract."

"If only the world worked that way, right?"

"You're right. They wouldn't go for it," Northfield said. "They've all got the prickly disposition of someone who crabs at you for forgetting the anchovies on their pizza when you know damn well they didn't order them."

Jameson laughed, and he said, "Don't say that, man. You're making me sad. I used to hate Pizza Kingdom with a passion, but man, you don't know what I'd do to get a slice again."

"As strange as it may sound, I actually miss their wings. You know, those crappy wings you could get as a side?"

"Those wings are disgusting. A Spoonbills fan and a Pizza Kingdom wings fan? What kind of degenerate am I driving with? Why the hell would you miss those?"

Northfield laughed. "My wife had a dairy allergy, so we wouldn't really get pizza. But sometimes she'd get a craving for those breadsticks they have. I wasn't gonna order a whole pizza for myself, so I'd get the wings instead. And yeah, they were low-grade, but they kinda grew on me."

Jameson chuckled and shook his head. "Being subjected to eating those wings? You sound like you were whipped, man."

"Willful sacrifice, man," Northfield said with a laugh. "Willful sacrifice."

The truck ascended the parking ramp and exited on the fifth floor. A guard flagged them down and directed them to a parking spot. Three Death Corps guards approached the truck, one of them holding a clipboard. Jameson and Northfield disembarked, leaving their gear and weapons on the seats, and Jameson approached the agent with a clipboard.

"Papers?" the guard asked him. Jameson handed him the delivery papers. The agent read the ID number, found it on his clipboard, and announced to the other two agents, "Food ration delivery, boys!" To Jameson, he said, "Any weapons I should know about?"

"Yes. Only on the driver and shotgun seats," Jameson answered. After patting Northfield and Jameson down, the guard nodded and relayed the information to the other agents. A few minutes passed as Northfield and Jameson watched them closely inspect every nook and cranny of the semi-truck and trailer. The guards gave each other a thumbs-up, and the one with the clipboard radioed to the Network room on the floor.

He approached them and said, "You're good to go. Everything checks out. Your job is hereby completed. Go to the Network room for your payment. Leave your weapons here."

Jameson and Northfield walked to the Network room, warily watching the machine guns in the wall slits trace their movements, their barrels centered on their chests. Once they reached the steel door, it cracked open with a loud hiss, and they rushed through. The Network room, like most rooms, had a filtration system to cleanse the air; it was a common courtesy to hastily enter rooms with filtration systems.

The room's tile floors and walls were all white. Panel lights on the ceiling flickered with a certain degree of what could only be described as sickness, as if the lights were a visible symptom of a disease that had infested the room. The whiteness of the walls and floor partially offset the dimness, but Northfield couldn't shake sensations of weariness and dread caused by the atmosphere.

Looking to his left and right immediately after entering through the door, he could see two guards manning the machine guns that had been pointing at him and Jameson when they approached. At the other end of the room, there was a desk with various files and papers stacked on top of it. Behind it was a man wearing circular glasses. He looked around sixty and had an exhausted expression and disarrayed white hair, presumably from working the night shift. On the wall behind him were nine lockers arranged in a three-by-three grid. Next to them, a steel door led to Little Empire; the ability to access the Network's secretive building was the primary reason for such tight security. One armed guard stood in front of the locker, while another stood in front of the door.

Jameson and Northfield took off their gas masks; after the long ride, their faces needed a break from the stuffiness. The weary-looking man behind the table held out his hand with an air of joyless expectation. Jameson handed him his ID card, which the man inspected. Then he looked down at the papers on his desk before handing Jameson his card, turning to the guards, and ordering flatly, "Fifty credit cards."

A guard opened one of the lockers and pulled out a stack of credit cards bound by a rubber band. He handed the bag to Jameson. The exhausted man looked down and sifted through papers on the table, paying Jameson no further mind. Obviously for him, their business had been concluded.

Jameson separated twenty-five cards from the stack and handed them to Northfield. "Here. You've earned it. Thanks for everything."

"Thanks for the ride," Northfield said. He addressed the old man and asked, "What floor's the trading room on?" In the trading room, he could exchange the credit cards for weapons, ammunition, food rations, and other supplies; in addition, he could rent a hotel in the city.

"Next floor up. The staircase is next to the car ramp. You're gonna need your ID for the guards to let you past the staircase," the old man said, looking up at Northfield with dismissive annoyance, as if he was the pebble creating ripples of disruption on his peaceful lake.

Northfield and Jameson put on their gas masks, left the Network room, and returned to the truck. Jameson unlocked it, and Northfield grabbed his gear from his seat.

After he shut the door, Jameson asked, "What are you gonna do?"

Northfield looked at him and repeated, confused, "What am I gonna do?"

"About your job," Jameson said. "You really gonna do it?"

"Don't really have a choice, do I?" he replied. "It's either my target or me at this point."

"I guess that's how you gotta rationalize it," Jameson said. "I'd do the same."

"Yeah. Doesn't really seem to make it any easier, though," he replied. He stuck his hand out and said, "Nice meeting you, Jameson. Been a while since I've had a friend. Have safe travels wherever you're going, alright?"

Jameson shook his hand and said, "The pleasure's all mine. Glad to know that there's still good people out here, you know? Good luck with what you have to do."

He got into his truck and drove toward the spiral ramp. Northfield briefly wondered if he'd ever see Jameson again. He subsequently wondered if Jess would like him or not. *God, make sure to keep my recent bad luck away from him, alright?*

He averted his gaze from the spiral ramp and found the U-shaped set of concrete stairs adjacent to it. A bulletproof glass wall surrounded the staircase. A glass door, guarded by two Death Corps soldiers on either side, allowed access.

He sighed. He felt like he was descending with each step he took on this journey. A descent into what, he didn't know. Maybe into some sort of shitstorm he didn't want any part of. Or maybe into hell.

Either way, going back didn't feel like much of an option. He climbed the stairs and approached a glass door with two Death Corps soldiers on the other side.

"Your ID," one of the guards shouted to him from the other side of the glass. After Northfield pulled out his ID and showed it to the guard, the guard said, "Come on through. Leave your weapons where they are."

Northfield complied and allowed a guard to search him.

Once the guard finished, the other guard nodded toward the far end of the parking garage and said, "Trading room's there."

From the outside, the Network room on the sixth floor looked identical to the Network room on the fifth floor, with the same concrete exterior and machine guns pointing out of slits on either side of the steel door. Once again, these machine guns traced his movements as he approached the room and waited for the door to open.

Because the Network room on the sixth floor was purposed for the trading of supplies and rentals for credit cards as opposed to the management of contracts and shipments, the interior looked much different than that of the fifth.

Similar to Francis's outpost, a window with bulletproof glass protected a Network merchant. Behind the window, a room contained gas masks, food rations, and other supplies, much more than was available at Francis's outpost. A number of weapons were also available for purchase, but they differed from those Francis offered in one key way.

Because Little Empire could be accessed through the trading room, weapons purchased here had physical locks. These locks prevented the guns from firing, and they could only be taken off by Death Corps soldiers at the facility's exits.

Although the merchant in the Network room held a similar occupation to Francis, she could have come from an entirely different planet than him; she was attractive with vibrant lips and blonde hair that curled to her shoulders. The only blemish on her face of any sort was a small mole above her upper lip, which still managed to add to her appearance rather than detract from it.

Fastened to the glass above the woman's right shoulder was a sheet of paper with four columns and *Hotels in the South District* for a title. On the same side of the glass as Northfield, two Death Corps soldiers stood with submachine guns. Their heads swiveled, following Northfield intently as he took off his gas mask and approached the counter.

"Can I rent a hotel?" he asked the woman, handing her his ID.

She said, "Take your pick."

He studied the table; the first column listed the hotels' names, the second listed their addresses, and the third contained bullet points that provided general information about them, such as security precautions. The fourth column listed the price of renting a room per night. Landlords and the Network each received a portion of the listed price; landlords presented an asking price to the Network, and the Network appended fees for additional services, which included random gas-concentration checks to ensure that the filtration systems were safe for guests.

"Any rooms available in the Cantina Inn?" he asked her.

She asked, "How long are you staying?"

"Just one night."

"One minute," she said. The woman used a small computer; hotels could be reserved from multiple Network locations throughout the city, and she had to ensure that the hotel still had availability. After reserving a room for him and returning his ID, she said, "Eight credit cards."

He took eight credit cards from his stack and slid them through the small opening in the glass. The woman printed out a ticket and handed it to him. "You'll be staying in room 873. You know where the Cantina Inn is?"

He shook his head and replied, "Been a while since I've been in the city."

She said, "When you leave, take a left out of the gate and walk straight for five blocks. You'll see the sign. Again, room 873. You'll get your room key at the hotel. You should already be in their system, but if you run into any issues, you have the ticket I gave you. Return the key to the hotel's front desk by 3:00 p.m. tomorrow. Follow the hotel rules. That means no stealing, no harassing, no vandalization, or anything of the like. Break those rules or any others, and we'll find you."

He understood the implications of her last phrase: the Death Corps.

"Anything else for you today?" the woman asked with a lighter tone, offsetting her last sentence.

He nodded and asked, "You got a grappling hook?"

"Four credits," she said, and after he slid the cards underneath the glass, she searched the room until she found a grappling hook. Small traces of rust had accumulated on the hook, but considering the state of most items in the wasteland, he considered it to be in pretty good condition.

From what he recalled from the contents of his job envelope, Nathaniel Salb lived in Heaven's Rebirth, which was an old Catholic church that had been repurposed by the Network for living spaces. The three-story church had a dual-pitched roof with gargoyles lining the ledges, along with an eight-story-tall nonfunctional clocktower that contained converted Sunday School classrooms currently being used as living spaces.

Heaven's Rebirth was private property; access was only granted to those who lived in the former church. Despite Northfield's assassination contract, legal and mandatory in the eyes of the Network, guards of Heaven's Rebirth could kill him with impunity or even sic the Death Corps on him for trespassing. As such, he was suspended in a legal limbo: killing Salb was authorized, but trespassing on Heaven's Rebirth wasn't. Although the limbo was strange, it wasn't uncommon; targets cognizant of the fact that they were being hunted often avoided death by hiding in buildings that assassins couldn't access without the Network's blessing or protection. The ingenuity required of Network mercs was one reason for their high payment, aside from their ability to fight outnumbered.

Northfield figured that the grappling hook could help him get onto the roof; according to the papers in the envelope, Salb lived in one of the converted classrooms on the fifth story in the clocktower. If he could find a window leading directly into Salb's room, he could get in, do the job, and get out quickly. Hopefully he wouldn't run into witnesses or anybody wanting to stop him. He wouldn't hurt anyone else; his blood would run cold in the dirt first. Though he knew his resolution was sincere, he doubted it was worth enough to pay for his soul's dry-cleaning bill.

He took the coiled grappling hook and he nodded at the woman, who reacted with a curt smile, flashing her pearly white teeth for just a moment before frowning and resuming her work. After putting on his gas mask, he left the trading room and returned to the parking lot, nodding to the two guards as he went through the glass door. He retrieved his backpack and weaponry, and he attached the coiled grappling hook to his backpack.

Northfield left the parking garage and crossed the grass lawn on his way back to the gate, all the while observing the Death Corps guards cooped up in the towers with their machine guns. The gate creaked open and he swiftly left the premises, recalling the woman's directions. *Take a left out of the gate when you leave and walk straight five blocks.*

He heeded her words and turned left after he passed through the gate, watching jet-black trucks and jeeps roll past him in both directions as they headed to and from the South Network Facility.

Neon signs crowded the first- and second-story walls of every building, begging for the attention of anyone with a few credit cards to their name. With the ever-present gas, store and building owners figured the best way to attract customers was through bright light, like drawing moths to a lamp. Regardless of the strategy's effectiveness, the resulting neon-lit buildings gave the street level of Cumulus an odd mixture of tones, both decrepit and lively.

The neon lights dimmed in Northfield's mind as his anguished thoughts weighed him down like a lead blanket.

Don't know the exact time, but I know it's gotta be past midnight, meaning late night or early, early morning, depending on perspective. Either way, I'm already onto a new day, which means that tonight I might kill a man. I might kill a man, and I may never find out why. He could've murdered a man, or he could've been screwed over for trying to do the right thing. Like me. I have no idea the good this guy's done, and I have no idea what bad this guy's done. But would knowing his life's story change what I might do or just make the task easier or harder? Would knowing what he's done make what I might do any more or less wrong?

He studied the neon lights, searching for a flicker or flash. *Maybe you could give me some sort of sign, God. If it rains today, this Salb guy's time to die has come. If it's sunny, he still has to complete a couple of bullet points on your life plan for him and doesn't get the fat ax dropping on his neck just yet. The short time he's got left better be damn worth it. Whoever put out the hit's gonna get a refund once the contract expires and probably put out a hit on Salb again. As many times as it takes until the deed's done.*

But if it's sunny or raining, how the hell am I supposed to tell if it's a sign or just a goddamn sunny or rainy day? See, that's your problem, God. You make this shit far too cryptic. Why the hell can't you have an angel just deliver an envelope or something and tell me what to do? Is the airfare just too expensive? Do those angel wings run on more than hope, like in that one Christmas movie? What one was it, again? Elf? Yeah, I think it was Elf. Well, either way, I'll be staying at the Cantina Inn, room 873, if you're wondering and have anything to drop off. But of course you knew that. You're omnipotent. And besides, we both know you're not giving me jack shit.

Maybe I just gotta come up with my own reasons for this guy being targeted. Who knows, maybe it'll make it easier. Let's see. What could Nathaniel Salb have done to incur Mr. Hood and Sickle's visit at his doorstep? First, I gotta think of who would put out a hit on him. His wife? Is he married? Or girlfriend? Was my new pal caught trying to get his rocks off and now his wife's trying to get him off of this rock? Damn, that'd be cold, but I've heard of it happening before. I know the hit's not for a breach of Network contract. The Death Corps would have been sent after him instead. He could have killed or robbed someone, and a family member wants revenge. I can only hope it's something like that, right? But who am I kidding? He's probably the poor sap behind the old animal abuse ads who just wanted to save puppies, and some jackass figured out who he is and wants to kill him as revenge for always souring the mood in the middle of Shark Week.

Well, that backfired. Thinking about what he did or didn't do is only making me feel worse. Who the hell put me in charge of judging who gets to live or die? Who the hell am I to make a decision like that?

He smirked. *Maybe he used to be a Spoonbills fan but now he prefers the Sox. Pro ball's not even around anymore, but damn, I'd understand putting out that hit. Hell, if he's a dirty Sox fan and I could put out a second hit on the guy, I'd do it.*

One hundred feet ahead of him, a blue circular neon sign jutted out from the second story of a light-brown building; red lettering crossed through the circle that read *Cantina Inn*. He approached the building's air-sealed door and looked up at a small camera.

Through an intercom to his right, a male voice said through heavy static, "Business?"

He held his ID and hotel ticket up to the camera and said, "My name's Mark Northfield. I've got a hotel reservation."

After a few seconds, the voice replied, "Name's on the list. Come in." The door hissed open. Entering the building quickly, he closed the door and waited for a couple of seconds, after which he took off his gas mask.

The lobby of the Cantina Inn appeared to be a converted barbershop; haircuts weren't exactly a priority for Cumulus citizens. Most people thought their valued credit cards were better spent on food and living spaces, and they figured that their grooming needs could be satisfied at home by the sharp side of a blade. As a result, many "luxury" businesses like barbershops and spas were converted to hotels and apartments to satisfy living needs. The black and white checkered floor was shoddily swept, with dust accumulating in the corners of the room.

The old barber seats had been converted into waiting chairs, and the mirrors were replaced with paintings of the Midwest countryside in cracked and seemingly homemade frames. A wooden kiosk with bulletproof glass resided in the far-left corner. Inside the kiosk, a man in his late twenties sat in a black chair with his feet up and resting on the wall. An AK-47 leaned next to him. Adjacent to the kiosk on the far wall of the room, a stained-carpet staircase led to the upper floors.

Northfield approached the kiosk. The man stroked his patchy goatee, looking him up and down and studying him with a mouth-half-open expression; Northfield suspected that the man's effort was borne out of boredom rather than concern for his own safety or a sense of duty to protect the hotel.

His eyes widened slightly as they fell on the submachine gun strapped to Northfield's backpack, inducing him to say, "Is that a Vector?" His voice was raspy and his tone distant enough that he could be orbiting Mars, leading Northfield to suspect that the man took acute advantage of the fact that vegetation could still grow in the gas, particularly certain types of plants.

Northfield nodded.

The man said, "Damn. Where the hell'd you scrape together the credit cards for that?"

"Need it for my job," he replied. "Figured that I could invest: people are less likely to fire at you when you're carrying a gun that looks like it's either from outer space or twenty years in the future."

"For sure, man," the man said, his gaze shifting to the assault rifle leaning against the wall in the kiosk. "Meanwhile, I've got a rusted AK that I swear is from the goddamned Vietnam era. I don't even know if the thing can fire in a straight line."

Northfield shrugged. "Well, that means you've gotta improvise, doesn't it? If you hold down the trigger and spray and pray, firing in a straight line isn't a huge priority, is it?"

The man smirked. "Heh. 'Improvise.' I like you, man." He set his feet down and leaned forward in his chair. "Could I get a closer look at your ID?"

He pulled out his ID and passed it through the glass. The man stroked his goatee and studied it, comparing it to a document he had pulled up on his computer. Satisfied, he grabbed a key from a cabinet underneath the glass and handed it to Northfield.

The man nodded toward the staircase and said, "You're good to go, Mark. If you ever feel God's light shining down on you and telling you to give up violence, you know who to give that gun to, you hear?"

Northfield smirked as he walked to the staircase. He called back to the man on his way up, "Giving up violence doesn't mean giving up your stick. It just means you can't swing it."

The dull red carpet on the staircase had suspect blotches and stains, along with tears and holes that revealed the rotting wood underneath. *With my luck, after I just took off my gas mask, I'm gonna breathe in mold spores or something.*

He ascended to the eighth floor and searched for his room number: 873. The floor had a faded red-gold floral carpet design that looked to be in no better condition than the carpet on the stairs, and the yellow and white striped wallpaper had yellow stains on the white stripes, making it seem as if the yellow stripes were bleeding. Lights in semi-circle lamps lined the walls. Half of them were either dead or flickering. He passed a broken lamp on his left; fragmented glass littered the carpet directly beneath it.

He found room 873 on the left side of the hallway. The doors were the only parts of the hotel in better-than-deplorable condition. The dark brown wood looked sturdy, and the silver doorknob and keyhole, if not exactly brand new, didn't yet appear to have been ravaged by time and wear. The condition of the doors made sense; people cared about security above all else, and the state of the hotel reflected that sentiment.

The room's interior was, well, not much. The room contained a twin-sized bed in the center, a bathroom with a toilet and sink, a small dresser with a lamp atop it, and a single two-by-two-foot window. Above the window, an unlit red warning light and sensor were housed in a cage. Most buildings in the city had a single filtration system per floor; putting a filtration system in each room would be far too costly. Instead, each room had vents placed around doors and windows, and they connected to the floor's filtration system, which was usually housed in a locked room to prevent tampering, along with a sensor that measured the concentration of gas in the air. If the sensor in a room detected that the air had a high enough concentration of gas to be unsafe, the red light in every room on the floor would turn on, and a small speaker underneath the lights in each room would emit a loud siren. Protocol directed people on the breached floor to put on their gas masks and seek refuge on another floor.

As the door clicked behind him, his shoulders slouched and he stared at the city skyline through the window. The iron hands of exhaustion firmly clenched his arms and legs, pulling him toward the bed. He couldn't tell if the lack of energy stemmed primarily from his body's need for sleep or if it could be attributed to the oppressiveness of his situation weighing down on him.

Studying the stars that shone through the sky and gas, the latter of which was much thinner due to his altitude, the thought occurred to him that he could pull off the job before sunrise. Although waiting until the following night would reduce the time he had to come up with a potential plan B if Salb escaped or wasn't in the building, he preferred the benefits of a sound night's sleep. Though this track of logic ran through his mind, he knew damn well that it was mostly an excuse to delay pulling off the hit until he felt a stronger sense of conviction.

He set his gear on the floor next to the small dresser. He turned on his gas mask's cleaning system, which produced the hissing noise he had long since gotten used to. Exhaling, he sat on the bed, and a twinge of pain stabbed him in his rear, prompting him to stand up quickly and twist to face the bed. He pulled off the worn tan and brown checkered blankets, and he saw a metal spring poking out of the mattress.

Great, he thought. *Made it through the long-ass journey filled with violence and despair to finally reach the safety of a hotel room, only to be sodomized by a mattress.*

He examined the rest of the mattress, searching for any further breaches due to springs or other hazards. Save for some suspect stains, which he was too tired to give a damn about, the rest of the mattress was clear. He sat down again, this time avoiding the metal spring. He opened his backpack and took out his framed picture of Jess and set it on the dresser so the image faced him. He proceeded to lie down, rest his head on the yellow-white pillow, and look at her.

Hey, Jess, it's your hubby again. How's it going? I know you're not a huge fan of talking back or anything like that, so I'm gonna assume that you're doing good. And I'm gonna assume that if you were gonna respond, you'd ask me how I'm doing. And, well, if I'm gonna be honest, I'd say I've had better days. You see, God and I are fighting again. I know what you'd say: "What's new?" But you see, this is an important fight. Not the usual shit that I bitch to him about. This is a big ol' grandaddy, end-of-the-relationship fight.

See, I made those promises to you. I need to live for you, and I need to keep the good that you always saw in me. Those promises are number one on my priority list. Someday, I'm coming back to you, Jess, and things with us are gonna be the same up there as they were down here. As long as I keep my promises, that is. I'm coming to you as the man you fell in love with, not some monster that this godforsaken world has spat out. And he's forsaken us down here, hasn't he?

He's given me two choices: suicide by defying the Network or assassinating a man, both of which violate my promises to you. And I've been waiting here for some sort of sign from him telling me what to do, but I'm still lost. I still have absolutely no idea what I'm supposed to do here. I feel like no matter what action I take, it's the wrong action. If I don't kill Salb, I might as well put the bullet between my eyes myself. The Death Corps are relentless and brutal, some of the most ruthless men in the wasteland. And considering that we're in a wasteland, where the prevailing way of living is every man for himself, that's a big statement. And for what? Another hit on Salb's gonna be put out, and someone else is gonna do the job all the same. What point would my death serve?

Or maybe, deep down, I'm afraid of dying and I'm using my promise to you as an excuse. I don't know. But that's exactly what I'm saying: I don't know. I need some guidance from up there in the clouds, where everything down here can be seen with just a bit more clarity. But God's not giving me anything. Not a single thing.

I feel like I'm living up to my end of the bargain, while God's slacking on his end. I'm trying to do what he wants, and all I require is a bit of guidance on what that good path is. Instead, God's flipping me the middle finger and telling me to figure it out myself. I wonder if there's heavenly lawyers who handle this sort of thing, who make sure both sides of heavenly agreements follow through with their promises and don't shirk on them. Man, could you imagine how a conversation like that would go?

"So, Mr. Northfield, it appears that God's not following through with his end of the contract."

"Yeah, I thought so. What's your advice, Counselor?"

"Well . . . I mean . . . He's sorta the grand creator of everything. So if he decides to screw you over, you kind of just have to take it."

"What? That can't be right. Isn't there the other guy?"

"I wouldn't advise that, Mr. Northfield. The other guy asks for a lot more and gives a lot less. And where you go after you kick the bucket is a lot worse. Fire, brimstone, and a whole lot of shackles and chains. Yeah, a lot of weird stuff goes on down there, I think."

"Bummer."

"Yeah. Bummer."

Yeah, I don't think litigation's gonna help me here, Jess. So all that being said, can you do me a favor? Can you talk to God for me? Convince him to throw me a bone if you can? Some divine intervention? I'll repay you with kisses and hugs when I see you, I promise. Thanks, Love.

He didn't know what awaited him, but he was certain that it would be a night he would never forget, for better or worse.

CHAPTER 5

Despite wanting to abandon the conscious world for a couple of hours, he slept fitfully. After realizing that spending more time letting his thoughts fester in this hotel would only drive him insane, he left.

He watched the orange sun as it rose between the tall buildings to the east like a comet. A rosy-pink halo encircled the sun, and the sky grew darker and bluer the farther he looked from the halo. With each minute, the streets grew even more populated as citizens rose from their moss-ridden beds, put on their gas masks, and ventured out into the city. He hoped the early walk would help clear his head, but he only succeeded in further clouding it.

Resolving to get more sleep before his job, he returned to the hotel, only to fail in his mission. He lay on his crappy mattress and stared at the ceiling, all the while deeply regretting not bringing one of his books. Eventually, he numbly packed his things, put on his gear, and returned his key to the front desk of the hotel, after which he left for the second time.

He spent one of his remaining credit cards at one of the few laundromats in the city, where he cleaned his clothes and removed any traces of mud from the prior night; he doubted a few granules of dirt would be what fucked him over during the job, but at least he felt somewhat productive.

His next stop was the bar; he told himself his dread and nerves about the impending future needed to be reined in before the job, although he knew this was an excuse. If he really needed a drink to calm his fears, he would have been an alcoholic years ago, given the nature of his job. As it stood, he rarely drank. He could've been doing something else to further the mission, such as scouting out Heaven's Rebirth in the daylight, when outside eyes would be less scrutinizing of him, but he didn't want to. Not yet. His trip to the bar was a way of him dragging his feet, like a dog resisting his leash being pulled. The delay, hopefully, would give him time to make an actual decision and put some conviction behind it. Slowly, he sipped the lone beer he purchased. He didn't want the bartender to see him with an empty glass; he would get harassed to buy another drink or leave. For all his delaying, by the time he left the bar, the clouds of indecision in his head only loomed darker.

As he made his way to Heaven's Rebirth, the sun had just disappeared behind the horizon; the west side of the sky had an ember-red glow that faded with each moment. In the east, blue-black mixed with the glowing colors of the gas.

When he saw Heaven's Rebirth's unique dual-pitched roof pop up in his view after traversing the maze of skyscrapers, he barely registered that he had reached his destination. Each moment, he felt like he was traveling farther into a labyrinth without leaving a trail of breadcrumbs behind.

Approaching the front of the building, he saw a circular stained-glass window that depicted Jesus and his disciples sitting at the Last Supper. The window was twenty feet wide, and due to the way the dual-pitched roof descended around it, the window seemed to burst out from the former cathedral's walls. Below the stained glass, two sets of double doors were made of oak. A silver chain and a lock sealed one set shut, while a hooded man with a gas mask and assault rifle guarded the other. In front of him, a line of ten people waited to gain admittance into Heaven's Rebirth. He assumed this was a routine every evening; the Heaven's Rebirth residents who left for the day wanted to return before nightfall. Each person in line would hand their identification over to the guard, who would allow residents in while rejecting non-residents. Nonresidents like Northfield.

He looked at the surrounding buildings; all of them were skyscrapers, rising higher than the ever-present gas. As a result, Heaven's Rebirth felt like a valley among mountains. The observation made him wish that he'd brought a high-powered rifle and tried to eliminate Salb from the safety of one of the surrounding buildings. The wish was an irrelevant one; he didn't currently have the funds to buy a sniper, and something told him that even if he did, he wouldn't have opted for that strategy. His already overburdened conscience wouldn't let him neutralize Salb using such cold, indirect means. No, if he was going to do this, he was going to face Salb. He wouldn't shy away from the horridness of what he was doing.

He decided to take a walk around the building. To avoid attracting the attention of the guard in front of the double doors, he used the sidewalks adjacent to the surrounding skyscrapers on the opposite side of the street of Heaven's Rebirth. He scanned for additional guards and points of entry.

The side walls of the building each had three stained-glass windows that depicted various events of Jesus's life, from birth to crucifixion, death, and the resurrection. The windows were rectangular with a semi-circle top and were bordered by brick pillars that extended to the dual-pitched roof. A gray gargoyle was perched on each pillar. Their wings curled around their bodies like blankets billowing in the wind, with the bottom corners of their wings almost touching their front talons. Grins stretched across their faces, baring teeth dulled by years of weathering, and they stared forward with knowing eyes that unsettled him. He felt as if they could see into the future and were laughing at him in the knowledge of his fate.

The defunct clock tower that housed former classrooms extended from the back wall of Heaven's Rebirth. The back wall was devoid of features save for a fire escape door, which was chained shut in a similar fashion as the first set of double doors at the front of the building. Although the door was chained shut, a guard armed with an M4 carbine stood in front of the door as an additional precaution.

He took brief glances at the surrounding buildings, noting a lack of neon signs in the area; the nearest walls of the adjacent buildings had only a couple of flickering signs. Although the lack of lights was advantageous to him, it nonetheless planted a seed of unease in his stomach. He felt like he'd entered the dark heart of a monster.

A plan formulated in his head. He'd go to one side of the building, wait until the coast was clear, secure his grappling hook to one of the gargoyles, and climb up the wall with, hopefully, no one the wiser.

He took the sidewalk back to the right side of the building. After looking left and right and ensuring that nobody was watching him, he hurried across the street to reach the wall. Standing directly underneath the left brick pillar of the middle stained-glass window, he unlatched his grappling hook from his backpack and hid it in his jacket. If a guard did see him, the grappling hook wasn't something he wanted to explain.

He waited for a couple of minutes, casually glancing from left to right again. He waited for two reasons. Although he didn't see any guards patrolling the property during his surveillance, save for the two posted at the front and back of the building, he wanted to make sure no guards would spot him halfway up the building and start playing pin the tail on the donkey, with their bullets being the pins and his ass being, well, the ass. In addition, the sky was blackening rapidly, and he wanted as much darkness as possible before he began climbing. Though the gas provided an ever-present glow, the power of the glow was more akin to the flicker of a candle than the shining of the sun; his surroundings would still darken considerably without sunlight. The night vision capability of his goggles was calibrated to work with the light of the gas, and they would give him an advantage.

Once convinced that guards wouldn't intrude on his little Spider-Man excursion, and he had enough darkness, Northfield put on his goggles and turned on their night vision mode. At the same time, he pulled the grappling hook out of his jacket. With the coil in his left hand and the end of the rope and grappling hook in his right hand, he started spinning the grappling hook and rope to build momentum. His head craned up as he eyed his target: the right scapula of a gargoyle, which protruded enough to hold the hook steady. At least that was what he hoped.

Alright, Mark, don't screw this up, he thought as he swung the grappling hook. *They always do this shit in the movies, right? Can't be that hard.*

He let go of the grappling hook, watching it sail toward the gargoyle. His heart crawled up into his throat as the grappling hook clinked against the scapula of the gargoyle, bounced off, and fell dismally back down to the earth with a loud *clack*.

Nuts, he thought, looking to his left and right to see if either of the guards in the front or back had heard the noise. He drew his pistol from his ankle holster and held it ready by his side; he wouldn't fire to hit the guards if they came. He still clung to his resolution to harm nobody aside from Salb, no matter what the consequences might be.

Instead, he'd aim over their heads, hopefully causing them to duck behind cover and giving him a chance to escape. From there, he'd figure out what to do about Salb.

The guards didn't come, either from being accustomed to random noises in the city or not hearing the noise in the first place. Sucking in air through his gas mask in relief, he picked up the grappling hook and swung it around once to generate momentum.

This better not be one of those "third time's a charm" things, or I swear I'm gonna pack my stuff and go home.

He didn't have to try a third throw; the grappling hook caught onto the gargoyle's right scapula. He gave the rope two sharp tugs to make sure the hook was fastened. The hook didn't budge, and he felt reasonably confident in its secureness. At least confident enough to try climbing the side of the building. The whole way up, however, he knew damn well that he'd be afraid of falling right back down and making a nice mess on the sidewalk.

As he held onto the rope and looked up at the gargoyle, he suddenly felt acutely aware of the idiocy of his plan.

I'm about to scale a wall with a grappling hook and break into a building. Who the hell am I? James Bond?

He couldn't deliberate further. If he did, there was a significant chance he'd just turn around and walk away, which might be the best course of action, but he still had no idea. God hadn't gotten back to him with his letter.

Alright, Marky boy, just one foot after another. That's it. Just one foot after the other and you'll be up the wall in no time.

Deliberately and with great effort, he scaled the wall, fearing with each step that he might fall.

About halfway up the pillar, he couldn't resist looking down. *What the hell are you doing, Northfield?*

He gritted his teeth and continued climbing. His arms and shoulders started to burn.

If I die here, that'd be a way to go, wouldn't it? I survived the apocalypse, yet I die by falling off a damned rope. I could just imagine the guards finding my body and trying to figure out what happened.

"Hey, how'd this guy die?"

"He tried to break into the building by climbing onto the roof with a grappling hook."

"What? He wanted to break into the building and that's how he decided to do it? With a grappling hook, for Pete's sake?"

"Yeah. Probably saw too many movies or something."

"Wow, this guy must have been some rare brand of idiot."

"Yeah, man, he probably was . . ."

He reached the top of the pillar and grabbed the gargoyle's wings.

"Excuse me," he muttered as he climbed over the gargoyle. For a moment, he wondered if he was crazy for his bizarre sense of humor. *Hey*, he figured, *sometimes you gotta make jokes just to make yourself laugh.*

He retrieved the grappling hook from the gargoyle's scapula and spun it back into a coil. He looked up at the clocktower, which was eight stories high from ground level. From Salb's file, Northfield recalled that he lived in a classroom on the sixth story of the tower.

He crept across the roof, acutely aware of his footsteps. He figured that the area directly below the dual-pitched roof was likely the former nave of the cathedral and had been converted into living space. Thus, there were probably a lot of people and a lot of ears below him.

He knew that anybody capable of hearing his footsteps would've probably already heard the clanks of his grappling hook. Still, his nerves implored him to minimize the sound of each step anyway.

Once he reached the clocktower, he looked at the sixth-story window. Unease lashed his stomach like a notched whip when he realized his target could be just three stories above him. Given the demand for living space in Cumulus and the poverty level of its citizens, an entire classroom would rarely belong to a single individual or family. Instead, the classrooms were often divided into four living spaces with partition panels, each individual or family occupying a corner of the floor.

According to the information in the envelope Northfield had received, Salb resided in the nearest right corner. In addition, the envelope provided a physical description of Salb, along with a few bullet points of information the client thought worthy to include. If the physical description matched someone inside, he would have his target.

The bullet points included details about Salb's sleep schedule; Salb slept best in the early night, but he awoke periodically in the later night. The client recommended conducting the hit in the early night, and Northfield chose to follow their advice. Although the other occupants of the floor were more likely to be up and about, he trusted his ability to avoid alerting them more than he wanted to risk Salb being awake. He had a direct path to Salb's room through the window. Hopefully he could avoid any neighbors, but if Salb saw him and made a commotion, the neighbors would undoubtedly be alerted.

Although the information in the envelope could be horseshit or merely inaccurate, he chose to believe it. If mercs were given incorrect or poor information, they often hunted the clients. Some mercs, if they failed their job, would hunt the client no matter what, which was why the Network kept clients anonymous. However, no precautions were perfect, and disgruntled mercs could still occasionally figure out the identity of clients, given enough time, wit, and suitable motivation. In fear of this, clients tended to give the most accurate and up-to-date information as possible when putting out contracts.

He threw the grappling hook at the sixth-story gargoyle to his left. When it caught onto the gargoyle, he grinned behind his gas mask. As he tugged the rope twice to make sure the hook was secure, he thought, *Wish there were some Spoonbills scouts who saw that toss.*

He climbed up the far side of the wall, as close to the corner of the roof as possible without getting the rope caught on the fourth- or fifth-story gargoyles. He stayed away from the windows as he ascended; he didn't want inhabitants to catch sight of him. His muscles started to ache, but he tried to pretend that the pain didn't exist; he had a lot more hanging and climbing to do. Fortunately, he could hold onto the brick windowsills when he made his entrance, but his forearms didn't relish the thought.

Once he reached the sixth-story gargoyle, he used its wings to pull himself up to sit on the statue's head for a quick break. Flipping his night-vision goggles up, he allowed himself a moment to drink in the view of the city. His eyes traveled from the streets to the dark skyscrapers, which looked like heavenly black pillars as they broke through the glowing yellow and orange cloud. The contrast between the neon-illuminated first two stories of each building and the darkness of the subsequent stories was as visually stunning as it was fascinating. High above, penthouses glowed with splendor. The city's rich and powerful, living in their own private corners of the universe.

Northfield flipped his night-vision goggles back over his eyes. Break time was over. He removed the grappling hook from the gargoyle and wound up the rope.

He pivoted on the gargoyle and looked at the nearest window. The ledge was within leaping range and wide enough for him to grab hold of, but because the gargoyle was on the corner of the building while the window was on the side, he'd have to jump and reach sideways to grab on. If he put too much power into his jump, his momentum would continue to carry him forward and peel him away from the ledge. If he didn't put enough power into his jump, well, the result would be apparent.

He briefly considered making some sort of safety harness, but he decided against it. He was so close to his target; bungling around with his clanky metal grappling hook sounded just as risky as making the jump. Besides, he wanted the grappling hook ready by his side if he had to make an escape.

Maybe I should pray. But God and I haven't resolved our spat. Would he be more angry if I prayed or if I didn't?

He considered for a moment before thinking, *Aw, fuck it. If I fall and die, I'll apologize to him in heaven.*

He leaped from the gargoyle, his arms outstretched. The ledge fast approached on his left; he reached out his arms and grabbed onto it. His momentum continued to pull his body, and his forearms strained to keep his fingers from tearing off of the ledge, but his grip held; he breathed hard in and out as his heart thudded in his chest. *What I'd give to never have to do that again . . .*

To see into the window, he pulled himself up so his chin rested on the ledge. The room behind the window was dark, save for the light from the gas outside, but his goggles enabled him to see with greater detail, albeit through a green tint. Partition panels divided the classroom into quadrants. In the section that he could see, there was a small dresser flanked by an unlit candle and a twin-sized bed. A middle-aged man lay in the bed, facing Northfield.

Northfield studied the man's face. Defined, dark eyebrows. Short black hair that was just beginning to gray. A flat, wide nose. Thick but also slightly patchy facial hair.

The man matched the exact physical description of Nathaniel Salb. Northfield had found his target.

Instead of relief, despair, or dread, his first immediate reaction was one of nausea. Salb was no longer an abstract idea, a moral qualm he had to deal with; he was a real, physical person just feet away.

Unrealistic alternatives flashed through his head. He considered somehow conspiring with Salb to fake the hit. It wouldn't work. The few times it happened, the Network always found out, always. Maybe he'd buy Salb a week, a month at best. For what? They would both die an awful death.

Windows in the city below the gas line could not be opened from the inside. The methods for inhibiting windows from being opened varied based on the type of window, but the methods were always as cheap as possible, like most things in the city. With resources as scarce as they were, resource management was key.

The window in front of Northfield had large screws drilled into it. The seal wasn't airtight, but whatever minuscule amount of gas seeped into the room would be cleaned out by the floor's filtration system.

He pulled himself up and balanced his feet on the windowsill. He held onto the rail of the window to keep from peeling back. He fished for his screwdriver in his backpack, and he started unscrewing. Every couple of moments, he would glance through the window to make sure his target didn't stir.

Stop. Stop thinking. It's his life or both of ours. It's his life or both of ours.

Yeah, Northfield. Keep telling yourself that, and maybe you'll be able to sleep again someday.

He removed the last screw and promptly opened the window, then slid through. He shut it as quickly and quietly as possible. He looked at the alarm above the window. The alarm light remained off, and no warning noises emitted from the speaker; he'd safely slipped inside before too much gas seeped in.

Once he took a closer look at Salb, he noticed that something was off: the man was sweating like mad. His sheets were drenched, and even in his sleep, he had a pained expression on his face. A bucket containing a snot-filled rag sat on the ground next to his bed. Salb was sick, very sick. That much was apparent.

"We've got to leave."

Northfield's heart jumped from his chest and clung to his throat when he heard the voice. It was hushed, and he could tell it belonged to a man.

His head snapped around to look at the partition panel behind the head of Salb's bed; the voice came from the room on the other side.

There wasn't just one person. At least two. If someone spoke, that meant another person had to be listening.

Please don't let them have heard me, God. Don't let them investigate. I won't hurt anybody but the target, but please don't test me. Right now, I'm being tested enough.

A woman responded, "We can't leave. Not with Salb in his condition. We're not going to make it. If we take him like this, we'll be giving the Death Corps a breadcrumb trail. There's too many people between here and there for nobody to notice, and the Death Corps will find us. Once they put the pieces together, we'll be painting a beacon to where we're going, even if we manage to get there."

His fear eased when he realized that they were in the middle of a conversation.

The mention of the Death Corps gave him pause. *The Death Corps are after them? After Salb?*

"I'm in charge here," the man replied. "And I say that we go."

The Death Corps being sent after you is essentially a death sentence. Hell, that's why I'm here. If Salb's sick, that death sentence is even more concrete.

The woman said, "Fine. You can go then. I'm staying put."

This puts a big wrench in my whole thought process here. If Salb's dying, killing him isn't the worst thing, right? I'm just accelerating the timetable.

"Christ, you're infuriating. Well, what do you suggest we do then?" the man asked. "We can't just wait here and let the Death Corps find us and kill us all."

"What I already said. Wait until the Coalition gets back to us. See if any of the sympathizers can find us a ride out of here," she said.

"And if they can't?" the man responded gruffly.

"Then we do what we have to do," she said. "But we need to check the safer option first."

The man replied, "Then we'd be wasting time for the practical option. Best if we start moving now."

While the man was talking, Northfield concurrently thought, *Don't kid yourself. This doesn't throw a wrench in anything. You're just searching for some reason, any reason, to stall making a decision. You have been since this contract fell in your lap. But these people could come in here any second. You're at the crossroads. The fork in the road. The point of decision. Right now. Kill Salb or run.*

She responded in exasperation, "You really think that moving won't kill us in this busy of a neighborhood? We'll attract way too much attention lugging his body over our shoulders."

"I'd rather chance it outside. No place to run in this stuffy room."

In reaction to the pause in their conversation, Northfield tensed himself and listened for footsteps; hearing none, he slipped a knife out of his backpack. He held the knife so tightly that it shook, but he couldn't bring himself to lift the weapon and bring it near Salb. The weapon felt like a swelling dumbbell in his hand. Thirty pounds. Forty pounds. Fifty pounds.

I've just gotta cup his mouth and stab, then let him fade away. Less than a minute and he'll be dead and this will all be over.

Breaking the pause, the female voice said, "This is just such a mess."

"You're damned right about that."

The knife continued to grow heavier, and he found himself struggling to not let it fall. Clenching it tightly before relaxing, he sighed. Time to be honest with himself.

You're not gonna do this, Northfield. You never were, despite the escapade this has been. I gotta stop with the nonsense and figure out what I'm actually gonna do. I'm sorry, Jess, that I couldn't do it to save myself. Although with the clarity I have after finally making my decision, I feel like this is what you wanted all along.

No, I know it is. Funny how obvious decisions seem after they're made.

You made me give you the first promise because you didn't want me giving up, wallowing in sorrow, and ending it all. But staying true to myself is the only way I live for you.

In all the blood and hell of this world, I'll try not to lose that, Jess. I promise.

He slipped his knife back into his backpack and stared at Salb, squinting behind his goggles.

My contract with the Network expires the day after tomorrow, at which point the Death Corps will be sent after me. If I leave now, I can try to get ahead of the Death Corps and get far away and disappear.

He started moving toward the windows before he looked back at Salb and thought, *But that brings me to the excuse I've been repeating to myself. Even after the contract expires, another contract's gonna be put on the market for Salb. His life's still gonna be in danger, even if I'm not the one who pulls the trigger.*

He watched Salb's breathing as he slept. Inhale. Exhale. Inhale.

Exhale. His eyes darted toward the edges of the partition panels as he listened for footsteps, every survival instinct in his body screaming that he was an idiot for delaying his departure even a second longer, but his feet were leaden by a question that kept him anchored in place.

Can I just leave a man who is sentenced to death and not even give him some sort of warning?

If another merc comes to kill Salb, it seems those people talking are gonna transport him, so the merc won't have any idea where the fuck Salb's gone. But then again, I have so little information that I can't tell down from up.

You can't help here, Northfield. You can't help when you have no idea what's going on. You gotta just wash your hands of this and walk away. Get out before these people find you and you either have to kill them or let them kill you.

He turned around and silently snuck to the window, during which he glanced at his reflection; clad with his goggles and gas mask, he looked like a demon in the night.

He slid open the window and stuck his foot through. He didn't get a chance to stick his other through.

His eyes widened. *Footsteps.*

He turned his head before something slammed into his left temple. Hands grabbed onto him and threw him to the floor. His goggles' display was disrupted by the impact. However, the temporary static mattered little, as the blurred green quickly dissipated into complete darkness.

CHAPTER 6

O nce Northfield came to, he could immediately tell that his body was restrained. He sat in an uncomfortable wooden chair, his wrists bound behind his back. His gas mask, earplugs, and night vision goggles were gone, but he could still feel the beanie on his head, which kept his dirty-blond hair from falling over his eyebrows. His head drooped with his chin touching his chest, and his body felt like lead sinking in water. Voices murmured around him, but he was too groggy to pick any words out of the fog. With quite a strain, he managed to lift his head.

Two partition panels were in front of him, leading him to believe that he was still in the same classroom as Salb. However, the windows, twin-sized bed, and dresser had different orientations, and Salb was missing. In addition, he could see part of a door past the edge of one of the partition panels, a door he couldn't see from Salb's living space. He surmised that if he was indeed in the same classroom, someone had put him in a different living space.

Spotting two pairs of feet, he lifted his head higher. A man and woman stood in front of him. They were tall, with the man standing a couple of inches over six feet and the woman standing around Northfield's height of five-ten. Both wore gas masks with opaque

91

eyepieces; he couldn't see their facial features. Because the air was safe to breathe, he assumed they wore masks to conceal their identities. In addition, they wore black pants with long-sleeve shirts, the woman wearing dark gray and the man wearing black. Underneath the long-sleeve shirts, Northfield could make out the outline of Kevlar vests. HK416s hung from slings on their shoulders, and a military-grade radio was strapped to the man's belt.

Northfield didn't need to be a rocket scientist to realize these were the people he heard talking behind the partition panel earlier. The man and woman appeared to be arguing about something, probably a continuation of their argument earlier. They promptly stopped conversing once the woman noticed Northfield looking around.

Oh boy. This is gonna be fun, he thought bitterly. He was angry at himself for taking so long in his decision. Otherwise, he might have been halfway out of the city by now.

"Who are you?" the woman asked with urgency and assertiveness, but not quite aggression.

On second thought, he wasn't angry at himself for the hesitation as much as he was for showing up at Salb's apartment in the damned first place.

"FedEx," Northfield said. "The door was open, so I thought I'd just drop your package off inside." The words came out slower than he'd hoped; his jaw still felt heavy and unresponsive. The room spun like a damned carnival ride on cocaine.

"A jokester," the man said to the woman. "Great. We don't have time for this. We need to pop him and leave."

The woman ignored him, and she said to Northfield, "Don't worry. I hit you hard, but not that hard. You should feel better soon."

He didn't respond, instead gritting his teeth and waiting for the spinning to subside.

"We need to go," the man urged. "This op is already FUBAR. We kill this jackass, and we get our guy out of here."

She ignored him and instead addressed Northfield. "What the hell were you doing?"

The man answered before Northfield could respond. "What do you think he was doing, delivering donuts?"

"I'm not going to kill him without at least knowing why," she said. "So out with it. Who are you?"

Northfield's eyes narrowed. He could feel his brain picking up, but the speed wasn't fully there yet. He asked, "Maybe I'm the one who should be asking that. Who the hell are you?"

She cocked her head slightly to the side, obviously studying him. Her facial expression was unreadable behind her gas mask. "Mark Northfield. That's what your ID said in that backpack of yours. Says you're a Network merc. But for all I know, that ID could be forged. If you won't answer my question, I have another for you. Why are you here?"

"Are you actually gonna believe me if I tell you?"

She said, "Depends on what you say. Right now, you confuse me."

He managed to pull his gaze up to the eyepieces of her gas mask. The spinning in his vision was subsiding, but the filters of her mask still seemed to float around her head like lethargic planets in orbit.

"Confuse me?" he repeated.

She could evidently see how his brain was chugging along, so she said, "I heard you open the window. I looked around the partition panel and saw you on your way out. If you're a merc, the only reason you'd be here would be to complete a hit, meaning that Salb wouldn't have still been alive by the time you were on your way out. If you're Death Corps, you wouldn't be alone—you would have breached the windows or door with your squad. Same goes for the Yellowbacks. So for the life of me, I can't figure out who you are or why you're here."

"Does it matter?" the man asked. "If we're not gonna kill him, for God's sake, let's just leave him tied up and go. He doesn't know where we're heading."

"I told you why leaving is a bad idea," she told him.

"And I told you why staying is even worse," he retorted.

His brain continued to clear as they talked, and their verbal spar reminded him of their argument earlier, particularly that Salb was being hunted by the Death Corps. Why, Northfield didn't have the slightest clue, but he wondered if it had anything to do with the hit contract that had been forced on him. A sick feeling welled in his stomach, one that told him he was aboard a canoe traveling down shit creek at blinding speeds. He wanted out of that canoe.

She turned to Northfield and said, "Right now, time isn't a resource we have a lot of. If you don't start talking, you're going to lose anything close to a good option. We'll just go with what he wants, and you won't like that. Who the hell are you? Why are you here?"

The man stared at Northfield with his arms crossed. Tension oozed off him like a strong cologne. Who the hell were these people?

Honesty might be the best approach. If I'm honest, maybe I'll get a bit of honesty in return and I'll find out what the hell is going on.

Feeling himself starting to win the battle against his abating dizziness, he took a moment to collect his thoughts and organize them. He said, "I'm a Network merc. The ID's real. I only take escort and protection jobs. I don't do hits. Ever. I'm not that type of guy, and I don't have the heart for it. Someone didn't like that, and he screwed me over and tricked me into taking this contract. I admit, I did come here to kill Salb to save my own life, but I couldn't go through with it. I was leaving, but then you people knocked me out."

"So you're telling me you're a merc that doesn't do hits?" the man butted in. His voice was weathered and gravelly. "Yet you took a hit.

Then you came all the way here and decided not to go through with it at the very last moment? I don't buy it."

"I can't make you believe me," Northfield said. "All I can do is tell you the truth. If you believe me or not, that's up to you."

"You don't seem very enthused to convince us to spare you," the man said.

"No, I'm just trying to cut out all the bull," he replied. "If you want to kill me, I can't stop you. And I don't know what else I can tell you to convince you to believe me. If you're going to let me live, I want you to make that decision fast. The Death Corps are gonna come after me. If I don't get a good lead on them, I'm a dead man."

"Do you live in the city?" she asked.

"No, I drove here last night," he replied.

"What entrance did you come through?"

"The south entrance."

"If you came through the south entrance, did you go to the South Network Facility for any reason? To get a room to stay in? To pick up supplies for the job?" she asked.

"Yes, late last night or early morning. For both of those reasons. I got a hotel and I picked up a grappling hook for the job. The grappling hook is in my backpack. So is the hotel ticket."

The man sifted through Northfield's backpack, locating the ticket and grappling hook. He asked, "What room did you stay in?"

"Room 873."

"If you're a merc, but you don't take hits, how do you manage to still get jobs?"

"Where I operate, I'm the best around with a gun. It lets me be a bit choosier about which jobs I take."

"What hotel is room 837 in?"

"The room number is 873, and I stayed at the Cantina Inn."

They looked at each other. She said, "His story seems to check out. No hesitations, odd facial expressions."

"Great, he's either telling the truth or has a good memory for lies," the man retorted. "Frankly, I don't care. Time to pack up and go."

"And just leave this guy here? You heard his story. He's hunted by the Death Corps. Are we really going to leave him tied up for them? Or were you just planning on shooting him?"

"You're assuming his story is true."

The woman's mention of the Death Corps spurred him to wonder why they left Salb alone in a room. He supposed that the Death Corps almost always employed brute-force methods over finesse. If they attacked, they'd breach from the stairwell. The section of the room that the man and woman had argued in earlier was adjacent to the stairwell; they probably wanted to argue away from Salb and give him peace to rest. If the Death Corps did strike from the stairwell, they would be between Salb and the Death Corps.

"What's wrong with Salb?" he asked, interrupting the man and woman's continued quarrel. Their heads twisted toward him like cracked whips.

"Why do you care?" the man asked dubiously.

"I wanna know if there's anything I can do to help him. By refusing to kill him, I've made myself a target for the Death Corps. If he just rolls over and dies anyway, what's the fucking point?"

The man and woman looked at each other again. The man said, "I still don't buy his 'nice guy' act. This isn't a good idea. He's gonna bite us in the ass or shoot us in the back the second we turn around."

"You didn't see him until he was knocked out," she said. "When I saw him, one of his feet was out the window. He was leaving. Why would he come in and leave except for the explanation he gave us? I don't know what he is, but he isn't what you think he is. I believe him."

"Your judgment's clouded," he said. "You're seeing what you want in him."

She didn't say anything for a moment. Then she said, "No, I'm not. Maybe it's a gamble, a big one. But my mind is clear."

"Okay, fine. You believe him. What are you gonna do? Just untie him and give him his gun? And we can sing campfire songs together?"

"Don't patronize me. I'm just going to talk to him. Maybe there's a way we can help each other. We've got enough enemies as it is."

He sighed, then threw his hands up and walked away. "Fine. Talk then. I'll check on Salb."

Once the man disappeared behind the partition panel, the woman turned to Northfield and said, "He thinks I should have killed you. Stabbing you in the back would have been easy. And safer. He has his instincts. I have mine. In this case, I think I made the right choice. Your story lines up with what I saw. You were leaving, and yet Salb was untouched. Your ID, room ticket, and grappling hook are solid evidence of what you say happened. But I'm going to need more than that. Even I'd consider myself naive if I just let you go and gave you back your gear. Help prove me right and him wrong."

No useful information that might help exonerate him popped into his head, but his thoughts kept returning to her first sentence. So he asked, "He thought you should have killed me. Why didn't you?"

"What?"

"Most people these days would have just stabbed without hesitation. Wouldn't have even bothered to notice that I was leaving."

She paused. "Would you have fired immediately without questioning the fact that I was leaving?"

Northfield sighed and looked down. "No. Then again, I have quite the knack for making stupid decisions that come around to bite me in the ass. Maybe I'm not the best example of what you should and shouldn't do."

She said, "Are you saying that I made a stupid decision?"

"Just a moral one," he said. "They're not free. Maybe that makes them stupid. I bet I don't exactly look like a genius tied up in this chair right now."

"Then why make them? You refuse to take hits, even when it would make you more money. You refuse to kill Salb, even to save your life. When you're tied up by two strangers, you still ask about Salb's condition."

He closed his eyes, and he was right alongside Jess under the tree. A soft breeze pushed her hair onto his shoulder, hugging his neck. "I'm no saint. I still came here, didn't I? I'm just trying to keep a promise." He opened his eyes, and he became acutely aware of the rope cutting into his wrists. He said, "You never really answered my question. Why didn't you kill me? Why do you give a damn?"

"The world has been a hard place for a while," she said. "We need to start helping each other if we're going to make things any easier. If I believe that, I have to be the one to start. Doing something like killing you as you were about to leave wouldn't fall into that category."

"A lot of people would call your thinking naive," he said.

"Naivety, optimism, call it what you want," she said. "I think we need some to make things better. Pessimism hasn't done us much good for the past ten years."

"I hope you're right," he said softly.

"You sound like my dad," she said.

"Your dad?" he asked, looking up at her.

The woman nodded toward the partition board. "The man who was in here, who's now checking on Salb. He's my father."

He paused. Her comment clearly wasn't made carelessly.

"My name's Mark, as, well, my ID says."

"My name's Elena."

"I'd shake your hand, but . . ." Northfield joked, looking behind him at his tied-up hands.

"Sorry about that. But we're not quite there yet."

"Understood," he said. "How can I prove that I'm telling the truth?"

"I believe you, but it would be stupid of me to just let you go on my hunch, no matter how strong that hunch is. Besides, my dad's technically in charge. Convince him, and then we'll figure out what to do with you."

Before he could respond, Elena's father stormed back into their section of the classroom. He cursed and exclaimed, "I told you we couldn't stay this long. I told you."

"What's wrong?" Elena asked.

He said, "Two jet-black Humvees are driving toward us. The Death Corps are here, and they're coming."

CHAPTER 7

"**L**et me go," Northfield asserted.

"Look, buddy, we still have no idea who you—" Elena's father said.

"The Death Corps have to park, then command the guard to unlock the chains on the back door and let them through. Including the time it takes for them to climb the stairs and get into breaching position, that gives you two or three minutes before they bust down the door. Two Humvees means six of them, maybe eight. For two people, those are some crappy odds."

"So we should just let you go and give you your guns?" he said incredulously.

"I'm a Network merc. At this point, whatever you think my motives are, you should at least gamble on that. Unless you can come up with a better explanation for my stuff. My job relies on my ability to fight while outnumbered. You've got a lot better chance with my help."

"And a far better chance of you putting a bullet through my head," he retorted.

"You're right. But if I end up helping you, your odds go way up. You don't trust me, that's fine. It's up to you what odds are worth taking."

"I vouch for him," Elena said. "Let him go."

Elena's father hesitated before he untied Northfield and said, "Your backpack and weapons are in Salb's section. Don't make me regret this. I'll be watching you."

They rushed into Salb's section. Northfield grabbed his Vector and backpack, and he put on all his gear while Elena put a mask on Salb. He gave a soft groan of discomfort and mumbled something; Northfield didn't hear what.

"Sorry, Nathan. I'll be quick," she said while reaching under his bed and grabbing an armored vest. The vest wouldn't stop a direct TAP bullet, but one that punctured another surface or ricocheted before reaching the vest might be stopped. While Elena manipulated Salb's limbs to fit the vest over him, she asked her father, "What's the plan?"

There was a gap between the stairwell door and nearest partition panel; the door could swing open unimpeded. As a result, someone who came through the door could immediately see into the nearest two sections. Conversely, anyone in the front two sections could see the doorway and whoever entered through it.

"I've studied the Death Corps and how they move," Elena's father said. "When they breach this room, they'll throw a flashbang and fan out into the front two sections. That's their standard MO when they want a captive. One of us stays back with Salb as a last line of defense. The other two attack from the front sections."

Before he could assign anyone to a section, Northfield half-pleaded and half-commanded, "Let me take one of the front two sections. My goggles have thermal functionality, and I have smoke grenades. When they open the door, I can pop a few smoke grenades and shoot them through the smoke."

Elena added, just as she finished fitting the vest over Salb, "I can fire into the smoke, too, disorient them while Mark picks them off."

Elena's father nodded and said, "The Death Corps won't fire blindly.

They can't risk hitting Salb. They need him alive. I'll stay with him. Cover your ears and watch each other's fire."

"Don't move, Nathan," Elena said. Salb mumbled something, but his voice drifted off.

They said nothing more; there wasn't time. Northfield rushed to the front-right section while Elena rushed to the front-left section. In the front-right section, there was a bed and a dresser, like in the other sections he had seen. Northfield took cover behind the bed's wooden headboard and flipped on his goggles, switching them from night vision to thermal. The headboard wouldn't stop a bullet, but crappy cover was better than no cover. His body would at least be concealed.

From his position, he could see the right half of the door; the left half was obscured by the partition panel. A window on the wall to his right cast a pale square of moonlight onto the bed. There were no windows on the wall with the door; the Death Corps couldn't peek inside before opening it.

He pulled a smoke grenade out of his backpack. He tried to steel his nerves while thinking, *What the fuck have I gotten myself into?*

He didn't have time to deliberate further; the door smashed open, breaking at its hinges, and a metal cylinder rolled through the opening: the flashbang. He tossed his smoke grenade and crouched behind the headboard, closing his eyes and hoping his earplugs could handle the flashbang's shock wave. To further reduce the chances of the flashbang's shock wave rupturing his eardrums, he opened his mouth.

The explosion hit. When he didn't experience sudden deafness, he counted himself lucky to have his earplugs.

He popped over the headboard with his Vector. A large cloud of smoke obscured everything in front of him, reaching from the doorway to the headboard and to the left and right walls.

Because the Death Corps wanted to capitalize on the effects of the flashbang, they rushed into the room a split second after the flashbang detonated and were momentarily disoriented by the smoke cloud. Through his goggles, the Death Corps soldiers' bodies appeared red-yellow, while the surrounding smoke appeared blue. As Elena's father had predicted, the Death Corps fanned out; three rushed into the right section, where Northfield was, and he assumed three had rushed into the left.

With his submachine gun set on fully automatic, he pulled the trigger and dragged his weapon from left to right and then right to left, unloading the entire magazine on the three Death Corps soldiers. They were in point-blank range; he didn't miss. As their bodies collapsed to the floor, he reloaded and rushed forward, pressing his back against the wall with the door. He kept a healthy distance between himself and the door; he didn't want to venture too far in Elena's direction for fear of catching one of her stray bullets. From his position, he could still partially see into her section. He made out the foot of the bed, but not the mattress or head.

Two Death Corps soldiers were sprawled on the floor, while another clutched his side with his left hand and held a rifle with his right. Elena had sprayed into the smoke like Northfield, but without thermal goggles, she was firing blind. As Elena's father had predicted, the Death Corps didn't fire back.

Northfield fired his weapon. The Death Corps soldier collapsed, his rifle falling out of his hand and clattering to the ground. He scanned with his goggles, but he didn't see any more Death Corps soldiers. The coast was clear, at least for now.

He waited until the smoke cloud dissipated before he called out, "Clear!"

"Clear!" he heard Elena shout.

"Clear!" he heard her father shout.

They regrouped around Salb's bed. Salb was unharmed and awake; the gunshots clearly hadn't helped him fall back asleep. His head slowly rolled back and forth in search of the commotion that had roused him while he coughed deeply, discharging mucus. Quickly, Northfield noticed that his glossy eyes had a far-away look. He suspected that Salb wasn't entirely lucid. *Why the hell is this guy so important?*

"What's happening?" Salb asked. His voice was soft and incredibly weak as he quivered from the struggle to form each syllable. A cough doubled him over like fingers folding fresh paper, and the accompanying wet sound probably meant a glob of mucus had splattered the inside of his gas mask.

"Don't worry, Nathan," Elena said to him gently yet with firmness. "I'm just going to put a coat on you, okay?" She dug around his clothing drawers and picked out a baggy coat off the floor. While she put his hands through the sleeves, she said soothingly, "We'll keep you safe. You need to rest. Close your eyes, and you'll feel better soon."

"But . . ."

"Sleep," she said as she zipped up his coat. He listened, closing his eyes. She looked at Northfield and her father, then said, "All things considered, that wasn't too bad."

"Not bad?" Northfield protested. "We just had to kill six men to stop them from killing us. What part of that's not bad?"

"Calm down," Elena's father commanded.

"No," Northfield said, pointing at him. "Minutes ago, I was gonna leave this room and put my life at risk just to avoid killing a man. Now I've killed four. I need to know what's going on."

"We need to leave. Now," Elena's father said. "The Network only sent six soldiers this time. They wanted to take Salb with discretion. Obviously, they didn't expect us. Next time, they won't give a damn about discretion, and there will be more of them. You can be sure of that. This conversation can wait."

"He's right," Elena said. "We have time for this later. I'm sorry, but we need to go."

Elena's father said, "If you need to address me, you can call me John."

Northfield nodded and said, "Mark."

John said, "We need to get him to our doctor."

"We can take one of the Death Corps' Humvees and carry Salb the last leg of the journey," Elena said. "I hate the idea of walking and taking the chance of being spotted by the Corps, or some random person willing to report us, but we need to dump the vehicle. Once the Death Corps find it, they'll find us pretty quick if we're too close."

"Good thinking," John said. "Northfield, grab Salb. Elena, search the bodies for a key to one of the vehicles."

Northfield picked up Salb in a fireman's carry.

Salb awoke from his slumber, and he asked faintly, "What's happ—"

"We're getting you to a doctor," Northfield said. "Don't worry, buddy . . . Can I call you buddy? Probably not there yet . . . You're gonna get better soon." But was he going to get better? Northfield didn't even know what the hell was wrong with him. This was all so frustrating . . .

Salb didn't answer, and Northfield figured that he'd either fallen asleep or just wasn't protesting. Either was fine with him. Northfield carried him to the door, and on the way, he stepped around the Death Corps bodies. He felt a spear stab into his midsection, the tip spinning around and tearing up his insides. *Jess, what am I doing? Lord help me, look at this shit. Still, something's keeping my feet moving. One of those feelings, I guess. Please let me not be wrong. You would stop me if I was, wouldn't you?*

Elena found a key on a soldier in the front-left section. They walked out of the room and reached the stairwell. Without delay, they descended the stairs. Northfield glimpsed out of the windows on each floor as they made their way down. The bright white circles of stars were visible through the orange and yellow gas, vaguely reminding him of an apocalyptic version of Van Gogh's *Starry Night* painting. The buildings were rectangular silhouettes against the backdrop, and for a small moment, despite the desperateness of his situation or perhaps because of it, he couldn't help but wish for just one more glimpse of a city with lights illuminating every floor. This moment quickly passed, and he refocused on carrying Salb's limp body down the stairs.

"What am I, a pledge at a frat house?" he joked as a knee-jerk reaction to the sadness that pricked his heart. "You always make the new guy do all the work?"

"Not always," John said, his head turning back to face him. "Just the dumb ones." Northfield scowled as he imagined the satisfied grin behind John's gas mask. Because he had never seen John's face; the image in his head was of a strange clown's grin in a black void.

Before the final flight of stairs, John held up a hand, signaling for Northfield and Elena to stay put as he moved toward the closed back door. Presumably, the guards on the other side of the door would wait for the Death Corps soldiers to return to their Humvees before re-chaining it shut. John knocked on the door three times. The guard opened it, and he jolted in shock at the sight of John pointing his assault rifle at the center of his chest. Instantly, the guard knew that he couldn't possibly bring his own weapon to bear before getting shot. Elena, Northfield, and Salb were out of the guard's sight; he could only see John.

"Drop the gun. Turn around and put your hands over your head," John commanded. The guard obeyed; once he faced away from John and put his hands over his head, John smashed the butt of his rifle into the back of the guard's skull. The guard crumpled to the ground, and John signaled for Elena and Northfield to join him.

"Aw, hell," Northfield said as he passed the guard's sprawled-out body.

"He'll wake up—with a hell of a headache—but he'll wake up," John said, continuing forward without turning around. "Which one, Elena?"

She clicked the unlock button on the key she had picked up, and the leftmost Humvee's lights flashed. There weren't any Death Corps soldiers guarding the Humvees; the soldiers generally didn't fear their vehicles being stolen. On the list of stupid things to do in Cumulus, grand theft auto of a Network vehicle ranked highly.

Once they reached the leftmost Humvee, John opened the rear passenger door and said, "Mark, put Salb in here. You sit in the back with him. Elena, hand me the keys. I know where we're going, so I'll drive. You take the passenger seat."

Northfield said, "Letting me sit alone in the back seat? With my weapons? You trust me enough for that?"

John replied, "You killed Death Corps soldiers. They're gonna be after you now. Even if you gave us up to them, the best they'd do is kill you quickly. I don't know if you're with us, but you're definitely against them."

While Northfield set Salb in the seat and inserted his seat belt for him, he muttered, "Well, when you put it that fucking way . . ."

Salb drooped in his seat, still asleep, and it was apparent that the only thing keeping him remotely upright was the seat belt. His breaths were heavy and labored, and his body quivered with every exhale. *Whatever's wrong with you, man, I hope there's a way to fix you.*

Northfield closed the door and made his way to the other side of the vehicle, where he entered the Humvee. John put the key into the ignition, and the Humvee roared to life. The vehicle sped across the street and turned right. Through the rear window, Northfield watched as Heaven's Rebirth disappeared, swallowed by the orange gas and surrounding buildings.

CHAPTER 8

Northfield stared at Salb's slouched figure and replayed the shootout inside the classroom over and over. Again and again, he watched the Death Corps soldiers collapse as his finger squeezed the trigger, and again and again, he stared at the bodies on the floor with Salb on his shoulders.

While these images flashed in his head, something Elena had said nagged at him: "All things considered, that wasn't too bad."

Six Death Corps soldiers had tried to kill them. Sure, they came out of the ordeal unscathed, but they still had to kill six men. From what Northfield had seen of Elena, she didn't seem like the callous type. Because of that, he could see only two reasons she would say the fight "wasn't too bad." Either she had expected a worse fight then or she expected a worse fight later. He suspected the latter.

Small murmurs came from Salb's lips, and Northfield couldn't tell if they were cries of pain. Maybe they were elicited by nightmares or hallucinations. Either way, the guy didn't look good. What could be so important about this sick middle-aged man? What must the violence and bloodshed be worth?

"Lord . . ." he muttered.

"What?" Elena said, turning in her seat to look at him. Suddenly, it occurred to him that her voice was gentle, soft, and soothing. Just like Jess's.

John held his radio while he drove, and he kept repeating the same phrase into it: "Shepherd, this is Eagle Five. Do you read? Over." The radio's static was the only reply, and after a few moments of waiting, he would try again. Periodically, he'd blurt out an expletive between attempts.

"I've killed before," Northfield said to Elena. "The blood on my hands could fill a river. But I've always had a reason."

"You had plenty of reasons," Elena said.

"Sure, I was protecting myself, protecting Salb," he answered. "But why? When Yellowbacks attack, I know why. They're trying to rob you, maybe kill you. I don't know why the Death Corps attacked. Maybe they were even justified."

"They weren't, Mark. That I can promise you."

"How do I know that? Right now, I don't have a clue what's going on," he said, taking a deep breath. "Earlier, when I asked what was going on, you told me there would be time later. I think we've got some time now."

Before she could answer, a masculine voice crackled through John's radio. "Eagle Five, this is Shepherd. What's your sitrep? Over."

"Finally," John muttered. He relayed the previous series of events to whoever was on the other end of the line.

After he concluded, Elena said to him, "I think it's time we informed Mark about the situation."

"Hell no," John said. "Are you crazy?"

"You said it yourself. He's against the Death Corps. He's gotta be. They'll kill him if they find him."

"That doesn't mean he's a friendly," John retorted. "We don't know this guy from Adam, Elena."

"The evidence corroborates his story," she said. "And so do his actions."

"No," John said, shaking his head. "No. I mean, come on, Elena. This is insanity. Trusting someone we just met? With the information we have? Textbook naivety."

Northfield didn't exactly like being talked about as if he wasn't present, but he decided to remain silent. He had a feeling that his input wouldn't help the situation much.

"It's not naivety," she said. "It's a calculation. You saw Mark's skill with a gun back there. Having a guy like him by our side during a fight is something I want. How can he screw us over, exactly? Like you said earlier, the Death Corps will find out about his involvement eventually. There's no going back from killing Death Corps. Even if he gave them information, they'd still kill him."

"Okay, say we tell him about the operation. Say he refuses to be a part of it. He goes his own way and ends up being caught by the Death Corps. They'll torture him to get information, and they'll kill him only after he's compromised the whole op."

"Christ, Dad," she said. "When he learns about the op, what we're trying to do, he'll help us."

Northfield couldn't help himself, and he muttered quietly, "You guys need to talk about this in private? I can just jump out the window."

Elena and John didn't hear him; they were too focused on their argument.

"What cockamamie mental math did you use to arrive at that conclusion?" John asked.

"What he's already done. What he's already said," Elena said in exasperation. "Add those to his life already being in danger, and I'm pretty confident."

"Trust needs to be earned, Elena," he said. "Far as I'm concerned, there is a fat river between where he is and where trust is. What he's already done doesn't bridge the gap. We've just met him."

"What are you planning on doing with Mark, then?" Elena asked. "You took him with us. You let him keep his weapons. You told him where we're going."

"I told him we're going to a doctor. You, Salb, and I are going. Not him," John said. "Telling him that we're going to the doctor isn't the same thing as giving someone a map with a big red X. As far as the other things go . . ." He flashed a glance at Northfield before he added, "You helped us stay alive back there. We owe you. I'm letting you keep your weapons. I'm getting you away from the scene. Past that, our obligation to you ends."

Northfield nodded, and he turned to look out the window. He said, "I understand. Just tell me one thing. Whatever you're doing . . . is it good?"

"It is, Mark. I promise," Elena said. She asked, "If you take my promise seriously, would you be willing to help us?"

"Heaven above, you can't drop an argument," John muttered, gripping the steering wheel tightly in frustration.

Northfield ignored John and answered her. "The way I see it, my life's been on a timer since I opened that window. My choices look like either getting shot running away or getting shot doing some good. I'd prefer trying my hand at the latter before falling into the pit, you know?"

I'm gonna fight against that timer, Jess. I'm gonna keep kicking and screaming to live. I haven't forgotten my first promise. I won't go gently or willingly—that's for damned sure.

"Why would he lie?" Elena asked, turning to John. "Just to get information that the Death Corps will torture out of him? Or do you really think he'd sell our information to the Yellowbacks? If he was after money, he would have killed Salb without a second thought."

"Look, Elena . . ." John said dismissively.

She pushed on. "Dropping him off somewhere will slow us down, too. Who knows how close on our tail the Death Corps are? We're safer taking him with us."

John remained silent for a minute, and his head rigidly faced the road ahead. He slowly turned and asked her, "This is really what you think is best?"

"Yes," she answered.

His grip on the steering wheel relaxed slightly. He said with resignation, "At this point, arguing with you, I'm more likely to have a heart attack than get killed by the Death Corps. Having an extra gun by our side could help us survive. If this is a choice we regret, I just hope you know that I did everything I could for you."

"I know, Dad," she said. Her hand reached over and rubbed his shoulder.

She turned to Northfield and asked, "What do you know about the Network?"

"I know that calling the organization shady would be like saying that a double-decker bus has a couple seats," he replied. "Once you work as a merc long enough, you get hints that the Network is more than the producer, protector, and neutral adjudicator of deals that it claims to be."

"What do you know about NRD?" Elena asked. The acronym NRD referred to the Network Research Division.

He said, "I only know NRD by the products it has produced. Filters, filtration systems, that sort of stuff. I'd wager that most of NRD's research goes to weapons and defenses for the Death Corps, like those faceplates that make them top runners for the most menacing dinner plates I've ever seen."

"NRD has been working on something big for a while, Mark," she said. "Two years ago, the Network discovered a small independent research team in the middle of Wisconsin. The team was building a dispersal device, one that would distribute a yet-uncreated agent across a large area. The lab that the scientists worked in was a shoddy, ragtag setup. Pretty much what you'd expect for a bunch of scientists gathering materials in the middle of nowhere. The scientists had trouble getting their hands on resources, but they still made genuine progress on the device. Geniuses in resourcefulness as well as their studies, I guess."

She sighed, and her voice took on a somber tone when she continued. "Death Corps soldiers stumbled across the lab. They killed the scientists and wasted no time stealing their device. The Network didn't just let the device rot, though. The device continued to be developed under a project named Zeus's Mercy. A sister project, Code Blue, developed the neutralizing agent that Zeus's Mercy would disperse. Using Zeus's Mercy, the stagnant gas that's been over the city for ten years could be eradicated overnight."

John said while keeping his eyes on the road, "NRD finished Zeus's Mercy and Code Blue, Mark. One month ago, the Network declared both to be in operational condition."

"What?" he exclaimed. He felt like his ears had betrayed him, and he was tempted to ask Elena and John to repeat everything they had just said. There was a device, right at that very moment, able to expunge the gas and make the air breathable. A device existed that could make tomorrow a day he could walk outside without a gas mask. That could make the world normal again, maybe even make people normal again.

Questions struck him like a flurry of thunderbolts. He asked, "How does Code Blue neutralize the gas, exactly? How does this all work?"

"I don't know the specifics," Elena said. "When Salb's lucid, ask him. He was one of the scientists who worked on the project."

A thought occurred to him, and his hope quickly faded, replaced by pessimism and dread. "If the Network finished this device a month ago, why the hell hasn't it been used yet?"

Elena said, "The Network is the most powerful entity in the region. At the top of the food chain, so to speak. Why would the Network want anything to change? Change could mean a loss of power. Think of it: at this point, pretty much everyone is dependent on the Network to buy filters, unless you've got an expensive gas mask like yours, also conveniently produced by the Network, and even then you'll eventually have to stop in at a Network outpost to buy new filters after a couple years, maximum. And that's not even including the Network-made filtration systems that you or your landlord has to pay for."

John added, "Sure, if you can produce breathable air like the Yellowbacks, there's less dependency. Thing is, most people don't have the resources to do that shit themselves. If the Network detonated Zeus's Mercy, it would lose that dependency. Some of the Network's power would follow."

"Why finish the device, then?" Northfield cried, frustrated. "Why waste the resources and time creating a device to fix the goddamned apocalypse if you're just gonna sit on it?"

"Again, power," Elena said. "The Network wants control, and that control includes power over the gas. But it goes deeper than that. The Network plans to use the device to gain complete control over the people."

"How do they figure that, exactly?"

"This is America, or it used to be, anyway. It hasn't been long enough for people to take too kindly to being ruled over and controlled. If the Network pushes too hard, the organization can expect a certain amount of pushback, which is why it has always grabbed at power with a degree of tact."

"I don't disagree, but where does Zeus's Mercy play into what you said?" Northfield asked.

Elena continued. "Zeus's Mercy is the sweetness in a Venus flytrap. By lulling people with the dream of the gas being gone, the Network can exert more control and squeeze tighter and tighter without as much pushback or anger, at least not until the trap is closed. The Network can disperse water vapor across the city, or maybe launch Code Blue over a limited area, to prove the device's existence to the public and give rise to that hope. While the Network claims work is still being done on the device, more and more controlling practices and rules are put into place."

She allowed Northfield time to absorb the details before she added, "As far as why the Network actually finished Zeus's Mercy, the device also serves as a fail-safe. If the Network closes the jaws of the trap too hard and too fast, and people become aware of what's happening, there might be danger of revolts. In that case, the Network can set off the device at its full capacity. It would serve as a public-relations shot in the arm. While people are elated by the new safe air, provided courtesy of the Network, the organization can stop an uprising or at least delay any resistance long enough to successfully contain and manage it."

"Sounds like a lot of work when there's a different fail-safe staring me in the face. The Network produces the gas masks and filters for the city," Northfield said. "If there was a danger of a rebellion big enough to ruin them, why not just take the filters and gas masks away and choke out the resistance?"

"The first thing a resistance with the power to take down the Network would do is find a way to keep breathing. A resistance would either stockpile gas masks and filters or find another option, like the Yellowbacks have. To make sure a resistance couldn't access the

Network's filters or gas masks, the Network would have to take them away from everybody, and that would be a surefire way to push people into the arms of the resistance. If you take away people's means to breathe, they won't react well."

"Christ, all of this . . . This is all one of the most despicably calculated things I've ever heard," Northfield said.

"Not the first despicable thing the Network's done," John said. "That's why the Coalition formed. We're made up of people that are aware of what the Network has done. Most are either victims or perpetrators of those sins. Until now, the Coalition has stayed under the radar. The Network's just too damned big and powerful for us to go against without being crushed."

Elena said, "But we've been waiting for an opportunity, and Salb has given us one. If we set that device off, we've not only saved the people of Cumulus, but we've taken the first step toward dismantling the Network's hold. The Coalition doesn't have the resources or manpower to be the large-scale resistance needed to take them down, but we're hoping that we serve as a spark. Even if the whole Coalition is killed trying to set off the device, we're willing to risk it."

For a moment, Northfield thought he saw John's hands tighten around the steering wheel, but unsure if his mind was just playing tricks on him, he instead nodded toward Salb and said, "You say that Salb gave you an opportunity. What opportunity are you talking about?"

Elena answered. "Salb was the second-in-command scientist on the Zeus's Mercy project, working under the lead of a scientist named Kayden Knox. Salb had the impression that the device would be used to help people instead of being squirreled away by the Network. He found out the truth when the device was finished, and he sought out the Coalition not long after."

John said, "Zeus's Mercy has a master key, and the key is required to activate the device. Kayden Knox had the master key until Salb stole it from him this evening."

"Hang on," Northfield said. "If Salb stole the key, why didn't he activate Zeus's Mercy?"

John answered. "Zeus's Mercy takes three minutes to launch Code Blue after activation. Somebody, either a scientist or one of the guards patrolling the lab, would have noticed if he tried to set off the device. A loud warning siren goes off throughout the entire building if Zeus's Mercy is activated. Salb didn't think it was possible to activate the device and launch Code Blue before the Network stopped him. Even if he could, the Network would kill him pretty damn quick after, and that wasn't a price Salb was willing to pay. Instead, he hid the key and agreed to give the Coalition its location under one condition: we get him out of the city and to a safe location."

Elena said, "We planned on escorting Salb to a meeting location with the Coalition so they could get him out of the city. We rented out the other rooms on Salb's floor. When the time came to retrieve him, we wanted easy access inside Heaven's Rebirth. We also wanted to eliminate the fear of adjacent neighbors eavesdropping on Salb when he was communicating with us over radio. Although we rented out the rooms, we didn't actually stay in them. John and I used fake IDs to get into Cumulus, and we wanted to be in the city as little as possible to avoid detection. Our IDs are decent but not able to hold up to intense scrutiny. The longer we stay in the city, the more times we have to use our IDs, upping our chances of being caught."

John said, "Originally, Salb was supposed to steal the key tomorrow evening, and we were supposed to escort him to the meeting location that same night. But yesterday, Salb said he had to move the theft up to today. The Coalition couldn't move their plans forward because they still needed to finish outfitting the smuggling vehicle, and they needed to wait for their weapons and fighters to arrive. Because Salb also said he was starting to feel a bit under the weather, we arranged to stay at Dr. Flynn's for the night so he could get a final examination before leaving the city. There won't be many doctors around when he's in hiding. Still, we didn't realize how sick he'd be when we arrived at his room section tonight, either because he didn't let on how bad it was or because he got significantly worse. He must've managed to hide the key somewhere before collapsing on his bed, because we couldn't find it anywhere in his room."

Elena said, "His poor state threw a wrench in our plans. Between Heaven's Rebirth and Dr. Flynn's neighborhood is one of the most heavily populated areas of the city. We had a longer, more indirect route mapped out. The route avoided busy streets, wound at some points, and had shortcuts that circumvented some roads altogether. The aim of the convolution, as you can probably guess, was to make it difficult for the Death Corps to piece together our path and destination from potential witnesses. However, the route involved crossing some physically taxing obstacles, mostly by climbing."

Northfield started to put together the rest. "But with Salb as sick as he is, you couldn't take the longer path. Even if you could lug Salb the whole way and pass those obstacles, his condition would slow you down too much to keep ahead of the Death Corps. Probably bring you unwanted attention and potential witnesses to boot. In the end, the long path would have been your greatest chance of getting caught."

"Right," Elena said. "We argued about what to do until you showed up. I wanted to go through our sympathizer contacts in the city to see if any of them could pick us up. John thought doing so would be a waste of time. The sympathizers provided the Coalition with funds, but they're beyond reluctant to stick their necks out into danger. If one of them volunteered, their car would stand a good chance of being seen by witnesses and tracked back to them, and the Death Corps would be on the hunt for them, too."

John said, "I thought we stood a better chance if we just started moving and tried a straight shot through the city to Flynn's, playing Salb off as a drunk guy. I hoped we could stay ahead of the Death Corps and not leave a trail of witnesses, which honestly had a good chance of still happening. Either plan would've probably failed, but then you showed up."

"Lucky me," Northfield muttered, then asked, "Why didn't you get a car yourself?"

"Cars are hellishly expensive," Elena said. "Even though the sympathizers provided funds, the Coalition is still working on a tight budget. For instance, our IDs and the ID of the Coalition's main smuggler are the only fake IDs the Coalition could spend cards on. With all the weapons, ammunition, and combat vehicles needed for the assault, the Coalition didn't have the cards to buy another car. Even if we got one, we would ultimately have to dispose of it. Seeing as everyone in the Coalition is wanted by the Death Corps, we'd have to use one of our fake IDs to buy a car. The Death Corps would quickly find out the IDs that rented the rooms next to Salb are the same fakes, and they would hunt the car. We would have had to dump it. That's a lot of resources for just one or two trips, no matter how valuable those trips are."

Northfield nodded. Renting cars wasn't an option for anybody anymore; cars were too valuable to trust with anybody else, even for a fee. If someone without a vehicle wanted to get from point A to point B, they had to hire a Network driver to take them.

John added, "As much as we would have liked the sympathizers to give us more funds for a car or fake IDs, they didn't have any. They already gave us whatever resources they had to spare."

He pulled the Humvee into an alley and parked. The alley was pitch black and contrasted heavily with the neon-lit streets on either end. The headlights of the Humvee illuminated the walls, and Northfield could see graffiti letters scrawled all over the bricks. The lights shut off when John took out the key, and the walls blackened. He said, "We're dumping the vehicle here. I'd bet all my chips that the Network's already sent an alert to the Death Corps about it. We should be far enough from Heaven's Rebirth to make it to Dr. Flynn's apartment before they find it." He added, "Walking with Salb in his condition is conspicuous, but we're past the most densely populated part of the city, where we'd get spotted and reported for almost certain. If we move quick and keep our eyes peeled while acting natural, we should hopefully make it without drawing much attention."

"Positive thinking," Elena said. "I like it."

They exited the car, and both Northfield and Elena made their way to Salb's door.

"I can carry him," Northfield said, moving to open the door. "I skipped leg day, so I gotta work the glutes somehow."

She put her hand on the door and said, "We both should. Like John's prior plan, we should make it look like he's drunk and we're helping him home, at least from a distance." He nodded, and she opened the door and shook Salb firmly yet gently, saying to him, "You've got to move a little bit with us, Salb, alright? You think you can?"

Roused from his sleep, Salb muttered, "I'll try. I feel quite weak."

As she maneuvered him out of his seat and put one of his arms over her shoulder, she said, "It won't be long. We'll make this walk as quick as possible."

When Northfield put Salb's other arm over his shoulder, he said, "When's your old man gonna take a shift on Salb duty?"

John, who was waiting at the end of the alley behind the Humvee, said, "I supervise."

"Yeah. 'Supervise.' Right," he said.

He could sense John's patronizing smirk behind his gas mask. "Perks of being in charge."

Northfield and Elena, supporting Salb, moved to John. Salb's feet dragged, and he let out a throaty cough every handful of seconds. Still, the ruse of Salb being a drunk man they were helping home would hold from a distance.

Northfield's presence helped alleviate suspicion; once the Network discovered that Elena's and John's living spaces were rented using fake IDs, it would put together that Salb had two accomplices with him. However, the discovery of Northfield's involvement, although inevitable, would take longer, meaning the Network and its Death Corps' search would be for three people fleeing Heaven's Rebirth, not four, and the reward for information leading to Salb's capture would reflect such intel.

As a result, honest citizens would be less likely to report them, and there would be many dishonest reports that the Death Corps would need to sift through from people hungry for money. While the Death Corps knew it was entirely possible for Elena, John, and Salb to be traveling with a fourth person, with so many reports to sift through, the Network would prioritize sightings of three people rather than four. Of course, that would be if anyone even reported them; drunkenness was common at night, and their weaponry wouldn't stand out, as many people openly carried in the city.

The true risk came from people closer to them, either walking or driving past, who could tell that Salb was sick rather than drunk. Physical evidence in Salb's living space, such as mucus on his bed, would point to him being ill, information the Death Corps would include in their reward. If anyone realized Salb was sick and could describe Salb's sickness to the Death Corps and convince them they had accurate information, their report would drastically rise in priority.

John stepped out of the alley, onto the sidewalk, and turned right. Elena and Northfield followed him.

Few capable doctors remained in society, so Flynn's services were in high demand, enabling him to live in comfort compared to the rest of Cumulus's citizens. He lived in one of the nicest and safest neighborhoods in the city, aside from those occupied by inner Network officials. As such, the neighborhood occupied a happy medium of being peaceful at the dead of night, with almost no locals outside, while simultaneously being less patrolled by Death Corps soldiers than other areas of the city.

Trees lined the sidewalks, with thick sections of leaves bubbling out from them like clouds. This pleased Northfield because the trees would obscure them from people looking through the windows above, of which there would be few.

When they started walking, the only pedestrian also on the sidewalk was a withered old lady wearing a brown gas mask and facing them. She wore a puffy brown coat and a red floral shawl over her head, and the features of her face and body couldn't be discerned as a result, save for her short height. Her head drooped down, and she seemed to be staring at her feet. She shuffled past Northfield without glancing up. Elena and John looked over their shoulders and studied her for a moment after she walked past. After determining that she had truly paid them no notice, they paid her no further notice in kind. Northfield studied her as well, but his stare lingered a little longer.

Jess, you always used to joke about what you'd do when you found your first gray hair, how you'd have your midlife crisis and buy yourself a nice car that you knew you couldn't afford. Sometimes, when I look at that picture of you I always carry around, I think about what you'd look like as an old woman, what you'd look like fifty years into our marriage. I know it's stupid, and I don't know why, but when I miss you the most, I often think of that.

"We go straight and turn left," John said. "Then we'll reach Dr. Flynn's apartment."

The rest of the journey to the doctor's apartment was uneventful; they only saw a handful of pedestrians on the sidewalks. All of them had trouble walking and stumbled around as if someone was shaking the ground under them. In such an affluent neighborhood, Northfield assumed the occupants enjoyed their peaceful nights away from the noise and dinginess of the rest of the city. The neighborhood seemed to have no nightlife, devoid as it was of the copious neon signs found near the South Network Facility.

Without a nightlife, most of the late-night adventurers in the area were alcoholics or drug addicts, presumably on their way back from a bar or shoot-up spot. Alcohol and drug problems were bad even in affluent communities, Northfield mused. Based on how intoxicated the pedestrians were, if they even remembered seeing Salb and his protectors, the Death Corps would take a while to piece together their disjointed stories.

Two vehicles drove past them on their way to the apartment. The first, a motorcycle, was driven by a man with a leather jacket that had some shining symbol on the left arm, although the motorcycle sped by too fast for Northfield to identify it. A spike of fear went through him, but he calmed himself somewhat upon realizing that the driver didn't even glance their way and that he traveled too quickly to see them as anything more than a blur even if he did. The second vehicle, a red armored Lamborghini, similarly sped too quickly down the street to even notice them. The richest in the city, those that lived in even nicer neighborhoods than Flynn, habitually took armored luxury cars on joyrides at night. The Network and Death Corps' mass search for the killers of their soldiers hadn't yet reached a mile out from the epicenter at Heaven's Rebirth. But soon enough, their vehicles would be swarming the streets.

They reached Dr. Flynn's apartment, a red-brick building with white window frames that had an old-fashioned and homey flair. A concrete staircase with metal railings on both sides led up to the door from the sidewalk. Dark-green bushes lined the staircase, and two dark trees rose up on each side of the building. Their leaves faintly brushed the bricks with each breeze, creating a soft rustling noise.

They stood on the sidewalk. John pulled out his radio and said, "Shepherd, this is Eagle Six. We're at Scalpel's apartment. Tell him to let us in. Over."

A reply crackled through the radio. "Copy, Eagle Six. Relaying message to Scalpel. Over."

"Is there a guard inside that we need to worry about?" Elena asked.

"No," John said, "Dr. Flynn bribed the guard to take a little break. People don't enter or leave apartments at night often in this neighborhood. Nobody else is coming in or out to notice."

"What about the guard himself?" she asked. "We sure we can trust this guy?"

"Flynn says so, but I can't say for sure. It's the best we're going to get right now." He nodded toward the staircase. "Let's go. Dr. Flynn will open the door for us."

They climbed the stairs and promptly heard an electronic buzz as the door creaked open. A man of medium height and build held it open for them; Northfield assumed he was Dr. Flynn. The man wore a black gas mask along with a plaid shirt and jeans. After they entered, the doctor shut the door.

They found themselves in a hallway with a dusty wooden floor and sea-green walls, all dimly lit by lamps spaced across the ceiling. At the far wall, the hallway expanded into a room containing an inoperable elevator and a door leading to the stairwell. Between the elevator and door, a room that typically housed the security guard was empty. Doors lined both sides of the hallway, key-readers above each handle.

Dr. Flynn led them down the hallway without a word being uttered; they all understood that conversations were better held in the safety and privacy of a room. At the farthest-left door in the hallway, Flynn stopped and pulled out his keycard. He swiped it across the key-reader, and he opened the door.

Despite the neighborhood, Northfield still found himself surprised by how nice Flynn's apartment was, although he couldn't tell how much of his surprise could simply be attributed to the fact that he hadn't seen a nice apartment in a long time. Flynn's apartment had a living room with a leather couch in the center, along with a small coffee table in front of it. To the left of the living room, cutlery hung from the wall in a small kitchen, and an oak table with four wooden chairs sat at the kitchen's center. To the right of the living room, there were two doors, and Northfield figured that one led to the bathroom while the other led to Flynn's room. Two candle lamps on nightstands illuminated the living room while two lamps illuminated the kitchen. Northfield gathered that Dr. Flynn was economical, saving money on electricity even when he could afford not to. The clean white carpet and white walls reminded him of an operating room, a correlation aided by the pristine condition of the couch and nightstand.

Flynn took off his gas mask, revealing the face of a man in his mid-fifties. His paper-white hair and thick eyebrows made him appear older than the relatively few wrinkles on his face would otherwise indicate. His soft yet icy-blue eyes reminded Northfield of his own, although Flynn's had heavy bags under them.

Elena and John took off their gas masks, and Northfield saw their faces for the first time. Both had light-brown skin. Elena had shoulder-length brunette hair, while John was bald. She had a soft chin, high cheekbones, wide brown eyes, and tightly arcing eyebrows. John's eyes were beady in comparison, and his square jaw and chin contrasted with Elena's softer features. Although they didn't look much alike, their relation to one another showed through their noses; both were pointed with defined C-shape curves.

While Northfield took off his gas mask, goggles, and earplugs, Doctor Flynn said to John, "I don't like this one bit. I hear you've already gotten into a shootout."

Elena carried Salb to the couch, laid him down, and took off his gas mask, jacket, and armored vest. As she did so, John said, "Things got hairy, but we're through."

"You sure they're not on your trail?"

"Not now, at least."

"Then we should be okay, at least for a little while." Flynn sighed and said, "It'll have to do."

Flynn looked toward Salb, and John said, "We need you to figure out what's wrong with Salb and fix him."

"I figured as much," Flynn said.

He walked to the couch, and John followed, standing by Elena. Northfield went into the living room, but he leaned against the wall instead of approaching the couch. He figured that he wouldn't be much help, and he didn't want to get in the way.

Flynn knelt next to Salb, who was moaning quietly on the couch and narrowed his eyes. Observing that Salb was sweating profusely, he put a hand on his forehead and said, "Fever. A bad one." He took Salb's temperature with a thermometer and announced, "Hundred and three. What other symptoms has he shown?"

"Chills and sweating," John said. "And his breathing's been off. Lots of coughing, too."

Flynn rubbed his chin and continued to study Salb. After listening to Salb's lungs with a stethoscope, he said, "I'd say it's a bad case of pneumonia. Pneumonia is as common as the letter E these days, and there's a new strain of pneumonia-causing bacteria that hits harder and faster than other strains. I've seen people walking and talking, and then, just a couple hours later, they're in a condition like this. You might know the strain by its informal name, Mask's Kiss, which comes from the common occurrence of bacteria contacting the interior of gas masks and exposing users when they put them on and inhale. The gas masks keep us alive, but they're a haven for pathogens. For starters, Salb needs a new mask. I have a spare he can take."

"Pneumonia? That's treatable, right?" John asked.

"Depends if it's bacterial or viral," Flynn said. "If it's bacterial, specifically Mask's Kiss, antibiotics will work as treatment. I've stowed away some of the most powerful that used to be made. Not much, but enough for a rainy day. For the information this man holds, I'll be happy to part with some pills. He'll still need a week or so to recover to one hundred percent, but I'd say that he'll show vast improvement by morning. Lucid and hopefully even able to walk and talk. The silver lining of Mask's Kiss is that antibiotics hit the bacteria harder than other strains."

"And if it's viral?" Elena asked.

"Then there's not much I can do, especially with the limited medical tools in my apartment. He'll just have to ride out the sickness."

"Shit," John muttered. "Is there a way to tell which type he has?"

"No," Flynn said, standing up. As he walked to the cabinet in the kitchen, he said, "I'll just have to give him antibiotics, and we'll all have to hope his symptoms clear up soon." He opened the cabinet, which was filled with pill bottles, gauze, bandages, and other medical supplies. He fished around the cabinet and grabbed a translucent orange pill bottle. After filling a glass with water, he brought it and the pill bottle back into the living room. He asked, "You don't have anywhere else to go, correct?"

"Yeah. You're it, Dr. Flynn," John said.

"In that case," Flynn replied, "You can stay here, if you need. But only tomorrow. Any longer I can't allow, for all of our sakes. The Death Corps are going to be on high alert, searching everywhere for Salb. Stay in one place for too long, and they'll eventually find you."

"Understood," John said.

Flynn knelt by Salb with the pill bottle and water. He inserted a pill into Salb's mouth and held the glass of water to his lips.

"Drink this," he ordered. "It will help you swallow the pill."

Salb, although only half-lucid, complied. The task seemed to expend more energy than he possessed; once he swallowed, his eyes shut, and he fell into a deep sleep after a strangled wheeze.

Flynn stood up and faced John. He exhaled and said, "Now all we can do is wait."

"Thanks for everything, Doc," John said.

"I just want to be able to walk outside without wearing a gas mask. Seems worth the risk to me." He looked at the kitchen. "I assume you haven't eaten recently. I'd be a poor host if I didn't feed you, wouldn't I?"

"Thanks, Dr. Flynn, but we won't take your food. You've done enough for us," John said.

"I've got a few rations left in my backpack," Northfield offered.

"Nonsense," Flynn said, waving his hand. "I'm fortunate enough that my income allows me to purchase enough food to spare, and not that ration rubbish you fancy eating. Come on, doesn't a cooked meal sound nice?"

John deliberated and said nothing. After a moment, Elena said, "We'd love that. Sorry about my dad. He has a hard time accepting food from other people. One of his weird quirks." John glared at her, and she shrugged.

"Ah, I see." Flynn waved his hand, ushering them to come into the kitchen. "Well, take a seat at the table."

Northfield, still leaning against the wall, watched the three of them go into the kitchen. *How long's it been since I've eaten a meal with others? Christ, I can't even remember . . .*

Elena, noticing that he hadn't come into the kitchen, peeked her head out into the living room. She said, "You need food, too. Gumption only gets you so far."

He set his backpack down and joined them. Dr. Flynn pulled pork out of his refrigerator.

Northfield took a seat in the chair opposite John. Awkward glances darted around the table; what should they talk about?

"I take it that you're a Spoonbills fan," John said, looking at Northfield's hat and jacket.

"Oh, shit, you found me out," he said. "I hope you're not a Sox fan. We might need to have a duel."

John smirked. "Actually, we're originally from New York. We're Yankees fans."

"Oh God, that's worse."

John chuckled and said, "You'd be surprised how often we get that."

"Everything makes sense now. All of the pieces are lining up," he said, looking around wide-eyed. "The Death Corps weren't after Salb, were they? They just found out that a Yankees fan was in the city and decided to do the world a favor by coming after you. Salb was just a cover-up for your lie."

"He found us out, Dad," Elena said. "Do we need to kill him now?"

"You try that and the Death Corps will be the least of your concerns," Northfield said.

John said with a wry smirk, "I could shoot a gun before you were even in diapers."

"Pretty soon, you're gonna need diapers . . ."

"If you start punching each other, I'm not going to bandage your cuts and bruises," Dr. Flynn said wryly. He turned on the gas stove and placed a pan on the bottom-left. He spread some butter before dropping chunks of pork onto the pan. They sizzled, and a savory scent wafted through the air.

"You'd be surprised," Northfield said. "I just met a guy that gave me crap for being a Spoonbills fan, too. I swear, there are none of my loyal brethren left in this tin pot of a city."

"That's surprising," Elena said. "It seems like I can't stick my leg out without kicking a Spoonbills fan in the ass. You must be some sort of social butterfly to meet so many non-Spoonbills fans in this city."

"Me?" he said, chuckling. "Oh, I'm not the social butterfly type."

"Then what type of person are you?" she asked. "What were you doing before the attacks?"

"The attacks?" he repeated. "You mean like ten years ago?"

"Yeah," she said. "Did you have a job? Or what were you up to?"

"Hmmm. Well, my wife and I had just gotten back from our honeymoon, and we were trying to figure out where to live. Guess the apocalypse got me out of making that choice."

"That's one hell of a silver lining," she said, a soft grimace disappearing as quickly as it appeared.

He asked, "What about you? What were you doing before the attacks?"

"High school," she said. "Just turned sixteen. I remember trying to convince my dad here"—she nudged John—"to get me a car for my birthday."

"I told her public transportation was good enough," John said, looking at her, "and that she wouldn't need the car."

"He was right, but I didn't listen," she said. "I remember saying to him, in my stupid teenage angst, 'It'll be the end of the world if I don't get a car.'"

"Did you get a car, then?" Northfield asked.

"No," she said. "And ever since, I've joked to my dad that the apocalypse was his fault because he didn't get me that car."

"And you put up with that?" Northfield asked John, laughing.

He shrugged and said, "I just throw her comment back at her. I tell her that if she didn't make that cursed premonition and jinx us all, the world wouldn't have ended. And then we go back and forth with our comments with no end in sight. It's been ten years, and I don't think we'll make progress anytime soon."

He chuckled and asked, "What were you doing ten years ago, John?"

"Like you, I was trying to figure out what to do with my life. I'd served a couple of tours in the Army. When I got back, I just couldn't find my footing. I hopped from job to job for years, and then, well, this all happened." John leaned forward ever so slightly and said, "The way you handled yourself back there . . . you must have served, too."

Northfield nodded. "Raven 404."

"You served in that outfit? Hell," John muttered, his eyebrows quickly rising and falling like the flicker of a flame. "You didn't mention that."

"Yeah, well, that wasn't before the war," he replied, and his eyes lowered from John's to stare at the table. John leaned back in his chair.

Dr. Flynn set a large bowl in the middle of the table, and he handed plates to his guests.

"What about you, Dr. Flynn?" Elena asked. "What were you doing before the attacks?"

Dr. Flynn sat at the table. "Hmm . . . well, I started my twentieth year at Halbot Memorial. Pediatric care. Other than that, well, my life was pretty standard, now that I think of it."

"Nothing wrong with standard," John said. "Nowadays a standard life sounds better than the lotto."

"Yeah," Northfield said. "You know, it's the damnedest thing. I can't remember very well what life used to be like. The memorable events, sure, but the day-to-day events? Pretty hazy. I just remember that it was great."

They sat in silence. Dr. Flynn broke the stillness by gesturing to the food, and he said, "Well, I didn't make food for you all to just stare at it. Dig in."

They reached into the bowl and put pork squares on their plates. The golden-brown squares had black seasoning on them, and they were dry enough for reasonably clean finger-eating. Northfield tasted one and instantly shut his eyes; he relished the smoky and tender taste.

They ate without talking, all focused on the meal. Fresher food than ration packages was expensive, and most people saved buying "real" foods for special occasions. Dr. Flynn, due to his in-demand and much-needed job, could afford buying "real" food more often. *Should have gone to med school*, Northfield thought as he relished another bite.

After he finished his food, he said, "Thanks for the meal, Dr. Flynn. I haven't eaten that well in ages. Nice eating something that doesn't taste like a basketball for a change."

Elena and John shared their thanks as well, to which Dr. Flynn replied, "My pleasure. We all might die soon, so might as well eat like it." He looked down at the remaining pork in the bowl. "While I clean up, one of you might want to take these squares to Salb to see if he can eat. Best for him to get some energy to fight the illness."

Elena and Northfield both stood up to grab the bowl. He said, "I can feed Salb."

"Let me," she said. "He recognizes my voice. I talked to him in his living space. In his semi-lucid state, it's probably better that I do it."

He opened his mouth to protest, but figuring that she was right, he sat back in his chair. As she left the kitchen and Flynn started washing the dishes, John asked, "Do you have any kids, Mark?"

"No, my wife and I never got the chance to," he said.

Understanding the implication of his remark, John didn't push further. Instead, he nodded toward the living room and said, "It's funny. She's younger than me, a lot younger, but she seems to remember the old world a whole lot better than I do. She clings to it and what it held more than anyone I've seen. She's convinced that the only way to bring it back is to act like it still exists: doing the right thing and everything that comes along with it, like having faith in other people." His head shook softly as he said, "I'm convinced that she'll either save the world or be killed by it."

"If those are the possibilities, I really hope for the former," Northfield said.

John turned toward him and said, "She thinks you're of similar stock. She sees something in you, Mark. She's never been dumb. Her faith in others is drawn from a conscious choice, not idleness. Whether she's right or wrong, well, she's willing to chance being wrong."

"And you?"

"I need to make sure the world doesn't kill her," John said, his eyes narrowing. Northfield noted that he didn't directly answer his question. "There are some truly evil people out there. If anyone can bring the old world back, it's her. I believe that. Someone just needs to fend off the assholes as she tries. But make no mistake, Mark. Whatever's out in that gas, she is my world. You don't have kids, so I don't expect you to understand, but I expect you to know that's how I feel."

"I didn't have kids, but I understand what it means to have someone be your world," Northfield said, his voice momentarily pulling away from the earth like a receding tide. "God, I miss that."

John took a moment to study Northfield before he said, more softly, "She's got her reasons for having faith in you. On the surface, you do seem like a rarity. One of the few decent ones. But we've known you for less than twenty-four hours. The only thing you can know about a man in less than twenty-four hours is his shadow." John's voice hardened as he added, "So take this warning, Mark. You show any sign of betrayal, even the smallest hint that you might hurt her, and I won't just kill you. I'll cut and burn what's left of your soul before I extinguish it."

Northfield let his words settle between them before he said, "I get it. Her protection is number one. But tell me, then, why are you on such a dangerous mission with her?"

"She volunteered for the mission first. She's an adult. She makes her own decisions that I don't always like, and she wouldn't be Elena if she didn't volunteer for this. I've got more military experience than most people still kicking these days. Way I see it, I'm the shield to her spear." He hesitated, then said, "But it's more than that. I've had to do a lot to keep us safe. Stuff not worth mentioning, but stuff you can probably imagine. I'm tired of it. I want this world to change. Like everybody else, I guess."

"This world's funny," Northfield said. "You do everything you can to keep your hands clean, and this world tries everything to make you dirty them."

"You think there's a way to keep them clean?"

137

"I don't know. The more I try, the deeper God digs his shovel into the dirt to pile on me."

Coughs echoed from the living room as Elena attempted to feed Salb.

John said, "You asked if you could help Salb when we were questioning you. Even though you were in a bad way, you worried about him instead of yourself. You're either someone who genuinely wants to do the right thing or someone who's damned good at acting like it. Why?"

Northfield thought for a moment, and he said after a soft exhale, "The old world just feels like it's slipping away more and more each day—and me along with it. Gotta hang on, I guess, and save what's left."

John's eyes bored into him as he said, "We all face danger. Every day in this hellscape. But this mission, Mark, is danger like we've never experienced. Not even during the war. If you've been skirting death's knife, now your cheek is going to rest against the blade. You need to be aware of that."

Northfield met his gaze and said, "My life's not what I'm worried about losing, John."

"If that's true, then we can use you," John said, standing from his chair. "I'm going to report back to the Coalition one final time. Then we should get some shuteye."

Dr. Flynn, who had just finished the dishes, said, "I'm sorry. I don't have any spare blankets or pillows."

"Don't worry about it," John said. "Elena and I, and I assume Mark, have slept in far worse conditions. The ground is fine."

Dr. Flynn nodded. He turned to Northfield and said, "Feel free to stay up, but I'm going to extinguish all of the lamps in a few minutes."

"Sounds good, Dr. Flynn. I'm going to catch some sleep, too."

He followed John into the living room. John reported to the Coalition using his portable radio. He was quiet and minded Salb, who was sound asleep on the couch. Elena sat on the adjacent coffee table and watched Salb. Concern showed through the creases on her mouth. The bowl sat empty next to her.

"Not much more we can do for him," John said after finishing his report. "Best we get some sleep and keep our own strength up. We don't want to catch the shit he has. I'll take the first lookout shift. Elena, in a couple of hours, I'll wake you to take the next shift."

She nodded in agreement. Northfield grabbed his backpack and lay behind the couch. Elena stood up from the coffee table and lay to the right of it. John sat on the coffee table and faced the door. Northfield pulled out the picture of Jess from his backpack. *You used to love the Spoonbills, too. I wish you were here. I'd feel comfortable taking on these two heretics with my Spoonbills buddy at my side. Yankee fans in our territory, can you believe it? One versus two, I don't like those odds. But two versus two? We'd fight them and win, babe. Sorry if you were talking to God or something and I interrupted you, Jess. I just had to see you and talk to you again tonight.*

He put the picture back in his backpack and set it against the couch. After pressing the button on his gas mask to clean the filters, he rested his head on the carpet and stared at the ceiling, gravity pulling on his eyelids harder each second as air hissed out of his mask.

CHAPTER 9

Tiny red gremlins with hairy chests and protruding beer bellies tormented him throughout the night as he hung by chains over a boiling pot. They submerged him, and he somehow found odd comfort in his nightly drowning even though his suffocation felt somewhat more prolonged and severe than usual. Irritated by his serenity, the gremlins jabbed him forcefully with absurdly long pitchforks and scimitars. One of the little rascals might have been poking him with the pointed corner of a potato chip bag, but he couldn't entirely remember. When he woke up in the morning, the entire dream seemed absurd to the point of being laughable, although he didn't feel much like laughing.

He heard voices coming from the other side of the couch; Elena and John were already awake. Shortly after, he heard a faint voice offer a quiet response to whatever they said. With a small burst of measured relief, he realized that the voice belonged to Salb. He stretched for a moment, working out the kinks in his body from sleeping on the carpet, and he stood up and walked to the other side of the couch. He stood behind Elena, who was sitting on the coffee table in a similar manner to the prior night. John rapped on Dr. Flynn's bedroom door to wake him.

Salb would be mistaken as a Martian before a healthy man, but he nonetheless looked significantly better. His skin was pale, and his breathing was labored and difficult, but Northfield could see a more alert and lucid look in his eyes, suggesting that the fever-induced delirium might have passed. The storm might have been a nasty one, but the worst of it was over.

"How are you feeling?" Elena asked Salb.

He thought for a moment before replying. "Better. Still like a ragged bucket of trash, but better. I don't feel like I'm on another plane of existence or like I'm going to die anymore."

"Good. That's good," she said, not bothering to downplay her exuberant relief.

Dr. Flynn came out of his room and knelt next to Salb's head. He put a hand on his forehead and muttered, "Fever seems like it's declined. I'll grab a thermometer to check."

After Flynn received the tool, he promptly inserted it into Salb's ear. After a beep, he pulled out the thermometer and said, "It says 99.5 degrees Fahrenheit. An improvement over last night. His fever has definitely gone down."

"Does that mean the antibiotics are working?" John asked.

"It seems like it," Flynn said. "At the rate he's improved, I'd say that he won't be in pristine shape by tonight, but with enough rest throughout the day, he'll be capable of moving with you . . . Perfect timing for you all to get going." With a brighter tone, he added, "I'm going to make breakfast."

After Flynn left, Salb looked around and asked, "Where are we? Everything has passed in a haze . . . I know you and Elena are my escorts to the Coalition but not much else."

"Mark here is escorting you, too. We figured that with the Death Corps' lethality, the extra help would be appreciated," John said.

Northfield noticed how deliberately vague he was being. John didn't want to tell a man who just woke up from a half-comatose state that Northfield was sent to kill him. No need to scare the poor sap before he even got his bearings. "The guy who stuck a thermometer in your ear is Dr. Flynn. If you remember, when you told us you were feeling under the weather, we decided to bring you here. Good thing we did."

"Thank you," Salb said. "So what do I have? Or did the doctor not determine the cause yet?"

"Pneumonia, probably. Mask's Kiss," John said. "But Dr. Flynn's given you some antibiotics. If you keep taking them, the illness should clear out."

"Good. That's good to hear. I believe a couple of scientists in the lab were out with Mask's Kiss last week, so that diagnosis sounds right," Salb said, nodding only slightly either out of weakness or the desire not to make himself dizzy.

"Lie down a bit longer, Salb," John said. "We can talk more when breakfast is ready."

"Okay." Salb rested his head against the couch and shut his eyes.

A couple of minutes later, Dr. Flynn called from the kitchen, "Breakfast is ready."

"Let me help you," Elena said. She assisted Salb in getting to the kitchen. John and Northfield followed.

Four fried eggs rested on plates around the table. Elena pulled out a chair for Salb to sit before she took a seat herself. John sat beside her, but Northfield remained standing. Dr. Flynn, who was near the stove with a pan in one hand and a spatula in the other, asked, "Aren't you going to take a seat?"

He shook his head and said, "You've done all of the cooking and work, Doc. There's only four seats. You take the last one."

Dr. Flynn smiled slightly and said, "And here I thought politeness was dead in this godforsaken era. Thank you, but I'm going to go outside and check on the Death Corps' search progress. They've surely found the vehicle you ditched by now."

"Good thinking," John said. Northfield expected John eventually would have asked Dr. Flynn to do so anyway. The doctor was the only person who could walk outside without much risk, after all.

Dr. Flynn used the spatula to scoop the last egg off the pan and drop it onto a plate. He handed the plate and a fork to Northfield, who said, "Thanks, Doc."

After the door closed behind Dr. Flynn, Salb asked, "Has the plan changed since I've last heard?"

John went over the plan in detail, which Northfield suspected was to inform Salb of any changes while also refreshing his memory, given his state. "The Coalition is outfitting a semi-truck for smuggling. The floor of the trailer has been elevated to allow for a compartment underneath, where weapons and Coalition fighters will hide. The truck will drive into the city, deliver them, and drive back out with you in the compartment. The Network will be searching for you at the checkpoint. Soldiers will heavily scrutinize anyone who crosses. Unfortunately, the Coalition could only afford one quality black-market ID that'll hold up to such an intense examination, and it's for the driver. This way, you and the fighters won't even have to face the checkpoints or need IDs. We figure that this is the safest bet, and it kills two birds with one stone."

"Sounds logical." Salb attempted to suppress a cough but failed as he asked, "Are we still meeting tonight? And where?"

"The truck will be here tonight," John said. "Gramercy and 8th Street. Then you should be on your way to safety." He added assertively, "After giving us the location of the master key."

"Of course," Salb said. "A deal is a deal. My safety for the key."

Elena asked, "How did you manage to steal the key from Kayden Knox, anyway? That must have been quite a feat."

Salb, who hadn't yet touched his egg, inhaled with resolve and said, "The master key was kept within a safe in the lab. Knox is the only scientist entrusted with the code. With how complex the safe is, I couldn't hope to crack it. Fortunately, the key has to periodically leave the safe."

"And why is that?" Northfield asked.

"The master key has a critical role, aside from keeping unwanted actors from detonating Zeus's Mercy. The master key serves as what you might call version control. The Network is paranoid about bad actors tampering with Zeus's Mercy. The device is made up of complex software and hardware components, and even small modifications to either could have drastic consequences. Someone with malicious intent could change the code or the way a mechanism is wired. Someone could turn Zeus's Mercy into a bomb that would blow up the entire building upon activation, or someone could plant a virus that would gather diagnostics about Zeus's Mercy, or any number of other unforeseeable attacks on the Network."

He paused and put a hand over his chest while he gathered his breath.

Elena said, "So that's where the master key comes in?"

"Yes," Salb said. "Zeus's Mercy is surrounded by a blast-proof shell. Anything with a big enough punch to destroy the shell would surely destroy Zeus's Mercy along with it. Only the master key can open the device and any of its components. Thus, modifications to Zeus's Mercy can only be made with the master key. New lines of code that are added to the operating system, new hardware, and revisions to old components must first be checked and verified by a certain number of scientists, depending on the proposed change."

"Why require a key?" Elena asked. "Why not just use another security measure? A password, fingerprint scanner, or something else to get into the device. A key seems like an unnecessary step, doesn't it?"

Salb didn't answer for a couple of moments, instead using the time to build his energy. When he felt enough strength to continue, he said, "Knox's personal design choice. For how mathematically brilliant he is, his arrogance and paranoia still dwarf his intelligence. Knox doesn't trust anything or anyone except himself. Any security precaution can be surpassed, anybody can betray him, and he stands as the only entity incapable of compromising the security of the project. The master key was specifically designed to be difficult to replicate, even by the Network. By his logic, it stands that if the Network could replicate the key, a mole that had infiltrated the organization might be able to, as well.

"Knox carries the key on his person in the lab, and where he takes it afterward, I cannot say. I'd assume he has multiple locations he safe-keeps the key, where nobody else in the Network would know. Or, rather, his arrogance clouds his judgment. Whenever Knox left the lab, he'd lock the master key in a safe. But when he was in the lab, he'd keep the master key in his pocket. Two days ago, I learned that he planned to spend the day consulting with scientists at the North Network Facility, making the key inaccessible to me, which is why I had to push things forward and try to steal it yesterday."

"Why would he keep the key in his pocket?" Elena asked. "Would he really think the key would be safer there and in a safe or something in the lab until it needed to be used?"

"Not if you're Knox," Salb replied. "But as I said, Knox is as arrogant as he is paranoid. He didn't think somebody could pickpocket or otherwise trick him without his knowledge. No, he's far too intelligent and perceptually aware for anybody to outsmart him. In his mind, the odds were significantly lower than someone finding a way to break into a safe. Also, I think he enjoyed the idea of having the key to change the world in his pocket and within his grasp." Salb took a moment to raggedly inhale before he said, "I never liked the man. Narcissism and sadism rolled up into one person." A longer pause. He breathed in and out. In and out. "Despite me being his second in command, we never got along. But the Network knew we were the most capable scientists on their roster, so they put us on the same projects."

"Then you become a master of pickpocketing?" Northfield asked, picking at his egg with his fork.

Salb smirked for a moment before a bout of coughing wiped his expression clean. After spitting mucus into a napkin, he said weakly, "After we finished Zeus's Mercy and I learned how the Network only intended to use the device as glorified insurance, I formulated a plan to steal the key. I ramped up my aggression toward Knox, jabbing his ego whenever I could. Naturally, our clashes grew more and more severe. When the time came, I dredged up something to fight about and started a shoving match with him. In the commotion, I snatched the key from his lab coat."

Northfield took another bite of egg, the gears spinning in his mind. "He must've really hated you, right? Enough to put a hit out on you."

"I wouldn't put it past him," Salb said. "But why do you ask?"

"An assassination contract was put out for you," Northfield said. He started scratching the back of his head. "I, ah, was sent to kill you."

Salb tensed. Elena reached her hand out and said, "It's okay, Salb. It's a long story, but he's with us now. He risked his life to save yours. He's still risking his life to save yours."

John said nothing, his eyes moving between Salb and Northfield with a coolness akin to a drifting iceberg.

Salb's muscles relaxed slightly, although he continued to stare at Northfield. "If you take contracts, you're a Network merc, I suppose?"

"Was," he said. "Though I forgot to hand in my two-week notice. I'm just hoping it doesn't screw up my 401(k) plan. That would really kill me."

"I know you're being sarcastic . . . but you don't seem old enough to even care about what a 401(k) plan was back then," John said.

Northfield shrugged and said, "Yeah, I'm talking out of my rear."

Salb, ignoring them, was deep in thought. He said, "If there was an assassination contract put out on me, it had to be Knox. Makes sense."

"Did you ever tell him about your sleep patterns?" Northfield asked. "In the envelope I got for your hit, your sleep patterns were mentioned."

Salb took a moment to shuffle through his memories before answering. "A long time ago, before our relationship soured to the point where we became bitter enemies, we used to talk more. I believe we might have had a casual conversation or two about sleep. He must have filed details about my sleep away in his brain as important in case he ever needed them for something like this. He has a frighteningly good memory. Even if he didn't, he's conniving enough for me to believe he would write such information down about his coworkers just in case he ever needed to plan for their death."

"You really think he'd commit to the act, though?" Elena asked. "You're the most useful scientist to the Network aside from him. Would he really screw up the Network's agenda?"

"I don't know why anybody else would want me dead," Salb said. "Provided he can avoid getting caught, I know he's a large enough prick to eliminate me for the sake of his ego, the Network's agenda be damned. And he would get away with it."

"Hit contracts are anonymous," Northfield said, nodding. "So there'd be no trace linking back to Knox. Rumors might circulate, but no actual evidence to verify any claims."

"Precisely. And when I began coordinating with the Coalition, we arranged for me to move to Heaven's Rebirth. Many employees of the Inner Network lived in the same building as I used to, and I was wary about planning with the Coalition while near so many hostile ears. The move didn't draw much attention. It isn't uncommon for Network employees to move into cheaper housing due to rampant gambling and drug addictions. No circle of society is immune to those ills nowadays, it appears."

Salb took a couple of moments to catch his breath, and Elena filled in for him. "If Knox became fed up with you to the point of murder, your move would make a hit viable. Hits don't occur much at the buildings of the Inner Network due to how much security they have, but at Heaven's Rebirth . . ." Salb nodded at her, and she muttered, "If this guy is really killing you just for the sake of his ego, man, he must really be compensating for something."

"Believe me, he isn't compensating for anything," Salb said with harsh, subsequent coughs that seemed to accentuate his point. He again spat into his napkin before bitterly stating, "He's just a prick."

"Well, if we run into him at the South Network Facility, I'll give him a nice welcome for you," Elena said. The sentence confused Northfield at first before a realization dawned on him.

"Zeus's Mercy is at the South Network Facility, isn't it? That's where you worked?" Northfield asked Salb.

"Yes. The lab is on the top floor of Little Empire. Zeus's Mercy is housed inside glass walls."

"Shit," Northfield said. He turned to John and Elena and asked, "So that's the Coalition's target? That giant fortress?"

Elena and John nodded. She said, "The facility is formidable. The Network thinks it's impenetrable, but that works in our favor, too. The Network won't destroy Zeus's Mercy, at least not yet. Why would you scrap a multiyear project just because a scientist stole the master key? They think they can afford to hunt Salb and the key for a little while."

"Surprise is on our side, too," John added. "With a well-timed and coordinated attack, we're hoping we can break through the Network's defenses and activate Zeus's Mercy, though we're still on a limited timeframe. Eventually, the Network will find a way to crack Zeus's Mercy and make the key useless. If they can't do that, they'll destroy Zeus's Mercy. Either way, we'll lose our chance."

"Coast looks clear. For now," Dr. Flynn said upon reentering the room. John nodded in acknowledgment.

"Damn it all to hell," Salb muttered, rubbing his temples with his fingers. "There's something you need to know."

"What?" John asked.

"There's another project in the South Network Facility that I recently caught wind of. Some sort of experimental exoskeleton armor for their Death Corps troops. Something that turns a man into a walking tank and is able to withstand a volley of gunfire without bleeding, including TAP rounds. I don't have any further details, but the fact that I even heard about the project probably means that they're close to finishing. Whether close means months, weeks, or days from completion or an already-working prototype, I have no idea."

"Christ," John exclaimed, aghast. Elena and Northfield shared similar reactions.

Because the armor worn by Death Corps soldiers was penetrable by TAP rounds, opposing forces like the Yellowbacks or Coalition stood a fighting chance, provided they could get access to TAP rounds. This project was undoubtedly a result of the Network's desire to achieve complete physical dominance. Northfield didn't want to imagine a future where the streets of Cumulus and the outer country were patrolled by masses of Death Corps soldiers in hulking suits of exo armor, unable to be challenged or stood up to by anyone for their abuses of power.

"If the project is indeed finished, only a few prototype armors likely exist, although there's a chance they could have more. But they still might decide to use them, if able," Salb said, breaking the frightened pause in the air.

"I wish you would have told us this sooner," John said, pulling out his radio.

"I didn't have a chance to," Salb said. "Network personnel aren't allowed to communicate with unauthorized personnel about their respective projects. The punishment for doing so is death, which as you can imagine makes one reluctant to share information with un-authorized colleagues. Even a potential infiltrator would be hesitant about spreading information throughout the ranks of the Network. I can't imagine a much quicker way to alert the Network of a bad ac-tor and direct them to the actor's location. The leak would have to come from someone assigned to the leaked project, either a mem-ber of the research team or a Death Corps guard tasked with security. Because of this, information about other projects doesn't often spread, and the Network only informs us about projects when they are near completion."

John asked, "If the Network informed you about the project, why don't you know if the project is complete or not?"

With slight defensiveness, Salb said, "I said they inform us about projects when they are near completion. Near can be anywhere from a few months left of development to already having been completed. It depends on the project. Often, they inform us earlier if they need additional scientists to work between projects. I found out about the exoskeleton armor shortly before stealing the key, and by the time you arrived at my place, well, you saw how I was."

"I know," John replied. "I'm not blaming you." He said into the radio, "Shepherd, this is Eagle Five. Over."

"Eagle Five, this is Shepherd. Over," a male voice crackled through the radio.

John relayed the information given to him by Salb.

Shepherd replied, "Eagle Five, we appreciate your update. We'll recalibrate our plans to take these potential exo-armored soldiers into account. But right now, we've just learned of a bigger problem on our hands. Over."

"A bigger problem? What bigger problem? Over," John asked through gritted teeth.

"Rolling Moses's engine broke down," the man said. Northfield assumed "Rolling Moses" was a codename for the truck smuggling weapons and Coalition soldiers into the city. "We're going to replace the engine, but Rolling Moses won't arrive in the city until morning. Over."

"Shit," he said. "We don't have any Coalition soldiers in the city yet, just sympathizers, right? Over."

"Correct," the man said. "But none of the sympathizers are willing to take you in. We'll keep asking, but you know how they are: offer resources from a distance but aren't willing to walk near crosshairs. Over."

"Cowards," he muttered. "So what are we supposed to do? Over."

"Just give it time. Hopefully someone changes their mind. Otherwise, we'll have to come up with something else. Out."

"Out," he muttered in return and put the radio back on his belt.

Using Elena and John's fake IDs to rent a room was out of the question. They had used them to rent the rooms adjacent to Salb; the Network, in its investigation of Salb, would have already run the names of Salb's neighbors, only to realize the names on the fake IDs used to rent the living spaces didn't exist. The fake names would subsequently be tagged, meaning John and Elena couldn't rent another room without alerting the Network.

Northfield couldn't rent a room, either. Although his hit contract didn't expire until tomorrow, after which he'd be marked for death, the Network likely regarded him as a person of interest due to his contract's suspicious alignment with the Death Corps' hunt for Salb. If the Death Corps sought him out for questioning at whatever room he rented, they would discover Salb, Elena, and John. Either way, they would eventually figure out that Northfield helped Salb, if they didn't know already.

"Someone will volunteer soon," Elena said. "People are already risking their lives for the cause. They won't get cold feet now."

"You overestimate people, Elena," John said, sighing.

"Hopefully you'll be pleasantly surprised, then," she retorted. "The Coalition isn't going to leave us hanging out to dry. They'll get someone to take us in."

"How would the Coalition do that, exactly?" he replied. "Threaten to rat them out to the Network? After all the money the sympathizers donated, I'm sure that conversation would go over well. Maybe one of them would prefer giving us up over being extorted."

"Well, no," she said. "I was thinking along the lines of talking to them. Persuading them."

"I don't know," Salb said nervously, wheezing after a deep cough. "Maybe they're onto something."

"What do you mean?" he asked. "Who's onto something?"

"The people not taking us in," Salb said. He started to crack his knuckles before having to cough into his forearm.

"And how do you figure that?" he said tensely.

"The Network is searching the city high and low for us right now," Salb said. "What if we're spotted? I highly doubt the sympathizers know how to use weapons effectively, if they even have any in the first place." He let out a small flurry of coughs before continuing. "Which means only you, Elena, and Mark will be armed and capable of fighting. I don't like those odds. I don't like them one bit."

Dr. Flynn, who had been silent during the conversation, said, "You can't stay here. The Death Corps will focus their resources on chasing whatever leads they have. But they won't stop there. They'll also conduct door-to-door searches. Searching every room in all directions from the vehicle you dumped will take a while, but they will eventually get here."

"Like the odds or not, we don't have any other choice," John said. "Dr. Flynn's right, and even if he wasn't, he's done too much for us for me to disrespect his wishes."

"The way you're talking, Salb, makes it sound like you have another option," Elena said.

"Yes. There is another choice." Salb hesitated for a moment before saying, "I have a brother who lives in the city."

"A brother?" John echoed.

"Yeah," he said. He hesitated again before adding, "His name is Geralt."

"Wait a minute . . ." Northfield said, his eyes widening. "You can't mean Geralt—"

"Geralt Salb," Salb interrupted, sighing. "The leader of the Yellowbacks. The one they call King."

"Christ," Northfield muttered.

"Why didn't you tell us this before?" John asked. "Seems like a pretty big damned detail to leave out. How didn't the Coalition know about this?"

Salb sighed, and then he said, "My brother and I haven't talked for years. Many years. The last time was long before the bombs, even. You can hardly call us brothers anymore. Up until now, I've refused to talk to him, refused to ask him for help. Our relation is my best-kept secret. Not even the Network knows. Otherwise, I wouldn't have been allowed within a mile of a project like Zeus's Mercy. As far as the Coalition is concerned, I didn't think it was relevant information to share. I suppose my habit of keeping our relationship a secret dies hard."

"And now?" John asked.

"Now it's become relevant."

"What, exactly, are you suggesting?" Northfield asked. He couldn't suppress the edge in his voice; the Yellowbacks weren't a group he ever imagined allying with.

His reaction didn't stem from hate or condemnation. It wasn't his job to sit in a moral highchair and decry every last Yellowback as a sack of shit. Instead, the ugly sensation in his chest came from fear.

If he allied with the Yellowbacks, he worried about participating in their bad deeds he'd witnessed. His concern grew about the direction this mission was taking. *Deeper and deeper we go, it seems.*

"Geralt Salb lives in Cumulus," Salb said. "With a group of those closest to him in command, plus his guards. The Network and the Yellowbacks have a cease-fire within the confines of the city."

Northfield nodded and said, "You know, that doesn't surprise me. I've heard rumors."

Salb again massaged his forehead and temples to assuage an oncoming headache. He stifled a cough. "The Yellowbacks are more powerful than the Network lets on. If the Yellowbacks fought the Network in Cumulus, it would be a full-out war, and the order the Network proclaims to preserve in the city would disintegrate. That is why the Network offers the Yellowbacks haven in the city, provided they don't conduct their business within the city's confines or wear their uniforms. Specifically, they are prohibited from wearing their air tanks or anything yellow. The presence of the Yellowbacks inside Cumulus and their agreement are to be kept secret. Outside of the city, however, it's open season for both groups."

Northfield's eyes widened before narrowing, and he added, "So Cumulus serves as a sort of central hub for the Yellowbacks, a place safe from the Network, where they plan their extortions, kidnappings, and thefts outside of the city."

"Precisely," Salb said with a nod. He cringed immediately after the movement, which probably exacerbated his headache.

"So if I'm getting this right," John said, "you're suggesting that we stay with your brother until Rolling Moses arrives in the morning."

"With the cease-fire, there's a chance the Network won't attack us, even if Death Corps soldiers see us enter my brother's apartment. The Network doesn't want to start a war. The soldiers may wait for us to leave or try to pressure the Yellowbacks into giving us up, but it's better than the alternative."

John nodded and said, "If the Network finds us, and we have no other option, we could maybe hold out in your brother's apartment until Coalition reinforcements arrive from Rolling Moses."

"And even if the Network attacks the Yellowbacks to get to us, they have firepower. Our odds of survival aren't great, but they're better than staying with a Coalition sympathizer," Salb added.

Northfield decided to speak his mind. "Hang on. This is the Yellowbacks we're talking about. I've spent the past few years of my life protecting people from them, and let me tell you, getting into bed with them isn't something to think about lightly."

"I realize that," Salb said. "Why do you think I haven't talked to my brother in years? Morally, they're bankrupt. Abhorrent, even. As terrible of a man as my brother is, I'm still family. And that means something to Geralt. That's the one virtue he still holds. He'll take us in. Trust me," Salb said.

"I'm not doubting you," Northfield said. "But whether the Yellowbacks will take us in isn't my biggest concern. And my point isn't that they are morally bankrupt. But knowing what I know about how they operate, this isn't gonna be free. Your brother would be doing us a favor, and the Yellowbacks don't do favors out of charity. I'm worried about what we'll have to do in return."

Salb shook his head and said, "We would merely be staying at his apartment. Nobody is asking you to rob a truck or kidnap a child."

Salb was about to say something more, but he was overcome by a series of coughs, during which Elena said, "It's a smart play, Mark. This sounds like the best move. You have a point about the Yellowbacks. Maybe they'll expect us to return the favor in the future. But we have something to bargain with: our mission. Clearing the city of the gas is something that everybody wants. Except the Network, obviously. Our mission will be advantageous to the Yellowbacks."

"I think this is a problem for another day," John added. "If we survive and complete our mission, that's when I'll worry about whatever favors we might have to do for the Yellowbacks. We don't have much to offer them now. Any repayment would probably be sometime in the future."

After Salb recovered, he said, "As I was about to say, I don't think my brother will ask us for repayment. Like I said, family's everything to him. Because it's me, he'll help without thinking about gains for him or the Yellowbacks. It's in his nature."

Northfield shook his head and said, "I'm just getting a bad feeling about this."

"Your opinion doesn't matter," Salb said. "This is the best chance for my survival. So this is what we're doing."

John's eyes narrowed. "You act like you're the one in charge here."

Salb stared him down. "I am. I'm the one with the information you need, and in order to receive it, you must deliver me out of the city. You will never discover the location of the key unless I'm safe, and I refuse to stay with the sympathizers until Rolling Moses arrives. You can try to force me to stay with them, but then you'll be fighting me as well as the Network and get us all killed. Which is an unnecessary path, considering that you seem to agree with me, John." He turned to Northfield and said after recovering from a wheeze, "You're the one not on board. Unless you're going to beat me for the information to avoid staying with the Yellowbacks, and I can't imagine you'll break me until the Network catches up with us, this looks like your only option."

Exasperated, he said, "I'm not going to beat you, Salb. What the hell kind of thing is that to say?"

After a brief silence that solidified the tension in the room, Salb said softly, "I'm not just another selfish man worthy of contempt in this city. The reality is, I'm risking my life to help the Coalition detonate Zeus's Mercy. Without me, none of this would be possible. I've done my part. I've done enough. Now I'm going to survive. I've earned that at least, damn it. It's only fair."

"It looks like this is our plan, then," John said. "Mark, is this going to be a problem for you?"

He sighed. What the hell could he do about it? "No. Don't get me wrong, the plan's not exactly peachy-keen to me, but I'll go along."

"Good," John said.

Salb's shoulders sagged in tandem with his eyelids; guilt pressed into Northfield's chest like a heated needle after he realized how long and how much they had made Salb talk, especially when considering his condition the previous night. Of course, given the danger they all found themselves in, information needed to be relayed and plans needed to be discussed, but Northfield wondered how much of the conversation could've waited or been at least spaced out. He couldn't imagine how much energy or willpower Salb had exerted to power through his illness and talk. He felt a measure of respect for the man, even though they disagreed.

Elena had the same line of thought as Northfield. She said, "Get rest, Salb. You need it."

Dr. Flynn added, "I second that. Rest. I'll bring you your antibiotics when it's time."

Salb slowly stood up and said, "Thank you, Dr. Flynn."

"Don't worry, Mark," Elena said after Salb left. "We're not going to do the Yellowbacks' bidding. If anyone tries to force us, I'll be the first one by your side with a gun."

"Thanks for the thought. But these things have a way of screwing themselves," he said.

John squinted as he focused on countless moving parts. His eyes darted to Dr. Flynn, and he asked, "Are you sure that guard downstairs is reliable?"

"I'd bet my life on it," Flynn said. "I saved his brother's and mother's lives when they needed help. At a time when he couldn't hope to pay me, no less. In addition, I've provided his mother with her medication without charge, which I knew they also couldn't afford. He's indebted to me, and he's told me that he would do anything to repay that debt. He's a good man. He won't turn me in for whatever award the Network offers, no matter how big."

"Even if this man doesn't have malicious intent, are you sure the Death Corps won't find you?"

"I don't think so. All he has to do is deny that we entered the building if there are any reports of you four entering. I think he can handle that. At night, the people in this neighborhood who aren't high or drunk are asleep. It's very unlikely that there was more than one sighting of you entering the building, if there was one at all. It's his word against that of whoever spotted him."

"The Death Corps would err on the side of caution, though, and suspect that the guard is lying. What stops them from torturing him to get the information they need?"

"What you must remember is that even in this rich of a neighborhood, lots of people are starving for money, mostly to feed their addictions to drugs and alcohol. Desperate people in every direction from that vehicle you left are bound to send in false reports, hoping for a chance at the reward money. With so many false reports, the unreliability of torture comes into play."

"What are you getting at?" John asked.

Dr. Flynn explained, "It's one thing to torture someone you know has information that can be verified. It's another thing entirely to torture someone who might be telling the truth. If the Death Corps torture every guard who denies a report of you entering their building, every single one of them will eventually point a finger at someone they know. In turn, all those people will point more fingers, creating even more false leads and dead ends. In the end, a brute-force door-to-door search after the Death Corps exhaust all expedient leads would be faster, and they can punish any liars appropriately if they find Salb. But by the time that happens, you'll be gone, and the Death Corps won't even know you were here."

John nodded and asked, "Do you have a plan to go into hiding, just in case this doesn't work out?"

"No, I'm staying right here."

Shaking his head firmly, John said, "No. No, no. Dr. Flynn, if things go ass-sideways, it's not just a risk to you. It's a risk to the Coalition, the sympathizers . . ."

Dr. Flynn, with an equal amount of firmness that surprised Northfield, said, "If I run and hide, the Death Corps will realize for certain that I'm an accomplice of yours, and I will not be able to continue my practice. Regardless of if Zeus's Mercy goes off or not, I have patients that rely on me, and I will not abandon them. Their ill health and deaths from my departure will not be a burden I carry."

"This puts the mission at risk, Flynn."

"Yes, but if I leave, patients of mine will die for certain," Flynn retorted. "I explained to you why my involvement won't be discovered, and I bet my life on it."

John sighed but said nothing more; he knew that further arguing wouldn't go anywhere.

Dr. Flynn, as consolation, said, "I have a red SUV you can use. The windows are tinted, which will hopefully keep you from being spotted by the Network. Just be sure to take off the plates and dispose of them before you dump the car. Obviously, I don't want the Network tracing the vehicle back to me."

"Thanks, Dr. Flynn. For everything," Elena answered for all of them.

Dr. Flynn opened his mouth to say something but shut it. Instead, he said, "I'll go get the keys."

He left the kitchen and went to his bedroom. While he did so, Elena declared, "Salb needs rest. It will take a while for the Death Corps' door-to-door search to reach here. I'd bet sometime at night. I say we still leave at sunset."

John nodded, looking down while thinking out loud. "If we leave later, fewer cars will be on the road, meaning less traffic, meaning a lower chance of Death Corps soldiers stopping us for whatever reason they can gin up. If we leave just before dusk, the sun will be setting. We'll be able to take even more advantage of the car's tinted windows than if we leave during the day. I agree."

"Okay then," Elena said. "Sunset it is."

Northfield looked down, exhaling as he thought, *Here we go again, Jess. How could this possibly go wrong?*

CHAPTER 10

They departed in the red SUV as the setting sun reddened the world. The blood-red color mixed with the glowing orange-yellow of the gas. When Northfield looked around, he half-believed they were driving through the hottest depths of an inferno.

The vehicles they passed were a mix of Network-owned and civilian-owned. Most of the Network's consisted of jet-black jeeps and Humvees, while the civilians' were beat-up trucks, SUVs, and sedans with a couple of flashier cars thrown into the mix. Elena drove at a measured pace, matching the speed of a dented blue truck in front of her. John sat behind her while Salb sat in the right-back seat; John wanted to discuss with Salb the master key and his transportation out of the city. Consequently, Northfield sat in the passenger seat.

"You'll be taken twelve miles away from the city, where you'll be set up in a Coalition safehouse for a few months," John said to the scientist. "Once things cool down and we're able to get more funds, we'll issue you a new identity . . ."

John's explanation and Salb's coughing faded into the background as Northfield stared, mystified by the faux fire show around him. Each time a Death Corps vehicle passed in the opposite lane, his chest tightened, and he wondered whether machine-gun fire would tear into the vehicle. Perhaps the fear was slightly irrational, as the Death Corps wouldn't just rip apart the SUV without first stopping it and verifying that their targets were inside. Even if the Network knew to be on the lookout for three men and one woman, the gas masks that concealed everyone's faces meant that a lot of cars driving in the city would be carrying people who matched such a description. Despite his rationalization, the paranoia didn't leave. Fortunately, machine-gun fire didn't come.

When he inhaled, the air somehow felt thicker. He wondered whether the observation was an invention of his imagination or if the state of stress he constantly found himself in was taking a toll on his body.

Elena took note of his heavy breathing and asked, "You alright?"

"Yeah, I'm alright," he muttered. "Just tired."

Her head was slightly turned toward him; he could feel her eyes studying him from behind her mask. Whatever she observed, she didn't say, and she returned her attention to the road.

The turmoil in his head moved through his body like a storm, spreading to his stomach and creating nausea. *Not too long ago, I fought Yellowbacks. Watched their bullets shred the grass around me. Now I'm driving to their leader. If somebody told me last week that this would happen, I would have laughed them out of the room.*

Don't let me let her down, God. Don't let me let her down. I'll say it as many times as I have to.

Thoughts of her, thoughts of the Death Corps, and thoughts of the Yellowbacks pressed around him like collapsing walls. He attempted to zone out and forget his worries by staring out the window, but to no avail.

To distract himself, he turned to look at Salb and asked, "So how does Zeus's Mercy work, exactly? I assume it's not like a confetti cannon."

Salb coughed a couple of times to clear his throat before saying, "To understand the device, you must understand the gas. The gas isn't merely a chemical compound—it's composed of robots on the scale of microns, designed to specifically destroy human lung tissue, which is why plants and other animals are immune. Once a high enough concentration of gas enters a pair of human lungs, about the amount of a full inhale, they enter an attack mode."

"Robots?" he exclaimed. "You're kidding."

Salb suppressed a cough that would have unleashed a fit of hacking, and he said, "That's how the gas stays in place. Within minutes of being released, the bots fix to a geographic location. After any disturbance, like the wind, a human hand, or a truck, the bots eventually return to their pinpointed location. The attraction of the bots to their pinpointed locations works like a tether. The attraction is weak over short distances, but this attraction grows as the distance between the bots and their fixed locations increases. The weak attraction over small distances allows for human inhalation and subsequent death by lung damage, as well as movement over short distances to fill any gaps of low-density gas. Picture how sand fills a hole on the beach. However, the strong attraction over long distances prevents wind from blowing gas long distances. The principle behind the design is that you could bomb a single city without harming another city a dozen miles away . . ."

Unable to hold back the cough any longer, Salb suffered through a fit of hacking. Starting to regret having asked a question that Salb felt compelled to explain at length, Northfield asked, "You okay? Take a break."

"I'll be fine," Salb said. He moved to wipe his face before he remembered his gas mask. "This information is important. You should probably hear it. And honestly, I enjoy talking my head off about it." After taking a few more breaths, he continued. "The bots are the most concentrated near buildings. The filters drive the bots out of a building, only for the bots to try to reach their original geographic position inside the building in a constant cycle. This is why opening windows or doors can often result in gas, or the bots, entering the building in high densities. Though a design for the filtration systems to destroy the bots instead of just expelling them outside is conceivable, the Network currently designs and distributes all the filters in Cumulus. Given the Network's demonstrated desire to keep the bots intact and the people inundated in the gas, such a design would be counterproductive.

"The bots, powered by solar, are incredibly efficient, absorbing the minimum amount of sunlight required for their functions while allowing remaining sunlight to pass through. The majority reaches the ground, enough to enable the survival of most plant life requiring energy for photosynthesis. The bots use a portion of the absorbed power to emit orange and yellow light, which serves as a fear tactic for the human population inundated in the gas. As I'm sure you've witnessed every day for the past ten years, the landscape is hellish and, well, fear-inducing."

As Salb shook from coughs, Northfield said, "Don't kill yourself, man. Just take a second."

Between staggered breaths, he continued speaking despite Northfield's warning. "The designer was a genius, I'll admit. The bots were designed to conquer land while keeping it intact. You unleash the bot-composed gas in an area, wait for the people to die, and release a neutralizing agent to eradicate it. The plants, animals, and infrastructure remain intact, although, as how these things go, nobody bothered creating the neutralizing agent before deploying the gas."

Northfield hated watching the guy struggle through his words.

"Take a break and breathe for a couple of minutes, Salb. You sound horrible."

"I will," he replied, gratefully sucking air in through his gas mask. After regaining his energy and composing himself, he proceeded. "The neutralizing agent, Code Blue, is composed of microbots as well, which are designed to target and destroy the bots that make up the gas. Zeus's Mercy is designed to use Little Empire as a launching mechanism for Code Blue. In this way, the Network improved upon the design from the scientists who originally conceived the device, increasing the radius of Code Blue's effectiveness.

"The payload travels through the antenna-like structure that juts up from the top of the building, and the structure serves a similar function to the barrel of a gun: it makes sure the payload shoots in a straight trajectory and gains as much altitude as possible. Zeus's Mercy launches a payload of Code Blue into the air, which detonates and disperses the neutralizing microbots horizontally. While they descend, they destroy the gas. As I already stated, because the gas-composing bots are geographically fixed, the city will remain clear of the gas."

Northfield said, "Ideally, you could put multiple of these devices around the country and eradicate the gas entirely."

"Ideally. Of course, the Network has other plans," Salb said. After a few moments of silence, he added, more softly, "Ninety-nine percent. That is the calculated odds of Zeus's Mercy successfully launching. The difficulty of working on Zeus's Mercy is that, for obvious reasons, it couldn't be fully tested by launching Code Blue. We had to settle on ensuring that each component works, running simulations, and checking, double-checking, and triple-checking our math, the device, everything. After we completed the device one month ago, the calculated odds of success were ninety-seven percent. The last month has been spent searching for errors, adding an additional two percent of confidence."

"Sounds like decent odds. I guess the real gamble for us is making it to the device in the first place."

"You would be correct with that sentiment."

He gave Salb a few more minutes of rest before asking any further questions; he didn't want to continue torturing the poor guy. He reflected on the fact that Elena and John didn't react much to what Salb had said. From what he recalled, Elena stated that she and John hadn't heard the specifics of how the gas worked. Maybe the news didn't surprise them, or maybe they were just focused on the mission ahead. *Or maybe they figure that I'm bombarding the sick man with more than enough questions.* He felt a twinge of guilt at the thought, which was made worse by the fact that he had further questions that needed answers. Given his history with the Yellowbacks, he had to be prepared for where they were going. When Salb seemed refreshed enough to continue speaking, he asked, "What's your brother like? What should we be prepared for?"

"It's hard to say," he said. "I've always had trouble reading my brother, and after having not seen him for years, I can imagine that problem will be exacerbated. What I can say is that loyalty and truthfulness are his biggest values. Those who are loyal to him and keep their word know that they'll be treated well. If they break their word or are disloyal, well, I'm sure you've heard some of the stories."

"Yeah, about that," Northfield said. "As a Network merc, I've scrapped with quite a few Yellowbacks. That's not gonna be a problem, is it?"

"Not if you don't tell Geralt," he said. "Again, he's a hard man to read, and that's coming from his brother. I could see him understanding the nature of your job. On the other hand, I could see him wanting to cut your throat. He's an angry man. But if Geralt found out you used

168

to be a merc, I'm sure I could protect you. But why risk a problem by bringing it up?"

"Oh, don't worry," he replied. "Telling the Yellowbacks that I'm an ex-merc is the second-to-last item on my to-do list. The last being just shooting myself and expediting the whole process."

"Two more things," Salb said. "First, we all know the sins the Yellowbacks have committed, but don't moral grandstand. I give Geralt enough of that myself. We don't want to piss him off. A mad Geralt is not a fun Geralt."

"I'll bet," he muttered. He tried to form a mental image of Geralt Salb.

"Second, don't insult the spiderweb patches that the Yellowbacks wear. They're a symbol that the Yellowbacks in the city take deathly se-riously, and they don't take kindly to their symbol being trampled on."

"I think we were going to try our best to avoid insulting them either way, but good to know," Northfield said. "What's the significance of the symbol?"

"As I said before, the Yellowbacks, in accordance with the agree-ment to keep their presence in the city a secret, are not allowed to wear anything that explicitly identifies them as Yellowbacks. But that hasn't stopped them from developing a unifying symbol that represents their defiance of the Network: a spiderweb. In my brother's words, they are a spider to the Network because they're treated with disgust, abhor-rence, and scorn. But the Yellowbacks believe that when they come out of hiding, and when they show their fangs, they'll instill unbridled fear in the Network."

Northfield nodded and said, "They do like their symbols, alright. We won't bring it up."

Although the spiderweb symbol didn't explicitly defy the Yellowbacks' agreement of secrecy with the Network, because it wasn't yellow or an air tank, the symbol still went against the agreement in spirit. Despite this, Northfield could see why the Network would tolerate the spiderweb. Rumors probably circulated about the Yellowbacks being in the city because of the symbol. Some of those rumors might have even been confirmed by a few prideful Yellowbacks. But most would honor the agreement for Geralt Salb and his leadership and keep quiet, meaning none of the rumors would solidify into anything concrete, nothing that would really convince the public that the Yellowbacks had any significant presence in the city or convince the public that the Network didn't hold all the city's power. In fact, the symbol would work in the Network's favor as well; many citizens who had heard the rumors and believed them would see the spiderweb symbol in contrast to the normal Yellowback yellow as a sign of the Yellowbacks' submission to the Network, leading to possibly an even greater perception of the Network's power. Plus, the symbol allowed the Network to keep better tabs on the Yellowbacks, which the Yellowbacks must have been aware of. For how much the Yellowbacks valued their group solidarity and defiance of the Network, though, the potential setbacks would be worth it to them.

"What about the other Yellowbacks at his apartment?" John asked. "Can we trust them not to rat us out?"

"Any Yellowback that is a personal guard for Geralt Salb can be trusted. Only Geralt's best and most loyal people are even allowed on his property."

"You sure about that?" Elena asked.

Salb shrugged. "I suppose we'll find out."

"Tonight just keeps finding a way to get more exciting," Northfield muttered.

"Are the Death Corps a concern?" John asked.

"They are not allowed within a certain range of Geralt Salb's property without establishing reason, as per the agreement. Nor are they allowed to gatekeep the boundary, which would run counter to their desire to keep the Yellowbacks' presence in the city discreet, anyway. If we make it to his apartment, we should be safe."

"I need your directions from this point, Nathaniel," Elena said, her eyes focused on the T-intersection in front of her.

Salb instructed her, and they drove for five more minutes before parallel parking on the side of the street. He examined the building they had parked in front of and said, "From what I remember, this is the place."

The building was five stories tall and composed of red brick with long rectangular windows that formed neat rows and columns. A white porch extended from the second floor, and white roman columns descended from the porch to the ground for support. An oak door provided access to the porch. Underneath the porch, a concrete staircase led up to the front door from the sidewalk. Trees with golden leaves lined both sides of the staircase.

At the top of the staircase, two guards, one man and one woman, stood armed with pump-action shotguns. Northfield found the absence of their signature uniforms and air tanks incredibly off-putting. Never had he seen a Yellowback without them. He was sure they had a stash of air tanks somewhere in the city, ready for an emergency.

Upon seeing the red SUV park in front of the building, the male guard approached it. Once he reached the passenger window, Northfield could see a small spiderweb patch on his shoulder. The other guard remained stationed by the door. Elena rolled down Northfield's window, and the guard peered into the vehicle.

"This is private property," he said. His voice was gruff, and the implicit threat of violence dripped off the edge of each word.

Salb rolled down his window and said, "My name's Nathaniel Salb. I'm here to see my brother, Geralt."

"Brother?" the guard asked. "King doesn't have a fucking—"

"Ask him," Salb said, cutting him off. "He'll want you to treat me with respect. I guarantee it."

The guard stood still for a moment. Just slightly, his grip on his shotgun slackened. He said, "I'm going to go check this out and confirm. I'll be back. Don't get out."

The guard walked back up the staircase and spoke into an intercom next to the door. From this distance, Northfield couldn't parse any of the guard's words.

The guard returned and said, "He'll see you. You and your friends exit the car and walk in front of me. Any sudden movements, and I'll shoot. Not that I'm discouraging you. I've been bored all day."

From his tone, Northfield imagined that the guard had uttered the last sentence with a toothy grin behind his mask. Quiet enough so the guard couldn't hear, he muttered, "Great. Another tough guy."

They exited the car and walked in a single-file line up the staircase with Salb leading. The guard followed, his shotgun leveled at John's back, his finger hovering over the trigger. The other guard opened the door for them, and they quickly entered the building. When the door shut behind them, the building's filter made a loud whirring noise as it worked to purify the air. Turning his head, Northfield could see the guard still training his shotgun on John.

They found themselves inside a hallway that split into an ascending staircase on the left and a corridor on the right.

"Keep walking," the guard commanded, nudging them toward the corridor. They walked through the corridor and arrived at a spacious kitchen and dining area with eight chairs arranged around a circular oak table. On the other side of the room, a guard hunched over an open refrigerator and searched around for a snack or drink. Two windows on either side of the refrigerator gave a view of the building next door.

"Sit there and wait," the guard ordered, nodding toward the oak table. The four of them obeyed. They took off their gas masks, and Salb liberally coughed into his wrist to unclog his system as much as possible. Sheepishly, he wiped his wrist on his thigh.

"Interesting that they're letting us keep our weapons," Elena said, glancing at the assault rifle hanging from her shoulder.

"My brother holds the opinion that a man without a gun is a man without a . . . well . . . you know," Salb said. Elena cocked an eye at him, prompting him to say, "His words, not mine. He believes that a brave man should allow another man into his home armed, and if the guest causes problems, they should fight on equal terms. He thinks very highly of honor."

"How many Yellowbacks do you think are in the building?" Northfield asked.

"I'd wager ten or so, knowing my brother," Salb said, rubbing his chin. "We've seen three so far. I'd bet there's a few behind the apartment and a few upstairs."

"Ten versus four," he muttered. "If those are equal terms, I'm an astronaut on the moon."

"We can take them, I'd bet, if need be," John said quietly so the guard searching the fridge wouldn't hear. "The guards here may be the best-trained of the Yellowbacks, but they're still Yellowbacks."

"It'd be one hell of a fight, that's for sure," Northfield said. "Let's try to avoid it, though, huh?"

"Don't need to tell me twice," John replied.

The growing sound of footsteps came from the hallway staircase.

The guard shuffling through the refrigerator stopped and attentively faced the sound, his back ramrod-straight. As the footsteps grew louder, his eyes widened from either the utmost fear or respect, if not both, for the man they belonged to.

Geralt Salb walked into the dining area, and the guard who had previously escorted them followed closely behind. The guard stopped where the hallway met the dining area and kitchen, and he turned around to monitor the hallway and front door.

Northfield didn't know exactly what he expected the leader of the Yellowbacks to look like, but at first glance, Geralt Salb seemed like a man who could have easily been his neighbor years ago. He wore a plaid robe loosely tied around his waist, black and gray chest hair poking through. He was fit, with toned biceps and forearms, yet he wasn't physically imposing in the traditional sense. But Northfield could see the source of his underlings' intimidation: Geralt Salb's sharp brown eyes had a look of pure intensity and drive, practically goading people to challenge him and see what would happen. His thick, downward-angled eyebrows only added to the ferocity of his eyes. His square chin and accompanying scowl offered no hints of softness as a reprieve from his other facial features.

"At ease, son," he said to the guard near the refrigerator, who relaxed slightly in response. He turned toward the table, gawked at Nathaniel Salb, and exclaimed, "What the fuck are you doing here?"

Whatever energy Nathaniel Salb still possessed further diminished, either from his sickness or the prospect of a verbal spar with his brother. "Never one for pleasantries, were you?"

"I'll save pleasantries for people I've . . ." Geralt said, trailing off as another set of footsteps, these ones softer than his own, headed down the staircase. "The fuck's he still doing here?"

A man with disheveled hair walked into the kitchen, patches of soot spotting his body like a starving Dalmatian; he clutched a bag of tools, which was similarly blotched.

Thrusting his eyes into the man like a spear, Geralt said menacingly, "What the fuck took so long? You were supposed to be done by sundown."

"The filter had more issues than I originally thought."

Geralt Salb clamped his eyes shut and massaged his cheeks, growling, his eyes darting toward Nathaniel Salb. The King was clearly perturbed by his brother's presence.

"Jesus, King, I'm sorry," the man cried. "I just thought you'd want the filter done . . ."

"Got two damn filters in this joint," he almost yelled. Abruptly, his anger faded, and his mood switched to calmed reservation. His voice quieted to the extent that perhaps even signified embarrassment by his outburst as he ordered to one of the guards, "Message the Yellowbacks in the city. Tell them to stay indoors tonight." He flashed a look at his brother before continuing. "No bar drinking. None of that shit. Streets are gonna be dangerous tonight. The Death Corps are on the hunt. Tell them that if they don't lie low, and I hear about it, I'll make sure they aren't a fucking worry to me."

Uncomfortable looks were exchanged at the table. *What sort of guy are we dealing with here? His anger both rose and fell so quickly. He's got a boiling temper—that much is clear. But did he quell his anger to show his men that he's in control of his emotions? Or does he feel genuine remorse?*

Geralt Salb asked his brother, "Do they know? Do they fucking know we're brothers?"

Nathaniel Salb shook his head and said, "If they had the means to find out, they would have known long ago."

"Did they track you?"

"If they did, I suspect they would already be here."

Exhaling forcefully, Geralt said to the repairman, "Stay here to-night. I don't want people coming in and out of here. You'll sleep on the floor next to the other men."

"I'm . . . I'm sorry, King. I thought you wanted the filter fixed."

"Not your fault, son. Now go and take it easy."

The repairman nodded and left the room. Moments later, Northfield heard his footsteps as he ascended the stairs. Geralt Salb betrayed no emotion; he turned to face the group at the table, his chest steadily rising and falling.

"Still have that hot temper, huh?" Nathaniel said.

Geralt flashed his teeth in a snarl and retorted, "Still an arrogant prick, huh?"

Nathaniel jerked forward and let out a short burst of coughs, and he glared at his brother with half-open eyes, taking a few measured breaths to expel whatever insults initially entered his mind.

Geralt studied his brother. With a harsh tone betraying the slightest hint of softness, he said, "What the hell's wrong with you?"

"Mask's Kiss," Nathaniel muttered. "I'm fine. I'm on antibiotics."

A moment of silence followed as Geralt surveyed Elena, John, and Northfield. He gestured with his hand around the table and said, "You brought friends, too? I haven't seen you with a lot of those since grade school."

"We've both changed considerably since then, Geralt," Nathaniel said flatly.

"I know. That's what you said to me right before you told me you never wanted to see me again," Geralt said. "Which leads me to the question again: why the fuck are you here?"

Nathaniel started to say, "Right now, I'm being hunted by the Death Corps—"

Geralt cut him off. "I know that. Of course I know that. Everyone in the damned city knows that. You're the most wanted man since, well, since before the bombs dropped. So why now of all times do you show up on my doorstep?"

Nathaniel Salb turned to look at John. After exchanging glances, Nathaniel said to Geralt, "Some things are confidential. If you could tell your guards to leave the room—"

Geralt interrupted him again. "You have the balls to come into my house and tell me what to do with my people?" He shook his head. "No. My people are loyal. They stay."

Nathaniel glanced at John again. John's expression communicated a clear sentiment: *Sometimes, you have to play ball.*

After holding his wrist to his mouth and forcibly clearing his throat once more, he said, "Okay, Geralt. I'll tell you what happened."

Nathaniel Salb started with the creation of Zeus's Mercy and Code Blue, and he went on to explain the Coalition and his theft of the master key. From there, he explained how Elena and John showed up to escort him out of the city, his sickness, Northfield's appearance, and their stay at Dr. Flynn's. Lastly, he explained Rolling Moses and its delay.

"So," he concluded, "we needed a place to stay. We figured that your house was the safest place for us, considering the Network and Yellowbacks' cease-fire in the city, as well as your armed guards."

Geralt took a moment to absorb his words. He said, fury apparent in his voice, "That cease-fire is damned valuable to us, and we do a lot to maintain it. A fucking lot. The Death Corps soldiers are pieces of shit, the lot of them. They look down on us and disrespect us at every turn. The Network doesn't authorize it, or I'd be the first to rip the Death Corps in half with bullets, but the Network doesn't do much to stop it, either. We stomach it to stop an all-out war."

Geralt pointed at himself and said, "We don't wear our uniforms in the city. We don't wear our air tanks in the city. We don't wear our fucking identity in the city. All so the Network can keep its damned illusion that we've been driven out into the countryside. Some days I'm tempted to make their lies true, just pack my boys up and head out of the city, but Cumulus is the center of everything for over a hundred damn miles. Being able to plan all of our operations from a central hub like this without the Network trying to blow us up every two goddamned seconds is too valuable to just throw away." Geralt took a moment to breathe. Seething, he said, "And you decide to come here, knowing about the cease-fire, knowing that you might fuck that delicate agreement up? An agreement already on precarious terms? And disrupt our entire planning operation in the city?"

Nathaniel didn't respond for a moment, measuring his words. He said, "You're my brother, Geralt. Where else would I go?"

"Don't play that 'brother' bullshit on me," Geralt said. "You can't refuse to see me for over a decade and then pull that card on me now."

"We have our . . . differences," Nathaniel said. "But we're still family. And that means something to you. It has to."

Geralt grinned bitterly and shook his head. He said, "People always gave me flak for being the manipulative one, but, Nathan, you've always one-upped me."

Nathaniel's lips curled into a reserved frown, and he asked, "What do you mean?"

"I see what you're trying to do," Geralt said, shaking his head. "You're taking advantage of my loyalty to family to get me to do what you want, even though you don't even share the same loyalty. If you did, you wouldn't have left."

"I can't believe you," Nathaniel said, aghast. "You're trying to take the moral high ground? You?"

Geralt interrupted once more. "I'm family. You don't manipulate family. That's low for anybody."

"Christ," Nathaniel said, gritting his teeth and shaking his head. "I don't need to deal with this. I'm trying to save the city here." He looked around the table and continued. "We're trying to save the city. And if you don't help us, you're just proving right everything that people say about you."

Northfield, Elena, and John exchanged more awkward glances, but they kept their mouths shut; nobody wanted to jump into this mess. Anything they had to say would only add heat to an already-uncomfortable fire.

"What a load of bullshit," Geralt said. "You're not doing this to save the city. You're doing this for yourself."

"What the hell are you talking about?" Salb cried, rising to stand in righteous fury before a ferocious cough forced him to remain in his seat.

"You love grandstanding," Geralt said. "You always fucking loved being the best in the room in every type of way. The smartest and the most virtuous and whatever else you could find under the sun. This is just more of your moral grandstanding garbage."

"That's false," Nathaniel said. "I'm putting my life in extreme danger to help—"

"Oh, shut up," Geralt said. "You're not even giving the Coalition the location of the master key until you're on your way out of the city. You're not helping anyone until you make sure your own needs are met."

"I'm doing more for this city than anyone," Nathaniel said with a subsequent harsh cough that accentuated his indignance. "Ridding the city of the gas and reversing the apocalypse wouldn't be possible without me. There's nothing wrong with making sure I live to see the changes I've brought about."

"Keep telling yourself that's what you're doing," Geralt said. "If you were a real hero, you'd give the Coalition the key's location and wait to be escorted out of the city once the job's done. Instead, you're making these people"—he looked at Northfield, Elena, and John—"risk their lives just to ensure your personal safety."

Nathaniel inhaled sharply before he said, "What do you want, Geralt? What's the point of this drivel?"

"I don't want anything. I'll give you a place to stay for the night," Geralt said with a harsh grin. "I just wanted to take you down a peg. I can't stand your moral posturing."

"Don't try to claim moral equivalency when there is none, Geralt," he said. "We're not the same. We're not."

"Are you done?" Geralt asked. "Is this really the way you want to treat the man you're asking for help?"

He took a moment to think and catch his breath. With a scowl he barely attempted to conceal, he asked, "Where do you want us to stay?"

"Upstairs," Geralt replied. "The room with the balcony. There's a queen-sized bed and a couch, and hell, there's more than enough room for the four of you to sleep on the ground if you wanted."

"Balcony room?" Nathaniel echoed incredulously. "That's very generous of you."

He shrugged and said, "It's not my room. Mine's on the opposite side of the floor. I just hate that balcony and those windows. Even with the curtains drawn, I feel like eyes are on me. Drives me insane."

"Never thought you'd devolve into the paranoid type," Nathaniel muttered.

"In my position, paranoia's what keeps me alive," Geralt countered. "Some of my guards stationed here usually sleep in that room. But I'll pay them a bit extra and they'll be happy to find other places to sleep in the house."

Nathaniel's mouth opened before abruptly shutting and curling into an unsure grimace. "There's one more thing, Geralt. The Network has been working on a prototype exoskeleton, something that can make a man bulletproof. Make a man able to lift multiple times his own weight."

"Bulletproof? For fuck's sake," Geralt said. "This is what you decide to bring up last?"

"I don't know much about the project," he said. "They could still be months from finishing, or they could have a couple prototypes finished. And even if they do, who knows if they're going to be put in the field? I debated telling you, as I'm hoping it's a nonissue, but it felt wrong not to."

"You're telling me you didn't know much about this project? The second-in-command scientist?"

"Of the Zeus's Mercy project, I am," he said. "But the Network doesn't cross-pollinate projects. I generally have no inkling of the Network's other endeavors. Not until they're close to finishing, anyway."

"Was hoping you could give me better than that," Geralt Salb muttered, running his hand through his hair. "Best to assume these suits exist and are kicking. I'll have my guards get together the explosives we currently have, but our best defense is doing everything in our power to keep the fact that you're staying here a secret. If we start hauling truckloads of extra guys and weapons here and stir shit up in the middle of the night, the Network has a better chance of finding you here. Our agreement states that the Network's not allowed to be anywhere within a block of this place without justifiable reason, and I don't want to give them a reason to sniff around. I'll arm up the nearest backup to handle an exo freak or two and whatever else the Network can throw at us."

Nathaniel Salb struggled in vain to articulate his thoughts, and all he could manage to say was, "Thanks, Geralt. For what it's worth, I'm sorry I roped you into this."

With a softness Northfield didn't expect, Geralt said, "No number of years is too long, at least in my book. I'll have one of my guards bring you and your friends a meal. Follow me. I'll show you to your room."

Nathaniel Salb and his allies followed Geralt in a single-file line. The two guards in the kitchen trailed behind them.

On the second floor, Geralt pointed to the door at the end of the hallway and said, "That one leads to the bathroom. Only flush if it's not yellow. I'm not trying to go broke from my water bill."

He opened the door on the right side of the hallway, beckoning them to enter. Inside, Northfield surveyed the room.

Light from the toxic gas came through windows on the far wall, and this light was currently the only source of illumination in the room. Soft winds made the gas ebb and flow, creating a fish-tank-like effect as waves of gentle light and shadow moved across the walls and floor.

True to Geralt's word, there was a queen-sized bed and a couch. Next to each stood small nightstands with lamps.

Geralt announced, "There's matches in the drawers if you want to light the lamps. The apartment's got electricity, but again, it costs me enough credit cards to choke an elephant, so don't use it unless there's some emergency." After a pause, he said, "I'll have a meal brought up for you four in a couple minutes. I'll also have my men prepare a meal for you just before dawn, when you leave."

Before Nathaniel, Northfield, Elena, or John could respond or offer thanks, the door slammed shut, leaving them alone. Nathaniel reached into the nightstand next to the bed, pulled out a pack of matches, and proceeded to light the lamps.

"So, uh, how's the sleeping situation gonna work here?" he asked, his eyes swiveling from the bed to the couch.

"Elena takes the bed. Salb takes the couch. You and I take the floor," John directed.

"Hang on," she said. "Salb's still recovering. He should take the bed."

"Okay then, you and Salb switch. You're on the couch, and he's on the bed," John said.

"I can sleep on the floor," she insisted. "You take the couch."

John smirked and said, "I'm not quite that old yet, El."

She turned to Northfield and said, "Or maybe Mark can sleep on the couch."

He shook his head and said, "You should see the mattress I sleep on at my house. In comparison, this floor is a bed of feathers. Nah, I'm good."

"Fine," John said, throwing up his hands. "I won't turn down a good deal. You two sleep on the floor, then."

Elena turned to Salb and said, "You should sleep. And take your meds."

"I will," he replied. "But not until after I eat. I'm starving."

There was a knock at the door, and John opened it. One of Geralt's guards, a man with facial hair slightly longer than Northfield's, carried a platter with four bowls filled with oatmeal, spoons, and napkins. He placed the platter on the nightstand near the couch and left without acknowledging their presence.

"Thanks for the—" Northfield said after him, but he was cut off by the shutting door. He shrugged and made his way to the food.

John and Salb sat on the couch while Elena and Northfield sat cross-legged on the floor. Each of them, save for John, grabbed a bowl and commenced eating. Salb eagerly snagged a couple of the napkins. With relief comparable to a man finally finding his way out of the forest, he coughed into them. He crumpled the used napkins and stuffed the unused ones in his pocket.

John stared at the remaining bowl of oatmeal, prompting Elena to say, "I know you're not a fan of eating food other people offer, but you've got to keep your strength up, too."

He muttered something inaudible before tentatively taking the final bowl.

Northfield, scooping up a heap of oatmeal, said, "Oatmeal? Don't get me wrong, I'm not complaining. Just didn't expect it from your brother. He doesn't exactly seem like a grains type of guy, you know?"

"Not if you knew him better," Salb said after swallowing a bite. "The man likes oatmeal more than he likes booze. He eats two bowls a day, I think. And considering that it's the cheapest non-ration food available, he probably doesn't want to spare any more expenses on us than he has to."

"Makes sense," Northfield replied between spoonfuls. "I used to hate oatmeal. But man, after eating so many rations, I think raw sewage would taste great in comparison."

"That reminds me of a crazy story," Elena said. "Once, I saw this guy who was so sick of food rations that he tried selling his daughter for a loaf of stale bread and a box of fruit snacks."

"What?" he said, his spoon freezing mid-bite. "You can't be serious. That's a joke, right?"

"I wish it was," Elena said. "It does sound like a joke, though, if you have that sort of dark humor."

"Man," Northfield said somberly, poking at his oatmeal with his spoon. "What's wrong with people these days?"

"Heh," John uttered with a sly grin. "You sound exactly like I used to before the bombs dropped."

Northfield looked up from his fat scoop of oatmeal and asked, "What, you'd complain about how much better things were in your younger days?"

"Pretty much," John said. "Like a man twice my age. Well, double my age at the time. My daughters got pretty sick of it."

"You never run out of understatements, Dad," Elena said with a wry shake of her head. "That's for sure."

When John said "daughters," Northfield almost dumbly asked if he had another daughter or asked Elena if she had a sister before he stopped himself. Instead, he said, "Yeah, well, maybe I'm just reaching old age prematurely, too. Stress tends to do that to you. If the last ten years haven't been pure stress, then the moon better be made of cheese."

"I'd drink to that," John said. "If I had any booze, that is."

"With how high my blood pressure has probably been, I should start digging my damn grave," Northfield said. His eyes narrowed, and he added with a melancholic smirk, "Digging. Huh. Never even thought of that. If each of the microbots that make up the gas is geographically located and not designed to rise or lower, would you not need a filtration system if you lived underground?"

"It depends," Salb answered. "You'd have downdrafts to worry about. If you inhale gas that's been temporarily displaced into your living space by wind, your life is over. Even if you can guard against downdrafts or other forms of gas infiltration, no safeguard is infallible. Who knows what coincidental, unimaginable ways gas could enter your living space? Having a filtration system is still a safe precaution, especially for what little benefit you'd receive otherwise."

"Yeah, I guess you'd still have to come to the surface eventually to get food and supplies, meaning that you'd need a gas mask, meaning that you'd need Network-produced filters, meaning that you'd still be dependent on the Network. Unless you're a Yellowback, that is. So I guess digging to avoid needing a filtration system is a moot point."

Salb nodded. "Even so, the Network doesn't want the idea to even occur to the populace. Most people haven't a clue how the gas works. In the city, I've heard that the Network installs two filtration systems on the deepest underground floors just to deceive people. In the country, I've heard of Death Corps patrols scouring the land in search of underground complexes to destroy them and whoever lives in them."

"Christ," Northfield muttered.

"When you were building Zeus's Mercy, did you truly believe the Network planned to rid the city of gas?" Elena asked.

Salb took a moment to cough, perhaps to give himself time to think of an answer. Softly, he said, "I looked the other way. I ignored all the rumors about the Network and believed what I wanted to, which was its version of the truth. The Network said the goal of everything it was doing was to keep control until we finished the device and could save the city. That couldn't have more obviously been a lie. But it was easier believing it than realizing that I was helping a monster. Most of my colleagues are still stuck in this state of mind. After I learned of the Network's true plans for the device from the mouth of Kayden Knox, everything clicked. Those rumors I had brushed away suddenly became real."

"You're brave for doing what you did, Salb," Elena said.

He nodded wordlessly.

They finished eating, and they decided to call it a night to maximize their sleep. John, Elena, and Salb placed fresh filters in their gas masks, and Northfield turned on his mask's cleaning system. Salb also tried scraping as much dried mucus off the interior of his gas mask as he could with one of the napkins he'd taken from the tray.

"I'll take the first night watch," John said. "Elena, you take the second. Mark, you take the third. Wake us at dawn. I want to reach Rolling Moses by morning."

Northfield concealed his surprise at John's order; John had asked him to keep watch. Was his trust in Northfield growing? Could this be some sort of test? Or did he simply figure that Northfield wasn't in a position to harm Salb or his escorts in Yellowback territory?

"Do you really think that's necessary?" Salb asked, collapsing on the bed. "My brother has at least ten armed men in or around the building. They'll keep us safe."

"I'm not exactly keen on trusting them," John said. He looked at the windows and added, "Wouldn't hurt to have another pair of eyes watch the street and next-door buildings, either."

"You're not keeping watch anyway, Salb. You still need to recuperate," Elena said. "Wouldn't you sleep better knowing that we're keeping an eye out on you?"

Nathaniel thought for a moment, and he said, "I see your point." He pulled the blanket over himself and added, "I'm going to catch some shuteye, then. I have a long day of traveling ahead."

Northfield set his backpack on the floor and leaned against the back of the couch. He pulled out his framed picture of Jess. The picture flickered from the combination of ebbing candlelight and the glowing gas outside. Even when the picture was the most illuminated, he could only faintly make out her figure and flowing black hair; he recalled her facial features, and he tried to paint them in the shadows.

"Is it okay if I put out the candles?" Elena asked him after noticing the picture in his hands.

His response was delayed. First, he had to break out of the trance the image and ebbing light had put him into. "Yeah . . . Yeah, that's okay. I gotta catch some shuteye, too."

The candlelight vanished. Elena made her way to the front of the couch, where she lay between it and the wall.

Now he could barely distinguish any features of the picture. With only the faint glow coming from outside, all he could make out were lines where the changes in color contrasted the most. Sighing, he put the picture in his backpack, and he lay on the floor, staring up at the ceiling.

God, at this point, I figure that you and Jess are getting sick of my complaining. Maybe now you're taking shifts. Or, hell, maybe you're both listening and you're laughing at my whining together. You're laughing because you know I'm exactly where I'm supposed to be in your cosmic plan.

Or maybe you're crying because the opposite is true.

See, this is why your book's dogshit. You left things far too vague. Why do I feel like half of the time I have no idea what to do? How am I supposed to have a relationship with you if I don't ever know how you're feeling?

I hope she's laughing, God, even if it's at my expense. I never liked being the butt of jokes, but for her, it would be worth it.

I hope she's not crying. I just hope she's not crying.

And I'm too scared to ask her myself.

CHAPTER 11

Some mysterious force pushed and pulled his body. Back and forth. Back and forth. When he opened his eyes, sunlight blinded him. His hand moved to shield his eyes, and his vision cleared from the initial disorientation. Blue skies surrounded him while wispy clouds crawled across the air. He felt a roughness on the bottoms of his feet, and he realized that he was standing on wooden planks. In front of him, a large wooden rod jutted into the air with three perpendicular wooden poles attached, each evenly spaced. Large sections of black fabric were attached to the horizontal poles, the largest of which had a white skull and crossbones painted on it.

The wooden components constituted a mast, he realized, and each section of black fabric was a sail.

Am I on a pirate ship? he wondered, suddenly becoming acutely aware of the fact that he wasn't wearing a shirt. Looking down at his legs, he saw a pair of dirty brown breeches, and he could feel a bandana tied around his forehead. Haggard shouts and cries surrounded him, and he realized that a dozen other men accompanied him on the ship, manning the cannons that lined the deck.

Jameson appeared by his side. He wasn't sure if Jameson had

already been standing there and he just hadn't noticed or if Jameson had, in fact, materialized next to him.

"Where did you . . . What?" he uttered, beyond confused.

"Northfield," Jameson said, flashing a toothy, albeit cynical, grin. "Looks like another trip we're on, huh?"

Cannons exploded on the ship's port side, causing Northfield to jump in shock and instinctively cover his ears. He followed their trails of smoke, and he saw a ship in the distance. Its prominent red, blue, and black sails billowed in the wind. The cannonballs fell short, crashing into the ocean and causing clouds of water to erupt from the surface.

"Get down!" Jameson cried over clashing waves. Averting his gaze to the red, blue, and black ship, Northfield could immediately see why Jameson had yelled.

Flashes of fire followed by plumes of smoke emitted from the red, blue, and black ship's starboard side. The sounds of explosions quickly followed. He copied the other shipmen as they threw themselves to the deck and buried their heads in their arms.

Cannonballs tore through the ship like knives through heated butter. A cannonball obliterated the mast, sending splinters of wood raining down on them. Shards cut through his arms and back. Some even embedded in him.

"Water's breaching the hull!" one of the shipmen cried out in desperation. Northfield raised his head. Fountains of water bubbled from holes on the deck, which was covered in an increasingly thick layer of water. The ocean began to slowly consume the ship, greedily pulling the vessel down inch by inch. The opposing ship fired no further cannonballs; evidently, the enemy already considered them sunk.

Jameson echoed this sentiment. "The ship's sinking! Abandon ship!"

As men began diving off the deck and into the surrounding blue, Northfield asked Jameson, "Where are the lifeboats?"

"Don't have any," he replied, watching his men jump. As captain, he waited for his men to abandon ship before he followed.

Perplexed, Northfield asked, "Why don't you have any?"

"Didn't think we'd sink," he said, shrugging. Seeing as he and Northfield were the only men left on the sinking vessel, he trudged through the rising water toward the starboard side and launched himself off the ship.

He was gone before Northfield could even ask, *But who expects their ship to sink before leaving port?*

Northfield was now up to his ankles in water, and the only option was to follow Jameson. He sloshed his way across the deck and stood on the edge of the ship, looking into the swirling water below him. He bent his legs slightly, priming his muscles to jump. Before he committed to the leap, he noticed a white figure appear on the horizon. Initially, he thought it was simply a wispy cloud, but as the figure grew nearer, he made out the shape of a woman in a billowing white dress. Her hair was long, straight, and raven-black, and it flowed down her shoulders in a manner akin to the ocean currents beneath her hovering frame.

"Jess?" he asked. For some strange reason, terror coiled around his heart like a kraken's tentacles.

She hovered and stared down at him, now only a scarce few feet away. She opened her mouth to speak, but before he could hear her words, he found himself submerged under water, sinking right along with the ship. The thought of swimming didn't occur to him. As he continued descending with his arms relaxed by his sides, he stared up at the surface, watching the sunlight shimmer in incandescent waves that slowly dulled as he fell into the deep. His world darkened, but he could still see her and her flowing dress.

He thought she would follow him. No, he expected her to. But as he watched her slowly dwindle from view, the horrifying realization that she wasn't coming struck him. His eyes widened in pure panic as the sensation of drowning overtook him.

I can't breathe. I can't breathe! His brain cried out in fiery letters that scalded his skull. He thrashed with his arms and legs, unable to stop the darkness consuming the corners of his vision. But the surface was too far away. He wouldn't reach it. He'd never reach it. The realization only pushed his panic further, pushed his limbs to the brink of exertion in the vain attempt to pull his body out of the endless blue cage that was killing him.

His fright only succeeded in exacerbating his death. He drew in deep breaths of salt water, feeling a searing pain in his chest as his lungs revolted against the water's presence. For a moment, he thought he closed his eyes, only to realize that they were wide open, begging for light.

He awoke with a gasp, jolting into a sitting position. He hesitantly breathed, having to remind himself with each inhalation that he wasn't under water.

"Nightmare?" Elena asked. If his heart hadn't already been racing faster than a horse on cocaine, he might have been startled. She was standing near the doors leading out to the balcony; he figured it was her turn on lookout duty.

Shadows concealed her face. However, she could probably discern his expression from the glow coming through the windows. She added, "You've been thrashing around for the past twenty minutes."

"You've been watching me?" he asked, rubbing his eyes.

"Hard not to," she replied. "Your thrashing has been the most interesting thing that's happened for the past two hours."

"Glad to entertain you, I guess." He looked past her and stared through the window. His focus melted into the orange and yellow. "Yeah, I had a nightmare. Drowning."

He didn't exactly know why he told her that. His eyes moved away from the window and back to her silhouette.

"I'm sorry," she offered.

"I'm alright," he said. He stood up and groaned; sleeping on the floor certainly wasn't doing his back any favors. He stood next to her, leaned against the window, and said, "If you want, you can go to sleep. I don't mind taking up my guard shift early. You know, seeing as I'm up already."

"That's kind," she said. "But if you can, I want you to get more rest. It's best if we're all as alert as possible tomorrow."

He shrugged and said, "Well, if you get twice as much sleep, you'll be twice as ready. That should compensate, right?"

"I'm not sure it works like that," she said.

Next to her, he could now see her expression. Even so, he couldn't decipher it, making the added visibility useless. Still, there was a tinge of sorrow in her voice, one he found hard to ignore.

Why does she remind me of you? What piece of you is in her?

So instead of trying to read her face, he went the old-fashioned way.

"What?" he asked.

"Nothing," she said. "It's just . . . It must have been a bad night-mare. I'm sorry."

He turned his gaze back to the gas. "It's okay. Dream I've already had, kind of."

"So it's recurring?" she said. "That makes it sound worse, not better."

He leaned forward as he let out a soft sigh. "I guess. It's not usu-ally quite as bad. Or, I don't know, maybe it is." Shrugging, he added, "Who doesn't have bad dreams these days? I bet eighty percent of the people in this city see the same horrors every night."

"Yeah, you're probably right," she said. "I don't think it diminishes them, though."

"Sounds like you've got some nightmares of your own."

She turned away. "I don't really have dreams when I sleep. Just close my eyes and wake up, you know?"

"You're lucky," he said with a hint of a smile.

"Yeah, I guess so," she said. "But at the same time, I don't have good dreams either. Having some nightmares for the chance at a good dream every so often? I don't know, sounds like it could be worth it." She met his gaze and said, "Easy to say for me, though. Grass is always greener, right?"

Outside, the wind picked up. The gas spilled through alleyways and swirled around the streets like a churning whirlpool.

He closed his eyes and tried to let the howling sound transport his mind to another place. However, he couldn't get an image to crystallize. When he opened his eyes and glimpsed the gas once more, he only felt weary.

Apparently, she could tell that his exhaustion extended past a mere lack of sleep, because she asked, "If you're having doubts about what we're doing, I can—"

"No, it's not that. It's just . . ." he said. "It's just, well, maybe. Maybe I am."

She asked, "Are you worried that we won't be able to pull it off?"

He shook his head and said, "Don't get me wrong, I wouldn't exactly bet on our horse right now. But no, that's not what's getting to me." He exhaled deeply, fogging the window. She patiently studied him as he drew in a breath and added, "There's gonna be blood. Maybe more of theirs, maybe more of ours. Either way, a lot will be spilled, and I just keep asking myself if the mission is worth it."

While she contemplated his words, he watched the fog fade from the window.

When the last trace of fog had disappeared, she said, "If we manage to set off Zeus's Mercy, we'll be saving millions of lives."

"Yeah," he said. "Believe me, I know. Yet I can't . . . I've . . . I'm just sick of rationalizing the killing, you know?" He pressed his lips together. "Nowadays, people do it all the time. The Yellowbacks, Network, Death Corps, take your pick. When I look at them, and when I look at me, I can't stop thinking about how much I've done it. Maybe I'm . . ." He took a breath. "Maybe I'm running out of rationalizations."

She didn't say anything for a while. When she finally spoke, she said, "I understand. Killing . . . it's never sat right with me. It's not something I take lightly. Once you start dictating when human lives are worth losing, you enter dangerous territory, a territory I'm not sure I'm comfortable being in for long."

She paused. Her eyes were soft, glimmering by the glow of the gas.

"At the same time, besides this mission, I don't know what to do," she said. "Things have been bad, you know? I just . . . I don't think I can do nothing. I have to do something."

He slowly absorbed what she said, taking in one word at a time. The howl of the wind grew louder, filling the void in their conversation.

Eventually, he pushed himself away from the window and stood straight. "That's just the thing, isn't it?" he said. "I don't think I can do nothing, either."

"I'd hate asking you to rationalize again," she said. "But I think if there's any time, now's probably one of the better times."

"I know. Millions of lives," he replied with a grimace. "I'm not going anywhere, don't worry."

And God forgive me because of it.

"Good. We'd hate to lose you." She briefly glanced at her father before continuing. "And not just because you can shoot."

He turned to John, then turned back to her. "Thanks, Elena."

Before she could respond, she yawned, leading him to say, "Really, you should get to sleep."

She shook her head with stubbornness and said, "No, it's not the end of my shift. If you can sleep—"

"Are you really gonna make me fight to stay up later?" he said with a good-humored smile. "I'll be alright tomorrow, I promise. I got enough sleep already."

"I doubt that," she said, squinting. "But if you're staying up either way, I won't say no to more sleep. Just wake me if you need anything. Or if you think you can sleep."

"Will do," he said. "Hope you have that dream."

"Thanks. I hope so, too."

Soon, she was asleep; he heard her deep breathing as he stared out the window.

While her sleep was peaceful, Salb had periodic fits where he thrashed around and coughed, but each time, he eventually succumbed to his sick and weary body. His coughs ceased, replaced by soft snoring.

From the window, Northfield could see the far half of the street and sidewalk; the balcony obscured the closer half of the street and the sidewalk adjacent to the apartment. He put his forearm on the glass and rested on it, letting his mind wander. Eventually, he entered a state of half-consciousness and absentmindedly gazed at the non-changing street and buildings. Every handful of minutes, a car would travel across the street, and in these moments, Northfield's attention would snap back until he realized that the passing car wasn't going to stop anywhere near the building. Sighing, he'd fall back into his state of semi-alertness, his mind continuing to fade until the next car passed.

Eventually, dawn approached; to the east, the sky brightened ever so slightly, morphing from a jet black to a dark blue.

The changing sky returned his brain to full consciousness, and he thought, *I should wake them soon.*

Any further thoughts were interrupted as he watched a black Humvee race across the street in the farthest lane and screech to a halt directly across from the building.

Oh no, he thought as another Humvee parked behind the first, followed by a truck towing a trailer.

He didn't need to wait until Death Corps soldiers stepped out of the vehicles to know they belonged to the Network.

Adrenaline surged through him like icy sludge. Darting from the window, he woke up Elena, John, and Salb.

After he told them about the Humvees, John said, "I'm going to alert the Coalition and the Yellowbacks, if they haven't seen the vehicles already."

As John left the room, Elena peeked out of one of the windows. Northfield checked out the same window, as well. Salb stayed away from the windows; he was the Network's primary target, after all, and he didn't want to risk being spotted.

"This isn't good," Elena muttered, watching Death Corps soldiers step out of the vehicles. Five soldiers exited each Humvee. Three soldiers got out of the truck, and they opened the trailer.

"What are we going to do?" Salb asked.

"Nothing yet," Elena said. "With the cease-fire, there's a chance the Network won't attack the Yellowbacks to get—"

Before she even finished her sentence, a metal tank of a man stepped out of the back of the trailer.

His feet thundered when they crunched the pavement. Thick plates of black armor covered his body, reminiscent of a dark medieval knight, and he wore a gas mask with large circular filters over both cheeks. Red piping attached to his forearms and calves connected to a red power pack on his back: his exoskeleton. He carried a machine gun that weighed far too much for a man of ordinary strength to hold. Two large ammo bags hung from his belt; he had enough to eliminate a small army.

"Holy hell. Is that . . ." he said softly, his voice trailing off.

"Christ," Elena muttered.

"What?" Salb asked, taking a calculated risk and briefly peeking out the window to see what they were gawking at. He crouched out of sight and said, "Their exoskeleton project. This is not good."

"You're right about that," Northfield said, shaking his head. "You're damned right about that."

"What about explosives?" Elena asked. "Grenades or C4?"

"I assume the exo armor has a fair amount of resistance to shrapnel, but perhaps a direct hit by an RPG or grenade well within its blast radius would do some damage. I don't have any idea, but it's worth a shot," Salb said. "Do you have any grenades?"

"No," she said. "Let's hope the Yellowbacks have some for us."

Northfield added, "I've got a couple smoke grenades left that would be good for a diversion."

John rushed back into the room with a sling bag over his shoulder. He pointed to Salb and said, "There's a safe room. You're going to hide with your brother. Go! The Yellowbacks will show you where."

Salb didn't bother questioning him. He put on his armored vest and hurried out of the room.

John opened the sling bag and passed magazines to Elena and Northfield, as well as a couple of grenades. "Take these. Get your gas masks on and get your weapons. Odds are, we're going to have a fight on our hands. There's soldiers out back, too."

Elena and Northfield followed his instructions, gearing up with everything they had.

John said, "Our timing couldn't be worse. I updated the Coalition, but they're about to pass through security to get into the city, and they had to cut off communication with us until they're through. Border security in and out of the city has been beefed up since the key's been stolen. Rolling Moses should make it through, but it's going to take time."

"Just what we needed," Elena muttered. "So they're not altering plans?"

"Not yet. At this point, they've got two choices: enter the city or bug out. Seeing as Nathaniel Salb's our only shot at setting off Zeus's Mercy, they're not willing to give up yet. Once we can communicate again, I'll update them on our condition, and they'll assess whether to meet at the rendezvous if we make it out, provide us backup, or do something else if everything goes to shit."

"Let's hope not the latter," she said. "What's the game plan, then?"

"We're surrounded, outnumbered, and outgunned. There's nowhere we can run, and we'll lose in a prolonged fight. Our best chance is to hold out until Geralt Salb's reinforcements show up. He just called them in."

"What about Death Corps reinforcements?" Northfield asked. "They may have a numbers advantage on us right now, but if they're smart, they're arming and mobilizing another large attack force this very second."

"You're right," he said. "But the plan is to avoid Death Corps reinforcements entirely. They would normally get here first, but remember, Geralt Salb's reinforcements have been prepared to head our way since last night. They should get here before the next wave of Death Corps. When the Yellowbacks arrive, there'll be enough of them to ward off this wave of Death Corps and escape with Nathaniel Salb. The problem is surviving that long."

"You're damned right about that," Northfield said. "Did you see the guy in the exoskeleton? The fucking tank man? Any plans to deal with him?"

"Yes, I saw him," he replied, positioning himself next to the central window. Elena and Northfield took up a position next to the windows on either side of him. "The Yellowbacks have more grenades. If the Death Corps start shooting, we focus our heavy stuff on the exo soldier. Don't waste them on the normal guys. Backup's got something to deal with the exo, from what I've heard; we just need to hold out. Until then, dig your feet in and plant like a tree. Elena and I will hit the exo. Northfield, you focus on the others."

Northfield nodded and said, "I've got some smokes I can throw out to give us a little breathing room. Like Heaven's Rebirth, I can pick them off using my goggles."

"Good idea," John said. "Hopefully it will work as well this time."

Northfield peeked out the window. The Death Corps soldiers stared at the building. Their expressions were unreadable through their uniform faceplates. Most took cover behind their Humvees, expecting a barrage of gunfire from the building, waiting for the order to begin their assault. The imposing figure in the exoskeleton stood in front of the Humvees, unafraid of an attack. With his sheer size and motionlessness, he seemed to taunt the forces in the house.

A question tormented Northfield, one he hesitated to ask because part of him didn't want to know the answer. But part of him needed to know. "How did they find us?"

"They got him," John said, his head lowering. "They got Flynn."

Northfield's shoulders drooped; he felt like he got punched in the gut.

"Shit," Elena exclaimed. "They're going to get the sympathizers, aren't they? They're probably on their way to get them right now."

John said with a hard voice, "Dr. Flynn was the rapport between the sympathizers and Coalition. He'd get the money from the sympathizers and get it to us. The Death Corps now have the names of everyone who funded us. Every fucking one."

Elena slapped her hand onto the wall and held it there in what seemed like an attempt to vent all the anguish and frustration in her body. Northfield's head fell, and he clenched his weapon tighter. "God help them."

Help us, too, while you're at it. What's the point of omnipotence if you're not gonna spread it around?

Another moment passed, and they soaked in the anguish. Elena's voice was initially concrete like John's before an aching empathy steadily seeped through the cracks. "The mission has been complicated, but not completely screwed. Flynn didn't know where the Coalition is meeting or how we're smuggling the fighters into the city. The sympathizers don't know anything about the mission. So the Network doesn't know that information, at least. But it now knows we're planning an attack on the South Network Facility. The Death Corps will be prepared." She sighed and continued, her voice filling the void in the room. "So good and bad news. Not enough to make the taste of their deaths wash down any smoother, although I don't know if any news could." After another breath, she added with resolve, "We'll figure it out. We're going to do this, damn it. We're going to complete the mission."

Northfield tried to figure out if Flynn had betrayed them or if the Death Corps discovered their plans through some other means, perhaps if they had left evidence of their presence in Flynn's room when the Death Corps inevitably conducted their door-to-door search. *It doesn't matter, Mark. You don't know if that happened, and maybe you never will. Flynn was just trying to do the right thing, God, and you did this to him. Got him tortured and killed by the Death Corps.*

Why are people always punished for trying to do the right thing? What's your goddamn logic with that design?

Stop thinking about this, Mark. It's not doing anyone any good. Focus on the present. That's all you can do.

"Maybe there's a chance the Death Corps try to negotiate before attacking," he said, thinking out loud. "Doubt they want to break their agreement with the Yellowbacks and start a war. And if they attack, they might kill Nathaniel Salb and lose their chance at finding the master key with him. Wouldn't mean we'd be home free, but it'd give us time to think, at least."

"That's what I thought, but the more I think about it, the more pessimistic I get," Elena said. "The master key is more important to them than the agreement. Worse yet, they're probably betting that we want to keep Salb alive, too, and that we'll keep him as far away from the action as we can."

"Well, they'd be right on that count," he muttered.

"I hope they try, though," she said. "I don't think anybody wants this fight."

"Even if they try to negotiate, a fight's inevitable," John said. "We're not getting Nathaniel Salb out of this any other way. He's trapped here."

"Yeah, maybe," she agreed, adding, "But it would buy us time. Time to think, time to plan."

"Look," Northfield said, peeking out of the window. The exoskeleton soldier lifted his machine gun and pointed it at the building. The other Death Corps soldiers followed, with half of them aiming at the windows on the first floor and the other half aiming at the windows on the second floor.

"Oh, hell," John muttered, training his weapon on the soldiers. Elena did the same, while Northfield reached into his backpack and fished out his remaining smoke grenades. With his submachine gun slung over his left shoulder, he held a grenade in each hand.

The gunfire came all at once. John, Elena, and Northfield were forced to pull away from the windows, bracing against the wall as bullets shattered the glass, fragments darting across the room, shredding the couch and blankets and splintering the wooden frames of the bed and nightstands. The gas crawled into the room like a hungry demon from hell given access to a saint's soul. The gas quickly became invisible as it dispersed, as if the demon had stepped into darkness and faded from view, although his presence remained known and feared.

"I guess that's our answer," Northfield hollowly muttered to himself, his voice inaudible over the chaos. After pulling the pins on his grenades, he popped in front of his shattered window and hurled them onto the street, then quickly took cover again behind the wall.

He waited until the enemy fire died slightly, although "slightly" was a relative term; the Death Corps' fire was still loud and violent enough to make him think that he was in some sort of bullet-precipitating hellstorm. The exoskeleton soldier's machine-gun fire was distinctive and could be heard even above the rest of the chaos. However, the Yellowbacks returned fire from the other windows and lobbed grenades. The incoming fire and explosions, along with the smoke clouds, created a sense of confusion and disarray among the Death Corps. It would dissipate shortly, but Northfield fully intended to capitalize on the momentary advantage.

He aimed his submachine gun out the window, peering through the holographic sight. Through his goggles, which were set to thermal mode, he viewed the world in shades of red, yellow, and blue. The smoke clouds appeared navy blue, with lighter shades of blue throughout adding definition. The enemy soldiers appeared red at their core, this red fading to orange-yellow at their extremities. The red pipes on the exoskeleton man showed as bright yellow, almost white, and the man consequently looked like a Christmas tree in the middle of a midnight desert. But following John's plan, Northfield didn't expend his ammunition on the exoskeleton man; instead, he focused on exposed Death Corps soldiers who were either blindly firing their weapons at the building or simply disadvantageously positioned where he could hit them. After he set his weapon's sight on each of them, he double-tapped the trigger and watched each body collapse before acquiring another target. Out of the corner of his eye, he saw explosions bombard the exo soldier, but the exo soldier shrugged off each attack and continued to make his way toward the apartment.

Northfield had eliminated four Death Corps soldiers before he noticed one of them pulling a long cylindrical object out of the trunk of the leftmost Humvee. Not until the soldier pointed the weapon at the house did Northfield realize what it was.

"RPG," he muttered to himself, then, eyes widening, screamed, "RPG!"

He turned to make sure that Elena and John had heard him, and seeing as they were running away from the windows and seeking cover, he sprinted toward the bed and dove over it.

Everything that happened next occurred too quickly for him to completely register. The RPG detonated on impact—where, he didn't have any clue—exploding in a hellish white inferno and sending shrapnel flying in all directions. The shock wave hit the bed full-force, lifting the three-hundred-pound frame and mattress into the air and throwing it against the wall. Northfield was hit by the bed as it traveled through the air, and he was sandwiched between the mattress and the wall on impact, his goggles shattering as he fell to the ground and the bed landing on top of him.

His submachine gun lay sprawled on the floor just a couple feet in front of him. He thought to reach for it but lost consciousness as he lay limp beneath the bed.

CHAPTER 12

His veil of darkness was torn open by the sharp scream of an alarm. When he roused, a high-pitched ring in his ears intermingled with the alarm.

Aside from harrowing sounds, the first thing he noticed upon awakening was a copper taste in his mouth. *Blood,* he quickly realized, panicking briefly as the thought of his gas mask being broken occurred to him. *That alarm means that there's an unsafe level of gas. If my gas mask broke, I'd already be dead.* Tentatively, he drew in a breath, and after detecting nothing amiss in the air, he felt a bit more comfortable. He heard that the gas had a sort of sulfur taste when inhaled orally, although he never knew if that statement was a fact or just a rumor. Verification seemed like an exercise in suicide.

What the fuck happened? he thought, reeling as the darkness surrounding him spun; he hadn't yet opened his eyes. *Christ, I feel like I drank too much and have the spins. Maybe this whole apocalypse, world-ending crap's been some sort of drunken stupor and I'm gonna wake up as a college kid. Just have midterms to worry about instead of all this bullshit. Yeah, I can hope for that, can't I?*

Except I never drank much back then. Always time to start, right?

Piece by piece, the last few minutes before he lost consciousness returned to him. The Death Corps' arrival, the brief fight, the RPG, the bed falling on him. *Yeah, the headache and ringing in my ears definitely aren't the result of a drunken rager. Guess I'm trapped in this hell a little while longer. But man, I'm lucky my gas mask didn't break, aren't I? Fine, God, I'll give you a point for my good fortune. You have a little bit more to do before we're square, though, I think.*

He opened his eyes. His vision lagged, remaining blurry for a few moments. When his eyes did clear, what he saw looked like hell on earth.

The room resembled the charred remains of a forest fire, with black burn patches from incendiaries and grenades spotting the floor, furniture, and walls. Small flames flickered in these patches, like embers nearing their dark death in a grill. Bodies littered the floor, both Yellowbacks and Death Corps soldiers. He put the story together in his head: Death Corps soldiers fought through the house, pushing the Yellowbacks up into this room, where they made their final stand. A stand they evidently lost.

What about Elena and John? he thought, snapping his gaze from the floor to hip level. The rapid movement caused a brief dizzy spell to come over him, blurring his vision for the duration.

His eyes refocused, and he spotted Elena and John on the opposite end of the room. This observation sent a pang of relief through him before a look at their surroundings shot a disheartening arrow through his positivity.

Elena and John were on their knees with their hands clasped together behind their heads. Two Death Corps soldiers stood behind them, pointing the barrels of pistols at the back of their skulls.

A shadowy figure swallowed up a large part of the room like a black hole. The exo-armored soldier. Only a handful of feet away from him.

The exo soldier lorded over Elena and John with crossed arms. His machine gun was strapped to his back, and in his right hand, he carried an obscenely large Desert Eagle pistol. His faceplate, like all other Death Corps soldiers, was devoid of emotion, leaving Northfield only able to imagine the man's cold grin.

"Spiderwebs. That's the key. You two aren't wearing spiderweb patches," Northfield heard the exo soldier say to Elena and John. His voice was deep, brassy, and filled with a natural disdain that Northfield had a strong suspicion was an inherent part of his speech.

The high-pitched ring in Northfield's ears was already fading thanks to his earplugs, which had miraculously protected his ears despite the intensity of the explosion.

The exo soldier continued. "Sometimes the Yellowbacks take them off to escape our notice. But don't even try to tell me that a Yellowback wouldn't wear that patch inside Geralt Salb's apartment." The soldier took a deep breath, and then he said, "But you two aren't wearing those patches. Which means you're not Yellowbacks, which means you both have IQs scraping past the single digits. But not much higher, considering that, with Nathaniel Salb being here, you must be part of the Coalition. Don't bother telling me I'm wrong on any of this, or I swear to God I'll start by chopping off your arms. I won't buy that shit, not for a second. Your friend Dr. Flynn sang like a bird."

"What did you do to him, you sack of shit?" Elena growled.

A loud *whrrrrr* noise came from the pipes on the exoskeleton soldier's arm as he whipped her in the head with his pistol. As she cried out in pain, John instinctively burst out, "Elena!"

The soldier pointed his Desert Eagle at John and said, "So she matters to you? Good to know. Word of advice: don't give information like that away so easily." He pointed his pistol at Elena. "What the hell do you think we did to him? Use your damned head. We hurt the doctor. A lot. Expect worse if you don't cooperate." The exo soldier paused before he added with satisfied spite, "Don't let the worry of being the first rat who screwed everyone else over stop you. That guard you bribed? Ratted out the doctor the second we walked into the building."

Stabbed in the back by a man he trusted, Northfield thought, reeling from the news of Dr. Flynn despite expecting nothing less. *If the guard gave up Flynn only when the Death Corps walked into the building, he probably did so out of fear rather than malice. Saw the Death Corps' offer of amnesty for information and decided to be safe. But does that make the betrayal any less treacherous?*

The mattress and heavy bed frame pinned Northfield down. His left arm was immobile, trapped between the floor and his chest. His right arm remained free, resting in front of him. His submachine gun lay nearby, and he reached out to grab it. But even with his arm straining from the extension, the weapon's folding stock, the closest part of the gun, remained a few inches out of reach.

Is this a test, God, or are you just taunting me? he thought, gritting his teeth as he tried to stretch his arm even farther. His eyes remained focused on the Death Corps soldiers. They probably thought he was dead, and he wanted to keep that false belief intact, at least long enough to start blowing them to hell. *Blowing them to hell? Jesus, if I keep talking like that, I'll end up down there right alongside them . . .*

"Where is Nathaniel Salb?" the exoskeleton soldier demanded, leveling his pistol at Elena's head.

"I don't know. Honest to God, I don't know," she said. "The Yellowbacks escorted him and his brother away as soon as they saw your men, and I don't have any clue where."

In response, the exoskeleton soldier reared back to hit her again.

"Wait!" John cried out savagely. Despite his combat gear, Northfield could see how tense his muscles were. "She's telling the truth, I swear.

I know more than her. If you want to see if she's telling the truth, beat it out of me. But not her."

Northfield hadn't seen John like this before. Up until now, he had been levelheaded, cool, and calculating, even in the heat of a firefight. Now, even without the ability to see his facial expressions through his gas mask, Northfield could see the raw fear coursing through him. He was rigid and tense yet also shaking like a leaf desperately hanging onto a branch during a tornado.

The exoskeleton soldier looked at his fellow soldiers, and he asked, "How long until our reinforcements arrive?"

"Ten minutes," the soldier behind John said.

If he's mentioning reinforcements, there's probably not a lot of Death Corps soldiers left, he thought, eying his submachine gun as he continued straining to reach it. *If I can take these three guys out, we might still have a chance of making it out of here. The guy in the exoskeleton's bulletproof, but just maybe if I pump enough lead into a concentrated spot, it'll do the trick all the same. It's a long shot, but it's the only shot we've got right now.*

"When they get here, tell them to help our guys downstairs search the building. They wouldn't have escaped without us noticing. They have a safe room somewhere," the exoskeleton soldier commanded. He inhaled deeply, seeming to savor not just the air filtered through his faceplate but also imminent victory. Pointing his pistol at Elena once more, he said to John, "You said you know more than this woman. Time to put that to the test. If you can't give me Salb, you're going to give me something better: information the good doctor didn't have. Give me the location of where you're meeting the resistance to hand off Salb."

"And why would I do that?" he asked. The soldier hit Elena, eliciting another scream from John.

"Because if the information you give me satisfies me, I'll let her live. I'll kill you, but I'll let her live."

"Why should I believe that? Why the hell wouldn't you just kill us both?"

"John, you're not actually thinking of telling him anything . . ." Elena said, disbelief, disappointment, and, above all else, fear present in her voice. Not fear for her safety, Northfield assumed, but rather fear that the mission, the hope, the future was crumbling right in front of her.

He needed to reach his damned gun.

"What reason would I have to kill her if I end your little resistance?" the soldier said. "What's she gonna do? Fight the Network by herself? After I kill you, someone who obviously cares for her, right in front of her eyes? When I show her that we can reach and kill anyone? Crushing the resistance and setting an example for any dumbass who might have similar ideas in the future is worth letting her live. An ant's not gonna cause a beehive trouble."

John didn't respond. Instead, he stared at the floor, his body frozen, his mind obviously millions of miles away. His shoulders slouched as years seemed to pile on his body and weigh on him, and he resembled a millennium-old tree, withered bark peeling off and drifting away with each gust of wind. His words from the other night, when he and Northfield sat at Flynn's table, pounded into Northfield's head. *I've had to do a lot to keep us safe. Stuff not worth mentioning, stuff you can probably guess, but I'm tired of it.*

Northfield almost screamed as he reached, determined to either move himself or the world to reach his gun. *Don't make this another one of those times, John. Don't doom the Coalition for her, not yet. Not yet. Damn it, God, let me save them. Please, don't let me let them down.*

Elena said, "John, he's just going to kill us anyway. Don't tell him anything, plea—" The soldier hit her again, drawing another cry from John.

"Just . . . just stop hitting her, alright?" he said weakly. He was a man hanging onto the last vestiges of free will, a man feeling himself being pulled away and losing his grip, a man drawn toward the decision he'd always made, the decision he'd always needed to make.

"That all depends on you, John," the soldier said. "Her safety depends on you."

"John, please, for me," Elena begged. "Don't tell him anything. It's not worth it."

John's gaze lifted to her face; Northfield couldn't see his eyes through his mask, and he didn't want to. "I only took this job to protect you, Elena. You know that. You're all I've got left. Without you alive, it's not worth it to me."

"This is bigger than both of us, John," she said. "Christ, think of all the people we could save."

"It's not bigger to me," he said.

Northfield swore his shoulder would pop out of its socket any second, yet he tried to push his body even further. As his teeth clenched in exertion, he thought, *You wouldn't have kept me alive for nothing. If you really wanted to kill me, that RPG shot would have finished me. You wouldn't have kept me alive just to be killed by the Death Corps or left to die under this wreckage. I'm alive for a reason. You and I both know that. So, damn you, let me reach my gun and save them before John gets everybody killed.*

"You may hate me, Elena, but I need to make the choice that gives you the best chance. Right now, this is it." He looked at the exoskeleton soldier and said, pain and guilt dripping off of every word, "This morning, in half an hour. In the underpass on Gramercy Street beneath 8th

Avenue. That's where we planned on taking Salb. His safety out of the city in exchange for the key. The whole Coalition will be there, twenty armed men and women, crammed under the trailer like sardines."

"John, no," she muttered in despair, her head lowering as if an anvil had been placed on her shoulders. Northfield kept reaching for the Vector, his middle finger almost scraping against the frame.

The exoskeleton soldier pressed his finger on a square object on the side of his head; Northfield realized that it was an earpiece. The soldier said to the presumed Death Corps soldiers on the other end of the transmission, "We've located the resistance group. A half-hour from now, they're meeting in the underpass on Gramercy Street beneath 8th Avenue. Crush them." The exo said to John, "That radio on your belt. I assume you use it to communicate with the Coalition. And I assume you alerted them of our presence once we arrived on Salb's doorstep. Did you manage to send out an alert that you were going to lose before we subdued you?"

John shook his head softly, staring at the ground and saying nothing. The man was on the verge of breaking, if not broken already. He kept her safe, for now, but the burden of the Coalition's fate now rested on his shoulders. Northfield could only imagine the other burdens weighing on him.

"You've made it this far, John. Might as well complete the race. I'm gonna take your radio and hit the transmit button. When I do, you're gonna tell them you've shaken our trail and are safe with Salb. Most importantly, you're gonna tell them that it's safe to meet in the underpass. And lastly, you're gonna come up with an excuse for dropping contact with the Coalition without worrying them enough to skitter off. I'm not giving you a chance to have a change of heart and warn them by staying in contact. That's all you've got to do, John, and she's safe. Calm down. Breathe in and out. You're gonna need to be calm to be convincing. This won't work if you're fucking breathing and shaking like that."

"John, it's not too late. You can still fix this. Warn them," Elena pleaded.

"Choke her," the exo said, and the soldier behind Elena complied, putting her in a chokehold. A startled gasp escaped her throat before only faint gurgling noises could be heard.

"You bastard!" John cried out, about to lunge toward her in his kneeled position before being pistol-whipped by the soldier behind him.

"Calm, John. Calm. We're choking her to prevent her from warning the Coalition when you do as I instruct," the exo said. "You tell them what we need you to, and she's free. Breathe. Remember that. And calm yourself. But if you refuse to speak to the Coalition or if you try to warn them . . . Don't let it come to that. Same goes for if you try to trick me. If the Death Corps report back that the Coalition's gone, deal's off."

"I get it. I fucking get it," he cried in defeat. "Grab my fucking radio already!"

The soldier behind John looked in Northfield's direction, his head slightly tilted. "Sir, I think I might see something moving under the bed."

Shit, shit, shit.

"Check it out," the exo soldier ordered, leveling his gun at John with one hand and grabbing his radio with the other. He held the radio up to John's ear, and he said with dark amusement, "She must be your daughter, right? You wouldn't do this shit except if it was for your daughter."

I'm not gonna reach it, Northfield thought, staring at the Vector in front of his outstretched arm as he heard boots crunch fragments of wood and flecks of ash. He ignored the sound, keeping his eyes focused on the gun, even though it might as well have been a million miles away. *Damn you, God, I'm not gonna reach it.*

The exo clicked the transmit button on the radio, jabbing John in the head with the barrel of his pistol. Masking his despair as well as he could, John said, "Shepherd, this is Eagle Five. Over."

Before Northfield could open his mouth to scream and warn the Coalition, or before he could even consider not doing so to possibly save Elena, a boot rammed into his throat. On instinct, he gasped for breath.

"I fucking knew I saw something alive," the soldier stepping on him whispered, his voice inaudible to the Coalition on the other end of John's radio.

Although Northfield couldn't make a sound, the soldier's foot couldn't stop him from screaming mentally. Fear and frustration plummeted into his stomach like meteors, launching fiery fragments to every inch of his body upon impact.

A voice crackled through the radio. "Eagle Five, this is Shepherd. Is the nest padded? Over." Assumedly, the question was addressing whether John was in distress.

John answered, his voice steady. "Nest is padded. But the batteries in my radio are fucked. Blast hit too close and now battery life is dying, fast. Thing is going to die in a couple minutes. Over."

"Copy that, Eagle Five. Given your complication, Shepherd will briefly discuss further action. Can your radio hold out until then? Over."

"Affirmative, Shepherd. Over."

The exo soldier took his hand off the transmit button, and the soldier choking out Elena released his grip to let her breathe. While she gasped for breath, the soldier with his foot on Northfield's throat took the opportunity to say, "I don't see any patch on this guy. I think he's with them. You want me to kill him? If I do it between transmissions, the Coalition won't hear a thing."

The exo soldier answered, "Not yet."

Before she was being choked again, Elena managed to say, "John, come on."

John said nothing, slightly turning his head away as if she'd slapped him.

As Northfield braced for a bullet to pierce his skull despite the exo soldier's words, he could only frantically grasp at why his life continued to inch forward. Maybe the exo soldier wanted John as calm as possible to sell the lie to the Coalition. John was already shaken, although he hid his fear well enough; the exo soldier might think that blowing a friend's head off would push him past what he could hide. If that happened, the Coalition would be spooked.

The Coalition responded, "Eagle Five, this complication is unfortunate to hear, but at this point, with no alternatives, we'll have to make do. Are the feathers shaken? Over."

"Feathers are shaken. Over."

"Can you confirm that the shake is complete? Over."

"I can confirm a complete shake, Shepherd. Heading to Rolling Moses now. Over and out," he said. He slumped to the point that Northfield thought he would simply collapse to the floor. His spirit, his motivation, and his will all seemed to escape his body, leaving a failing, broken husk behind.

"Copy that, Eagle Five. Rolling Moses will proceed as planned. Over and out."

The exo dropped the radio, then lifted his left leg, and the electric *whrrr* coming from the metal pipes on his leg almost eclipsed the crunch of the radio as he stomped on it. He commanded, his voice booming, "We're done here. Kil—"

The exo was cut off by the sound of a shotgun blast echoing through the room. He looked down and saw blood oozing out of a scattering of holes in his armor, all of them burning with white flames that spat out orange sparks like a constellation of dragons. The exo soldier collapsed, his heavy metal frame crashing to the floor with a loud *thump*. The other two soldiers, stunned by watching their supposedly infallible comrade topple, turned their heads toward the door. Before they could lift their weapons in retaliation, two more shotgun blasts tore fiery holes through their bodies, and they collapsed in a similar fashion. Blood filled the cracks in the wood around the soldier next to Northfield like rills on a hillside during a storm. The blood neared him as he watched with rapidly blinking eyes and shaking hands.

Three Yellowbacks charged into the room, wearing their trademark air tanks with tubes that latched onto their mouths. He flinched at the cracks of further gunshots, squeezing his eyes shut as if his eyelids could protect him from bullets, realizing with a hollow absence of relief that the shots came from the floor beneath him. The Yellowbacks' weapons swung around the room, scanning for remaining Death Corps soldiers. Once each of the Yellowbacks called out "clear," they helped Elena and John to their feet.

Northfield stared at the floor, which was inches away from his eyes, waiting for a bullet to burst through and puncture his skull; he wouldn't even see the damn bullet if it came, but he just needed an excuse to not look up. Short moments, or perhaps an eternity, passed, and he heard no further gunshots. The Yellowbacks struck the first and second floors simultaneously to surprise the Death Corps and keep them from killing any captives. He didn't want to, but knowing he had to, he peeled his eyes from the floor.

"Over here," he called out between shaky breaths. Elena, John, and the Yellowbacks lifted the heavy bed frame and mattress off him.

Columns of smoke rose from smoldering holes of metal and flesh on the exo's body; whatever heat the Yellowbacks packed definitely burned. *How many times do you have to stare at a gruesome scene like this before the horror fades and gives way to weariness? How many times do you have to experience the rattlesnake's poison before an immunity builds up?*

He looked at Elena and John, and he said, "I'm sorry. Christ, I'm sorry. I tried my damned hardest to reach my gun and I just couldn't do it."

"This isn't your fault, Mark," John said. "It's mine."

"We have to warn the Coalition," Elena said. "It will be a massacre if we don't."

"We can't," John cried in frustration aimed entirely at himself. "Even if there's another radio around here, we can't. Coalition radios have electronic scramblers built into them. If any non-Coalition radio tries to pick up on Coalition radio signals, the message will be scrambled, and vice versa. The only way to warn them would be to get there physically, and the Death Corps are already on their way."

"Then we've got to get moving." She turned to one of the Yellowbacks and asked, "Where are Geralt and Nathaniel Salb?"

"Downstairs by the dinner table," the Yellowback said. Promptly, Elena made her way to the stairs, with John and Northfield following close behind.

The kitchen and dining room looked like they had experienced their own apocalypse. The refrigerator and cabinets in the kitchen were charred and riddled with dents and puncture holes caused by both bullets and grenade shrapnel. Coolant leaked out of the refrigerator in white tufts of smoke, which intermingled with the gas seeping through entry points in the bullet-torn windows. They both faded as they dispersed across the room. The oak table in the dining room was flipped onto its side. Entire sections of wood were missing; high-caliber bullets had torn out chunks rather than simply piercing through. Blood stained the remaining wood, and the bodies of two Yellowbacks rested behind it.

The story was clear. The Yellowbacks tipped the table over to use as cover, which had obviously proven inadequate. More bodies littered the kitchen and dining room, those of both the Yellowbacks and Death Corps. There were so many bodies that the floor beneath was hardly visible, and blood pooled like some sort of death lake. *And reinforcements just got here . . . Christ, how fast—how brutal—must this fight have been?*

He walked past the corpse of a Yellowback that froze him mid-step. Dried blood caked the body, and a large section of the stomach was missing, torn out by shrapnel from a grenade. The wound was horrid, but no worse than any other in the room, no worse than what Northfield had seen countless times in the past, but what made the body stand out was that Northfield recognized who it belonged to, even with a gas mask concealing the face. The body belonged to the man tasked with repairing Geralt Salb's filter, the one whom Geralt Salb had ordered to stay the night.

This guy was here just to repair a filter. He wasn't here to fight in a damned battle. I don't get Flynn, and I don't get this guy. God, I know I'm not the hand of judgment, but I can't for the life of me make any sense of this. How am I supposed to work insanity like this out?

One of the Yellowbacks knocked three times on the floor where the oak table used to be centered. Northfield realized that, aside from the air tanks, none of the Yellowbacks were wearing patches, or yellow, or anything else that could identify them as Yellowbacks.

A square tile of the wooden boards, three feet in length, lifted from the floor and slid sideways. The Yellowback helped the Salb brothers out of the safe room.

Nathaniel Salb took in his surroundings. Each burn mark, each bullet hole, each spatter of blood hit him like a shot of alcohol, his knees wobbling with an increasing loss of balance that made Northfield worry he might fall over.

"My God," Nathaniel Salb muttered, his eyes moving from body to body. "My God, this isn't . . ."

Geralt Salb also looked at the bodies, but his gaze ignored the Death Corps, only pausing momentarily at the sight of each of his fallen men. "The bastards," he muttered under his breath. To the remaining Yellowbacks in the room, he said, "We can grieve later. Or hell, think of payback. But now, we've got to move. The Death Corps are sending reinforcements this way. I'm sure of it."

Elena didn't waste a moment. She approached Geralt and said, "The Death Corps are going after the Coalition. They know where the rendezvous is. We need your help."

"What? How—" Nathaniel started to say.

"Not now," she cut him off, letting the urgency in each word serve as an explanation for her interruption. "What matters is that the Death Corps are heading there now. And we can't warn them through radio."

Geralt Salb sighed and said, "Too many of my people have died today. Now's the time to lick our wounds, not start another fight. A war might start because of this shit. I need everyone I've got."

Elena nodded. There wasn't time to argue or persuade, but she had two more requests. "Do you have a vehicle we can use? And can you spare any of the ammunition you used to take out that exo soldier?"

They couldn't use Flynn's vehicle, regardless of if it was still operable after the battle; the Death Corps would know to look for it.

Geralt nodded to some of his men and ordered, "Give them some of your thermite rounds. And someone get them keys to a vehicle."

While Geralt's men handed red-taped magazines to them, she said to Northfield, John, and Nathaniel, "We're going. The Death Corps might already be there, but damn everything if we don't try to get to the underpass first and warn the Coalition."

"I'll drive," John said. "I know the fastest route there."

Geralt said, "My brother comes with us."

Nathaniel Salb took another look at the bodies. He said after a quiet cough, "No. I'm going with them."

"What?" Geralt asked. "Don't you want to get out of the city? You go with them, you're just going to get killed."

Nathaniel shook his head and said, "Look how many people have already died trying to get me out of the city. I'm not going to hide while the Coalition is slaughtered on my account. I can at least show up at the meeting location, seeing as they may have died by planning to meet me there."

Geralt sighed. "I said you weren't a hero. I didn't mean to imply that you need to be." He didn't try to convince his brother to change his mind; all parties realized that time was of the essence. He put his hand on his brother's shoulder and added, "You change your mind or things don't work out, I'll be at the Kelley Apartments. We've got a stronghold there, and it's a secret from the Death Corps. The guards are all with me. Announce yourself at the front with the codeword 'python'. Ask for me."

Nathaniel replied, "Thanks, Geralt—for everything. I can't repay you."

"You don't need to," his brother said. "We're family." He nodded to one of the Yellowbacks, who handed John a pair of car keys.

The guard said, "Car's out front, parked on the other side of the street. Least shot-up car I saw out there."

"Let's go," Elena said. Northfield, John, and Nathaniel followed her as she rushed out of the house and to the car.

As they ran, Nathaniel Salb asked Northfield with urgency and pain, "How did this happen? How the hell did they find us?"

Northfield's muscles tightened, and he grimaced behind his mask. "Flynn. They got him and all the sympathizers."

"Oh, no. No, no, no . . ."

Despite all the gunfire and explosions, the car was relatively unscathed, save for a smattering of bullet holes on the passenger side. Bullet holes in vehicles, while not exactly common, were not uncommon, either; the violence of their world left scars in many ways and places, especially on vehicles that regularly traveled in and out of the city. The holes wouldn't attract much attention and stand out as anything worth reporting. Still, given the Death Corps' hunt for them, anything might be worth investigating in their eyes. As if they needed more reason to reach their destination rapidly.

A pained screech from the wheels echoed through the neighborhood when John slammed on the gas pedal. The scene of carnage quickly vanished; the last vestige of the battle that Northfield saw was smoke pluming from the fires still raging in the aftermath.

CHAPTER 13

Before they could see the underpass, they saw smoke floating over skyscrapers and climbing into the troposphere. The jet-black smoke contrasted against the brightening sky like a coffee stain on a pale dress shirt. The sun was fully over the horizon, albeit barely, with its bottom curve almost touching the horizon. Without the gas, the west side of the sky would appear navy blue, but it distorted the color to a mild gray. Colors to the east, a mixture of pink and yellow as the sun's rays reflected off clouds, were heightened by the gas's orange and yellow.

Salb let out a soft trio of coughs, all dry-sounding, which Northfield considered a small pebble of positive news among boulders of bad news. During the drive, Salb only coughed a handful of times, a vast improvement over the previous day. *Either the medicine's really working some magic or he's trying his best to play tough given everything that's happened. Probably a combination of both.*

"Is that smoke coming from the same direction as the underpass?" Elena asked. She pointed at the column of black with a tone that indicated she dreaded the answer.

"Yes," John answered, his hands clenching the steering wheel tighter.

"Man," Northfield muttered. "Does the Coalition stand a chance?"

"Not a good one," she said. "The Coalition is small. We stood a chance assaulting the South Network Facility with a well-coordinated surprise attack. But when the situation is reversed . . . and the Coalition are the surprised party . . ."

Northfield said, "What chance do we have, then? If the Coalition has a couple more fighters on their side, would that really change the outcome?"

Elena sighed and said, "Probably not. But that doesn't change much for us. Without the Coalition, there isn't a force to attack the South Network Facility, and there isn't a way to reach Zeus's Mercy. We have to try."

"I didn't mean to give up," he replied, shaking his head. "I just meant there's a way to be smart about this. Maybe there's a way I can stage a distraction, something to keep the Death Corps' forces at bay long enough for you to help whoever's left of the Coalition escape."

"If someone's got to be a distraction, it'll be me," John said.

"Or me," Salb offered.

"Nobody will be a distraction. I won't just leave one of us to die," she said. "Besides, the Death Corps probably have the Coalition surrounded. Just escaping wouldn't be easy. We'll probably have to fight our way to the Coalition and fight it out with them."

She didn't take her eyes off John. Northfield didn't need to read her expression to understand her concern.

John's shoulders were slouched like every gram of the world was pressed on them, and he gripped the steering wheel as though it was the exposed throat of a Death Corps soldier.

John's distress was severe enough to impair his judgment, and Elena naturally stepped in as the leader of their little four-person group. With her resourcefulness and sheer drive, Northfield didn't doubt her ability to handle the job. What remained uncertain, however, was whether John could bring himself to clarity and take the reins anytime soon. Or even if he could, would he want to?

Elena momentarily peeled her eyes away from her father to look at Salb. She said, "You're not fighting, Nathaniel. You're the only one who knows where the key is. No way we're risking your life. When we get there, find a place to hide."

"I didn't come just to spectate. If I wanted to be safe, I would have gone with my brother." After a moment of hesitation, he said, "The Weston construction building. A building half-built before the bombs dropped and never finished. On the top floor, under a pile of cinder bricks. That's where the key is."

"I thought you were waiting until you were out of the city to give us the location. What changed?" she asked.

"To detonate Zeus's Mercy, we all need to fight. I cannot stand by and watch," Salb said. "It wouldn't be right. It just wouldn't be right."

"You're gonna need this," Northfield said, grabbing his pistol and handing it to him. "You know how to use one, right?"

"A gun?" he said. "Yes, of course I know how. These days, who doesn't?"

John parked the car on the side of a street with a steep incline; at the top of the hill, the road melted into the sky as billows of black smoke rose into the air.

He pointed at the top of the hill and said, "The underpass is on the other side of this hill. I figure it's best if we park here and scope out the situation on foot."

Elena nodded. "If the Death Corps is fighting the Coalition, they will shoot first and ask questions later at the sight of any car driving toward them. Good thinking, Dad." Her voice, despite the obvious anxiety and despair, sounded slightly hopeful. John seemed to be holding himself together, albeit barely. Northfield made the same observation about himself, although he wondered whether his hold would last if all that lay ahead was the Coalition's eradication.

They got out of the truck and climbed the hill. Gramercy Street winded down the hill, straightened out when the terrain flattened, and ran under 8th Avenue. Because of Northfield's distance from the underpass, as well as the haziness caused by the black smoke, he couldn't see the situation in the underpass very clearly.

However, what he could see jammed an icy spear through his heart.

A truck with a large trailer, which he assumed was Rolling Moses, sat in the middle of the underpass. Flames ate at the truck like ravenous demons, vomiting smoke that filled the underpass and escaped in billows. The same billows Northfield saw on the other side of the hill.

Through intermittent pockets of less-dense smoke, he could glimpse large dents and holes that covered the semi-trailer. Any parts of the trailer that were not dented or punched through had scorch marks that could be mistaken as simply parts of the smoke cloud. All the air had escaped from the punctured tires, and the trailer was unhinged from the truck, its front end resting on the pavement.

On both sides of Gramercy Street in the underpass, concrete walls supported 8th Avenue running above. At the front and back of the underpass, Death Corps vehicles boxed in Rolling Moses. Their vehicles ranged from Humvees to Jeeps to trucks. Within the boundary the Death Corps' vehicles created, bodies littered the ground, but they were too far away for Northfield to discern if they belonged to the Death Corps or Coalition, although he had suspicions that he desperately hoped were wrong.

"Christ," Salb muttered. "The Coalition didn't even have cover."

"Why would they?" John said, each syllable pained. "The meeting was supposed to be low profile. The Coalition was planning to avoid a fight, not get in one."

Elena took out a pair of binoculars and peered through them. "No . . ." She gasped, and Northfield didn't need to look through the binoculars to see what she was seeing. She said in barely a whisper, her voice cracking, "They're . . . gone. They're all gone."

"Oh God," Salb said, putting his hand on his forehead. Northfield watched the smoke rise from the semi-truck, and his eyes followed it to the sky, a brief reprieve from the hell below.

"Let me see," John said through gritted teeth, his voice tense and hoarse, like he was holding back tears. Northfield didn't want to know if he succeeded or failed; he had trouble pulling his eyes away from the sky.

Elena pulled the binoculars to her chest and shook her head, attempting to speak but choking up. Her breathing was labored, and the binoculars shook in her hands.

"Let me see," John said, his voice even hoarser and now cracking.

"John," she said softly, forcing the name out. Her words seemed to fall out of her mouth and plummet to the ground like teardrops out of bloodshot eyes. "I don't want you to see this. Not—"

"I need to," he said, his tone unequivocal. Reluctantly, she handed him the binoculars. Northfield forced his gaze down, only to watch John's spirit fall further than he imagined possible. John held back a choked scream, painfully aware of the Death Corps' forces at the bottom of the hill. Instead, he channeled his despondency and rage on the binoculars, lifting them into the air and threatening to throw them onto the pavement.

"Wait," Northfield said, holding his hand out. John managed to restrain himself, and he passed the binoculars to Northfield.

He knew what lay below, but he still had to see for himself. Steeling his nerves, he held the binoculars to his eyes.

The bodies in the underpass, by and large, had civilian clothing, with some of them wearing armored vests. The Coalition. A few of the bodies belonged to Death Corps soldiers, which he chalked up to a few lucky shots from the Coalition before . . . before . . . *Wait a minute,* he thought, his eyes widening.

A single body, a woman wearing an armored vest over a brown coat, moved slightly; she used her arms to pull herself across the gravel, away from the smoking truck. Northfield didn't process the other bodies. He couldn't; he could only focus on her. There was a bullet wound in her leg, blood pooling around at a frightening rate, but she was crawling nonetheless. Alive. His brain spun as he frantically thought of how to get her out of there, how to keep her alive. This wouldn't be all for nothing. He'd save her, damn it. He'd save her, at least.

He opened his mouth to tell the others, but he spotted something. His tongue numbed, and his jaw froze.

He wasn't the only one who spotted her. An exo soldier took notice.

The soldier pointed her out to his comrades and approached. He carried a heavy shotgun with a drum magazine. He put the barrel of the gun on the back of her head; she hardly took notice and continued to crawl without pause, absorbed in her determination. The exo pulled the trigger, and the resulting explosion was loud enough for Northfield to hear not once but many times as the noise echoed off the surroundings.

He dropped to his knees. The tears welling in his eyes blurred his vision. Salb asked for the binoculars, but the words didn't really register in his head. He handed them off without being aware of his actions. His eyes again drifted upward to look at the brightening sky.

God, I heard you have a soft spot for your sinners. I'm not seeing it. You make mountains look like marshmallows.

I just want to get back to Jess. I don't care what I have to go through. Just lead me back to her. Promise me that, alright? That's the only promise from you I need. Just get me back to her. Guide me to where I need to go, and I'll take care of the rest.

"We should leave," Elena said, each word raw. "Let's go back to the truck. From there, maybe we can figure out what the fuck to do next."

Nobody argued or protested.

She sat in the driver's seat while John sat in the passenger seat. Northfield watched Elena with concern. She seemed to be holding herself together the best, but he imagined she could only do so for the sake of her father. Earlier, he could see a glow in her eyes. Sometimes she even looked around as if she had already found herself in a world free of the gas. When he saw her eyes again, he wondered what would be there.

"This is my fault," Salb said after a few minutes of tense silence. "If I hadn't been so selfish, if I had given up the key and just waited until after the mission to be extracted, the Coalition would still be alive, too."

"We're not playing this game. I don't want to hear any guilt Olympics," Elena said more harshly than Northfield had ever heard her speak. "It won't help anything. Let's just focus on what to do next."

"And what would that be?" Northfield asked.

"Get the key," she said. "We—"

John cut her off. "No. Absolutely not. You're alive, Elena. What happened won't be for nothing. It won't. I'm getting you somewhere safe."

"I don't follow," Salb said. "What are you talking about?"

"Death Corps in your brother's apartment gave my dad a choice: my life for the location of the Coalition," she said, bubbles of anger popping with each syllable like a pot of water over a stove.

"What?" Salb cried.

"It happened," she said. She took a moment to banish the acidity in her voice. "No going back. Right now, anger is useless. Like I said about blaming ourselves, we won't accomplish anything if we're mad at each other. He made a choice to save someone in his family. How many of us would make that same choice? Or how many people in today's world would've even tried to find a way to just save their own life instead?" She looked at John and continued. "You traded me for the Coalition. How can I not use my life to help set off Zeus's Mercy? Would my life have really been worth saving at such a cost if I do anything else?"

John didn't respond. Instead, he stayed quiet, enduring each word like a physical blow.

"I'm on board for figuring out how to finish the mission, but there is one problem with your logic," Salb cut in. "How would we set off Zeus's Mercy? There is an entire Network facility between us and that device, and there are only four of us."

"I've got one idea," she said. "We get your brother to help us, get him to use the Yellowbacks to storm the compound or at least provide a distraction."

Salb shook his head and said, "You don't know my brother like I do. Even if a full-scale war breaks out between the Yellowbacks and the Network over what happened—something I bet he still wants to avoid, by the way—he wouldn't help us attack the facility. He would focus on leaving the city. He knows the Yellowbacks would fare better using guerilla tactics in less-populated areas."

"That is why we need to get the key before confronting him," she said. "We stand a better chance of convincing him if we have the key on us."

"How do you figure that?" Salb asked, coughing twice softly.

"If Zeus's Mercy is detonated, and the gas is expunged from the city, change will follow. Change that might include loosening the Network's hold on the city. Your brother is aware of this. Right now, detonating Zeus's Mercy is a hypothetical in his eyes. If we present the key to him, it might change that hypothetical to a real possibility."

"You have made it clear that you have no love for the Yellowbacks," Salb said. "Neither do I. They're not much better than the Network. Would you truly be okay with the Yellowbacks simply replacing the Network as the city's power center?"

"I don't think they will," she replied. "When the gas is gone, the people will have more power to push against groups like the Yellowbacks and Network."

"I'm sure Geralt is aware of that fact, as well. If the Yellowbacks might not end up with more power after helping us detonate Zeus's Mercy, why would he help us?"

"With war on the horizon between the Network and Yellowbacks, if that war isn't here already, I think he would rather have the Yellowbacks or the people of this city in a position of power rather than the Network."

He shook his head once more and said, "Again, you don't know my brother like I do. I think he will focus on self-preservation and the preservation of his organization rather than try to make a power play."

Northfield listened to the conversation, but he didn't speak. Instead, his hands were clasped together between his knees, and he thought, *Remember our conversation, God? If I'm supposed to help activate Zeus's Mercy, please let us decide to find the key and convince Geralt. If you want me to get out of Dodge and avoid all the violence, please let the decision follow your desire. Maybe the decision's arbitrary and you're not guiding me to shit, but I'm not gonna believe that right now. I'm putting my trust in you. Lead me right. Lead me to Jess.*

"What do you suppose we do then, Salb? Give up and get out of the city?" she asked in exasperation.

Northfield observed John, who was wringing his hands on the barrel of his assault rifle; at this point, his body was poised to split down the middle.

He doesn't know what to do. Like me, he's probably waiting to see how this conversation between Elena and Salb plays out. I'm not sure if we're sensible or cowardly for being so torn.

"I'm not saying that," Salb responded defensively. "There are too many bodies on my shoulders for me to say that. I want to set off Zeus's Mercy as badly as you do. I am simply saying that you need to understand what we're getting into if we keep fighting this fight. We all do. My brother is not an easy man to convince, especially if whatever plans he already has serves his interests better than ours."

"He seemed to do the right thing by you," she observed.

"I'm family. Family is different for Geralt. You have to remember, he's the leader of the Yellowbacks, the leader of thieves and extortionists and kidnappers."

"That's what I'm saying," she said. "He'll listen to you. You're his soft spot. You can convince him. If anyone can, it's you."

"If anyone can," he repeated. "That is the problem. I'm not sure anyone can convince him." He exhaled in resignation. "If you want to try, we can try. Just don't be too disappointed if Geralt rejects us."

"I'm okay with that," she said. She turned to the others, and she asked, "Everyone in agreement?"

"Let's do it," Northfield said. "For everyone who's died so far for this, let's do it."

"Dad?"

Meekly, John nodded; his hands continued to twist and wring to keep him from exploding. Her eyes lingered on him for a few more moments before she put the truck in drive and they headed away from the underpass.

If this is the direction you're taking me, God, then please forgive me for all I'm going to have to do. Make this all worth it, God. For my soul. For her. Please.

CHAPTER 14

Salb directed Elena to the Weston building, and after a drive-by, they sought out a place to park. They found a location a ways away to be inconspicuous. They'd have to walk, but they weren't afraid of being spotted; they had their masks, and Salb wasn't noticeably sick anymore.

The surrounding apartments and townhouses were spread chaotically, with alleyways twisting between them like strands of a broken spiderweb. The Weston stuck out like a sore thumb, dwarfing its competition. As a further distinction, the Weston was also unfinished. Work on the building was interrupted before the bombs dropped and never resumed. The top six floors were little more than concrete floors with arrays of girders and pillars holding everything together. A skeleton sitting atop a pile of ash and debris. At least, that's how it felt to Northfield.

Salb pointed at the unfinished floors and said, "People pay a lot to live up there. Did you know that? There aren't any ceilings to protect you from the wind and rain, the floor is harsh concrete, and there are nails and other rubbish everywhere. And yet, people pay more to live up there than in any apartment under the gas."

"But up there, they get to breathe outside without a mask. Tradeoffs and benefits, I guess," Northfield muttered.

"How did you manage to get up there to hide the key?" Elena asked.

"Some forgery," Salb replied. "For all buildings accessed by the public, Network inspectors perform tests on filtration systems to ensure that they meet an acceptable safety standard. To be considered operational, filtration systems must be able to filter a certain amount of gas for a certain amount of time. Building owners are responsible for making sure the filtration system on each floor meets this safety standard.

"Network inspectors have free rein to conduct tests. Building owners don't know when they'll come. They don't know how often inspectors will come, either. Could be three times in a week. Perhaps once every six months. Owners have little to no warning, either.

"With my Network resources, acquiring the apparatus for filtration system tests was not difficult, nor was acquiring fake identification. The day before I stole the key, I presented myself as an inspector to the front desk of the Weston and said I needed to take my tests."

Salb allowed himself two quick coughs to clear his throat before continuing. "As per Network policy, the security officer gave me access to every floor, so I could choose at my discretion which two floors to test. I had access to the highest floors, even though they are above the gas. After I stole the key, I returned to the Weston, and I hid it on the fifteenth floor. Despite my advancing sickness, I managed to return home before I collapsed on my bed."

Elena had another question. "The Coalition didn't have IDs to pose as inspectors. How did you figure we would retrieve the key?"

Sheepishly, he said, "I didn't. At the time, I figured that was your problem."

"Fair enough," she said without accusation, just tiredness.

"Why here?" Northfield asked.

"The people who live on the unfinished upper floors of the Weston are called rich ghosts. They pay an obscene amount of money to live in shoddy conditions, save for the breathable air. As you know, the use of any drugs that produce smoke is highly illegal anywhere inside, so the upper floors of the Weston are a few of the only living spaces where people can smoke without fear of Network punishment. Because of this, most of the people who live on the upper floors are drug addicts, albeit addicts with money. The inhabitants are transient, often only living at the Weston until they burn through their money. When someone leaves, another person with money and the desire to escape their sorrow moves in."

"Sad," Northfield muttered.

"Very," Salb said. "The Network wouldn't suspect me to be in this building. I already downgraded to Heaven's Rebirth, and if I could pay rent here as well, I wouldn't have needed to move out in the first place. There isn't a reason for me to be around here." Salb coughed and cleared his throat again; although his health was improving, the constant talking couldn't have been helping his cough much.

"Still seems like a lot of trouble," Elena observed. "You couldn't have just brought the key with you?"

Salb glanced at her before looking down. "If I did, what would have stopped the Coalition from just stealing the key from me? I had more leverage by hiding the key off my person. At least," he added quietly, "that was my train of thought at the time."

Northfield said, "Nobody can fault you for being too cautious then, huh?"

Salb pulled out his forged ID. "We'll see how far my caution gets us. Assuming my ID holds up, still I don't know if I can get the three of you access to the upper floors. You'll just have to wait in the lobby."

"I don't like this plan," John interjected. "There's a lot of heat on you, Salb. Your picture is plastered everywhere. Everyone is on the alert for you. The last time you used your ID to hide the master key, you weren't wanted by the Network. But now . . ."

"You're right. There's a good chance the ID won't work," Elena said. "But if that happens, we'll figure something out. Given the creek we're rowing down right now, improvisation is inevitable."

John sighed. "What if the security officer you encountered last time already reported you to the Death Corps? As I said, your picture is everywhere."

"I doubt it," Salb said. "I grew out my facial hair as a disguise for my fake ID photo. I kept my gas mask on around the guard at the front desk, save for a few brief flashes to show him that my face matched the photo. He likely remembers my ID photo or my gas mask far better than my shaven face. He didn't scrutinize me too closely, anyway. Most security officers want Network inspectors out of their hair as soon as possible." He gently coughed before continuing. "The only pictures the Network has posted around of me are clean-cut, from their biannual photo days for our ID cards. I doubt the officer put two and two together and reported me."

"This is insane," John muttered. "Probably the furthest plan from easy or safe as possible."

"In the last ten years, has anything been easy or safe?" Elena asked.

They reached the front double doors of the Weston and clicked a buzzer on the right side of the doors. A haggard male voice crackled through the intercom. "Weston living spaces. What can I do for you?"

"This is Arnold Kaine," Salb said, holding his fake ID up to the camera above the double doors. "I'm the Network inspector from earlier this week. I'm here to conduct follow-up filtration purity tests."

"I remember you. More tests, really? And what's with the company?"

"Things are heating up between the Network and Yellowbacks out here," he said smoothly. "I paid for a couple Network mercs for protection. It's not safe out here, man. Don't worry, though. They can stay in the lobby. I just need my supplies from them."

Good thing Northfield had his backpack, which Salb could pretend had his testing apparatus inside. Hopefully the officer wouldn't ask to look inside the backpack.

While the presence of Northfield, Elena, and John might have increased Nathaniel Salb's conspicuousness, they still decided to accompany him. If anything went wrong, they didn't want him to be alone in the building.

The doors unlocked, and they hurried into the building. Northfield surveyed the Weston lobby. Blotches of brown and gray stained the white floors, and there was an unknown mossy, yellow material rising from cracks in the tiles. Dim fluorescent lights flickered sporadically, with a few bulbs threatening to fall out of their lamps. Red flecks of paint had fallen from the walls and lay on the tiles; if Northfield squinted, the flecks of paint resembled splatters of blood.

"Damn," he muttered to himself. "Can't there be a single nice building in this city?"

On the far wall of the room, between two elevators, an array of metal bars blocked a stairwell to the upper floors. A door in the center of the bars granted access. A red light hung on the ceiling directly above the metal bars, indicating that the door was locked.

In the far-left corner, a concrete and bulletproof glass contraption encased the admissions security officer, along with a chair, desk, and various supplies on and around the desk. The bulletproof glass window had a semicircle opening. A single heavy metal door served as the entrance into and exit out of the contraption.

Salb approached the security officer. The man had light-olive skin, a chiseled jaw, and spiky black hair. He drank from a yellowing coffee cup, which he set on the desk before he wiped his mouth. "ID please," he said, gesturing toward the opening.

Salb took off his gas mask and slipped his faux ID through. The security officer studied Salb's face and the face of Arnold Kaine on the card. His eyes moved up and down, alternating between the two faces. Northfield's skin crawled and tingled as the seconds passed by like a stick dragging through mud.

The officer's eyes drifted to Northfield's backpack, and Northfield was terrified he would ask to look inside. His fear abated only slightly when the officer's eyes moved back to Salb.

"You really have to check this building again?" the officer asked.

"I don't make my routes," Salb said. Northfield noticed the clamminess in Salb's hands, which he attributed more to anxiety than sickness. Despite Salb's nerves, his voice remained steady as he said, "I'll be in and out of your hair as soon as possible. I want to get home, you know?"

"Should I expect you tomorrow then? Or the day after that? This gonna be a weekly thing now?" the security officer asked, rubbing his jaw.

Why the hell is he being so snotty? Northfield thought, thankful his gas mask covered his expression. *I suppose it's normal to be annoyed, but God, he seems like he's stalling. Yeah, he definitely seems like he's stalling. Or is it just me? Maybe I'm becoming paranoid and I'm just freaking out.*

"You know I can't say," Salb said. "Look, you don't want trouble. I don't want trouble. Just give me access—"

He was cut off by a loud buzzing noise; someone was at the entrance to the Weston. The security guard glanced at a monitor inside the contraption, the screen of which they could not see. He unlocked the front doors. Curiously, or ominously, no verbal exchange occurred between the security officer and whoever wanted to be let in.

Maybe they're residents the security officer knows. But then again, everyone wears gas masks outside. He can't see anyone's faces. So unless whoever's here immediately held their IDs up to the camera, or he knows the type of gas mask and clothes the Weston inhabitants wear by heart . . .

The air rushed out of his chest like a sucker punch to the gut as he watched three Death Corps agents walk into the Weston lobby. Adrenaline coursed through his body and flooded his brain, and everything that followed seemed to happen simultaneously. The Death Corps soldiers recognized Salb immediately. One of them pointed at him, another began to raise his assault rifle, and the third pulled out a radio and started yelling into it, assumedly alerting other Death Corps soldiers of Salb's position. Northfield, Elena, and John aimed their weapons and fired, prioritizing the soldier aiming his rifle, then the soldier talking into the radio second, and finally the one pointing. Before Northfield had a chance to blink, the soldiers were sprawled out on the stained tiles, rivers of blood flowing from their bodies and seeping into the cracks.

Take care of them, God, he thought as he numbly knelt along with Elena and John by the bodies. *Give them more grace than any of us deserve.*

A voice crackled through the Death Corps soldier's radio, which now rested on the ground a half-foot away from its owner's body. "X1, reply. X1, reply. Gunshots heard on your end. Over." After a few moments of pause, the voice said, "Death Corps soldiers en route to your position. Over."

"Just stay the fuck where you are," the security officer screamed, brandishing a revolver behind his fortress of bulletproof glass and concrete. Luckily, Salb had the sense of mind during the commotion to move away from the semicircle opening, which prevented the security guard from having a clear line of fire on him.

Did the officer recognize Salb and alert the Death Corps? Usually, security officers had alarms in their kiosks; he probably had one under his desk. Or did he see the Death Corps buzzing to be let into the building and he did so as per the law? Did it really matter? No. All that mattered was that the Death Corps were coming.

"We need to get out of here," John urged them. "This whole thing just went belly up."

"The key is upstairs," Elena cried, emphasizing the last word. "We get it, and we get out of here."

"We'd get trapped up there when the Death Corps come. We have to leave. There's no other option," John commanded.

"The Network will wonder why we're here, why Salb's here," she said. "Pretty quick, someone will realize that the key's here. They'll tear this building apart piece by piece until they find it. There won't be another chance."

"If we go upstairs, the odds are almost zero that you survive, you understand?" John cried in frustration, his focus on Elena.

"Too many people have died to get this key," Salb said. "I'm willing to add my name to the list."

"Christ, if I could physically stop both of you, I would," John said through gritted teeth. He pointed at the door in front of the stairwell. "How are you even planning to get upstairs?"

"Stay the hell away from me," the security officer cried, angling himself away from the semicircle opening so bullets from the other side of the glass couldn't hit him.

I remember when you taught me a breathing technique. It was one you told your patients to calm them down, Northfield thought as he searched one of the fallen Death Corps soldiers. *Breathe in, count to five. Breathe out, count to five. In and out, in and out. Hell, even hearing you describe it to me was relaxing. I'm gonna try that now, Jess.*

He picked up a grenade from the body. Even through his gloves, the metal surface chilled his skin. Or maybe it was just his imagination. He approached the security officer's kiosk, his finger threateningly hooking the pin of the grenade.

"Maybe we can't shoot you from here," he said. "But this grenade will do the trick all the same. Let us upstairs."

The officer's eyes moved from the grenade to his face. Northfield's gas mask only covered the bottom half, leaving his eyes exposed. He could feel the chill of his own eyes touch his heart. "Okay, okay! Christ Almighty, I'll open the door."

An electric buzz reverberated through the room, and the red light above the door turned green. Northfield, Elena, Salb, and John hurried through and charged up the stairwell.

"Good thinking, Mark," Salb said as they ran.

"You wouldn't have done it, would you?" Elena asked. "Thrown the grenade?"

"No," he replied. "It was a bluff."

I promise, Jess. It was a bluff. I wouldn't have thrown the grenade. The guy was innocent, as far as we know. Please believe me, Jess. I need you to.

After sprinting up two stairs at a time, his lungs and legs screaming holy murder in protest, they stopped at the door to the fifteenth floor. On the journey up, they saw dozens of Weston inhabitants rush down the stairs; the security officer had probably called for an evacuation, and the sound of gunshots so close had likely induced the building's inhabitants to act with more than a little haste. Undoubtedly, most would be wondering why the four of them were heading up the stairs instead of down, with military-grade weaponry no less, but nobody stopped to inquire or engage them. Curiosity could kill the cat, indeed.

"This is the floor I hid the key on," Salb said between deep breaths and short, staggered coughs exacerbated by the strain on his lungs. "The first unfinished floor."

"We get the key, try to blend in with the people evacuating, and get out," Elena said, inhaling deeply afterward.

"Elena . . ." John started to say.

"I'm doing this, Dad," she said. "I'm doing it."

For a painful, brief, grinding, wasted moment, he said nothing. His hands wrung around his assault rifle even more intensely as he said, "You should breach the room with your rifle as Mark opens the door, and I'll follow from behind and watch our backs."

They followed John's advice, and they continued on.

The concrete pillars seemed to drip from the concrete ceiling, pooling to form the concrete floor. Twenty-by-twenty-foot sections of the ceiling were missing on the far-right side of the floor. Almost a quarter was missing in total. Ladders were propped up on the concrete edges of the missing sections, granting the inhabitants of the fifteenth floor access to the seventeenth floor and vice versa. Pallets of cinder blocks were scattered on the floor like oats in a gray vat of cereal.

Only five people besides Northfield, Elena, John, and Salb remained on the floor; the rest had already evacuated. Two of the floor's inhabitants rested against the pallets, their eyes glazed over, occupying some fantasy world concocted by whatever drugs they had taken. The other three inhabitants shared similar half-conscious expressions, although they simply lay on the floor.

None of them wore gas masks, reminding Northfield that the air at their current elevation was safe to breathe. Lord, how long had it been since he'd inhaled fresh, nonfiltered air? He debated taking off his mask but decided not to. If he needed to quickly descend and reenter the gas, he didn't want to fumble around putting it on. He noticed that Elena, John, and Salb had kept their masks on, as well; they either hadn't yet remembered that the air was safe or they had come to a similar conclusion as him.

"The key is hidden there," Salb said. He pointed to a pallet of cinder blocks directly in front of them. The concrete floor extended five feet past the pallet, at the end of which was an eight-story drop to the apartment complex behind the Weston.

They hurried to the pallet. While Salb tried to wedge the key out of it, Northfield stood on the ledge and stared at the city skyline. Dark clouds covered the sky, blotting out the sun like thick ink stains. Looking down, he saw a carriage designed for window washing four stories below them. Even on an unfinished building, the landlord found a nifty way to leech every last credit card from tenants. The carriage swung slowly back and forth, like a body on a noose. Alleyways scattered in panic from an apartment building located directly below the carriage. He was in the center of a labyrinth, and he half-expected the soggy breath of a minotaur to dampen the back of his neck at any moment.

"Got it," Salb exclaimed, holding up the master key. Northfield stared at it for a moment, dumbfounded by how pedestrian it looked. Aside from the faint neon-green bar running along its length, it was just a normal golden key. For all their struggles, for all the chaos they had endured to find the key, he expected something more.

It's a key, he thought. *What the hell was I expecting, exactly? Probably more high-tech than my meager brain can imagine, too.*

Gunfire roared.

The sound came from the barrel of John's gun, and a flurry of gunshots crackled from the stairwell in response. Northfield heard him yell; he was probably warning them of danger, but the surrounding chaos was too overwhelming for Northfield to make out his words. Bullets smashed cinder blocks, cracking them and causing large puffs of smoke to materialize in the aftermath. Bullets penetrated and rico-cheted off steel girders, resulting in large reverberations as the metal cried in pain. The battle started too suddenly for Northfield to sense how many soldiers were firing at them.

Determining if the number was two or one hundred could wait; all that mattered was getting behind cover. His nearest refuge was the cinder block pallet where the master key had been hidden. However, he figured that the four of them couldn't safely hide behind one pallet, so he lowered his head and sprinted to the nearest concrete support beam, which was to his left and ten feet nearer to the stairwell.

Out of the corner of his eye, he could make out blobs of black near the stairwell, presumably Death Corps soldiers firing at them. Because he was running, he still couldn't make out exactly how many soldiers there were, but he now had a better idea. Four or five, or at least some-where in that ballpark.

I could live with a couple more than that, if I needed to. But please, God, don't let there be an exo.

Even with the thermite bullets the Yellowbacks had given him, he didn't even want to picture one of those behemoths thundering toward him. Who knew how much range the bullets had, anyway? Maybe they fizzled out eventually.

Once he reached the support beam, he pushed his back against it. He clenched the grip and foregrip of his submachine gun tightly, brac-ing as bullets ripped pieces of concrete off the support beam. Shards hurtled through the air with enough velocity to fly off the building and plummet to the apartment complex.

As he gritted his teeth, squinted, and endured the chaos, he couldn't shake a strange numbness. While fear and adrenaline should have been coursing through his system and sending his brain into a frenzy, a hollowness materialized in the pit of his stomach and spread to the rest of his body like a virus. The hollowness manifested into an out-of-body experience, and he felt like he was watching his body from afar.

What a shitshow this has turned into. What an unequivocal mess, he thought dismally as he hoped a ricocheting bullet wouldn't hit him in the midsection.

Okay, focus, Northfield. Focus on the facts. It's only been a couple of minutes since the Death Corps called in reinforcements in the lobby. Not enough time for full-fledged reinforcements to arrive. These guys shooting at us are probably a random group of Death Corps nearby that caught wind of what was happening. We take these guys out, maybe we have a chance before the big guns arrive. Maybe.

The gunfire stopped, leaving an ominous silence that couldn't possibly be construed as anything but the lull before another storm. *They're either reloading or repositioning.* Regardless of what caused the break in gunfire, he capitalized on the situation by checking on Elena, Salb, and John; he wanted to make sure they were okay, and he also wanted to formulate some sort of game plan, if possible. He looked back at the cinder pallet that the master key had been hidden under.

Elena peeked over the top of the panel while Salb glanced around the side; gunfire from the Death Corps abruptly returned, forcing them back behind cover.

He turned his head left thirty degrees and saw John behind a similar concrete support beam equidistant from the pallet as Northfield. They eyed one another, and he could tell that they had the same thought. *Gotta take care of this now, before reinforcements arrive, if they haven't already. The safe, cautious route won't work here. Sometimes you gotta be reckless.*

He poked his head around the corner and quickly pulled back as gunfire tore more shards off the support column. He recalled the brief image he saw, and he formulated a plan. *They moved up, alright. Their rifles are propped up on cover, and they're just itching for us to pop out. One of the soldiers is behind a cinder pallet, and another's behind a pile of steel girders five yards behind the pallet. Two more are farther back, both behind cinder pallets and girders. There's a cinder pallet ten feet in front of this column. I pop around cover and dive behind that as John provides suppressive fire.*

Not possessing the luxury of time to assess his plan, much less come up with another one, he tried to signal to John what he was thinking, as the others were still behind the cinder pallet. He wasn't sure if John understood, and even if he did, he wasn't sure if Elena and Salb would catch on when they returned fire. *Either way, the choices here aren't exactly bountiful. Gotta just go for it and pray I don't get turned into bloody swiss cheese.*

Aw, screw it. Go!

He braced himself and charged around the column, beelining to the cinder pallet while discharging rounds from his submachine gun at the nearest Death Corps soldier. It felt like a physical cloud of death was passing him as bullets whizzed past his body, the grim reaper taking swings with his scythe but missing him each time.

After what felt simultaneously like two eternities and less than half a second, he dove behind the pallet. Taking a moment to collect himself, he realized that bullets were flying toward the Death Corps soldiers. John had evidently understood his signal and provided suppressive fire, which probably explained in part why he hadn't been shot to oblivion. That, and luck. *Or you, Big Man. I'm too high on adrenaline to tell what the official score is between us with this grudge match, so let's just call this an even start, okay?*

John stopped firing to reload, and Northfield sprung up to take some shots. The Death Corps soldier nearest to him popped over his pallet at the same time, and both aimed their weapons at each other. Northfield was the first to the trigger; bullets left his Vector and struck the soldier in the shoulder and forehead. He ducked again to avoid incoming fire from the soldier behind the steel girders, and John sprayed more bullets in the soldier's direction, this time joined by Elena and Salb.

As they suppressed the soldier, Northfield fired at the two Death Corps soldiers farther back to keep them at bay. He hid when two more retorted with gunfire, and Elena and Salb fired at them to keep the pressure on.

John stopped shooting to reload. The soldier he had been suppressing detected that the gunfire had abated, and he took aim. Northfield pumped rounds into him, continuing to fire until he saw the soldier's blood stain a concrete support beam behind him. Crouching, double-checking that his body was well covered, he reloaded his submachine gun and gestured to Elena, John, and Salb, hoping they understood.

At the sound of cover fire from his allies, he ran around the pallet, wary of bullets flying at him from the remaining Death Corps soldiers. He vaulted over the pallet that the soldier he'd just shot had been using for cover, and he hid behind the blood-stained concrete support beam. He waited a few seconds, then peeked around the support beam, just in time to see a bullet fired by Elena tear through the chest of a Death Corps soldier who had popped out from behind a pile of steel girders.

That means there's one more of them, I think, he thought, shrinking back behind cover. *I think there were four, right? I only saw four of them firing. That means, unless the Death Corps started hiring ninjas, there's only one guy left behind a pallet.*

He peeked around the corner again. He could only watch as the final black-clad Death Corps soldier shot at Elena and Salb, hitting one of them. He heard a loud cry, so sharp that he could already picture the blood flowing from the bullet wound. He bared his teeth as he fired at the soldier and forced him behind the pallet.

The scream echoed in his brain, an ambiguous enough sound that either Elena or Salb could have been hit. Falling behind cover, he searched for Elena and Salb. He could only see the bloodied pallet.

Gotta finish this quick, he thought. *Reinforcements might already be here. Too many for us to fight, especially with one of us wounded. Or worse.*

Don't think of that. Don't think of that. Just finish this, Northfield.

He waited until he heard a burst of fire from John. He let out a small grunt to flush out his fear, then sprang out from behind the support column and sprinted toward the enemy. He centered his holographic sight on the top of the pallet, where the soldier would most likely show himself; his Vector was set to fully automatic. Once the Death Corps soldier peeked up, Northfield pulled the trigger and held it until his magazine was expended. He wasn't sure how many bullets hit the soldier, but it was enough to send him to the ground. Permanently. Northfield slid to a halt, breathing heavily from a potent mix of exertion and adrenaline.

He called out, "Clear!"

"Clear!" John called back.

The question weighing on Northfield's mind was answered when Elena called out, "Clear!"

Northfield thought that knowing who was wounded would somehow relieve him, but he didn't feel any damned better. They ran to the bloodied pallet that Elena and Salb were behind. Along the way, Northfield's eyes darted left and right, scanning the bodies of the drugged-out Weston inhabitants. Amazingly, none of them were hit by bullets, but the dead, absent looks in their eyes as they rolled back and forth would indicate otherwise. *Normally, I'd pity them,* he thought, *but man, right now I wish I was them. What horror am I gonna see behind that pallet? What new image am I about to see that's gonna be the new face of my nightmares?*

Northfield absorbed the scene before him. John, on his knee, stared at the blood that pooled around Salb. Elena, also kneeling, pressed her hands on a stomach wound only half successfully; blood trickled between her fingers. She dressed the wound with cloth torn off of Salb's clothes and did what she could to stop the bleeding, but without a first aid kit, there was little more she could do.

"Salb . . ." Northfield gasped, his gaze moving to Salb's pale, sweaty face. His gas mask was resting against a cinder block; he or Elena must have removed it to make breathing easier.

Salb groaned softly in pain and released a cough that sent a trickle of blood down his chin. After noticing Northfield, he grinned dismally and said, "I suppose we couldn't all last, could we?"

"Don't say that," he replied, taking a knee by him. He fished through his backpack and pulled out a first aid kit. "We're gonna fix you up, alright?"

"I don't think the bullet hit anything vital, but I'm not sure," Elena said.

"Did you check to see if there's an exit wound?" John asked.

She nodded and said, "There's an exit wound. The bullet went straight through both the front and back armor."

"An exit wound is good," John said, holding Salb's hand tightly for support. "Means the bullet went in and out instead of ricocheting around your insides or fragmenting. TAP bullets go through heavy armor on entry, but not always on exit. This is good news."

"See?" Northfield said, pulling out antibiotic wipes and gauze from the first aid kit. "You're gonna make it out of this. This is just gonna be a cool scar that you can show the ladies in a couple of months."

"Never been much of a ladies' man," he said, pausing as a grimace tore across his face like a streak of lightning. "My studies kept me away."

"Well, this badass scar might change that," he replied. "Consider it incentive for you to pull through for us, alright? Now, sorry, this might hurt."

After removing Elena's improvised dressing, he disinfected Salb's wound as well as he could with the antibiotic wipe. His efforts elicited another pained groan, and he started working to stop the bleeding.

As he did so, John looked around and said, "How are we going to get out of here? We can't stay here."

Elena's shoulders rose and fell with a labored sluggishness, moving through the thick, viscous dread in the air. "I'm not sure. We try taking the stairs, it's going to take a while with Salb, and I'd bet my right arm that the Death Corps will be waiting for us by the time we reach the lobby. Fighting our way out is the only option I see, but I don't like those odds."

"I don't even consider those odds at all," John said, his teeth gritting hard enough behind his mask to reduce granite to powder. "If we go that route, there will be more than we can handle and probably more exos. We don't stand a chance."

"There's another way," Northfield said after he finished applying gauze.

"Yeah? Like what?" John asked.

"There's a window-washing carriage on the side of this building. I've still got my grappling hook. We descend the carriage's supporting ropes. Then we can use the grappling hook on the carriage to reach the apartment complex."

"We'd have enough trouble just getting Salb down the stairs. How would we—" John started to say but was cut off by Salb's intense coughs, which stemmed from either his sickness or injury; Northfield couldn't tell.

"We fasten his arms to me using the straps of my backpack. Not the comfiest for either of us, but it'll work, I think, as long as we tie the straps well."

"It'll take at least as long to get down as the stairs, if not longer," Elena said. "How would that—"

"It might take longer, yeah. But the thing is, by the time we make it down the stairs with Salb, the Death Corps would be waiting for us in the lobby, but it'll take longer before they reach us up here. Think of the situation from their perspective. We took out their last batch of guys on this floor, sure, but they're smart enough to know that we're gonna try to escape the building."

Elena nodded and said, "They'll be expecting us to head down the stairs while they're heading up, and they'll have to be prepared for the possibility of us hiding on any floor or point in the stairwell to either jump them or hide from them. That means they have to ascend more carefully, and more carefully means slower."

Northfield concluded with haste, "And even though they might have the ground floor of the Weston secured before we can escape, it'll take longer for them to fully secure all possible exits through the cluttered maze of alleyways. We take random alleyways, lose the Death Corps, make it back to our truck, and get out of here."

"I like it," she said.

John muttered, "Better than anything I can think of right now."

Northfield asked Salb, "You okay with this plan? This isn't gonna be fun for you."

"If I wanted a fun time, I wouldn't be here," Salb said. He cracked a grin, which contrasted with his watery eyes.

Northfield's stomach churned.

"Yeah, well, I guess that's true," he said. He stood up and approached the ropes supporting the carriage. He grabbed onto one and pulled hard twice; he bet that the rope could hold both his and Salb's weight.

If not, there's worse ways to go out than falling, I guess.

"Can you stand?" Elena asked Salb.

"Yes," he said. He pressed his palms against the ground and tried to stand, but he grunted loudly and fell to his butt. "Maybe with some help," he added quietly.

Elena assisted him to his feet; his legs shook as she used the straps of Northfield's backpack to fasten his arms around Northfield. After making sure her knot was secure, she helped him put on his gas mask.

"Just hold on," Northfield said to his passenger. "I'll try to make this go as fast as possible." He said to John and Elena, "Probably best if one of you watches the stairwell and the other watches us as we climb down. If something looks like it's about to give, warn us. Maybe we can brace and get lucky enough to land on the carriage."

They nodded in agreement. Northfield approached the ledge, essentially carrying Salb, whose feet dragged on the floor. When Salb coughed, he could feel the vibration on his back.

Northfield grabbed the support rope tightly. He descended the side of the building, his feet walking down the wall. Immediately, he regretted not spending more time doing pull-ups. Pain escaped both men's lips in exasperated grunts.

"Not exactly a day at the spa, huh?" he said, attempting to inject some levity into the situation.

"No," Salb replied faintly.

God, he's sounding worse by the second.

"Just hold tight, buddy. Just hold tight, and I'll take care of the rest. Close your eyes, and this'll be over soon."

"Mark?"

"Yeah?"

"I think I'm bleeding through—"

"What?" he cried, snapping his head around to look at Salb. Out of the corner of his eye, he saw drops of blood splashing onto the black window-washing carriage below, creating a twisted checkerboard pattern. *If he's bleeding that much through the gauze already, this could be worse than we thought.*

Despite his distress, he said with as much confidence as he could muster, "Once we reach the carriage, I'll patch you up again and you'll be good to go, okay?"

"I don't think that's going . . . going to do much . . ." Salb said with a weak cough that made him sound like he was choking on feathers. Each word was a monumental struggle to formulate and utter.

Salb was fading. Fast.

"Hey, don't think like that. We gotta stay positive. There's so much shit against us that staying positive is the only thing we've got right now."

"Guess that positivity is hard . . . for me to see at the moment," he said, inhaling sharply. He paused to regain his strength and asked, "You believe in God, then?"

"Yeah, I'm Lutheran," Northfield said, ramming his teeth together to combat the rings of fire traveling up his overworked arms. "But God and I aren't exactly on steady terms. Haven't been for a while."

"I never believed in karma, but . . . been on my mind more and more lately," he said, breathing raggedly. "All those people dying for me . . . or because of me . . ."

"There's darkness dogging me for what I've done. Trust me," he said. "But we're gonna make things right. I believe that. I've gotta believe that." He looked over his shoulder again. The carriage was ten feet away. "Just a little longer. We're three-quarters of the way there. You're doing great, man."

He felt the fiddling of fingers on his chest; it took him a second to realize that Salb was trying to untie himself. He cried out, "Hey, what are you—"

"Half of me is in the grave, Mark," he said. "I won't take you, Elena, and John with me. Nobody else is dying for me. Not one more."

"Damn it, Nathaniel, don't!" he urged with everything in him, but he was powerless. His arms were too exhausted. If he took even a few moments and devoted one of his hands to stopping Salb from unfastening himself, he'd lose his grip on the rope, and they'd both fall. Even if they landed on the carriage and the ten-foot fall didn't seriously hurt him, he'd land on Salb, killing him all the same, given the severity of his injury.

"Finish the mission, Mark," he said with a resurgence of strength and steadiness. Northfield felt the master key slip into one of his pockets. Salb had conviction. Damn him.

"Please, don't do this," he begged, but it was too late. Salb had unlatched himself and pushed away from the building with what strength he still possessed.

He fell.

"No!" Northfield cried as he reached his right hand back to try catching Salb. His hand grabbed onto nothing but air, and his left hand almost let go of the rope from fatigue. In his heart, he knew that his effort was futile. Still, his hand remained outstretched.

His tongue felt thick and his mouth felt numb as Salb's back hit the railing of the carriage with a sickening *crack*. Salb rolled off the railing and continued plummeting. His body became more and more tinted with orange and yellow as he fell; the gas pulled his body down and swallowed him at the same time.

But the gas didn't consume him completely. Northfield watched Salb strike the roof of the apartment complex.

No, no, no, no, no, he frantically cried, unconsciously climbing down the rope until he reached the carriage. He stood on it and gripped the railing so tightly that the skin on his knuckles almost ripped. *No*, he kept repeating to himself, although he was certain that Salb was dead. He'd seen too many people die to not know.

You didn't have to, Salb. Damn it, you didn't have to. I wasn't going to give up on you. I would've tried to save you until both of our dying breaths.

He tore his gaze away from the body and looked up; Elena and John were now climbing down the rope. Without either of them having to support the weight of two people, they'd reach the carriage in seconds. Did they see? Did they hear? He didn't know, but his mouth felt like it had been injected with tar; he couldn't bring himself to say anything. But damn it, what was he supposed to say, exactly? How could he explain that Salb had just let himself die? He was still piecing what happened together in his own head, replaying his actions and trying to figure out what he could have done differently. What had he screwed up? Could he have saved Salb somehow?

I can't even count the number of people I've lost in my life. To say I'm an old hand at dealing with death is an understatement. But damn it, why does it still hurt like a bitch?

Elena, followed by John, landed on the carriage with a small *thud*. He couldn't see her face, but from her body language, he could tell that she was shaken. "My God, Mark. What happened?" She looked over the railing, gripping it as tightly as him. "My God, what happened?"

He tried to scrape together a coherent sentence, but his fatigued mind failed him, and the words came out funny and wrong. "He untied himself . . . I couldn't stop him. He just . . . He just fell."

"Oh, hell," she said, her voice distant. "So . . . you mean he . . . he did it on purpose?"

John held his hand out to Northfield and said, "Grappling hook."

He mechanically handed John the grappling hook and rope coil. John fastened the hook on the railing and threw the coil of rope over the edge. As it descended and unraveled, Elena stared at him, her head slightly cocked.

John said softly, "I don't like thinking about what's happened, either. But how many times have we watched family and friends die? We're used to this." Although John managed to keep his voice level, his hands clenched onto the railing and twisted back and forth like when his hands twisted around the barrel of his gun. "If Salb did this on purpose, this is what he wants. He didn't want to slow us down. And if we sit here and mourn him, we're slowing down, aren't we? We get the key, we get out of here. That's what he would want."

"He slipped the key in my pocket," Northfield said numbly.

John said, "Nathaniel gave his life to let us escape, Elena. And, by God, I'm going to make sure you do."

"Damn it. Damn everything to hell. Let's go," she said. "For Salb."

They descended the rope. The right side of the roof had a fire escape stairwell leading down to the spiderweb of alleyways.

Just a few feet in front of them, Salb's body lay face-down, soaked in a pool of blood. Northfield's tired legs and arms stop moving as he stared into the red, the gore sucking his own marrow dry. *I'm praying for you, man. I'm praying that you're up there with her. I know she'll give you a warm welcome.*

When he looked up, he saw Elena standing next to him, paying her own respects. John took a moment to honor Salb as well; the nervous twitch in his hands was even more pronounced than before. Moments later, Elena and John rushed to the stairwell.

Northfield took one final look at Salb's body. He briefly considered picking him up before remembering Salb's request: "Finish the mission, Mark." *The man died for us, and I can't even give him a proper burial. He's just gonna rot here or in whatever place the Network disposes of him. Damn this world.*

"I'm sorry, Nathaniel," he whispered, turning away. He ran to meet Elena and John at the fire escape. They bounded down, reaching the spiderweb maze of alleyways. At the end of the alleyway, a group of three Death Corps soldiers spotted them and fired their weapons. Without hesitation, John sprinted into an intersecting alleyway with Elena and Northfield following.

They navigated through the maze. To Northfield, the turns they took seemed random. Eventually, he lost all bearing on where they were. Evidently, so did the Death Corps soldiers; the gunfire nipping at their heels and grazing past their shoulders had ceased. Yet with every new turn, he wondered if a group of soldiers would be waiting for them, their weapons raised and fingers on triggers.

They broke out of the maze of alleyways; his lungs burned like they'd been roasting in an incinerator for the past hour. John and Elena were exhausted, too; their hands rested on their knees as they sucked in air.

John pointed and said through labored breaths, "Our car's a couple blocks from here. We'll be heading toward it from a different direction than we went to the Weston. Hopefully the Death Corps won't spot us on the way."

"We head to Geralt's hideout," Elena said. "Convince him to help us, then set off Zeus's Mercy."

"Sounds great and all," Northfield said, "but what plan of ours hasn't gone ass up so far? We just lost Salb. My God, we lost him."

"You're right. This sucks," she said. "But Salb wanted this city free, too, and I'm going to honor his wish. He deserves that much for what he's done."

"We have to keep moving," John said, his hand fiddling with the grip of his gun. "Not safe to stay here."

When they reached their car, Elena put her hand on Northfield's shoulder. She said, "Don't be strong in spite of him. Be strong for him. Keep moving."

"Yeah," he replied before saying, more softly, "I've held enough dying people close to keep moving. But that fact just makes me even more tired of it all."

They got into the vehicle, and without a moment's pause, they sped away from the Weston. As Northfield looked at Elena and John from the back seat, he thought, *What kind of world is this where people can just watch their friends die around them and not stop? Is it strength that we've all built up over the years or apathy? Are we just losing ourselves?*

God, I told you earlier to guide me and that I'd take care of the rest. I think I was wrong. I just don't know if there's enough of me still here to keep my end of the deal. I pray, please put the muscles back on my bones and will me to use them.

After a couple of minutes in the car, John inhaled softly and said, "I've done you wrong."

"Done me wrong?" Elena asked. "What do you mean?"

"Half-measures," he replied. "I've been taking half measures. I've been holding you back, and I've been putting you in danger by doing so. You volunteered for this mission, and I used my military knowledge to take control of the mission when you should've been the leader all along."

"Dad, that's crazy," she said. "With all your experience, I don't see why you wouldn't—"

"You have passion for the mission," he said. "You have the drive. I just want you safe. For all my experience, my goal isn't yours. Why am I leading when my eye isn't on the ball? I can't do what I need while doing what you need. I could've—I should've—just been at your side, helping with advice and protecting you. That way, we'd both be focused on our goals." He shook his head slowly, weighed down by every what-if. "I gave up the Coalition so quick to save you, Elena. If I held out just a couple more seconds, just delayed a little bit until the Yellowbacks arrived, both you and the Coalition would be safe. Hell, there's a good chance Salb would still be alive if you were in charge. Instead, now you're in even more danger. There are only three of us, and you're still going at this mission. Stopping you is impossible. I know that."

"Dad, that's ridiculous. Guilt is talking here."

"No, Elena," he said. "This is your mission. You lead it. I'm still here, like always. But you're safer this way."

"Dad," Elena started to say, but she stopped to look over at him. His entire body relaxed with a cathartic release, as if ropes that had been pulling his limbs in opposite directions had finally slackened. She lowered her head. "Okay. Okay."

CHAPTER 15

They managed to remain undetected by the Death Corps, and they reached the Kelley Apartments without trouble. Aside from the constant grind of tires rolling over poorly kept roads, the drive was silent.

While John parallel parked, Elena gripped the handle to her door tightly.

"Still don't know what we should say to him," she muttered. "This whole drive I've been thinking, and nothing. Nothing. Thought we'd have Nathaniel convince him, but now . . . Damn it. Now that we're here without him, I have no idea what we should say."

John put his hand on her shoulder and said, "If anyone can convince him, Elena, it's you. I believe that."

With some levity, she said, "Maybe I won't need to. You could always argue like a sonofabitch."

"Don't kid yourself. When it comes to arguing, you've always outpaced me."

"Yeah, well, maybe we can browbeat him together," she said, letting out a deep sigh. She turned to Northfield and asked, "You ready?"

"Ready as I'll ever be, I think."

She nodded and said, "Then might as well go and do this."

They got out of the truck and stepped onto the sidewalk. Northfield surveyed the Kelley Apartments, which comprised two brick buildings. Each was five stories tall, and they were connected at the base by a shared lobby. A copious amount of bright-green overgrowth wrapped around them, but other than the vegetation, nothing about the two buildings really stood out. *Probably why Geralt Salb picked the place for a hideout.*

They walked to the front door. Elena clicked the intercom and said into it, "My name is Elena. Their names are John and Mark, and we're Nathaniel Salb's escorts. We need to see Geralt Salb. The codeword is 'python.'"

There was a long pause as the security officer in the lobby examined them.

Northfield saw no reason for the guard not to let them in. The possibility that he, Elena, and John were Death Corps soldiers was highly unlikely. They weren't wearing Death Corps uniforms. The Death Corps would have also arrived in a larger number, ready to employ brute force. Stealth wasn't their style, especially not where the Yellowbacks were concerned.

A woman answered on the other end of the intercom. "Where is Nathaniel Salb?"

Elena lowered her head, presumably grimacing behind her gas mask. "He isn't here. It's urgent we talk to Geralt Salb. You can ask him to confirm who we are, if you need."

After another pause, the door emitted a loud buzz; Elena opened it and entered the building, followed by Northfield and John.

The lobby was drab. The walls were a dull brown with large flecks of paint torn off, revealing stained white beneath. They resembled a senile cow that had waded into a pool of piss. Four inoperable elevators, two pairs of two, were located on the left and right sides of the far wall, each pair corresponding to one of the apartment buildings connected by the lobby. In the far left and right corners of the lobby, doors led to staircases.

A kiosk stood between the elevators and stairs. Inside sat the security officer who had unlocked the front door. Two armed men stood on either side of the door leading to the left-hand staircase. Presumably, they were "associates" of Salb.

Elena, John, and Northfield took off their gas masks, and the security officer in the kiosk studied them, likely to ensure that they matched a physical description given to her by Geralt Salb. Without a word, she nodded at them, and they walked to the armed men. The one on the left beckoned them to follow.

They obeyed. The Yellowbacks went up the stairs and entered a hallway on the third floor. Red-striped wallpaper connected the doors like chains.

The hair on the back of Northfield's neck rose. For a split second, he thought the red stripes were constricting, forming a prison to entrap him. *Calm the hell down,* he thought. *What's next? Are the walls gonna start talking? I already have enough conversations in my head. I don't need more spirits to talk to.*

The Yellowbacks stopped in the middle of the hallway. One opened a door on the left and said, "He's in here."

Elena, John, and Northfield entered the apartment. The Yellowbacks remained outside, swiftly shutting the door behind them. A short hallway led to a living room. Doors on either side of the living room presumably led to bathrooms or bedrooms. Ragged blinds partially concealed two door-sized windows on the far end. Faint light from the overcast sky came through the holes and tears in the blinds, partially illuminating a couch pressed against the windows. A set of two chairs faced the couch, and a cracked coffee table was in the center.

Geralt Salb sat on the couch, staring at them as they approached.

He squinted, and his lips morphed into a scowl. He said, "What the fuck happened to him?"

Elena said gently, "Geralt . . ."

"He's dead, isn't he?" he said, rage threatening to break out of every word. "Don't sugarcoat it. He's dead, isn't he?"

Silence ripped through the room like grenade shrapnel. Northfield's hands were clammy. Nathaniel Salb's death was still fresh, and the thought of telling a family member about him made his throat constrict sharply, like a dog's jaw was clamping onto it. Although his tongue was entrapped in lead, he knew that he should give Geralt Salb a verbal answer, but he just couldn't.

"Yes," John said softly yet unequivocally.

"The fuck is wrong with me?" Geralt muttered. "Letting him go like that. Should've made him stay with me with handcuffs if that's what it took." He stared up at them, his barely concealed anger bubbling up from his scowl and showing through his eyes. "You were his escorts. You failed him, too."

A knife stabbed into Northfield's chest, twisting as he recalled Salb unfastening himself. He pleaded, he begged, but Salb still just . . . *I'm sorry, Salb. I should have figured something out. I should have thought of a way out, a way to save you, a way where you didn't feel like you had to give your life for us.*

"I'm sorry for your loss, Geralt," John said. "I truly am. In this world, we all know what losing loved ones is like. I'm sorry you had to experience that pain again."

"He was my last. The only one I had left," Geralt said. "And you know the damnedest thing? It hurts like a bitch, but I'm not shocked. I'm not dazed. I'm not reeling. You can't lose people ten, twenty times and have it shock you. At that point, you're either weak or fucking stupid."

Northfield couldn't tell if Geralt was sincere, if the shock hadn't hit him yet, or if he was good at concealing his horror. As the leader of a ruthless group like the Yellowbacks, he probably had a lot of experience hiding any signs of weakness a potential competitor could take advantage of. If he was faking, he sure was convincing.

"So what are you here for?" Geralt continued. The bubbling in his eyes faded as he tempered his rage. "I know you're not here just to deliver the news. What do you want?"

"To fulfill your brother's dying wish," Elena said. "He wanted us to detonate Zeus's Mercy. We can set it off. We have the master key. But just the three of us can't breach the South Network Facility. We need your help."

"And my Yellowbacks," he added. After a pause, he repeated, "Just the three of us? Your Coalition was wiped out, wasn't it?"

"We've been kicked down today," she said quietly. "But if we quit now, all of those deaths are going to be pointless."

He pondered for a moment. "Was this really Nate's dying wish?"

"Finish the mission," Northfield added. His words were hushed; he could still feel Nathaniel Salb on his back. "That's what he told me. 'Finish the mission.'"

Geralt Salb leaned forward and pressed his fingers together. "As of this morning, the Network and Yellowbacks are at war. Directly fighting them is suicide for us. We'd hurt them bad—even they know it. But in the end, we'd still lose. Getting out of the city, attacking their supply lines: that's how we were gonna fight them. To fight a giant, you pile on small indirect slashes to the ankles when it's not looking. You don't square up and try to stab it in the chest. Even one assault on a Network facility could result in heavy losses. 'Finish the mission,' he said. You never made things easy for me, did you, Nate?" He exhaled deeply, whispering, "But damn it, if this is your final wish . . ." He looked at them and said, "Convince me to help you. Convince me that it's worth it. I owe him listening to you, at least."

"In this war, you're not planning on taking out the Network, are you? They're too strong. At the end of the war, the Network will stay in power. So what's your goal?" she asked.

"You're right," he said. "We're not planning to overthrow them, just force them to back down first. Make them give us a more favorable peace treaty than the one they just breached."

"If you help us detonate Zeus's Mercy, you might be able to set your ambitions higher," she said. "Once the device is detonated and the city is free from the gas, things will change. Word will get around that the Network had the capability to get rid of the gas yet they refused to. People won't be happy. Wouldn't surprise me if a revolution started. At the very least, things will destabilize, a situation that your Yellowbacks can take advantage of."

Salb shook his head, saying, "True, but things are gonna destabilize for everyone, not just the Network. People hate us, too, and they have good reason. We're the assholes. The thieves. The extorters. If the people of Cumulus kick the Network to the curb, they're not just gonna welcome us in. I'd bet my left asshole they're not."

"What if the Yellowbacks get credit for setting off the device?" she countered. "You could be the force that liberated the city. You'll be the force that saved the people of Cumulus from the apocalypse. You'll be the heroes in this story. Circumstances can change in your favor."

"Maybe," he said. "But we've done a lot of bad shit over the years. Given, so has everyone else on this trash heap of a planet. There aren't many good people no more, not that I've fucking seen. But we've got a uniform and look that people can blame all their crap on. People don't forget so easily." He thought for a moment, then added, "Of course, I doubt you all want the Yellowbacks in power. You view me as the lesser of two evils. I'm an evil that can help you save the city and achieve a greater good. Past that, well, I'm not exactly good anymore."

"I'm entirely focused on detonating Zeus's Mercy," Elena said. "Whatever happens after that happens. If I accomplish my goal and manage to live through it, that's when I'll worry about who or what is in power. Either way, I'm banking on most people being better off without the gas."

Northfield looked at John; his expression was mostly neutral, but Northfield could tell that John's teeth were clenched by the tightness in his cheeks.

We've all done the risk assessment. He knows that Elena understands what she's getting into, but it must still suck to be him.

Come to think of it, my life's not a party, either. It's because I didn't buy any of those timeshares, isn't it, Jess? When the bombs hit, we could've been in Cancun. Life would still be anything but easy, but at least we'd be on a beach.

"You're asking for a lot," Geralt Salb said. "And I might not even get anything down the line. The Yellowbacks could benefit in a big way, gaining some or all of the influence that the Network has now. Or we could get fucked in the end, and a ton of my people could die just for us to lose out on what we have."

"We know the lives of your men are important. We don't plan on taking them for granted," Elena said.

Geralt pressed hard on his temples and rubbed them. "There isn't just the Death Corps at the South Network Facility I need to worry about. If we attack, soldiers from their other facilities are gonna swarm like horny honeybees. A fucking lot of them."

"Our plan is to detonate Zeus's Mercy before reinforcements arrive," she said. "I'm sure you're aware of the average Network response time. They can get a squad of four to six soldiers anywhere in pretty short order, but to amass a force equipped to reinforce or re-take a Network facility from a large-scale attack takes longer. From the nearest facility to the South Network Facility, it'll take twenty min-utes for proper reinforcements to gear up and arrive. We're not trying to take the facility, just detonate the device and get out. If we're not out by eighteen minutes, have your men withdraw."

"Either way, the South Network Facility is heavily fortified. I'm still gonna have some casualties." His brow furrowed, and he repeated, "Just eighteen minutes?"

"Just eighteen," she said. "With whatever Yellowbacks you can spare, we'll have most of them put on a show at the north entrance. Make it look like a massive force is attacking from that direction, enough to overwhelm the Death Corps and require all their resources to defend. They'll pull most of the facility's forces toward you. Once the Death Corps are distracted, we'll infiltrate from the south entrance with the remaining Yellowbacks."

"That second job will be dangerous," Geralt muttered.

"Yes," Elena said. "We only need a small number of Yellowbacks to help us. Speed is paramount to make our eighteen-minute mark. We just need enough Yellowbacks to push through whatever defenses we'll run into."

Salb didn't speak for a couple of moments. Then he said, "I'm guessing you'll need supplies." Before she responded, Salb shook his head and added, "Supplies aren't my big concern. I don't give a rat's ass about using some supplies when my people's lives are in danger. If I pull the lever, I'm gonna pull it all the way." Another pause be-fore he said, "I'm still not happy about the thought of losing some of my people."

"I know," Elena said empathetically. "As I said, we don't take their lives lightly. But here's something to consider. You're already in a war with the Network. Yellowback lives are in danger until the war ends either way. You just have to determine if this is a battle worth fighting, if this will deal a big enough blow to the Network to be worth the cost."

Salb said after thinking for a moment, "It would deal a blow to them, alright. Still, some questions bother me. How do you know Zeus's Mercy is still operable?"

"The Network put too much time and resources into the project to scrap it in just a couple days. It would allot the Death Corps time to find the key first," she said. "The Death Corps still don't have the key Salb stole, sure. But after what they did to the Coalition this morning, they're in no rush to destroy Zeus's Mercy. There is a chance they suspect that you have the key, because they now know of your relation to Nathaniel. Still, I bet the Network hasn't dismantled the device. It's aware of the fact that detonating Zeus's Mercy was the Coalition's aim, not yours."

Hints of pain and shock appeared on her face when she mentioned Nathaniel and the Coalition. After a pause to compose herself, she continued. "Like you said, the Yellowbacks don't have a chance of winning the war. If the Network thinks you have the key, it would never expect you to attack the facility. You know how much the Network despises the Yellowbacks, how cowardly and cockroach-like it thinks you are. The thought of you avenging your brother by fighting head-on is laughable to them. Guerilla warfare tactics outside of the city, and then using the key as leverage to get better peace terms, that's what the organization expects. Kayden Knox and the Network heads may be in talks about whether or not the investment in Zeus's Mercy is worth that leverage and whether to dismantle the device, but they won't throw away their invested resources so soon, not while the bodies of the Coalition are still fresh." She gritted her teeth, sparks in her brown eyes glowing in stubborn, agonizing determination as she said, "They won't expect an assault on the South Network Facility so quickly after a victory like that. We've got surprise on our side."

"Say you're right," Salb said. "If they decide to move the device, you're fucked."

"Zeus's Mercy is designed to use the South Network Facility building as a launching mechanism for Code Blue. The device can't be moved. It's part of the building."

Salb rested his forehead on the palm of his right hand and again massaged his temples with his fingers. "I'm not a good guy. Nate knew that. You all fucking know that. But I've survived in this world, haven't I? I've thrived. I'm not the king of the world, but I'm pretty high up. This . . . feels like the right thing to do. In a noble sort of way, I mean. And that makes me nervous. I didn't get here by being noble. Half the people who survived after the gas got killed from decisions like this."

"You've done a lot of wrong," Northfield said. Elena and John looked at him with raw concern for his sanity as he continued. "I've seen what bad shit the Yellowbacks have done, and I've heard stories of even worse, all under your leadership. I can only imagine what your brother's seen you do, and I can only imagine why he chose to distance himself from you."

"You done moral grandstanding yet? You pick that up from Nate?" Salb asked. "I'm aware of everything I've done. I know what I am."

"That's not my point," he said. "You've done bad things, but it's not for me to decide whether you're good or bad. Or Elena. Or John. Or Nathaniel. Or most of all yourself. That's for someone or something greater to judge. If you think of yourself as only a good or a bad guy, and you act accordingly, you're limiting your options severely. If you think you're a bad guy and think nothing can change that, you're cutting yourself off from redemption."

"Great, we've got a Quaker Oats granola bar over here," Salb muttered.

"I wish. I'd kill for a granola bar right now. And so would you. The food around here's dogshit," Northfield quipped.

Salb couldn't resist smirking. He said, "So what you're getting at, I'm guessing, is that this is my big chance to redeem myself? Right all my past wrongs? Turn into some sort of hero?"

"I don't know," he said frankly. "Again, that's not for me to decide. I'm not here to tell you how black your waters run or how to purify them. I just know that your brother sought redemption, and I like to think he ended up finding it for himself. And I know that he wanted the same thing for you. He wouldn't have slipped the master key in my pocket before he died without knowing we'd come to you for help."

Salb paused for a moment. "And you have the key?"

"Yeah," he said, taking it out and handing it to him.

Salb turned it over in his hands and exhaled deeply. "This might be the greatest mistake of my life. Or it might be the opposite. But I'll help you. For him, I'll help you. Give me more details of your plan."

CHAPTER 16

Geralt Salb told them that the entire floor was rented out to the Yellowbacks. As such, he offered them a place to stay while they waited for the assault on the South Network Facility, which was scheduled for tomorrow night. The layout of their apartment was like Salb's, with a hallway leading to a living room. They sat on two couches around the coffee table, Elena and John on one couch and Northfield on the other.

"What you said was a risk, Mark," John said, shaking his head.

"To be fair, coming here was a risk," Northfield replied, then said quietly, "Just felt like what I should say, I guess."

"Well, it worked," Elena said. She sank into the couch cushions. "It worked."

John narrowed his eyes and said, "I think we should try to get more Yellowbacks to help us push up through Little Empire. With the number we're planning—"

She shook her head and said, "You know how reluctant Salb is to risk his Yellowbacks. Plus, the more men we take, the longer our escape will take. Our exit plan will only work for a small number of us. We take more guys, we won't have enough time to get out."

"Do we even have enough time for our current plan?" Northfield asked.

"We'll find out," she said with a heavy sigh.

Jess, is any of this your doing? Did you finally get lonely without me and ask God to let me join you? It's been long enough, honey. I was worried you'd taken that whole "till death do us part" thing literally and found another man in heaven. Probably one of those guys who appears on the cover of romance novels with enough grease on his abs to coat a slip-and-slide. You always had high standards, Jess. But then again, you settled for me, so maybe they weren't too high.

"It's not too late, you know," John said. "We can get out of the city. Find somewhere to lie low."

"The Network's on alert of both our real and fake identities," she said. "We're not getting out of the city."

"Geralt could make us new fakes. High-quality ones, too," John said. "Your choice, Elena. I just want you to know all of our options."

"We're not running. If we don't set off Zeus's Mercy, who will?" She closed her eyes, her brow furrowing, and she said, "We didn't even know him long, did we? Not even a week. Still, his death—"

"Hurts," Northfield said.

John said, "He was a good man."

"Yeah," she said quietly. Her nose crinkled, as if each word coming out of her mouth tasted wrong. "He's gone. Flynn's gone. Everyone's gone . . ."

John opened his mouth to speak, but he cut himself off, instead placing his hand on her knee. He said, "We were moving before. Didn't have time to really think. But now, we have time, and I don't even know who to mourn first."

She nodded, then lowered her head as she pondered the same question. When she looked at John again, she had a smile whose glow stood out against the bleakness. She gently squeezed his hand and said, "They'll push us through what we've got to do. They will."

Northfield grimaced, and he averted his eyes to the table.

Despite the subtlety of the change in his expression, Elena noticed, and she asked, "What is it?"

"Nothing. I . . . It's nothing," he said. Elena's eyes didn't leave him. He exhaled and said, "It's just . . . I'm tired. I'm not even forty and I feel like I've lived through my whole life twice already. I'm on the end of my rope." He massaged his forehead with his thumbs. "Aren't you just sick of it all? The death, the killing?"

Elena and John gave his question some thought.

"I'm sick of the Network," John said. "I'm sick of our people being killed. I'd rather not see any Death Corps soldiers again. But if I can't do that, I'll damn well make sure they bleed."

After a pause, Elena said, "I hate all of this. I hate pulling the trigger." Her words settled over the room before she continued. "But the decision isn't in my hands. Everyone else put their lives down. We owe it to them."

John looked at Elena, his face a mix of admiration and love, both of which were overshadowed by sorrow. The emotion faded quickly; John wrenched them from her view.

"I don't care how much danger we're in, Elena," he said, attempting to inject some levity. "You better take every precaution possible to protect yourself. If I see any rodeo-clown hero moves, make no mistake, I will ground you."

"Ground me? Really?" she said with an amused smile. "Am I somehow a teenager again?"

Northfield joked, "You better stop. You're giving me flashbacks of high school, which is about the only thing that sounds worse than the apocalypse."

"Speak for yourself," John said. "Varsity football doesn't sound too bad to me."

"Could be worse," Elena said with a shrug. "Could be in middle school."

Despite all their sorrow and anguish, they laughed. Hell, they needed to.

When Elena stopped chuckling, she took a deep breath and said, "I wish we could laugh more. I wish everyone could laugh more, like how things used to be."

Northfield said, "People will get back to that. Someday, I guess."

"I think you're right," Elena said. "Still, I just hope we can speed that process along."

They talked for some time longer before hitting the hay. John again tried to convince Elena to sleep in the bedroom. She protested, and he ended up sleeping in the bedroom while she slept in the living room. Northfield slept on the other couch. Before his eyes closed and he drowned in his nightmares, he constructed pictures of Jess in his mind. Their whole life, what could have been, played in his mental theater. Kids. Jobs. Rooms, apartments, houses.

I know you miss me, Jess, and lord knows that I miss you. Man, do I miss you. I know that you're asking the Big Man to let me join you pretty soon.

But could you come to me instead? I need you down here by my side. I need your warmth. I need your conviction and blessing. Please let all the suffering I've been through be worth something. Please let all the suffering I've caused be worth something. I know I can't make things right, I know that's not how things work, but please let it be for something. Campaign, protest, and beg him to send you down.

Can you go on strike until that happens? Is there a heavenly workers' union that you're a part of?

I have faith you will, Jess, and I'll be waiting for you.

* * *

Sometime in the night, Northfield opened his eyes. When he looked around, his surroundings matched the apartment he had fallen asleep in. Still, he tensed his body, preparing for another nightmare to torment him. Maybe Dracula would come out of the shadows and make him drown in his own blood, with Jess watching silently from the ceiling. Maybe the walls would disintegrate and transform into a raging desert, one that would shove pounds of sand into his mouth until he suffocated, Jess again watching from a cloud.

When the dark surroundings of the apartment failed to change, and no strange apparition manifested, he realized that he might be awake.

He subsequently noticed Elena sitting up on the other couch.

He didn't know what time it was, but he knew it was late. Too late for her to be up for any other reason besides insomnia.

The room was dark, but he could make out her body. Her hand was pressed against her forehead, and her shoulders looked sunken.

He debated what he should do. He didn't know if he should just go back to sleep or if he should talk to her. He could imagine her wanting either.

Opting for the latter option, he started with a gentle, "Hey."

She jumped slightly, startled by his voice. She turned toward him and said, "Hey, Mark."

"You okay?"

"Yeah, I'm fine," she said, then repeated, "I'm fine. Just one of those nights. I don't know. I think about what could have been."

"I get it," he said, offering a smile as he thought about earlier. "It's been one of those nights for me, too."

"John, too, I bet," she said. "After everything that happened, who wouldn't?"

"Yeah, well . . ." he said, trying to figure out his words before just muttering, "Shit. It was a pretty bad day, even for these past ten years."

She nodded and looked down. When she looked back at him, she said, "Everything went to hell when I was just sixteen."

"Yeah," he said. "I'm sorry."

"I guess I just missed out on a lot, you know? There's so much I never got to experience. College. I mean, I had just gotten my license." She smirked as she added, "Never experienced a car crash, either."

"Believe me, that's one you're not missing out on."

There was a long pause.

"I never fell in love," she said. "Didn't even go on a date. I could try to blame that on my dad's strictness, but the truth is I was always picky."

"There could still be time," he offered.

"We'll see how tomorrow goes," she said. She spent a couple of moments thinking before she added, "I guess I'm lucky in a way. Never had to lose a love, either."

He nodded and said softly, "Yeah. Lucked out there."

"God, I'm sorry, Mark," she said.

His eyes felt wet, and he found himself glad the room was dark. He talked about her sometimes, but he couldn't remember the last time he mentioned her death to someone. Maybe never.

Neither spoke for a long while.

"Never gets easier, does it?" she asked.

"No," he said. Now his cheeks were wet. "It doesn't."

"Do you ever wish—" she began, then started over. "Do you ever wish you didn't know her?"

He closed his eyes. He took deep breaths, in and out, in and out. "I don't. Not for a second."

"I'm glad," she said. "She must have been very special."

"She was," he said.

His tongue felt heavy, and he couldn't bring himself to say anything more. Elena was quiet, no doubt focused on her thoughts. Neither spoke again. Not before the sun rose, surrounded by sweltering blood.

CHAPTER 17

The next morning, time passed at an agonizingly slow pace. Northfield was happy he didn't have a watch; if he constantly stared at it, every moment would pass even slower, and he'd just drive himself insane.

The more you're dreading something, the slower that thing takes to get to you. Is this how a pig feels before the butcher? Staring at the blade, waiting for it to drop?

Despite time passing slowly, it indeed passed. Eventually, he found himself traveling with Elena, John, and Geralt Salb in a van. They were on their way to Geralt's warehouse in the city to supply themselves and congregate with his men before heading to the South Network Facility.

Geralt told them, "This place is as safe as you can get from the Network in this city. The warehouse was my contingency in case the Network and Yellowbacks' deal ever went south, which, well, here we fucking are. Everything in the warehouse is designed either to escape from or fight the Network, and I've dumped massive resources into making sure this place has stayed hidden. My people have a protocol for coming here, the first being to remove clothes and gear that can identify them. They're trained to shake tails, too. The Network shouldn't know we're here."

"Shouldn't?" John repeated skeptically.

"Yeah. Shouldn't. If you haven't noticed, life ain't exactly perfect."

Elena said, "Were you able to get everything that we need?"

He nodded. "You asked for a lot, if I'm gonna be honest, but yeah."

"More of those thermite rounds?" John asked.

"Yeah. But do me a favor: only take as many as you think you'll need for exos. No more. My Yellowbacks need them, and I don't exactly have a truckload of them." He was about to say something, but he hesitated. After a moment, he said with a hard voice, "Did you use any thermite bullets when you got the key?"

Geralt Salb neglected to mention his brother's death, Northfield noticed.

She said, "No. Luckily, we didn't have to test them. I saw what those thermite bullets did in your apartment, but they still seem too good to be true."

"They'll work," he said, making a finger gun and pretending to pull the trigger. "Pump a few of those into those precious suits and they won't be alive to even feel the burn. Much."

"I don't doubt that the bullets themselves will work, it's just . . ." Elena said, pausing to choose her words. "Why haven't I ever heard of them before? And why would the Network expend so much money on an exoskeleton project to make soldiers bulletproof if thermite rounds can get through them so easily?"

"Because up until we blew those Death Corps soldiers to hell in my apartment, the Network didn't know they existed," Geralt said, eliciting a head tilt from Elena. He continued. "We're not as cowardly as the Network thinks, but we're not as dumb, either. They don't have the monopoly on all the scientists in the world. We've got our fair share of brainheads. And even though we don't have the Network's resources, we managed to make these thermite rounds. Originally, we designed them to shoot through armored vehicles, but they work just as well on those exoskeletons." He added with no small measure of spite, "It's funny: the Network designs exoskeletons impervious to bullets, and we're gonna take them down with bullets. I'm no poet, but I can recognize damned poetry when I see it. This sure as hell fits the bill."

"If you designed the thermite rounds to take out vehicles, why did you keep their existence a secret and not use them until now?" John asked.

"They were our trump card in case our agreement with the Network went ass up," he responded. "Why would I have my people use them on jobs in the country that they could handle already just to spoil the element of surprise in a situation like the one we find ourselves in now? Besides, on most jobs, my people are hijacking cargo trucks. Shooting through those with thermite rounds might ruin the cargo, making them damned useless anyway. The rounds are designed to be used against combat vehicles, and as I said, the Network's got more resources than us. I didn't want them to adapt to the thermite rounds if they knew we had them or if they thought we were even capable of making them."

"Well, we're lucky you have them," Elena said, then added softly, "Even if the Coalition had been able to continue the mission, they would've been killed all the same without anything to counter the exo soldiers."

Silence followed as they each pondered the possibility. Eventually, Geralt examined them and said, "Some better body armor is in order, too. Even if the Death Corps have those TAP rounds, you'll still want the best to protect against splash damage from grenades and bullets penetrating through other shit before hitting you." He focused on Northfield and said, "A Spoonbills jacket's not gonna protect you from anything."

"Maybe not, but after everything I've been through, I think the jacket's a lucky charm at this point," he replied. "And, well, I do have a light armored vest underneath."

"Get a better lucky charm," Salb said. "The number of grenades and bullets that have been slung at you until now is nothing compared to later. Like comparing condensation on a sippy bottle to the Niagara Falls. You're gonna want some better armor. I've got some you can wear and stay mobile."

"He says he's not a poet, and then he makes a comparison like that," she muttered to Mark so Geralt couldn't hear.

"Maybe we could write a poem together," Northfield muttered back. "I'm sort of a sculptor with words myself."

"If you don't stop, you'll regret not having that heavy armor right now," she said.

"It's a risk I'm gonna have to take," he replied. "Always have to for the sake of art."

They parked in a lot next to a gray warehouse. Vines crept up the side of the structure and strangled one another; they looked like an infection that had started on the side walls and was spreading to contaminate the rest of the building.

"Wow," Elena muttered. "The Coalition had enough trouble scrounging together resources to get fake IDs and bribe a couple guards. To hide a place like this . . ."

"Years and years of building influence, power, and resources," Salb said. "None of which the Coalition had. They did an admirable job with what they could work with."

Elena looked slightly taken aback by his compliment to the Coalition.

"You got more heads coming, or is this it?" John asked, looking around the parking lot at the other vehicles inside. There were around ten or so.

"This is probably it," Salb said. "As I said, my people gotta shake any Network tails before coming here. With this chaotic day and the

Network hunting us like damn rats, most of my people are just trying to survive and avoid getting killed. With four to five in each car, I bet we've got around forty to fifty."

When they stepped out of the car, a strong westward breeze pushed against them. The gusts of wind moved the gas across the city like the current of a river. When the wind subsided, the gas flowed in the opposite direction; the microbots composing the gas returned to their location prior to the breeze in a zero-sum game. Any trace of the breeze or the gas having moved was all but gone, like waves disappearing after a stone was tossed into a lake.

"Wish I would've asked Nathaniel more about how the microbots work," Northfield muttered. "Then again, I bet his explanation would have flown over my head."

"I'm not as curious," Elena said. "If I had a choice of getting rid of the gas or knowing exactly how each of the microbots composing it works, I'd choose to get rid of it."

"The Network doesn't agree, apparently," John muttered.

"You know, I bet the Network wasn't always this bad," Elena said. "Noble intentions and all. But now, the Network's a mad dog. That's how I see it. If we take down the organization, we'll be taking down a mad dog."

"Everyone's a dog that eats each other out here," Geralt said. "Sometimes you don't have a choice in it all. Sometimes doing bad things is what you gotta do."

"We've got a choice," Northfield said. "Sometimes the options are all shit, but it's still a choice."

"If it's between living and dying, it ain't really a choice at all," Geralt retorted. He typed a code in a keypad to unlock the warehouse door, and they entered.

The vines around the warehouse's exterior also infected the interior.

Large cracks wound around and crisscrossed the concrete floor. Vines and moss sprung out from them. Patches of brown stained the light gray concrete.

Vehicles of various shapes and sizes were parked on the concrete in rows. Shelves of weapons and armor lined the walls, with boxes of ammunition and magazines sitting beneath them. A mass of Yellowbacks talked by the vehicles, while a few lone Yellowbacks inspected the equipment on the walls. After the Yellowbacks spotted Geralt, they all stood at attention and silenced themselves.

Geralt said to his travel companions, "I'm going to address my people. Go and grab what you need."

"Ammo. That's first on our list," Elena said.

"Any SMG TAP rounds around here?" Northfield asked.

"Over there," John said, pointing across the warehouse. Looking to where John had pointed, he could see a set of SMGs hanging on the wall. A large box labeled *TAP* sat under the SMGs. He grabbed loaded magazines from the box and put them into his backpack. He noticed another box labeled *TAP*, but this one was red and had a small fire emblem over the letters.

He opened the box. There were far fewer magazines inside than the other box. *Must be the incendiary rounds we saw used at Salb's place,* he thought as he grabbed two magazines and stuffed them into his backpack. *I hope I don't have to use these. Then again, I hope I don't have to use any bullets at all, incendiary or not. Don't suppose the Death Corps would just surrender, would they?*

He had four thermite magazines in total. Heeding Geralt Salb's request, he refrained from grabbing more. Elena and John would have thermite rounds, too, and with the limited number of magazines in the box, he chose to leave the rest for the Yellowbacks. They would face the brunt of the Death Corps' defenses and consequently the brunt of the exo soldiers. Taking more just didn't feel right.

After finding a pistol that fit into his thigh holster, he picked up a first aid kit. He examined it and thought, *If somebody gets shot, I probably won't even have time to use this. Still, better to have than to want.*

He convened with Elena and John next to sets of armor plastered on the wall. John had replaced his assault rifle with a heavy machine gun. Slung over Elena's back was a metal contraption that looked like a combination of a gun and a tennis racquet. When Northfield saw the densely coiled rope attached to the mechanism, he recognized the portable zipline, an item Elena had requested from Salb. The tripod base of the zipline could be extended, and with a push of a button, the zipline could fasten itself in whatever ground it was placed on. Spikes would extend from the base, ram into the ground, and expand to prevent dislodging. From there, the zipline could be aimed and fired, the hook burrowing into its target.

She handed him and John a trolley, keeping one for herself. Also slung over her back was an RPG, which she handed to Northfield.

He said, "Can't tell if this feels like I'm receiving a Christmas present or a speeding ticket."

"Probably a present," she said. "The impending dread of tonight is throwing you off."

They examined the armor, searching for sets that weren't yellow and black. They weren't Yellowbacks, and they didn't want to offend them by dressing in their colors. They found sets with urban camouflage, along with red and blue lines running in the creases between armor plates. The armor sets were old Death Corps prototypes, abandoned in favor of the solid-black look.

They found some lockers and put on the armor. They looked

neither like current Death Corps soldiers nor Yellowbacks, forming a third faction with three lonely members standing among giants. They returned to Geralt.

He was in the middle of his speech, and his voice rose to a crescendo. "They think we're running with our tail between our legs, scared to even wear our colors. Well, ladies and gentlemen, now's our chance to give them the biggest bitch slap they can imagine. While they're thinking their facility's safe, they'll be partly right. It's true, we won't be wearing our uniforms. Not at first. But when it comes time to hit them, you'll be damned sure we'll rid of our disguises and wear our yellow masks, air tanks, the whole nine yards. When they bleed, they'll be looking at yellow and regret every damned thing they've done to us."

The Yellowbacks cheered in response. When they quieted down, he continued. "I told all of you the plan. Most of you will be tasked with distracting the Death Corps. The other task, as you know, is much more dangerous. I'm not going to force anybody to fight their way through Little Empire. It just wouldn't be right. If none of you volunteer, well, we'll either have to think of something else or head home."

He waited, letting his words sink in with the crowd. Then he said, "You would be part of something big, though. Probably the most good any of you will have the ability to do in your life. You make the choice you need to, but make it now. Whoever wants to volunteer, raise your hand."

The Yellowbacks were still, both their bodies and voices. John put his hand on Elena's shoulder. Northfield could tell she was holding her breath.

Then three hands shot up. They lit a spark, and within seconds, more hands rose into the air like a wide stretch of steam. By the time the Yellowback crowd was again still, more than three-quarters of their hands were lifted.

The intensity of Elena's exhale could have started an earthquake.

Geralt Salb smirked and said, "Well, that many of you can't volunteer. Figure out who's breaching Little Empire among yourselves. The most talented or whoever has the least to lose."

He waved his hand, dismissing them to prepare for the ambush. He approached Elena, John, and Northfield, and he said, "You've got your volunteers."

"Yeah, I can see that," Elena said, her astonishment apparent.

He said, "We're heading out at 8:00 p.m. to the South Network Facility. We'll attack at 9:00 and fight until 9:18. After that, I've given my boys the order to leave and regroup back here. If you can't exfil with us by then, you're on your own. Even if Yellowbacks are with you, I can't risk everybody else. You understand that."

"We understand," Elena said.

Salb nodded. "Follow me. I'll show you to your truck."

He led them to a jet-black armored truck with a ramming mechanism protruding from the grille. "It was a bitch to get a hold of this, especially under such short notice, but I pulled it off. Should be able to sustain small arms fire, no problem."

"And larger than small arms fire?" Northfield inquired.

"That's why we have this," John said, pointing to the RPG slung over Northfield's back. "You think you'll be a good enough shot with that thing? We can switch, and you can take this heavy-ass gun if you want."

"I'll manage," he replied. "I like my Vector."

"Don't have much food here, but we have some rations," Salb said. "You're gonna want to eat before the operation. Get your strength up."

They ate; afterward, Northfield had some time to himself. He found a secluded spot next to the wheel of one of the Yellowback vehicles, and he took out the framed photo of Jess from his backpack. He stared at the image and let memories warm him, temporarily ridding himself of the constant chill running through his bones.

In this moment, I feel your presence, Jess. Your arms are wrapped around me. Your heart's beating against my back, and I feel the heat of your body. Thanks for coming. I know you must've had to do a fat amount of convincing to get the Big Man to let you come. Lately, I've talked a lot about myself. Don't think I have much more bitching left in me. While you're here, I wanna hear about you. I know you can't talk back, but I'm gonna just ask you questions, if that's okay. I've missed you.

How are you? How have you been? Are you happy? What have you been up to?

Since you can't respond, I think I might just imagine your answers. Sounds comforting to me. And lord knows that I need that.

He imagined her short responses to some of his easier, surface-level questions, and he pictured her long-winded, soothing rants for questions that went deeper. After a while—he didn't know how long—he looked up to see Elena standing in front of him.

"Time to do this thing, Mark," she said, offering a small grin as comfort.

He stuffed the picture into his backpack and thought, *Thanks for sending her to me, God. I know I've been asking for a lot, but please give me that strength I asked for. At least long enough until I can hear her real answers.*

CHAPTER 18

For some reason Northfield couldn't explain, the South Network Facility seemed different than when he had seen it a few days ago. Yet the parking building and Little Empire looked the same, the fences and guard towers looked the same, and the green lawn looked the same. *So what's different this time?*

I think what's different is me. I'm scanning for threats and weak points, viewing the facility as some sort of death puzzle that needs solving. This place was always ominous, but now I'm tempted to run away screaming just by the sight of it.

"Hmm," Elena muttered.

"What?" John replied with concern.

"It's odd to think that Zeus's Mercy is just a couple hundred feet away," she said, pointing at the tallest floor of Little Empire. "At the same time, it feels farther than ever."

He put his hand on her shoulder and said, "We'll get there. We will."

She turned to look at him and cocked her head in a light-hearted manner. She said, "As long as you don't turn tail."

John let out an amused puff of air and said, "Never. You'd have to pry me away with a crowbar."

"Hope the same can go for them." She tilted her head backward, in the direction of the two armored trucks behind them. Inside were the Yellowbacks who would fight with them to Zeus's Mercy.

"They'll come through," Northfield said. "They're scared of death, but I bet they're scared of what Geralt Salb would do to them if they ran a good deal more."

Elena's radio crackled before a Yellowback said through it, "Come in, Wolf One, Wolf Two, Wolf Three. Final check. Over."

"Copy," Elena responded. "Wolf One, check. Over."

"Wolf Two, check. Over," replied the first armored truck behind them.

"Wolf Three, check. Over," replied the second armored truck.

"Copy that, Wolf One, Wolf Two, Wolf Three. Wildfire is a go. I repeat: Wildfire is a go. Out."

Within a minute, they heard an explosion on the other side of the South Network Facility, followed by rapid exchanges of gunfire.

"Here we go," Elena said with a deep exhale.

Northfield knew the wait would be agonizing. He wished they could get moving right away, but they couldn't, not until the Network's forces were drawn to the north side of the facility. If everything went to plan, the Yellowback offensive would look formidable enough to require all the Network's attention and make the soldiers think that, even if they wanted to send additional forces to guard the south, they wouldn't be able to without losing the north.

"You got that RPG ready, Mark?" she asked.

He held it up and said, "Ready to fire. I've got the four extra rockets on standby."

"We'll need them all," John said. "You remember the plan? What to shoot for?"

"Yeah, I'm not forgetting," he replied. "This is more important than a math test, you know? And I was good at remembering math."

John readied his machine gun, loading it with thermite rounds. He turned to his daughter and said, "No hesitation. Whatever happens, you keep driving, okay?"

She nodded and said, "Be ready on my word."

John climbed over the passenger seat and into the back of the truck with Northfield. He opened a circular hatch on the roof. The minutes passed tensely; Northfield tried to control his heartbeat by taking deep inhales and exhales. *Calm down, Mark. You've been in tough spots before. Your life's been in danger before. Remember her breathing technique. Breathe in, count to five. Breathe out, count to five.*

His breathing didn't stop his pulse from spiking when Elena said into the radio, "Wolf Two, Wolf Three. Charging. I repeat, charging. Over."

"Copy. Ready to follow. Over."

Elena glanced at John and Northfield once more before shouting, "Now!"

She stomped on the gas, and the truck lurched forward. John popped out of the hatch with his light machine gun, targeting the guard towers in front of the south gate.

He opened fire on the tower to his right. Gunfire quickly descended upon the truck like molten rain; bullets dented the armored vehicle with popping noises akin to popcorn in a microwave. Watching through the front windows, Northfield saw that the guard tower John was firing at had burst into a storm of white flames, sending orange sparks raining to the ground. The continuous thudding of John's machine gun prevented him from hearing any screams or cries of pain from inside the tower.

John eyed the second guard tower, but before he could swivel his gun toward it, a flurry of thermite bullets flew at the tower like an army of shooting stars. The tower burst into flames like the first. John glanced backward; smoke plumed from the machine guns wielded by Yellowbacks atop the other two trucks.

No bullets were shot at their truck, but Northfield suspected that the lull wouldn't last long. John reloaded his machine gun.

"Brace!" Elena screamed. Northfield and John obeyed, and he felt a hard jolt as the sound of screaming metal surrounded them; the truck rammed through the gate and pushed onward, scarcely losing speed.

On their way to the parking building, they passed three armored Death Corps Humvees on either side of the road. Most of the Death Corps vehicles were gathered at the north side of the facility, focused on the Yellowbacks' attack. Gunfire promptly spat at them from the vehicles, which quickly gave pursuit.

John and the Yellowbacks shot back. They managed to take out one vehicle, hitting it with enough thermite rounds to either kill the driver or the engine; Northfield couldn't tell which.

John was forced to duck back under the hatch; the shooters in one of the Humvees better calibrated their aim and came dangerously close to hitting him, following their armored truck as it neared the ramp to the upper floors. The other Humvee suppressed a Yellowback truck in a similar manner, leaving only one Yellowback truck to fire at the two Humvees.

"Ready?" John yelled over the sound of bullets denting the back of their truck.

Northfield nodded, and he set the loaded RPG on his shoulder. John sat on the right side of the truck, grabbing the handle on the left back door. Although opening it would expose them to gunfire, they had to take out the vehicles; Elena would soon have to slow the truck to ascend the building's ramp, and they couldn't risk the Death Corps ramming into them.

John flung the door open and, to get as far away as possible from incoming gunfire, pressed himself against the right side of the wall.

Don't let a random one hit me, God. I've gone too far to die from a random shot. If I'm gonna feel death, at least let me see it coming first.

Northfield leaned out from the right-side door, exposing his hands, shoulders, and head to incoming fire. Instantly, he felt like he had just entered a hailstorm with strong enough winds to throw ice parallel to the ground. Quickly, he took aim and fired at the Humvee firing at them, eyeing the soldiers poking out of the windows with their assault rifles and submachine guns. The rocket careened through the air, a trail of smoke painting its trajectory.

The Humvee exploded in a ball of fire and pain. He couldn't tell if the screeches originated from flying debris scraping against the gravel or from the throats of dying men. The explosion sent the other Humvee off the road; it swerved wildly and crashed at breakneck speed into the parking building.

The Yellowbacks followed their truck up the ramp.

As Northfield peeled his eyes away from the wreckage, he thought, *Don't think of how many soldiers were in each Humvee. Whether there were six, five, or four isn't gonna make you feel any damn better.*

Numbly, he loaded another rocket into his launcher. The truck exited onto the final floor of the parking building before the roof—the highest floor with access to Little Empire.

So far, everything was going to plan. Security was relatively light; most Death Corps were focused on the north Yellowback assault. *We'd be torn apart without that distraction. What's the saying again? The enemy of my enemy is my friend . . .*

However, for the Network, relatively light security still meant heavy security. Machine guns shot at the vehicle from slits in the Network room's concrete walls. Each shot was so loud and the rate of the fire was so high that Northfield felt nauseated.

Despite his stomach, he popped out of the hatch with his RPG. He set his sights on the Network room door as fast as he could, and he pulled the trigger. The door blasted away, and shrapnel was ejected in every direction in tandem with an expanding cloud of smoke. The Death Corps soldiers inside the Network room were dazed, and the machine-gun fire temporarily stopped. However, it quickly resumed as the truck sped toward the room.

"Get down and brace!" Elena screamed. She slammed on the brakes and spun the steering wheel counterclockwise. John and Northfield threw themselves on the floor, covering their heads with their hands. The loud screeching of the tires failed to overcome the thunderous onslaught of bullets that managed to puncture the right side of the truck. The vehicle stopped directly in front of the opening created by the blast, close enough that the machine guns in the slits couldn't hit the passenger side of the truck.

The Yellowbacks didn't rush the Network room, as only one van could fit into the blind spot of the machine guns. Instead, they continued to pepper the machine gun slits with their own fire to distract them.

Although gunfire couldn't hit the passenger door of Elena, Northfield, and John's truck, it could still hit the back compartment, which meant that they needed to move fast. Northfield got up from the floor, and he followed Elena as she opened the passenger door and rushed out. He readied his Vector, which was loaded with a regular magazine; he'd save the thermite rounds in case he came across the exo soldiers. John followed, taking slightly longer due to the weight of his weapon.

They breached the Network room. Elena pivoted left while

Northfield pivoted right; they discharged their weapons at the machine-gunners, who both collapsed. The short, stocky man behind the room's desk pulled a revolver on them and attempted to shoot. John fired, and the man collapsed just like the guards. Elena radioed for the Yellowbacks to advance. Meanwhile, John searched the stocky man's body, looking for a key to the door behind the desk. Finding it in his front pocket, he unlocked the door to Little Empire.

The Yellowbacks entered the room. There were twelve in total, six from each truck.

Elena radioed Geralt Salb. "Center, this is the Wolves. We're in. Over."

"Copy that. You've got thirteen minutes. Over."

"Copy. Out," she said, promptly holstering her radio. She turned to the others and said, "No telling what sort of defenses the Network has behind these doors. Be ready."

They nodded, and she opened the door. Two Yellowbacks stayed behind to protect the vehicles while the rest rushed through. Elena, John, and Northfield led the advance, with the Yellowbacks behind them.

They entered an opulent hallway with rose-colored carpet lined by glimmering gold. The walls were jet black accented with white lines and geometric shapes; lights housed in intertwining golden structures hung off the walls. Black lines crisscrossed the white ceiling. Semicircle black columns etched in gold stretched from floor to ceiling. Doors lined the walls between these columns, and a wide black-and-white spiral staircase at the end of the hallway led to the floors above and below.

"Good to see where this city's resources are going," Northfield muttered to himself as they moved, nearing the halfway point of the hall.

"Don't seem to be any Death Corps here, at least," a Yellowback also muttered.

Almost on cue, Death Corps soldiers sprung from behind pillars and doors, opening fire on them.

"Spoke too soon," Northfield said. Luckily, their combat formation took a surprise attack into account, and they were all in position to take cover nearby. Northfield rushed to the closest column on the right side of the hallway. John hid behind the same column; Elena took cover with a Yellowback behind a pillar on the left side.

The other Yellowbacks moved to columns farther back. One wasn't quick enough, or he was just unlucky. A bullet pierced his forehead in a splatter of red.

Northfield watched him fall; he could tell that death was immediate.

Bullets flew across the hallway in bright flashes of yellow light and burrowed into his pillar, chipping away small pieces.

John yelled to him over the gunfire, "Move. I'll fire high. You go low."

He tried signaling to the Yellowbacks and Elena. Northfield hoped most saw the signal to avoid shooting him on his advance, and he hoped the rest would have the sense not to anyway.

It was a risky, dangerous plan, even when he didn't take into consideration the possibility of friendly fire, but they didn't have time to try anything else. He nodded to John.

John leaned around the pillar and opened fire. Northfield crouch-ran out from behind the pillar; adrenaline drove his legs forward with the persuasiveness of a cattle prod as every movement became mechanical. Once he reached the next pair of pillars, he slid diagonally, aiming his gun right and spraying automatic fire at a soldier, then, while still sliding, aimed his submachine gun left and sprayed fire at a soldier hiding behind a pillar. His feet hit the wall, abruptly stopping his momentum. The bodies fell to the floor, the walls on either side of them bloody. He hurried behind the next pillar, pressing against it and re-loading his Vector.

His advance drew gunfire toward him and took pressure off the others, allowing them to move forward.

He popped out from behind cover just as a soldier two pillars ahead put his sights on him. Before the soldier could fire, three bullets tore into him, and he collapsed.

Northfield didn't know who to thank, but he hoped his rescuer knew of his gratitude. The others put steady pressure on the Death Corps.

Their advance was stopped nearly as it started. More Death Corps entered the hallway from the staircase, and not a second passed before gunfire washed over them like an avalanche. The sharp cracks of battle rifles mixed with the dull roar of machine guns to form a deafening wall.

Clearly, the Death Corps were aware of the second attack on their facility, and they were sending as many soldiers as they could spare without giving up the north gate. Maybe it would be enough.

Northfield was pinned down, and he knew the others were, too. They were bleeding minutes, and they couldn't wait until the gunfire abated, because it wouldn't. The Death Corps would also know that they were playing a time game and that they just needed to wait until their reinforcements arrived. The machine-gunners would switch off, staggering their fire to reload at different times, while the assault and battle rifles would pick off any of those who peeked out from behind cover.

Northfield looked backward. He saw two more Yellowbacks on the floor, unmoving. Blood pooled around them like sunsets.

He didn't have time to process the scene; Elena was signaling to him. From his angle, he could still see her behind a pillar.

Her signal was clear; they needed aggression. The seconds kept ticking by.

He signaled back, put in a fresh magazine, and switched to fully automatic.

Some of them would die. He was closest to the Death Corps, meaning that he would probably be one of them.

Be with me.

He charged with the others. In the chaos of movement, he couldn't tell how many Death Corps there were, but he swore there were enough to cover a night sky.

He ran with everything in him, firing at whomever he could. Black-clad bodies fell, maybe from his shots, maybe from those of others, but he didn't take much notice. He needed to reach the next pillar.

He nearly rammed into it. He took a single ragged breath, and he popped around the pillar. His adrenaline was at the maximum, burning in his stomach like a cocktail, and the world around him moved like syrup. He downed a soldier with a machine gun, swiveled, and downed another with a shotgun before the Death Corps returned fire.

When he aimed and took out another Death Corps soldier, he noticed something strange. Some of the soldiers' bodies were smoking.

He pulled back and reloaded. While he did so, he looked backward.

He almost dropped his gun.

John. It was John.

He was sprawled on the floor, his weapon lying next to him. Red leaked from his wounds. His chest and legs were all torn.

He wasn't moving.

Without thinking, Northfield sought out Elena with his eyes, but before he could find her, his attention was pulled away.

He heard deep, rumbling noises that lurked under the high cracks of gunfire—thunder rumbling under the cover of roaring rain.

Northfield peeked around the pillar, and he saw them. Two exos clambered up the staircase and entered the floor. Their armor was monstrously bulky, maybe even more than the exo they had encountered before, and each had a different weapon built into his right arm.

Northfield tried yelling to warn Elena and the Yellowbacks and tell them to use thermite magazines, but his voice was drowned out by the sound of a rocket screeching across the hall. It blasted apart a pillar, shredding a Yellowback with debris and launching him into the air.

Just as soon as the rocket exploded, another careened toward Yellowbacks hiding behind a column. Northfield didn't hear their cries over the detonation as he shoved a thermite magazine into his weapon.

He popped around the column and fired two shots that missed before, out of the corner of his eye, he saw a bright light.

Northfield snapped back behind cover as a cone of flame lurched toward him. *A flamethrower. Fuck me.* That explained why the rocket-launcher exo hadn't targeted him; his flamethrower buddy already had. The fire blasted into the column and rushed past the side of it. Flames licked the air around him like venomous tongues, but they didn't touch his body. The pillar protected him, at least for now. If—more accurately *when*—the flamethrower exo came closer and changed his angle, Northfield would be in for a lot of suffering.

Is this a taste of hell, God? he wondered, sweating profusely. The heat was intolerable, and he was effectively trapped. *Want me to repent that bad, huh? But I can't yet. I'm sorry. I gotta finish this. I've gotta.*

The cone pulled away from him, lashing to the exo's left like a whip.

With the heat off him, Northfield wouldn't let the opportunity pass. He swiveled around the corner again and took aim with his Vector. The flamethrower exo's left arm was smoking; somebody had hit him but missed his core. Northfield unloaded his entire magazine of thermite rounds. Explosions and flames engulfed the exo as each round tore through him, illuminating his black armor like fiery suns against the backdrop of empty space. With an agonizing scream, the soldier collapsed to the ground in a disorganized, sprawled-out heap, smoke rising from his body.

While the soldier collapsed, Northfield saw bright flashes out of the corner of his eye. Thermite bullets ate through the rocket-launcher exo, but he was already down, now nothing more than another smoldering heap.

He moved out of sight and reloaded with a normal magazine; he wanted to save the thermite rounds for exos. He prayed that if the Death Corps were willing to use flamethrowers and rocket launchers in their own building, they were desperate. He took it as a small sign that they had a chance.

Immediately after inserting his magazine, he saw Elena. She was shooting at the Death Corps with pure ferocity.

He popped around the pillar to help, but by the time he aimed, there were scarcely any soldiers left. He helped pick off the few who remained.

An eerie stillness washed over the hallway; even the war going on outside seemed quiet.

Elena moved to John immediately. She knelt by him and held his hand, but only for a second.

Northfield put together what happened. Before he saw John, he saw Death Corps soldiers smoking—smoking from thermite rounds. John had loaded his machine gun with them. Without any exos present at the time, there was only one reason he would do that.

Death Corps would prioritize someone firing thermite rounds. He was why Northfield wasn't hit. John protected them during their charge. He protected her.

"Elena," Northfield said, approaching her.

"No time," Elena said, her voice choking, unsteady. "There's not . . . There's no time." Before he could respond, she announced, "Let's go."

There were only three Yellowbacks left. Blood, bodies, and rubble covered nearly the whole floor.

Nonetheless, the Yellowbacks didn't seem discouraged. They paid their comrades one last respect and were ready to move.

They followed Elena as she pulled out her radio and headed toward the staircase.

"Center, we've reached the staircase. Over."

"Copy that. Nine minutes. Over."

They were behind on time, but the mission was still possible. In the plan, they gave themselves one more minute than needed to exfil. Now, they were just using that minute on the other end.

They reached the spiral staircase. Northfield took one last look at the hallway. First, his eyes rested on his friend.

I hope you're resting now, John. I hope you're resting.

Sprawled out and covered in blood, the Death Corps didn't look much different than the Yellowbacks. Four minutes to spill so much blood didn't seem possible. *I talked a big game to Geralt Salb about not weighing another man's sins, but this looks awfully like judgment. But I didn't want this. I didn't want to punish anybody.*

An end to justify the means. That's what you hear a lot. I never bought that shit. Gives people a way to excuse all their actions. Yet here I am, doing this shit in some attempt to save people, so what does that make me?

Just push through, Mark. Remember the people below, trapped in that gas hell. Remember why you're doing this, and just keep going. You gotta get through.

Elena addressed two Yellowbacks and said, "You, cover down. The rest of us will cover up."

She didn't look back. Her breathing was harsh and irregular, and she sounded like she could choke at any moment.

They ascended with no resistance; they all knew the break was temporary. The winds were calm now, but they'd pummel them all soon enough.

Once they reached the top of the staircase, they entered a hallway more opulent than any Northfield had seen. Gold showered everything like a cloud's heavy raindrops, and the white backdrop only highlighted the splendor. Doors on either side of the hallway mocked him with the arrogance of a king's sons. A pair of double doors at the end jeered the loudest.

There were planter boxes made of thick concrete before the first set of doors. Blood-red roses sprung out of them and loomed like dusk clouds. They were thorny and reminded him of knives instead of anything beautiful.

One floor white. One floor black. Maybe this entire building is just one big damned chessboard. Maybe they've already got a checkmate.

"Be ready," Elena whispered to them. Her voice was hoarse, so her words came out as growls. "Keep eyes on the doors."

After they took two more steps, the double doors sprung open, followed quickly by the doors on each side of the hallway. A flamethrower exo and a shotgun exo stood at the double doors, one slightly behind the other; they couldn't fit through at the same time. Four Death Corps soldiers materialized from behind the other doors.

Their gunfire tore apart two of the Yellowbacks.

Elena, Northfield, and the remaining Yellowback immediately opened fire, unloading their magazines as they dove behind the planter boxes. He was behind the planter box on the left, while Elena and the Yellowback were behind the other box. While firing, Northfield thought he might've hit one of the soldiers, but he wasn't sure.

The Yellowback popped over the planter box. He didn't manage to shoot; a bullet tore through his skull in an explosion of red, and he crumpled to the floor. Elena started to reach for him, but she immediately pulled back. He was already gone; she couldn't do anything for him.

Hell, Northfield thought, his eyes darting between bodies. *Less than five seconds. Less than five seconds and they're all gone.*

He couldn't afford to lament any longer. He loaded a thermite magazine into his submachine gun just as a cone of flame blasted through the middle of the room.

The flames arced toward Elena and crashed into her planter box, burning the flowers and sending glowing black flecks into the air. To avoid the fire, she pressed into the concrete and crouched as low as possible.

Northfield sprang up and snapped toward the flamethrower exo. He aligned his holographic sight with the exo's center mass, then pulled the trigger and held it, correcting for the Vector's recoil as thermite rounds exploded out of the barrel and destroyed the exo.

His vision blurred as bullets pounded all around him, some of them puncturing the concrete of the planter box on the opposite side of him and burrowing through the soil, while others tore off pieces of concrete that launched into the air and shredded the flowers. Quickly, he ducked and lifted his gun, emptying the rest of the mag without looking.

He reloaded and continued blind-firing thermite rounds. Elena took advantage of his distraction. In a flash of speed, she aimed and took out two Death Corps soldiers rushing them. She prioritized them over the slower-moving exo. If Death Corps soldiers managed to reach their side of the planter boxes, they would be done for.

Her decision was smart, but it was costly. Shotgun pellets tore into her right shoulder, and she dropped back down, clutching her wound. Unable to aim properly with her rifle, she took a pistol out of her ankle holster.

She gave him a nod to let him know she was alright, and he popped over cover.

The exo had the barrel of his shotgun pointed right at him. Northfield couldn't duck or aim fast enough.

The exo didn't have time to fire, either.

His head disappeared in an explosion of white-orange flame and sparks. The shotgun dropped to the ground, and the exo soldier fell on top of it, blood spilling out the burned remnants of his head like soda from a can.

Elena's pistol was smoking; she had it loaded with thermite rounds.

The instant after she fired, Northfield aimed and shot one of the two remaining Death Corps soldiers. She tried to aim at the other, but with her wound, she was too sluggish.

Northfield couldn't stop the soldier in time. With a stomach-lurching *crack*, the last soldier shot her in the chest. She stumbled backward, falling into the blood of the Yellowbacks around her.

Northfield shot the final soldier with three bullets: two in the chest and one in the head. Without hesitation, he ran to her, suffocating in the stillness that had overtaken the hallway.

"Elena," he said softly, sliding to a kneel next to her. Blood poured out of her chest, flowing down her sides and adding to the pool she lay in. He pressed his hands on the wound, hard, but blood still trickled between his fingers.

"Mark . . . go," she said; her voice couldn't rise above a whisper. Two violent coughs shook her body. Using the last of her strength, she pulled off her gas mask. There was a small measure of defiance in the movement, despite the feeble shaking of her hand.

"I'm sorry. I . . ." he said, looking at his hands. Helpless to stop the blood, his hands were even more feeble than hers. He scrambled for his first aid kit.

"Mark," she said. Suddenly, she squinted and bared her teeth. She managed to work through the pain and said, "Mark, please. Go. I need you to."

With one glance into her glistening eyes, which shined gold from the light reflecting off them, he knew her words to be true.

"Okay," he said. He lowered his head and curled his fingers. "Okay."

She nodded toward her radio; he reached and took it from her waist.

"And the zipline," she gasped. She started to turn her shoulder so he could grab it from her backpack.

He put a hand on her shoulder and shook his head. By now, the Death Corps would realize that the Yellowbacks at the north gate weren't trying to break into the compound, and they would realize that the Yellowbacks were only a distraction. Soon, the Death Corps would be running up the spiral staircase to reach them.

In their original plan, Elena had accounted for this. They planned to hold off the Death Corps until the device was detonated, then zipline to the roof of the parking garage. The two Yellowbacks guarding the vans would have driven to the roof and been waiting to bug out.

Now they were running out of time, and Northfield was the only person remaining of the primary infiltration team.

"Wolf Two, this is Wolf One. Exfil now. Over," he said into the radio. Elena reached her hand to him, and he held it tightly.

"Wolf One, are you sure? Is the op aborted? Over."

"No, not yet. Gonna give it our best shot. But you get out, you hear me?"

He watched her eyes go dark, and her hand fell limp in his. He closed his eyes.

"Copy that, Wolf One. Good luck. Out."

"Out," Northfield said. He holstered the radio and tore off his gas mask. The gas didn't extend high enough to affect him, and he just couldn't take wearing the thing anymore.

I want to feel your presence, Jess. I want you to come down, to cover me, to protect me. But, Jess, I don't want you to see this. I don't want you to see any of this.

He made sure his Vector was reloaded, and he hurried through the double doors as he thought, *Don't know what waits behind these doors, but, God, carry me through. You've gotten me this far. Help me reach the end zone. Take me after, but not a second before.*

CHAPTER 19

luorescent lights on the ceiling nearly blinded him; the pure white walls reflected the light and eliminated nearly every shadow in the room. His eyes adjusted, and he could see two rows of white laboratory tables with beakers, graduated cylinders, and other equipment on top of them.

In the center of the room, a large spherical contraption sat inside a glass cage with a glass door. Behind the cage, a row of windows provided a stunning view of the night sky and surrounding buildings. Four tubes extended from the contraption and connected to the center of the ceiling. *Zeus's Mercy uses the antenna on Little Empire to disperse the neutralizing agent . . . My God, I've found it. The damned, blessed machine is right in front of me.*

His excitement was dampened by the presence of a man standing between the cage and the frontmost row of tables. He was around fifty years old and had paper-white hair that screamed smug.

Northfield's excitement was further dampened by the two Death Corps soldiers on either side of him. One had an Aug A3 assault rifle and the other an M1014 shotgun, both leveled at him.

He dove behind a white table before the soldiers' incoming fire had the chance to tear him apart. After a couple of moments, he sprinted to a table on his left. As he ran, he sprayed his Vector to drive the soldiers behind cover.

When he reached the table, he pressed his head against it, fishing for his last magazine with normal rounds. Additionally, he had one thermite magazine, which he would save until he needed it. However, based on his situation, he might need it pretty damned soon. The pistol strapped to his ankle served as a last resort.

Just let my aim be true. They paid for my aim to be true. Don't forget that, God.

Just as he finished reloading, he noticed the incoming fire change direction.

Initially, bullets were flying directly over his head, indicating that the soldiers were in front of him. Now, the bullets were coming toward him from slight left and right angles, perhaps ten degrees either way.

The soldiers were attempting to flank him; they were moving from the scientist to the ends of the laboratory tables. To avoid crossing lines of fire, one soldier would be the primary flanker while the other hung back and provided suppressive fire. Northfield focused on listening to the gunfire to determine which soldier would draw nearer.

The left soldier. Knowing was only half the battle. Do or die.

He ran his fingers along the floor. *Slick,* he thought. *Slick enough.* He crouch-ran to the end of the row of laboratory tables, building speed. He dropped into a slide, taking aim with his submachine gun. As he suspected, a Death Corps soldier was running toward him.

The soldier aimed his assault rifle, but Northfield's sudden and strange movement took him too much by surprise. Bullets struck him and brought him to the ground. Northfield's feet hit the left wall; his legs bent, and he launched off the wall to slide behind a laboratory table. He and the last soldier proceeded to engage in a much deadlier version of whack-a-mole, although they were both simultaneously the mallets and the moles. One would pop up, fire, duck behind cover again, move to another piece of cover, pop up again, and fire.

Northfield's magazine ran out, and he swapped it for the thermite magazine. Cautious about wasting ammo, he focused on moving from cover to cover, letting the soldier fire more rounds than him, occasionally spraying his own fire to keep his enemy on his toes.

When he saw the soldier move behind a laboratory table to reload, he fired thermite rounds. White flames ate through the table and vomited a flurry of orange sparks in every direction; fragments fell to the ground like molten scoops of ice cream. He heard a soft *thump* and saw a limp hand fall as the soldier's shotgun clattered to the white floor. He had one bullet left in the submachine gun, but he wasn't clear yet. One potential threat remained: the scientist.

He crept around the room, keeping his footsteps quiet and his eyes alert. Northfield didn't know if the scientist was armed, but he wasn't going to take any chances. He rounded the corner of the final row of laboratory tables before the cage.

The scientist hadn't moved, apparently, and was still crouching in the same spot as when Northfield walked in. The scientist was facing the other way, holding his pistol out, waiting to see if his soldiers had won or waiting to shoot Northfield. Unfortunately for him, he picked the wrong side to look out from.

Northfield held his submachine gun to the scientist's head and said, "Set the gun down. I don't want to kill you."

"Now you try to get noble," the scientist mumbled with a disdainful scoff. "What's one more to you?"

"You really gonna make me do this?" he cried. "Put your goddamn gun down."

"Fuck you," the scientist yelled. "Everything was fine in this city. We brought it back from the ashes of hell. And you're going to ruin it all."

"Set down the gun," he barked. "I'll kill you, right here."

The scientist tried to spin around and fire; his head was a smoldering crater before his eyes even met Northfield's. *I'm sorry, God. I really didn't want to take another. I tried, damn it.*

While he reached down to grab his pistol, his eyes caught the scientist's name tag: Doctor Knox.

Knox? Why does that name sound so familiar? It clicked in his head. *He's the head scientist of the project, the arrogant prick Salb talked about. The man who hired a certain Network merc. Makes sense why he's the only one here. The other scientists must've headed home for the night.*

He rushed into the glass cage. Zeus's Mercy was transparent; he could see a dark-blue liquid with countless luminescent blue particles suspended inside. The liquid and particles looked like a navy universe rife with billions of shining blue stars. *Code Blue. Hope you're everything you're cracked up to be.*

A touchscreen device was mounted on Zeus's Mercy. Next to it was a keyhole. He took out the master key and stuck it inside. The touchscreen immediately lit up, and an electronic female voice announced, "Access granted."

The screen displayed a bunch of choices; he rapidly tapped through menus until he arrived at his goal.

"Would you like to detonate?" The automated voice didn't have any gravity in her tone. She as might well have been asking if he wanted coffee.

The touch screen then displayed two boxes that said *yes* and *no.*

He tapped the *yes* button fast enough to break the sound barrier, but he didn't experience a cathartic release. Instead, a wave of melancholy hit him in the stomach like an iron bar as the female voice announced the words displayed on the screen: "Detonation in three minutes. Two fifty-nine . . . two fifty-eight . . ."

A loud, wailing siren went off throughout the building; he assumed Death Corps soldiers were already rushing to Zeus's Mercy, but the sound would definitely put an extra spark in their step.

Each second the voice counted down hit him like a stone. He rushed to pick up the Aug A3 and M1014 from the dead soldiers, along with whatever ammunition he could find on their persons, and stuffed his pistol back into his ankle holster. *Elena, after you went down, I didn't want to hear how much time we had left, because I already knew. I already knew that we were running late, and with only me left, I would only move slower. The Death Corps are gonna keep coming. They'll just keep coming.*

I just need to make it three minutes. Right now, though, lasting three minutes sounds impossible.

A rumble came from the double doors, starting as quietly as a tired breath but steadily growing louder and louder. The sound of heavy footsteps trampled up the stairs and through the hallway.

Seconds now. He had seconds until they came.

Keep Elena's dream alive, God. You took her, but keep her dream alive, he thought, taking cover behind the second-to-first row of laboratory tables in front of the cage.

Death Corps soldiers burst into the laboratory room. They aimed at him, but he was quicker to the draw. Knowing he couldn't deescalate the situation, knowing he'd have to take more lives, knowing so many of his friends were gone, he let out a scream as he fired, downing a couple soldiers before ducking and reloading.

He stopped himself from thinking about Elena or John or Nathaniel or the Yellowbacks. He stopped himself from thinking about the fact that the Death Corps had entered the room to deactivate Zeus's Mercy and kill him. He stopped himself from thinking about how his three minutes were whittling down, for both good and bad.

Instead, he thought, *Hey, Jess. I think it's time to talk about real estate.*

He ran to the right end of the row of laboratory tables and aimed around the corner, shooting a Death Corps soldier running toward him. Caution clearly wasn't their foremost concern. They had the numbers to spare but not the time; funny how everybody felt short on time. *Seeing as how we've been apart for all these years, I suppose you're living alone in heaven. You never were the fondest of room-mates, and God's probably got enough space for everyone to have a single room if they want. Probably wouldn't be heaven if you couldn't even have a place to yourself, right?*

He sprayed his assault rifle at a few soldiers attempting to climb over the first row of tables. Man, they just kept coming. He didn't have time to count how many before he was forced back under the table by incoming fire. He reloaded and thought, *But as I was saying, Jess, we've gotta find a place to stay together. Somewhere that's within both of our budgets. Money doesn't mean jack up there, so I assume God takes your good deeds in life as payment. I know the Bible says that if you believe, you're gonna go to heaven, but it doesn't say any-thing about rent once you get there. That's where God gets you.*

He had to keep moving; he checked around the same corner, fired at another Death Corps soldier attempting to flank him, and crouch-ran to the other end of the row of laboratory tables.

As he ran and slid into cover, he thought, *I bet there's an asterisk in the Bible somewhere. Probably in such small print that people ha-ven't spotted it yet. When you get up there, he pulls out the Bible and puts on a set of big glasses that make his eyes look like bugs in a jar.*

Then he reads the fine print and tells you what type of room you can afford. "Fred, you were kinda an asshole in life, so you get a 450-foot single-room apartment with a forty-three-inch TV. HD, but not 4K. If you would've called your mom back a couple more times, you would have earned the 4K package . . ."

He held the trigger and swiveled back and forth, targeting the mass of Death Corps soldiers entering the room. Out of the corner of his eye, he saw a couple collapse before he returned behind cover. Nothing more than a drop in the bucket. They would overwhelm him soon.

In a bid to get some breathing room, he dove over the row of laboratory tables behind him. While in the air, something punched hard into his shoulder, although he didn't feel any pain. Once he hit the ground and cozied up behind the last row of laboratory tables, he checked his shoulder: a bullet wound, but just a flesh wound. With his rampant adrenaline driving away the pain, his shoulder's movement wasn't restricted. He paid the wound no further mind. Realizing that his assault rifle was empty, he switched to the shotgun. He rested his head against the back of the laboratory table, just for a second.

You're gonna have to carry the brunt of the bill, Jess. I don't think God's gonna give me a ton of brownie points for today. I'm just trying to save people, but I've ended up hurting a lot. The jury's still out. At best, maybe I get a slight net positive. At least enough to afford a good comforter.

Death Corps soldiers rounded the corners of the final row of laboratory tables; he fired his shotgun whenever a soldier appeared, barely keeping the sea of black uniforms at bay. After four rounds, he began reloading but stopped once he'd inserted two shells, wincing as a Death Corps soldier rounded a table to his left and opened fire. He aimed the shotgun and blasted him away, swiveling to drive another soldier behind cover by firing the other round. While reloading the shotgun again, he looked at the bullet holes to his immediate left and right; they'd missed his head and chest by inches.

This is his work, right? He's keeping me alive long enough to work this contract out, isn't he? Tell you what, Jess, you figure out our living situation with him. Right now, I think you know more about our finances than I do.

"One oh two . . . one oh one . . . one . . . fifty-nine . . ." the female voice announced from the touchscreen. *Just one more minute, Mark. Don't screw this up now.*

He fired the shotgun at Death Corps soldiers as they continued rushing to reach Zeus's Mercy. He could scarcely blink, and his gun was out of ammunition. Before he could reload, a soldier rounded the table to his left and ran toward the detonator while aiming his rifle at Northfield.

Northfield threw the shotgun at the soldier, stunning him as he drew his pistol from his ankle holster, then discharged two rounds. Slaps of wind hit his body as bullets whizzed past him: a soldier was behind him now, running from the right side of the table toward Zeus's Mercy.

He grimaced as what felt like a hammer slammed into his left thigh; again, he didn't feel pain, though everything below his thigh went numb, as if his leg was levitating. He dumped rounds into the soldier that shot him; he swiveled to look toward the tables and double doors and discharged the rest of his ammunition at whatever Death Corps soldiers he saw.

He crouched below the table, reloading and looking at his wounds as he thought, *I take it back. God's not keeping me alive to work out the contract, is he? He wants to punish me before I die. He's pissed about the whole New Testament thing. If I believe and earnestly repent, he's gotta take me, and he knows it. So before I meet you both up there, he's making me suffer a bit. That's really petty of God, you know that?*

He unloaded his magazine again, hitting a couple of the Death Corps soldiers vaulting over the tables, most of them disregarding him and recklessly trying to reach Zeus's Mercy. He ducked under the table and inserted his last magazine into the pistol. Turning the weapon back and forth in his hand, a bizarre mix of emotions washed over him, one part dispirited, the other calm. Although the logical part of his brain had no illusions about his fate since Elena fell, when he compared his dismal amount of ammunition to the sheer number of Death Corps soldiers looking to kill him, the small cowboy part of him finally accepted the idea that he wouldn't survive the night.

The female voice said, "Five . . . four . . ."

As the numbers dwindled on the touchscreen, he realized that he'd succeeded. The Death Corps couldn't reach Zeus's Mercy in time to stop it. He thought, *Screw it, if I'm gonna die, I'm at least gonna see the fruits of my labor.*

He steeled himself, fully cognizant of the fact that his impending actions would accelerate his death rather than delay it. Taking one final breath, he sprung to his feet, doing his best to ignore the numbness in his left thigh, and limp-sprinted around the glass cage to the row of windows, most of which were entirely shattered from the gunfire. He aimed his pistol backward and fired rounds in an attempt to deter the soldiers from pursuing or firing at him. Despite his efforts, a storm of gunfire rushed toward him. Three more hammers slammed into his body, one into his right tricep; his arm immediately went numb and limp. The second slammed into his left trapezius. The third hit his right calf.

He stumbled but didn't fall, not until he reached the backside of the glass cage, a brief reprieve from the gunfire. Everything was hazy, and he knew his muscles were moving and his lungs breathing, but he didn't feel like he controlled any part of himself. He approached the windows and collapsed, his eyes focused on the city.

When the Death Corps saw their adversary lying on the floor, they turned their attention in horror to Zeus's Mercy.

Ninety-nine percent. Those are the odds Nathaniel gave us. We never talked about that other one percent. We were already risking so much—we were going against so much—that none of us really wanted to think about it. Don't let me down. Don't let me down.

A loud *whirr* erupted from Zeus's Mercy as Code Blue traveled up the tubes and antenna of Little Empire, the blue universe of shining blue stars abruptly disappearing from the circular contraption. Within seconds, Zeus's Mercy was transparent. A thunderous shock wave knocked some Death Corps soldiers to the floor, stunned others, and shattered whatever parts of the windows remained.

The orange-yellow gas below appeared to pulse as it shifted and turned from drafts of wind, a heartbeat borne of death rather than life, one that killed the body instead of keeping it alive. Neon-blue cracks spread across the black sky like water rushing through a web of creeks after a drought, traveling in every direction away from Little Empire. Glowing blue particles gently fell from the cracks, glimmering like suns from the most distant galaxies.

When the blue particles collided with the gas, the effect was soft and subdued, but Northfield didn't think the view could be more beautiful. The gas quietly disappeared, bit by bit, inch by inch, appearing to recede lower and lower as the blue particles ate away at the poison like water dissolving a cube of sugar. Within moments, the gas was gone, like he was in the eye of a hurricane.

However, when he looked around, he realized that the hurricane was simply gone. The cloud, the poison, the hell that had plagued the city for over ten years was gone in less than a minute. Not in a cascade of explosions, not in a year-long expulsion campaign, but in a few quiet moments after a single loud burst.

The particles continued to fall slowly, floating back and forth from the crisp night breeze. He closed his eyes to absorb it all, absorb this moment, and store it away in his memory, however little time he might have left to recall it.

When his eyes opened, he caught a glimpse of himself on a broken shard of glass hanging off the window; his eyes blended with the glowing particles. He gazed back outside, drunkenly swallowing the view again.

I'm sorry, Elena and John. I'm sorry, Flynn and Salb. I'm sorry you can't see this. I finished what you started, though, and I hope you can at least take solace in that.

Finding newfound strength from the miracle he had witnessed, he tried to lift himself up, and he managed to sit up on his knees. He wouldn't die lying down, not while he could still stand; he wouldn't give the Network that satisfaction.

A hot, fiery sensation raced across his left arm; he didn't bother looking down to assess the damage, to see whether the bullet had punched a hole through his arm or if it was another flesh wound. He didn't bother looking back; he knew who fired, and he knew that he couldn't stop them. He found himself wanting just a little more time, just a few more sips of the view, although he figured that God had decided he'd had enough for the night.

Though he logically knew that only a handful of seconds had passed since he reached the windows, he couldn't say how many; he felt as if he'd been staring out them for both an hour and half a second simultaneously. For the feeling of an hour, he should be grateful, but the half-second sensation still left him wanting. Wanting but not quite resistant; he knew what was coming.

What are my last thoughts gonna be? Shit, I wish I would've thought this through earlier and come up with some sort of game plan.

I'll try to keep it simple and short, I guess. For how much I jabber in my head, I wanna make my last thoughts count.

His newfound strength was short-lived; he fell chest-first onto the floor again. His hands moved up toward his ears in a half-hearted attempt to break his fall.

I love you, Jess. That's the main thing I want to say. I didn't do as much good as I wanted to. I wanted to help so many more people, and I wanted to hurt so many less. I just hope, for you, it's enough. But either way, know that . . .

He hit the ground, his left cheek pressed against the floor. He stared at his right hand, which began blurring. Everything in sight decomposed into polygons and blobs, dimming in flickers like a fading fire.

Know that . . .

Figures moved toward him, holding long objects in their hands. He paid them no mind. They aroused no fear in him; where he was going, they couldn't touch him.

I love you.

Everything unraveled. The very words in his mind began dimming, growing quieter, becoming harder to discern. Before everything vanished entirely, one last phrase glowed dimly in the recesses of his mind.

Now and forever.

EPILOGUE

"**J**esus. You couldn't find a bigger shitshow in a goddamn sewer," the Death Corps commander muttered, kicking a soldier's body out of his way as he walked toward the shattered windows in the laboratory. His eyes narrowed as he peered through his faceplate, noting the newfound emptiness in the city due to the lack of gas swirling between every building. He gritted his teeth. "Fuck."

An officer stepped over broken glass and stood next to him. He asked, "How do you think New Medea will respond, sir?"

The commander snarled. The detonation of Zeus's Mercy couldn't be kept a secret from the Network in New Medea, despite how isolated it was from Cumulus.

He picked up a piece of glass. "I suppose we'll see," he said, turning the shard over in his hand before splitting it in two. "According to Flynn, every member of the Coalition was in Rolling Moses, except for the three Geralt Salb housed. Three bodies in Little Empire are wearing prototype Death Corps uniforms. These bodies are likely the last of the Coalition, affirming what Flynn told us."

"That sounds like good news, sir."

The commander dropped the glass. "I don't think so. The Coalition might be finished, but God knows how many copycat movements will arise in their wake. We need to nip this in the bud . . ."

"Sir?" a soldier said to him. "This one's still alive. Barely. And he's bleeding out, bad."

With paramount urgency, he ordered, "Do everything you can to save him. Everything. Go!"

Death Corps medics rushed to stop the intruder's bleeding.

The commander said to his officer, "We'll save him, if we can. Then we'll drain all the information he has, see if there's any details we could be missing. We'll use every tool at our disposal to rip the humanity from him, patch it back on him like a weathered Band-Aid, then tear it off again before blowing his brains out."

"And then we'll put him on display for everyone to see," the officer added.

"Exactly. This man better hope he's running toward the light. If he comes back, we'll make damned sure he only sees darkness."

ACKNOWLEDGMENTS

If I could thank everyone who has been a part of this novel's creation, this section would be at least a few chapters long. As such, I will do my best to keep it short. First and foremost, I want to thank my family for all their support during this process. The reading, the feedback, and the encouragement helped propel me across the finish line. The same acknowledgement goes to my beta readers, composed of many friends. Your feedback helped chop off some of the rougher edges of my story; I would shudder to think of what my novel would look like without you. I also appreciate the work of my editor, Bodie Dykstra, and my cover designer, Geoffrey Bunting. Your efforts truly propelled my novel into a commercial product. My final thanks goes to God, who makes all things happen.

ABOUT THE AUTHOR

As a native of Minnesota, Calvin Fisher learned to spend long winters tearing through pages and pages of novels. His desire to write for an audience bloomed early; as a child, he sold stacks of homemade comic books to family and neighbors. In the years since, his passion has refined and matured, but ultimately remains the same. His desire to bring characters to life is the engine that powers each work. He currently resides in Denver, Colorado.

Dear Reader,

Thank you for reading my novel. In the sea of books published each day, I am profoundly grateful that you chose mine. If you are so inclined, please share your thoughts by leaving an online review.